Julia

and

Maud

In *Julia and Maud*, author Joyce Faulkner presents a compelling tale told by Archie Biggs, the "steadfast," yet conflicted Huck Finn-type narrator. Biggs, often at the center of the action, whether he wants to be or not, reveals his own bias, while also showing the perspectives of complicated citizens during an evolutionary 1890s Fort Smith. The ebb and flow of popular opinion and the six-degrees of separation which connect characters throughout parallels many political stories and the ambitions throughout Arkansas history to the present. Readers are empathetic to the narrator, whose dialectal perspective, youth, and honor, are clear throughout. Some readers may find empathy for Maud, as reminded by Faulkner, this story has many sides.

Truth is stranger than fiction and as aided by the noted historian and author, UAFS Assistant Professor and Director of the Drennen-Scott Historic House, Tom Wing, the story is plausible, well-told, and intriguing. Faulkner's chapters will have some readers looking over their shoulders for Maud, as the chill crosses the room, laughing at the antics or language of some characters, or encouraging readers to look deeper into not only the well-known names, but also of those average folks in the blurry background, on the fringes of acceptable society, or those faces we recognize, yet their stories are untold or forgotten. Faulkner, Wing, with help from Cody Faber, Al Whitson, Calvin Evans, Joe Wasson, and Tom Dillard, among others, will keep this story, and many of Arkansas' unique people, places, and stories alive for generations.

—Kevin L. Jones, Ph.D.
Professor of English, Dept. of English, Rhetoric and Writing, and Media Communication, College of Arts and Sciences
University of Arkansas-Fort Smith

Julia and Maud

Joyce Faulkner
&
Tom Wing

Red Engine Press
Fort Smith, Arkansas

Cover Art by Sonny Robison
Cover Design by Sue and Sonny Robison

Library of Congress Control Number: 2023941280

ISBN: 979-8-9879576-4-6

Second Printing 2024

This book explores a real 19th century murder in Fort Smith, Arkansas, that remains disturbing to this day. The language is explicit and the events leading up to the final incident are shocking, even when viewed through a 21st century lens. The letters and drawings you will see are from the actual court documents that historian and contributor Tom Wing retrieved from the official records. While discretion is advised for everyone, parents must judge whether the subject matter is appropriate for their children.

This work is dedicated to my Great Uncle Cephas Rush (1915-1958) who was disabled at the age of twelve by an inherited paralytic disease. By the time I knew him in the early 1950s, he couldn't walk or talk or feed himself. I'd run into the room where he lay and either tell him fantastical stories I made up on the spot...or read to him from my stash of Little Golden Books. He couldn't smile because the muscles in his face were frozen...but his eyes followed me. He couldn't speak...but his grunts told me that he liked the tall tales I concocted for him. Near the end, he couldn't breathe without a noisy machine. I had to stand on a small step stool to see his eyes. He was the first person I ever knew who died.

I've often thought about the things he missed out on...like running across his front yard to buy a treat from the ice cream man...or going swimming at Creekmore Park...or watching Rodeo Parades on Garrison Avenue. So, I've created a "fantasy" Cephas for this book, a brawny one who rides horses and runs races and competes for girls. They are my vision of what the real Cephas' life might have been like but for...

Joyce Faulkner

Prologue

The Hotel Main, Fort Smith, Arkansas
August 1, 1941

"They think I'm crazy, but I'm not."

"Who'd say a mean thing like that, Miz Julia?" I set a breakfast tray down in front of the old woman.

"Everyone. It hurts my feelings, but they say it anyway." She picked up a spoon and dipped it into her bowl of oatmeal. "It's not hot."

"How do you know that without tasting it, ma'am?"

"The spoon didn't vibrate." She laid it down on her tray. "I can't eat it without the butter and brown sugar…and it has to be hot enough to melt them both. Sam knew that."

"I'm sorry, ma'am. We all thought Sam would live forever—and that he'd take care of you forever. So's I never learned about no vibrating spoon…" I filled her mug. "…but this here coffee's gonna be nice and hot."

She stuck a fresh spoon into it.

"It vibratin' for ya, Miz Julia?"

She looked up at me, raisin' one eyebrow. "You think I'm crazy?"

"No, ma'am. Jes particular. How about some toast?"

"Where?"

"Right there." I pointed to the tray.

"Oh, yes. Thank you."

As she buttered her toast, I picked up her bowl of oatmeal. Jes before leavin', I turned to look at her. She wuz starin' out the window agin. I sighed and went out, latchin' the door after me.

A short, gray man in a straw hat came outta the elevator halfway down the corridor. "Cold oatmeal again, Archie?"

"Yes sir."

"Wrong bowl?"

"No sir, vibratin' spoon."

The man sighed. "You have to wonder what's going on in her head these days."

"If I warn't doin' this fer Miz Julia, I'd be doin' somethin' like it fer someone else. It's my job and I'm happy to have it."

Fagan Bourland slipped a coin into my free hand. "I appreciate how kind you are to her. How patient."

"She's no trouble, really. Jes sits and stares out the window like she's watchin' fer someone. I peek out myself sometimes, but Garrison Avenue's too busy to pick out anythin' in particular—specially when I don't know what to look fer."

"She's looking for trouble, she told me one time—like we haven't had our share of it."

v

I pocketed the money. "I spose we all meet up with it from time to time."

Fagan sighed. "I love that old bat, but I haven't always been kind to her—or patient. Not in my makeup, I guess."

I nodded. "Ain't always easy with kin."

"No. It's not. But she's odd. Always has been."

"Ain't we all?"

Fagan chuckled. "I guess so—but Julia? Well, she's not like anyone else in the world. That's what drew me to her in the first place, I think. I never knew what she might do next. It's like living with something dark and fierce—and quite wonderful."

"Wonderful, sir?"

"She never gave up on me, Archie."

We looked down at her together. "She never gave up on any of us," I murmured.

We'd runned outta words.

"Well, then." Fagan took off his hat. "You go heat up that oatmeal. I'll hold the fort until you get back."

I wuz on the top step of the staircase when I heard a crash and someone callin' my name. I looked back down the long corridor.

Fagan Bourland wuz hurrying toward me. "Fetch the doctor, Archie. Julia's not well."

"I'm sure she'll be fine, Mr. Fagan."

"Hurry."

"Yes sir."

*   *   *

Julia? Jooo-li-ya!

Julia opened her eyes. "Did you hear that?"

Fagan shook his head.

"Did you?" She turned to me.

"I -I did. I heard it, Miz Julia."

It's time, you ugly old bitch.

Julia clutched at the quilt covering her. "Not yet. I'm not ready."

It won't be long now—you whore, you dog. You mother of hounds.

"Maud?" Julia raised her head off her pillow.

Fagan lifted her hand and kissed the palm.

"Do you hear her?"

"Hear who, darlin'?"

"Maud."

"No, sweetheart—not now, not then."

Sssssssss.

Julia cringed and I looked up at Fagan worriedly.

"It's okay, my darlin'," he stroked her cheek. "Maud's dead. Gone. She can't hurt you...us, anymore..."

A breeze lifted a fringe of curls off Julia's forehead. She held an index finger to her lips. "Shush. She's listening, Fagan. Waiting."

He held his hand to his ear. "I don't hear anything."

vi

Julia rocked her head from side to side on her pillow. "Why did you do it? Why did you...bring her into our lives?"

"That was a long time ago, sugar. I forget now."

"She's a demon—sure as Jesus lives." Sweat glistened on Julia's cheeks.

"Now Julia. Maud was no such thing. She was just a selfish, misguided girl. She's gone now and will be gone forever."

Maud be waiting for you, Joo-li-ya! Waiting to tell you how Fagan really feels about what you did to his sweet girl. Sssssssss.

Goose bumps raised the hair on my arms. I looked around the room. Nothin' but a breathy breeze from the open window.

"Fagan." Julia whimpered. "Fagan?"

"I'm here, darlin'." He squeezed her hand.

Just because you'll be free of that diseased carcass don't mean you'll be free, you ugly old whore. Maud's still here. She'll aways be here.

"What can I do, Mr. Fagan?"

"Stay with us, Archie. She knows you—and isn't afraid of you."

"Of me?" I straightened her blanket. "I've been takin' care of her a long time now. Ain't I, Miz Julia?"

She smiled up at me. "Like always, Sam."

I shivered. "Like always."

Sssssssss.

Historical Figures

Name	Relationships	Facts
Julia Bailey Bourland 1861–1941	Wife of Fagan Bourland Mother of Morton, James & Capola Bourland	Devout member of the Methodist Church and periodic attendee of tent revivals in Fort Smith
Wiley Bailey	Julia Bailey Bourland's father	Despite owning a slave, Wiley was a loyal Union man during the Civil War
Lucinda Linnard Bailey	Julia Bailey Bourland's mother	Lucinda's father was Wiley Bailey's business partner in Alabama during the Civil War
James Fagan Bourland 1862–1952	Husband of Julia Bourland Father of Morton, James & Capola Bourland	Businessman & Four times the Mayor of Fort Smith, AR
James Cook Bourland 1831–1904	Father of Fagan Bourland	
Anne E Spangler 1834–1900	Mother of Fagan Bourland	
Morton Bourland 1881–1932	Oldest son of Julia & Fagan Bourland	Merchant & Police Officer Died in swimming accident in 1932
James Fagan Bourland, Jr. 1884–1979	Second son of Julia & Fagan Bourland Married to Queen Branwell	
Capola Bourland 1886–1932	Youngest son of Julia & Fagan Bourland Married to Viola V. "Ola" Ulmer	Died of a self-inflicted gunshot wound, February 1932.
Maud Avery Allen 1874–1897	Wife of George Allen	Married March 1893 Divorced 1896
	Daughter of William DeLoss Avery & Clara De Bruler Avery Palmer	Maud, her mother, her father and her siblings are listed as "White" in personal documents available on Ancestry.com
	Siblings: Mabel, Stella, D, and Charles Avery	Mabel (13) and William DeLoss Avery (38) died of disease within weeks of each other in 1888.

George Allen	Husband of Maud Avery Allen	City Engineer
Dr. John Winchester Breedlove		Confederate Veteran, Physician/Coroner
Cal Whitson	Ancestor of Historians Cal Evans and Al Whitson	Civil War Veteran, Deputy US Marshal, Store Owner
Judge Edgar E. Bryant (Judge Eddie)		Circuit Court Judge (1890–1898)
Reverend William Mathews	Joyce Faulkner's Great Grandfather	Local Preacher
Bill Hatcher		Employee of Fagan Bourland Gambler, Scoundrel
Eliza Rogers	Widow of Hugh Rogers	Irish Immigrant
Milt "Freckles" Hinkle	Son of George Hinkle Buffalo Hide Dealer and Saloon Owner	Rodeo Star, Storyteller & Adventurer
Annie Schaffer		Rodeo Star
John Bourland	Younger brother of Fagan Bourland	Courts and marries Lily French
Louis Holder		Murderer Executed July 25, 1894
Crawford Goldsby (Cherokee Bill)		Murderer Executed March 17, 1896
Isaac Parker		United States District Court Judge for the Western District of Arkansas Died November 17, 1896
Corrine Southard	Wife of Dr. Southard	Quotes and time related incidents taken from her diary
Rosie Lee	Belle Starr's Daughter Pearl	A prostitute in Fort Smith
James Reed & J.B. McDonough		Julia's Defense Attorneys
Mr. Homann & Kate		Owned farm on Towson Avenue
Charles & Henry Birnie		Embalmers & Undertakers
George Winston		Judge Parker's Court Reporter

x

Section I

1893–1894

March 15, 1893
MARRIAGE LICENSE
State of Arkansas — County Sebastian
Fort Smith District
To any person authorized by law to solemnize marriage—greeting: YOU ARE
HEREBY COMMANDED to solemnize the rite and publish THE BANS OF
MATRIMONY, between Mr. George Allen of Fort Smith in the County
Sebastian in the state of Arkansas, aged Twenty Years, and Miss Maud Avery of
Fort Smith in the County of Sebastian and the state of Arkansas, aged nineteen
years, according to law. And do you officially sign and return this License to the
parties herein named.
Witness my hand and official seal, this 15th day of March 1893.
C.H. Howe, Clerk of the County Court
By R B Rutherford, D.C.

May 30, 1894
Note hanging on nail on Jethro's front door in Pope County, Arkansas:

Jethro Barnes and an orphan he took to work his farm have been missing for
three weeks now. Some say good riddance. Old Jethro ain't well liked in these
parts no how.

Chapter One

Rebirth

15 Jun 1894
DEATH OF WILEY BAILEY
Mr. Wiley Bailey, formerly a resident of this city, died at his home in the
Cherokee Nation last Tuesday, aged 68 years. He died from the effects of
cancer of the stomach. His funeral took place Wednesday.
The Weekly Elevator, Fort Smith, Arkansas

Rain bounced off the roof of the Frisco Station as the train rolled into Fort
Smith. As soon as it came to a full stop, everyone lined up in the aisle, eager to
get outta the stuffy car and stretch our legs. While we waited fer the conductor
to open the door, I tucked my little green book back into my pocket and helped
a young woman pull a bag down off a rack over her head.

"Thank you." She looked deep into my eyes.

I once tried flirtin' with a gal back in Pope County, but this'n made me feel
like I wuz butt naked and everyone else wuz dressed fer tea with Judge Parker
hisself. "My pleasure, ma'am."

She lifted her beat-up carpet bag with both hands and turned toward the
conductor who'd stepped out onto the platform.

He stretched out his arm. "Let me take that, ma'am."

"Make sure you don't drop it."

"No ma'am. Wouldn't think of it." He took it from her and set it on a cart
behind him.

"I have expensive things in there you know."

"Yes, ma'am."

"Very expensive things."

"It's safe and sound under the porch. Rain cain't get to it at all. See?"

The sides of her bag wuz dark with age and one of them handle straps wuz
rope. I smothered a snort. Miz High and Mighty.

"Let's get you down out of there afore's you get wet." The conductor
reached fer her hand.

"No, I don't need you." She turned sideways and pawed at the air with her
foot, teetering on the top step.

He wiped the rain outta his eyes. "I'll lift you off that step. No need you
ending up in a mud puddle."

"I can do it."

A short feller behind me rasped, "What's the hold up?"

"Tall steps, little woman," I said.

"It's an act. She's watching us watch her out of the corner of her eye."

"Shush," I said over my shoulder. "She'll hear you."

"Don't be a damn fool, boy. She likes us talking about her."

With a quick peek over her shoulder, the girl stepped down. Lightenin' startled her and she missed the second step.

"Whoa!" I reached fer her but the conductor caught her.

"Let go of me," she jerked her elbow outta his hand. "I can do it myself."

The conductor pointed toward the station. "Might wanna dry off in there before you head out on Garrison. It's mighty wet.

"Never you mind. I got me a husband wait'n." Chin up, she went into the station.

I hefted a burlap bag over one shoulder. It held everythin' I owned in the world 'ceptin' what I wuz a wearin'. "Hard to help wildcats," I said as I stepped down off the train.

The conductor grinned. "Aw, she's jes nervous. We get lil ladies like that a couple times a month. They's spinsters or wayward wives—coming back when they find out where they ran off to ain't any better than where they left."

I fished a couple coins outta my pocket and dropped 'em into his palm.

"That's too much, sir."

"She forgot."

"Thank ya, sir." He turned to the next passenger—and I headed on inside the station.

"Whoa, kid."

I turned around.

"You got folks here?" That raspy-voiced lil feller who'd been standin' behind me as we got off the train hurried to catch up.

"Naw, I ain't got folks no where."

"What're you here for?" He didn't come up any higher than my armpit and when he looked up at me, his round glasses slid down on his nose.

"Thought I'd get a job."

He thumped my bicep. "You got some muscle on ya. Farming?"

"Not if'n I kin help it. I played me some ball in Pope County though." I pretended to pitch ball.

"South paw?"

I shrugged.

"With the Yeller Hammers?"

"I wish. Chucked them boys some balls durin' practice sometimes though."

"I got a saloon on South Sixth. Connected to my store. Drop by sometime."

"I ain't much of a drinker..."

"Then you won't be drinking me dry,now will ya? Can you pour liquor out of a bottle into a glass?"

"I reckon I kin do that."

"Can you remember to collect the money before you pour whiskey for a stranger?"

"I kin manage."

"Fine. I need a bartender. Come by when you get settled. Ask for Fagan Bourland. That's me. He opened an umbrella.

I marveled at my luck while the rest of them passengers crowded around us. "Wait!" I called. "Don't you want my name?"

He turned. "Sure, sonny. What's your name?"

"Archie Biggs." I extended my hand.

"That's quite a paw you got there, Archie. Pope County must be growing 'em big these days."

"Yes, sir. I came up here hopin' they wuz gonna put a new baseball team together."

"Maybe, maybe not, I hear."

"If'n they do, I'll need me some time to prove to 'em I can do it."

"You want that job or not?"

I had fifty cents to my name. "It'll make things easier, sir."

"Good. Come on out to the store and I'll have Morty get you get situated." He turned to leave.

"Um...where exactly is yer store? And who's Morty?"

Fagan Bourland seemed disappointed in me already. "Ah yes. I forgot you just got here."

"I'm sure I can find it, sir."

"Good. I value resourcefulness in my employees." He turned on his heel and walked away.

I watched him cross North A and head South toward what looked like a big wide muddy avenue.

I went inside the Little Rock and Fort Smith Passenger Station. Whiles I wuz lookin' to ask someone how to find The Bourland Store, a young feller squeezed past me and yelled, "Maud!"

The girl who'd gotten off the train ahead of me frowned. "Where you been, George?"

"Waiting for you outside. Where'd you think I'd be?" He bent down to kiss her cheek, but she pulled back jes enough so's his lips didn't touch her. He straightened and took her bag. "I missed you."

"Buy me an egg?"

He picked up her bag. "How's your ma?"

"Nasty. What do you care?"

"Aw, Maud. Ain't you glad to see me?"

"I'm glad to be back in Fort Smith." Her eyes caught mine as she elbowed past me. "All kinds of interesting things here."

"Such as?" George said as they disappeared out the front entrance.

* * *

The rain'd slowed to a sprinkle when I came outta the station. A black man not much older'n me wuz pullin' up to the buildin'. He climbed down from the wagon and tied up the mule. "You that new barkeep Mr. Fagan found on the train?"

The mule gave me the evil eye and bared her teeth.

"How'd ya know it wuz me?"

"He said to look for a tall redheaded kid carryin' a burlap bag over his shoulder." He laughed. "I'm Sam. I work for the Bourlands. He told me to see if you needed a ride."

"Much obliged, Sam. I'm Archie. Right now I'm hungry and I ain't got enough change to make my pockets jingle. Any suggestions where I can pick up a cheap sandwich?"

"I could leave you off somewheres on Garrison if you want to eat downtown—but Mr. Fagan's store's better if you don't mind slapping your own sandwiches together."

"Bourland's then. Second problem is a place to stay. Any ideas there?"

Sam scratched his head. "Mr. Fagan owns a bunch of buildings all over town. At worst, he knows folks who let rooms for a good price. Course right now, he done gone off somewhere 'gain. Maybe Miz Julia knows. We can go by there first."

"Um... Miz Julia is?"

"Why that's Mr. Fagan's wife. Don't you know nothing?"

"Guess not."

The man grinned and I realized he wuz funnin' with me. "I shore appreciate it ... Sam."

"Give me a minute to pick up Mr. Fagan's stuff. You go ahead and toss your bag in the back there and climb up on the seat."

"I won't make that mule nervous?"

"You mean old Belle here? Only thing gets this lady riled is if'n you flap a towel or table cloth or something like that in her face. That'll piss her off plenty, but I don't see you aggravating her that way."

"I ain't aimin' to do anythin' like that."

After he disappeared into the station, Belle turned her head.

I held out my hand. "Whoa, Belle."

She twitched her ears.

"I ain't gonna hurt you so don't you go ahurtin' me." I waited to see what she might do next. She turned her face forward. "Okay, then." I took a deep breath and started toward the wagon. I warn't five feet from it when she turned to watch me agin. I froze.

"You ain't afraid of a mule, are you, boy?"

I spun around, my heart poundin' in my chest. A feller in a stovepipe hat stood on the sidewalk behind me, leanin' on a fancy cane.

"No, sir."

"Just grab ahold of them reins if she gives you any lip."

"I wuz jes plannin' on tossin' this here ..."

"What's going on, Dr. Breedlove? You okay?" Another man stepped onto to walkway. He had his hat pulled so low over the left side of his forehead that I couldn't see his eye.

"This here boy's afraid of that mule, Cal."

"I'm not afear..."

"That's Fagan Bourland's wagon," Cal said.

Doc Breedlove cocked his head. "You trying to steal it, boy?"

"Just tryin' to put this in the back." I held up the sack. "I came on the train with Mr. Bourland this mornin'."

"Where is he then?" The doctor scowled at me.

"Went on home, I reckon. He left right after we got off the train."

"And left Belle and the rig here?"

When Belle heard her name, she brayed so loud the hairs on the back of my neck stood up and I jumped back.

"See! He is afraid of that mule." Doc Breedlove elbowed Cal.

"I ain't afeared of no mule." My heart wuz poundin' so loud they could probably hear it. "Mr. Bourland offered me a job this mornin' and he sent Sam to fetch me. Really."

Doc Breedlove narrowed his eyes. "If that's so, then where's Sam?"

"Inside. Tendin' to Mr. Bourland's luggage."

A feller with fancy lip hair joined us. "What's going on, Doc? Someone hurt?"

"Not yet, Edgar. Of course, the day's young."

"Morning, Judge." Cal touched the brim of his hat instead of tippin' it. "Looks like this here stranger's eyeing Fagan's wagon."

"That true, boy?"

"No, sir. I ain't …"

"I saw him." Doc Breedlove pointed at me with his cane. "I walked right up on him. Only thing that saved the day was Fagan's old mule keeping this young fella at bay. He's scared of mules, don't ya know."

"Sam came to pick m…"

"You know Sam?" The judge folded his arms over his chest.

"Well, no," I swallowed. "Not really. We jes met."

"What's his family name?"

I tried to remember how Sam introduced himself. Nothin' but 'Sam' came to mind.

Cal took off his hat and slapped it aginst his thigh. It wuz then I seen that one of his eyes'd been put out.

When I tried not to look at it, he grinned real slow like he wuz used to folks starin' at him. "Well?"

"Well, what?"

"Sam's last name."

"I-I don't know."

"I think we better check this boy out."

"I should think so." Doc Breedlove hooked his cane over his forearm. "We've been getting riffraff coming into this town every day, lately. Can barely keep the Mexicans and the Indians and the Chinese at bay, but at least they're suited for Fort Smith weather. We may not like 'em but they can keep on workin' when the temperature gets way on up there. Now this pale face …" He pinched my arm between the end of my sleeve and my wrist. "… got skin the color of buttermilk in between them freckles. Not fit for workin' in the fields. He'll fry in ten minutes, pass out in fifteen."

"The doctor's got a point, boy," the judge grinned. "You're scared of mules and you can't tolerate the sun. What good are you?"

"I can throw a ball so hard it'll bust up a watermelon ninety feet away."

"The hell you say," Cal put his hands on his hips. "How big a ball?"

"Yay big." I held my thumb about three inches from my index finger.

"Can't be done, boy." The judge pretended to lose interest. "Besides, you're distracting these fine gentlemen from pursuing the answer to the larger question. Why are you lurking around Mr. Bourland's wagon, this fine wet morning?"

"And what have you done with Mr. Bourland and his man?" Doc Breedlove glared at me.

"And why're you scared of old Belle there?" Cal narrowed his good eye.

"I..."

A door squeaked and Sam backed outta the station's baggage room pullin' a trunk on a trolley.

I blew air through my lips. "Sam, can you tell these people who I am?"

Sam looked around, a slow grin brightenin' his face. "Maybe you should know who they be, Archie. That there gentleman with the cane is one of our Confederate veterans—Dr. John Winchester Breedlove. He been takin' care of folks around here nigh on fifteen years now. Yank or Rebel, Doc Breedlove tends to 'em all. "

I nodded. "Doc Breedlove."

"And this here young feller in that fine brocade waistcoat is Circuit Court Judge Edgar Bryant."

"Judge Bryant." I tipped my cap.

"And this here's Cal Whitson. He used to be a deputy U.S. Marshal a few years back. He's a constable here in Fort Smith, now. Owns a store out near Mill Creek."

"Mr. Whitson."

"And this here's Archie. I don't know much more about him 'ceptin' Mr. Fagan hired him this morning and I'm to bring him home with the supplies."

Doc Breedlove narrowed his eyes. "Were your folks North or South, boy?"

"Don't know, sir. I never knowed 'em."

"Well, ain't that too bad. You're mighty young to be out on your own like this. At least the James Brothers' got family."

"Yes, sir."

"Course lot of young fellers...younger than you...at least smaller than you...died on battlefields all the way from Pennsylvania down to the Gulf Coast."

"I warn't born until that ruckus wuz long over and done with, sir."

"Of course. Of course." The old man muttered. "Fort Smith was a little bit of both, I reckon. Ain't never gonna forget any of it myself." His voice rose. "Not ever..." Then he sighed. "Of course, I let go of all that a long time ago."

Cal and the judge looked like they wuz gonna bust out laughin' at that one.

"I wouldn't hold a boy accountable for something he had nothin' to do with anyway," the old man kept right in a talkin'.

"YEEEHAAA!" A tall boy on a tall horse galloped past us, splatterin' mud all over the place.

"Get some damned manners, Cephas Rush!" Cal Whitson wiped the muddy water off'n his face with the back of his hand.

The rider zipped in between wagons and carriages, jumped over a barrel settin' in front of a store and disappeared in the traffic headin' up a big wide avenue lined with businesses of one kind or another.

Belle shook herself, dousin' me with some of that mud. I almost cried. The front and back of my shirt wuz soaked and I didn't have another one.

"Don't get all riled now, boy!" Doc Breedlove dug into a pocket and handed me a folded handkerchief. "We all got splashed."

I looked around as I wiped my face. None of 'em except Cal looked damp.

"Thank you, sir." I handed Doc Breedlove's handkerchief back to him.

I still warn't sure if'n the good doctor wuz pokin' fun at me, but he winked. "Good to meet you, young man." He leaned forward on his cane. "Don't be afraid of Belle. She ain't got a mean bone in her body."

I smiled, "Yes, sir."

*　*　*

Judge Bryant and Doc Breedlove went into the station. And Cal Whitson headed on down toward the Arkansas River. Sam took my bag and stowed it in the back of the wagon alongside a trunk labeled 'Fagan Bourland.' He'd already loaded three other boxes and a couple crates of vegetables. "Miz Julia and young Morty'll keep you busy," he said. "Not just Mr. Fagan. Might as well expect it."

"I thought I wuz to work the saloon."

Sam kicked the mud off'n his boots and climbed up onto the seat. "That might be what Mr. Fagan say but that's not how it works in this family." He looked down at me still a standin' by the wagon. "What's wrong with you, Archie? Belle's all settled down now."

"It's not that." I avoided his eyes.

"What then?"

"I didn't expect you. Ain't got much on me fer a tip right now."

"Don't give that no never mind. Around here, we take care of each other. My time of need'll come soon enough. Besides Mr. Fagan might forget me from time to time, but Miz Julia always sees to it I get what I earn." When Sam smiled it wuz like the sun'd come out from a cloud. A body couldn't help but smile with him.

"I'll take care of you first payday. I promise."

"That'll be fine with me."

"Thanks, Sam." I climbed up onto the wagon.

"Get on, Belle!"

The sour-faced mule turned to look at us.

"She's not sure about me."

"She know who you be. Animals understand people better than people do each other."

I warn't comforted but I changed the subject. "Wh...what're the Bourlands like?"

"They come from good families. And they work hard to get ahead."

"Got to admire that," I said.

As we turned onto a wide muddy road, I seen a sign that said, "Garrison Avenue." About that time, we hit a rock or somethin' and my cap went a flyin'. It wuz the only head cover I had and I pert near fell outta the wagon tryin' to get it back.

"Whoa there, boy." Sam grabbed hold of my jacket. "Let's not drown first day."

Feelin' like a fool, I settled back into my seat next to him.

"Don't you worry, boy. I done took a header off this wagon a time or two my own self."

I grabbed the edge of the seat under me and hung on fer dear life. Banks and hotels and stores and restaurants lined Garrison Avenue. People wuz a sloshin' through the muddy street, both on foot or in carriages or wagons. I even seen an automobile parked in front of The Hotel Main. And there wuz a woman on some kinda wheeled contraption, a weavin' her way around the rocks and puddles. "What is that?"

"You never seen a pretty girl on a bicycle before?"

"I know about pretty girls," I grinned. "Never see'd no bicycle though."

"That particular girl works for Fagan Bourland too. Telephone operator."

I nodded like I knowed what that meant, hopin' he didn't take me fer the ignorant hayseed I wuz.

"We be at the Bourlands' soon's we get through this mess. It ain't that far." Sam turned onto South Sixth Street. At first, we plodded past some businesses, then there wuz a great big fancy buildin' with a clock tower.

I pointed. "What's that?"

"Courthouse."

"Shore is a fancy one."

"And a busy one too. That's were trouble goes to die."

"Think I'll steer clear of it then.'

"I would."

We'd jes crossed Parker Avenue when Sam pulled back on the reins and Belle stopped in front of a big white house on the corner of South 6 and South A. "Here we be, Archie."

I looked around. "Where?"

"At the Bourlands', of course."

Belle turned around and gave me the eye like she thought I wuz a durn fool too.

Sam grinned. "Calm down, boy. Belle likes to tease, don't ya know."

Actually, I didn't, but knowin' that dang mule wuz a teasin' gave me the heebie-jeebies anyway. Made me wonder what else she wuz a plannin' fer me.

Sam pulled the brake. "You might as well come on in too. Miz Julia'll want to meet you." He tied Belle's reins to a post and beckoned to me. "Jes know she lost her daddy a couple weeks back and she still be real sad."

I nodded and climbed down into the street.

"WATCH OUT!"

Heart a poundin', I pressed myself up side the wagon.

"Where you from, hayseed?" A fleshy feller scowled at me as he drove his team by.

"Don't you mind Bill Hatcher," Sam said. "He might act like a bully but if'n you look like you're gonna fight back, he'll run off with his tail between his legs."

I follered Sam up to the house. I no sooner stepped onto the porch than somewheres inside a dog started barkin'.

"Miz Julia?" Sam scratched at the door.

"Shush, Gertie! Need something, Sam?"

"Yes, ma'am. I got me a boy here that Mr. Fagan hired this mornin'."

A woman opened the door and stepped out on the porch. "A boy?" A little white dog peeked around her heavy black skirt and sniffed my leg.

"Yes, ma'am. This here's Mr. Archie Biggs. He's hungry and needs a place to stay."

Julia Bourland peered at me through the screen door. "What's Fagan think you're going to do, Archie?"

"Tend bar."

"You ever do that before?"

"No ma'am."

She sighed. "How old are you?"

I blushed. "Seventeen come January."

"Really?"

I lowered my eyes.

"Uh huh." She opened the door. "Come on in. I'm about to feed my boys. We got plenty."

I took off my cap. "Thank ya kindly, ma'am."

"Take off those muddy boots and leave them on the porch though. Wouldn't want Tawny to get after you for tracking up her nice clean rugs."

I looked down at my feet. "Yes ma'am."

She turned to Sam. "Give us an hour and then come back for him."

I pulled off my boots and set 'em on the porch. Gertie sniffed 'em first and then my toes through a big hole in my left sock.

Sam patted my back as I stepped into the Bourlands' home. "I'll leave Mr. Fagan's trunk on the porch for now," he said. "See ya later, Miz Julia."

"Come on back to the kitchen, Archie. What we have isn't fancy, but it's good."

"Thank ya kindly, Miz Bourland."

"Call me Julia. Missus Bourland's too uppity for everyday use."

I grinned. "Miz Julia."

As I follered her down a hallway, the smell of food made my stomach grumble. In the kitchen, three boys sat around a big table eating stew. A young colored woman hovered over 'em, demandin' that they 'eat ever bite.'

"Everyone, this is Archie," Julia said. "Your father hired him to help Hatcher with the saloon."

The oldest boy shook his spoon at me. "That kid ain't never been in no saloon."

"So he says, Morty. Seems that didn't matter to your father."

"You ain't gonna sit on your butt like the other one did, are you?"

"I aim to do a day's work fer a day's pay." All by itself my lower lip quivered.

It wuz quiet fer a moment as Morty sized me up. Then Gertie put her front paws on my knee. I could swear that little critter wuz smilin' at me. I scratched behind her ears and we wuz friends, jes like that.

"Sorry, Archie." Morty pushed a glass of milk my way. "I didn't mean to piss you off already. It's just that none of us got a clue what Pop's thinking most of the time."

I thanked him and threw back half the glass of buttermilk. When I came up fer air, my eyes wuz waterin'.

"Where you from, Archie?" The colored woman asked as she refilled my glass.

"Southern Arkansas. I came up here to play ball if'n they let me. Until that happens, I gotta eat and find me a place to sleep."

"Baseball?" The youngest boy sat up straight in his seat, his eyes wide. "What position do you play?"

"Third base. Like Ned Williamson."

"Really?" His eyes widened.

"When they let me."

"Archie, that's my baby, Cap." Julia smiled at him. "He loves baseball."

"Only cause our cousin, Bill Jr., talks about it all the time," Morty snorted. "Ain't none of us ever seen a real game."

"How about you?" I focused on the third boy who blushed and avoided my eyes.

"James, introduce yourself."

"Aw, Mama." The little dog trotted over to James and curled up at his feet.

"James is my reader. Aways has to have a book," Julia squeezed his shoulder.

"Oh, yeah? Whatcha reading now?"

"Tom Sawyer."

"What's it about?"

"A kid up in Missoura named Tom Sawyer."

I emptied my glass of buttermilk and wiped my mouth on my sleeve. "Would I like it?"

"Can you read?"

"Not as good as I can cypher. I mostly stick to newspapers—lookin' fer baseball scores. Never had me no real book."

"You wanna read one?"

I glanced around the table. All the little Bourlands and they's mother eyed me like a pack of hungry hounds. Not wantin' 'em to think I wuz the ignorant hick that I wuz, I said, "Well sure. If'n I had me a book and time to read it."

"I'll let you borrow Tom Sawyer if you promise not to bend down the corners of the pages."

"Thought you wuz a readin' it."

A hint of snootiness flickered in James' eyes. "I already read it four times— once to figure out words I never saw before, once for fun, once with Cap here, and this time cause my new book ain't come in yet and I'm bored."

"Well, maybe when that new book comes in, I'll take you up on it."

"When Pop came to tell us he was back, he said the Saint Louis order came in on the same train with him. Sam's taking it over there right now. Me and

Gertie here…,” he scratched her ears, “…and Morty are gonna go unpack and inventory the shipment this afternoon. My new books are bound to be there.”

“Well in that case, sure. I’d love to read about ole Tom.” It wuz a filthy lie and James knowed it. Heck, all of ‘em probably knowed it.

“When you’re finished we can discuss it.”

“Discuss it?”

“We can talk about Tom’s friends—Becky and Huck.”

“Oh?”

“It’s kinda like gossipin’ about folks that ain’t real,” the young colored woman said as she set a bowl in front of me and ladled stew into it. “Like goin’ to a play without leavin’ the house.”

“This here’s Tawny Jane. She cooks for us,” Julia said. “And pretty much takes care of us.”

I wanted to tell Tawny that I never see’d a play neither, but that stew smelled so good I forgot all about readin’ and shoveled it into my mouth, only stoppin’ long enough fer her to refill my bowl and cut me another piece of cornbread to sop it up with. Finally, I emptied one last glass of buttermilk. When I put the empty glass back down on the table, I saw that everyone wuz a starin’ at me. “What?”

James broke the silence. “Just how long since you ate anything?”

Tryin’ not to look at any of ‘em, I laid down my spoon. “Um, my …uh…my aunt…gave me breakfast yesterday and packed me an apple and a hunk of last year’s cheese to take with me.”

“Just how far south did you come from?” Morty raised one eyebrow.

“Didn’t say I came straight here, now did I?”

“Boys, stop pokin’ into Archie’s business,” Tawny said. “Let him rest up a bit. Sounds like he’s had a tryin’ couple days.”

“Tawny’s right,” Julia smiled at me. “If Archie’s gonna work in the saloon, there’ll be plenty time to poke into the intimate details of his private life.”

Mebbe things wuz goin’ to work out after all.

*　*　*

Someone knocked on the side door.

“There’s Sam,” Morty said.

The two younger Bourland boys pushed back they’s chairs and with Gertie a dancin’ around they’s feet, elbowed each other to get to the door first.

“Morty, remind your father that Joe and Alverda are getting married tonight. Rachel Mathews came by a few minutes ago to tell us to be there by six. Says the Reverend’s nervous as a cat in a room full of rockin’ chairs.”

“Why’s that, mama? He marries people every day.”

“It’s different when it’s your own baby.”

“We don’t have to go do we?”

“No, no. Not this time.”

“Thank you, Jesus.” Morty sighed.

“Better change your way of thinking, son. There’ll come a day when friends’ll come in handy.”

“Yes, ma’am.” Morty stood up. “Just hope it’s not anytime soon.”

James pushed the back door open. “Come on, Morty!”

13

"Coming." Morty sighed.

The door slammed shut and then opened agin. "Sam says he thinks Pa bought taffy, Morty," Cap called.

Morty growled and took his time going out the door.

Julia turned to me and sighed. "Boys!"

"Yes, ma'am." I laid down my last chunk of bread, unsure what to do next.

"Go ahead. Finish your lunch. The store's just around that corner and down aways."

"Shouldn't I go with 'em?"

"Are you still hungry?"

"Yes, ma'am!"

"Store's not that far away. You can walk."

"I gotta find me a place to live fer awhile."

"Eat, Archie." Her voice wuz like a smile. "The Bailey Hotel is catty corner from the store. My father owns it..." She sighed. "Used to own it, anyway."

The room got real quiet.

Julia looked at each of her boys in turn. I coulda sworn she wuz about to cry but she didn't.

I glanced at Tawny, but she shook her head.

"I'm sorry, Archie. I'm a little emotional right now." Julia blew her nose into an embroidered cotton handkerchief. "My father just died."

"Sorry, ma'am." I couldn't think of anything else to say so's I avoided her eyes fer a bit.

"More stew? Or maybe some peach cobbler?" Tawny lowered the pan she wuz holdin' and a sweet, cinnamony smell drifted across the room.

I forgot about Mr. Fagan's store or findin' a cheap room and watched as Tawny dipped me a whoppin' big helpin'. "Ain't the boys gonna want some?"

"They'll get some tonight." Tawny spooned another piece onto Julia's plate.

"So, Archie. Tell me about yourself," Julia said.

"Um...," My heart wuz beatin' so loud I wuz afraid them nice ladies could hear it. "What'd ya wanna know, ma'am?"

"You have much schoolin'?"

I let the second bite of cobbler dissolve in my mouth. "I kin read and write. And figger."

"Where's your family?"

"Dead, I reckon."

"Who took care of you growing up?"

I sighed and put down my fork. "To be honest, ma'am, I don't like talkin' about family."

Her eyes got real big."You're an orphan, aren't you?"

"Uh..." I glanced at Tawny who hid a smile behind her hand.

"How long since you lived in a real home with a real family?"

"Ma'am..."

"I knew it. I could tell by how worn your clothes are."

I glanced down at my shirt and pants. They wuz second hand, but not faded or filled with holes. "I'm fine, ma'am. Really. I kin take care of myself."

"If you could, do you think you'd be so skinny?"

Wonderin' what Julia Bourland seen that I didn't, I clinched my fist and felt better when my bicep bulged.

Tawny caught my eye and shook her head.

I blew air through my lips. Okay, okay. What do I care what some nosy housewife thinks? Miz Julia wuz bein' nice to me. At least, I thought that's what she wuz a doin'.

A knock at the back door made me jump.

Tawny opened it. "We're through, Sam. Go ahead and tote Mr. Fagan's trunk to his office."

"The boys are at the store, tearin' into that shipment from St. Louey," Sam said. "Only time James is excited to help unload is when he's expectin' somethin' hisself." He hefted the trunk up on one shoulder and squeezed past the table.

"And that's the truth," Tawny said.

"You ready to go find a room, Archie?" Sam said over his shoulder.

I figgered Sam thought I'd overstayed my welcome. "Thanks fer such a fine meal, ma'am." I pushed back the chair and stood up. "I need to get along now."

"Where are you planning on staying, Archie?"

"Dunno, Miz Julia. I ain't gotta a chance to look fer it yet."

"Mmhm." She looked up at Tawny who shrugged. "How much money you got?"

I blushed. "Fifty cents."

"Hmm." She squinched her face up and closed her eyes. When she opened 'em back up she said, "That's okay, Archie. You'll be working steady so The Bailey Hotel ought to be about right. It's not fancy but it's clean. The Sprinkles see to that. Breakfast and supper included in the rent. Plenty of places to eat nearby too. And you can't get any closer to our store."

I warn't gonna say no, of course so's I said, "Sounds fine to me."

"I'll telephone Lydia and find out how soon they can get a bed ready for you." Julia swept by me and disappeared toward the front of the house.

I glanced at Tawny who raised one eyebrow like she expected me to do somethin'.

Rubbin' my palms together, I stood up. "Sam has my stuff in the wagon. Should I go fetch it?"

"That mule'll eat you up if'n you try to take anything off that wagon."

I froze.

She smiled. "Don't get bent out of shape, Archie. I'm messin' with you. Sam'll take you to The Bailey."

I sat back down in my chair.

"Mary Kilpatrick cooks breakfast and dinner for the folks over there," Tawny said as she cleared the table. "It's plain but you won't go hungry."

"Miz Julia said that about eatin' here."

"Miz Julia sure got a way with words, don't she?" Tawny chuckled.

I relaxed. Fort Smith wuz lookin' good.

*　*　*

July 4, 1894

Kansas and Arkansas Railroad brakeman Samuel Collins was shot through the bowels after ejecting a drunkard for trying to steal a ride at Fort Gibson, Oklahoma; a tramp who was on the same car tried to run, was shot and died later. The assailant was Crawford Goldsby...

Indian Chieftain, March 19, 1896

*   *   *

GROCERIES, FLOUR AND FEED
FAGAN BOURLAND, 216 and 213 South Sixth Street
Groceries flour and feed. Bar in connection.
Most commodious and comfortable wagon yard in the city.

Chapter Two

The Lewis Holder Execution

July 6, 1894
Cherokee Bill (Crawford Goldsworthy) murdered Mississippi Railway
Station Agent A. L. "Dick" Richards. Later, Goldsworthy (Cherokee Bill)
boasted about it. Still later, he denied it.
Sacramento Daily Union, Volume 91, Number 21, 18 March 1896

* * *

Wednesday, July 25, 1894
7:30 AM

I opened my eyes earlier than usual. Sweat trickled down the side of my face when I sat up. Sarge Eacret, reekin' of last night's whiskey, kept right on a snorin' in the bed next to me. Mr. Cantrell'd already packed up and gone though. He wuz a carnival barker and he only came through town once or twice a year. He said he warn't much of a barker really. The carnival owner kept him on 'cause he wuz good lookin' and drew in pretty girls—and pretty girls drew in men eager to spend money on 'em. That kinda made sense, exceptin' Mr. Cantrell wuz a bit long in the tooth and walked kinda bent over. I guess there's no accountin' fer what women like.

I stood up and stretched. Today wuz the day Judge Parker wuz gonna hang Lewis Holder. I got dressed and hustled down the stairs.

"Why're you up so early, Archie?" Lydia Sprinkle peeked outta the dining room into the hall.

"Hangin' day, ma'am."

"The marshals won't let you anywhere near the gallows, boy," Tom Sprinkle said from behind his newspaper. "Might as well find fun elsewhere."

"That's not until noon anyway," Lydia said. "It don't take but ten minutes to get to the courthouse, eight if you run. Sit down and eat some breakfast. Mary made flapjacks this mornin' and we have some jam she made from blueberries Mr. Fagan ordered special for us."

I'd planned on grabbin' a bite downtown, but them flapjacks wuz smellin' pretty dadgum good. I took off my cap and held it aginst my chest. "Thank you, ma'am. I think I will."

"Coffee's still on the sideboard." Tom muttered from behind his newspaper.

"Thank you, sir." I took a mug and filled it halfway, using a slug of cream to lighten it a mite.

"Now take a load off." He gestured with the corner of his newspaper.

"Reverend Mathews," I said as I unfolded my napkin. "How's the family?"

"Takin' care of the Lord's business, doncha know."

"Seems like the Mathews family's all about that."

"We are indeed."

I reached across the table to grab one of Mary's rolls fresh outta the oven.

"What're you up to this early," Tom said behind his newspaper.

"Thought I'd go see the Lewis Holder hangin'."

"That execution got you excited, Archie?"

The disapprovin' tone of Reverend Mathews' voice surprised me. "Kinda."

"You think sending that man to meet his maker's gonna be fun?"

"No, sir."

"You planning on whooping and hollering when they hang him? Run around with your buddies like heathens on the warpath?"

"No, sir."

"Then why are you going?"

"Curious, I guess." I chewed my bottom lip, a tryin' to come up with a decent lie. "Never seen a feller die before."

"Never?"

"Only after they been dead awhile." Avoidin' the Reverend's eyes, I held out my plate fer Lydia to fill. "Any of y'all know him?"

Tom lowered the paper he wuz a readin'. "Not to speak of. He spent a night here a few years back. Him and his partner."

"The guy he kilt?"

"Name was Bickle...or Bickford. Something like that." Tom picked up the paper agin.

Reverend Mathews lowered his voice. "It's an ugly thing you're about to see, Archie. You sure you want to go through with it?"

"Ain't that why you're here, sir?"

"It is."

"But why? Certainly not to comfort that polecat down at the jail."

The preacher sighed. "Oh, maybe if he asked for me. But they'll have someone tend to him."

"So why do you go?"

"I go because it's my solemn duty to bear witness to what's happening," he went on "...and to look after those of you who might be sorry you saw what you came to see."

"You don't have to go, Archie." Lydia smiled with her eyes. "Only the four of us would know if you changed your mind."

I laid down my spoon. "I ain't changed my mind."

A woman in a white apron bustled in from the kitchen and set a platter of flapjacks on the table. "Y'all need more coffee?"

"I imagine we do, Mary," Lydia said. "And maybe open another jar of that jam? Our guests have been sneaking extra dollops."

"That stuff's blue gold," Reverend Mathews put in his two cents worth.

"Would you like me to pack you up a jar to take home to Miz Rachel and the kids, Reverend?"

"That sounds wonderful, but I won't be heading home for awhile. Thanks though."

"Don't you worry. I'll run it out to her after I finish up here."

"I'd be much obliged, Miz Kirkpatrick."

She went back into the kitchen.

"Well, it's time I get going." Reverend Mathews pushed back his chair. "Them fellers in the jail get nervous on hanging days." He picked his hat off'n a rack in the hall and put it on. "Ma'am." He nodded to Lydia who smiled back at him.

A door slammed above our heads. Then we heard, step thud step thud.

"Here comes Sarge," Lydia sipped her coffee. "He's running late this morning."

Sarge Eacret limped down the hall, mutterin' somethin' about 'some pantywaist rebel bastard.' Then, all of a sudden, he yelped—and then a crutch clattered down the stairs, landin' cockeyed agin the front door. And Sarge come crashin' after it, a'cussin' and whimperin'. When he hit bottom, he laid spread-eagle in the front hall.

"What in tarnation's goin on?" Mary came in with a platter of fried bacon.

"Sarge fell agin," I told her.

"Here ya go, Sarge." Reverend Mathews squatted down behind the one-legged man's head, slid his hands under his armpits, and hefted him to his foot.

I fetched his crutch and stood back lessen ole Sarge got it into his head to whack me with it.

Reverend Mathews patted Sarge on the back. "You okay?"

Sarge hung onto him to keep from topplin' over agin. "Do I look okay, Will?"

"You probably added a few bruises to your collection. Anything hurt so bad we need to get Doc Southard over here to patch you up?"

"Nothing a jug of whiskey can't fix." Sarge scowled.

"You ain't getting that from me." Reverend Mathews patted him on the back. "But after you get some food down your gullet, my wife has some bushes she wants trimmed back."

"She pays me in fruitcakes and cookies."

"Better for ya, Sarge." Reverend Mathews chuckled as he opened the front door. "Rachel's fruitcakes'll grow hair on your chest same as a bottle. Spare change'd just get you another night in the drunk tank."

After the Reverend left, I follered Sarge into the dinin' room. He stopped, leaned on his crutch, and made a big show outta sniffin' the air. "Flapjacks?"

"Come on in and join us," Lydia said over her shoulder.

"Thank ya kindly." Sarge's chair squeaked when he sat down.

I went back to my own seat across from him. "What're you up to?"

"Guess I'm weeding for Miz Mathews today, Archie."

"Big job?"

"Naw, I weeded there Monday."

"But...?"

Lydia caught my eye and shook her head.

I sighed and focused on drownin' my flapjacks in syrup.

* * *

8:45 AM

Even though the hangin' warn't supposed to happen 'til noon, I wuz tired of bein' cooped up. I'd been in Fort Smith since mid-June but I wuz either workin' or eatin' or restin' the whole time. So's after breakfast, I put on my cap and headed out to explore. I hadn't gone four blocks when I seen a burly feller wavin' his hat and yellin' at me.

"Archie!" Bill Hatcher crossed the street right in front of a lady on a bicycle.

She skidded into him and the two of 'em ended up in a pile of shoes, hats and wheels. Before I could get to 'em, the woman screamed and rolled on the road holdin' her arm.

"Shut up, shut up, shut up!"

From the scowl on Bill's face, I wuz skeered he might punch her in the nose, so's I stepped between 'em. "Whoa, you two. Calm down."

"My bicycle!" The girl tried to point with her good hand. "Look what he did to my bicycle!"

I reached down to help her to her feet. "You alright?"

She screamed and jerked away from me. "I'm fine!" A bruise wuz already formin' under one eye and blood trickled out the side of her mouth.

"No, you ain't fine. And that arm shore ain't fine. Let's get you outta the street and have Doc Southard come look at you."

"I cain't afford no doctor and I cain't miss my shift neither."

"I ain't used to no bicycles on this road." Hatcher sat up and rubbed his cheek where a fair-sized bruise of his own wuz a bloomin'. "I come and go this way all the time and never seen one of them damned contraptions."

"I ride it to work and back every single day and I haven't ever seen you neither." The woman tried to get up but her legs wuz a tangled up in her skirt. "Where you been?"

He stuck out his lip. "I been right here, lady."

I picked up her bicycle. "The front wheel's bent. You cain't ride it like this."

She put her good hand on her cheek and wailed. "How am I gonna get to work?"

"Where do you work?"

"At the telephone company."

I looked around. "It ain't that far."

"But what about my bicycle?"

I looked at Bill.

"Not my fault." He folded his arms across his chest. "Not my problem."

"Well, it's not mine!" The girl's voice rose another notch.

About that time, Sam and Belle showed up with Julia and Fagan in the wagon. Fagan leaned forward. "What's going on, Archie?"

"An accident."

"Oh that poor dear!" Julia climbed down out of the wagon and bent down over the girl. "Oh, you're hurt! Let's get you up on the wagon. Help me, Sam!"

"Yes, ma'am." Sam jumped down and handed me Belle's reins.

Belle gave me her evil eye, but this time, I took the reins and eyed her right back.

"It's getting late. I gotta get to work!" Blood trickled out the side of the girl's mouth and she wuz shiverin' even though it warn't a cool day.

"There now. It'll be okay," Julia pulled a lace-edged handkerchief out of her pocket and pressed it agin the girl's mouth. "Get her up here with us, Sam."

Whilest Sam helped first the girl and then Julia back up into the Bourland's wagon, Fagan turned to me. "What happened, Archie?"

Outta the corner of my eye, I seen Bill wrinkle his forehead. He mighta been meaner'n me but I wuz bigger. Lessin' he shot me, I figgered I could outrun him. And I heared he warn't all that good of a shot. "Bill here had somethin' to tell me," I said to Fagan, "...and he wuz so juiced up about whatever it wuz, he didn't see what wuz a comin' and he knocked that there lady off'n her bicycle."

"No, no, no!" Bill's left eye twitched and his cigar drooped outta the corner of his mouth. "That ain't what happened, I tell ya."

"Okay, Bill," Fagan sighed. "What do you say happened?"

"That idiot girl ran smack dab into me. Didn't even try to brake."

"Uh huh..." Fagan sounded worn out and it warn't even nine o'clock yet.

"What about my bicycle?" The girl sobbed. "It's all I got."

"Bill here works for Mr. Bourland," Julia said. "Let's get a doctor to look at you and then if you're okay, we'll take you to work. I'll have Sam come back for your bicycle and we'll get it fixed."

"I don't mean to be rude, ma'am, but I cain't jes leave it here. Someone'll take it and I ain't got money to fix it. And I jes started this job yesterday. They'll fire me if I don't get to work right now." She sobbed into Julia's bloody lace handkerchief.

"I guarantee no one will steal your bicycle, ma'am," Fagan said.

"How?"

"Randall!" Fagan pointed at a kid in the crowd that'd gathered.

Randall looked startled. "Yes sir?"

Fagan flipped him a coin. "Stay here and make sure no one but Sam touches that bicycle."

"Yes, sir!"

"Bill, you caused this mess. You pay to fix it."

Bill Hatcher clinched his fists and his jaws. "Yes sir."

Fagan turned to the girl a sobbin' in his wagon. "What's your name, young lady?"

"Arabella Plummer."

"It's more important that we get a doctor to look at you now, Arabella."

"How will I get my bicycle back?"

"I'll have someone bring it to you when it's fixed."

"But my job..."

"I own that telephone company you work at."

Her eyes widened. "You're Fagan Bourland?"

He winked at Julia who smiled. "Here's what we're going to do, Miss Arabella. Right now, my wife here'll take you over to The Bailey and call Doc Southard."

Red-faced, the girl lowered her eyes. "Sorry, sir."

Fagan leaned toward the boy who wuz still eyein' the coin in his hand. "Don't go anywhere until Sam gets back here, Randall."

"No sir."

Randall wuz still a grinnin' as they pulled away, headin' fer The Bailey. And Bill Hatcher? Well, he warn't happy about the whole shebang. He limped off a grumblin' under his breath. And me? I headed on over to the old Fort feelin' purty good fer a change.

*   *   *

11:25 AM

A rock wall circled the Federal Courthouse, the jail, the gallows, and the grounds. Cal Whitson stood at the gate. He had a pistol strapped on his hip.

"You got a gun, Archie Biggs?"

I held my arms out, palms up. "Wouldn't know how to shoot it if'n I had one."

"We'll find you face down in an alley one of these days then."

"I shore hope not, sir."

"You a relative of Holder's?"

"Not that I know of."

"How about Bickford? Know him?"

"Who?"

"The feller Holder shot?"

"Naw. I'm new to town. You know that, Cal."

"Ain't plannin' on breakin' Holder out are ya?"

"What?"

"Ain't gonna shoot or stab him?"

"Um…"

"How about throw rocks?"

I wuz flustered. "Jes gonna watch the hangin'. That's all."

"Why?"

"Curious."

Cal narrowed his good eye. "Ain't allowed," he said finally.

"Whatcha mean 'ain't allowed'?"

"You ain't related to Lewis Holder. If'n you was planning a getaway or murder, I'd tote you off for questioning. I don't think you're lying to me and being curious ain't a crime. You best get on along before I come up with a reason to kick your butt out of here though."

"Aw, Cal."

I'd already hiked around the outside wall, lookin' fer cracks, so's I headed fer a big oak I'd noticed when I first crossed Rogers. I jumped—and grabbin' the lowest thick limb—hoisted myself up on it so's could look over the wall. On my right, Reverend Mathews wuz goin' up a set of stairs to the courthouse. To my left, a marshal wuz leadin' folks toward the gallows. I couldn't see what wuz goin' on inside the fence though. "Dang." I put an arm part way around the trunk and slowly stood up on the limb where I'd been sittin'.

"What you doing there, boy?" It wuz a woman's voice. "Causing trouble?"

I looked down. The skinny girl I'd seen on the train the day I came to town stood at the foot of my tree. "I could say the same to you, ma'am." Balanced on

22

my limb, I took off my cap and held it agin my chest. "Don't ya know what's about to happen here? This crowd ain't big now but we're early birds."

She looked around, a dabbin' at her face and neck with a ragged handkerchief. "They say it ain't like the old days when folks came to party. Most people won't even bother to show up in this heat, especially since they won't let anyone in."

"My landlord, Mr. Tom Sprinkle, says there'll be all kinds of ghouls a pressin' up agin that wall by noon. Some not as nice as me. You shouldn't be down here without yer husband."

"How do you know Maud has a husband?"

"I came in on the same train with you a couple months back. I seen you with yer man."

"Ah." Her hat shaded her eyes. I couldn't tell if they wuz blue...or green...maybe gray?

"Seriously, ma'am, if'n you're gonna stay here, he oughta be with you."

"Maud."

"What?"

"That's her name. Say it."

"Miz Maud."

"Don't fancy it up. Just Maud."

"You teasin' me? Maud?"

"Now why would Maud do that? As you say, she's married. At least for now."

Fer now?

"What's your name?"

"Archie."

"Archie what?"

"Biggs, ma'am. Archie Biggs."

"Kinda fits you, now don't it?"

"Yes ma'am, I reckon, it do." That wuz why I picked it, but I didn't tell her that part.

"Can you see much up there, Archie?"

"I kin see the gallows if'n that's what you're askin'. But if'n you're wantin' to know if'n I kin see inside it, not so much."

"What if you climbed higher?"

"I'm about to try that."

She stretched up a thin arm. "Lift Maud up."

"Are you crazy? You cain't climb no tree in that get up."

"No?"

I shook my head.

"Okay then." She took off her hat and set it on the ground at the foot of the tree. Then she reached up under her skirt, pulled out somethin' that looked like a little pillow with long strings on each corner. Grinnin' and keepin' her eyes on mine, she dropped it at her feet. Then she started unbuttonin' the front of her top.

"Whu-whu-what'cha you doin'?"

"Taking off Maud's shirtwaist."

I tried not to look down at her but I couldn't help it. "Bu-but why?"

"You're right. These puffy sleeves'll get in the way."

"What're you two doing over there?" Cal bellowed from the gate.

"Nothin'!" I waved and grinned but my upper lip wuz a sweatin'.

"This here's a family town. We don't cotton to filth where God and everybody can see."

"You're a dirty-minded old coot, Cal Whitson!" Maud yelled back at him. "You think a crowd coming to watch a man die's gonna be offended by a woman with her shirtwaist open?"

"Button 'em up, Miz Allen. Now."

There warn't much he could do. His job wuz to keep ne'er-do-wells outside the wall durin' executions. Of course, he could shoot us or have one of them city cops run us in fer somethin', but I didn't figger he'd do that neither.

"Don't make me come over there."

I looked down. The girl'd taken off her starched jacket with the puffy sleeves, draped it over her shoes—and wuz busy unbuttonin' her blouse. "MAUD!"

"What?" She looked up at me, eyes wide.

"You're gonna get me arrested." I looked around. All kinds of people wuz a headin' to the courthouse now...includin' old biddies with picnic baskets, young gals a pushin' baby carriages, and gypsies tryin' to sell everyone somethin.' I covered my eyes with my free hand."Stop it!"

Maud grinned. "You're embarrassed!"

"Put that stuff back on before that lawman sics someone on us."

"Then come down and help Maud see the hangin' somewhere's else."

"I cain't even look at you."

"How old are you?"

I peeked between my fingers. "Old enough to know you're trouble."

She put her shirtwaist back on and buttoned it up. "Come on down and help Maud find a place where she can see what's going on."

She wuz havin' fun a makin' me feel like a fool, but I jumped down anyways. "Where'd ya suggest?"

She picked up her hat and pressed it down over her hair. "Let's see if we can climb up on the wall behind the gallows. Might be a crack or a peep hole. Maybe Maud can stand on your shoulders or something."

I warn't sure how that would help me see what wuz about to happen, but Maud seemed to think she wuz in charge. "Okay."

"C'mon then." She turned to our left and follered the wall.

"Wait!"

"My God, you're a pain in the butt, Archie. What is it?"

I held up the small pillow a layin' under the tree. "I have no idea."

"That's Maud's bustle."

"Okay?"

"They're going out of style, you know."

I didn't know—or care. "What should I do with it?"

"You got two choices. You can bring it to Maud or you can leave it there. Maud don't care which."

I figgered it fer a trick—and that she did care what I did with it. Very much.

"Well?" She stamped her foot.

I trotted over to her, bustle in hand.

*   *   *

11:45 AM

Maud squinted into the sun. "Can you see anything?"

We wuz behind the wall where the gallows backed up agin it. "All I can see is someone's hat."

"What color is it?"

"Black."

"Who do ya spose that might be?"

"The executioner or a preacher, mebbe?"

"Oh!" She pointed. "There's a peephole! Lift Maud up."

"Where?"

"It's right there. See it?"

I squinted. "Where?"

"There. If'n ya get Maud up high enough, she can see inside."

"Bu-but I won't be able see."

"Don't matter if you see, Archie."

"B-but th-that's why I came down here today."

"Lift Maud up!"

I cupped my hands and squatted down. She put her foot in my palms and her hands on my shoulder. She warn't that heavy, but I couldn't figger out how to get her onto my shoulders.

"Get closer to the wall."

I took a big step forward.

"Turn around."

"What?"

"Turn around and back up until you feel the wall."

With her feet in my hands, I did it.

"Back up...stop. Now lift me higher."

My muscles quivered.

"There we go. Stand up straighter."

The pressure on my arms changed and I guessed that she'd used the wall to help her step up onto my shoulders.

"Hold on to Maud's ankles, Archie."

"What? Why?"

"To help Maud keep her balance."

"Okay." I grabbed her right ankle and pawed through the folds of her skirt fer the left.

"Hold Maud tight now. Move to the left a bit...no, too far."

"Yeah," I grunted as I inched to my left.

"Stop. This here's perfect."

"Perfect fer who?"

"We're almost too late," she said. "Everyone's inside the gallows' fence."

"What're they a doin'?"

25

"Readin' somethin' from the Bible."

"Where's Holder?"

"Already got the rope around his neck."

"Is he skeered?"

"Can't tell. He's facing the same way we are."

"What's he look like?"

"The back of his shoulders ain't bad looking for a murderer." Maud shifted her weight and I staggered sideways. "Hold still," she squealed.

"You hold still."

"Didja hear about what he did when the jury convicted him?"

I gritted my teeth. "Cain't say I did cause I didn't."

"He cussed out Judge Parker!"

Now that wuz interestin.' "Why?"

"He said that if the judge hung him, he'd come back and haunt everyone."

"Haunt?"

"The courtroom, the gallows, the hangman, the marshals—and especially the judge."

I sighed. "Ole Jim Rutherford back in Pope County claims a wolf's been a hauntin' him fer years. Of course, I never seen no wolf and neither did anyone else—and Jim only seen the critter when he'd been at the white lightnin'.'"

"Maud'll do that too. Come back and scare the pee waddlin' outta everyone ever messed with her."

"Wouldn't ya wanna go on to glory? See Jesus?"

"Don't be a fool, Archie." She leaned forward and I staggered, bashin' my head into the wall.

"Dammit," I groaned. "Hold still, will ya?"

"Dead people ain't in no mood to suck up to no wimpy Jesus who didn't bother to fight back when they came for him. They got nothing to show for all the ugliness they had to put up with when they was alive...and they're mad as hell about it."

"How you know all that?"

"Where you been all your life, boy? Haunting's the only payback left a body at the end."

"Uh huh."

"Shush. There's a man in a fine suit and top hat. Maybe that's Judge Parker?"

"I doubt it. Reverend Mathews says the judge don't watch 'em die."

"A preacher?"

"Maybe some padre they invited to spend time with that varmint."

"Preachers ain't usually well to do, are they?"

"The only preacher I know in Fort Smith is Reverend Mathews and even if'n he ever had money, he's long spent it on his passel of kids. About all he does is marry people. Not sure that brings in enough to keep food on his table."

"This old guy has a cane?"

"Doc Breedlove?"

"How old would you say he is?"

"Old. He wuz already a doc durin' the war."

"Married?"

"Whatcha looking fer, Maud?"

"Is he married?"

"Well, of course, he's married. And if'n you're settin' yer hat on him, you should know he's old enough to be yer grandpa. Great grandpa, maybe."

"Maud ain't got eyes for no old man, Archie—but if they got pockets that jingle, she's got kin needing food...and a roof."

"I see..."

"Shush! The hangman put something over Holder's head. Wonder what he's thinking now?"

Goosebumps raised up on my arms. "Even he says he kilt Bickman. He's gotta be wonderin' if'n the devil's gonna treat him right."

"Probably made a deal with that ole bastard long time ago," she said under her breath.

"Is he sayin' anythin'?"

"Hard to make out what they're saying, especially with you going on and on."

"You keep bein' mean, I'll put you down and leave you fer Jim Rutherford's wolf."

"Don't you dare put me down now. It's about to happen."

"Does he look skeered?"

I felt her lean forward. "Naw, don't think so. But he's mad as hell, jes like Maud thought."

"You fibber. You never thought anythin' like that!"

"Did too...oh, there he goes!"

The words wuz no sooner outta her mouth than there wuz a loud crack...and then a kinda wheezy sigh, from the folks inside the fence. Louis probably didn't have no air to sigh with anymore.

"He's harder to see now, cause he's swinging back and forth," Maud said

"Is he a kickin'?"

"Naw, they got his ankles tied together."

I bit my tongue and waited. Finally I nudged her shoe with my cheek, "Someone a prayin'?"

"Maybe."

I waited several breaths longer. "Did ya see Lewis' soul go up to God?"

"You got strange ideas, Archie."

I waited, a wonderin' if'n Lewis Holder wuz still mad? Wuz he still hurtin'? Wuz he already bein' judged by the angels? Finally, I couldn't think about it no more. Or keep on standin' there. "Done?"

"Shush."

"Maud?" I nudged her shoe.

"WHAT?"

"Kin we go?"

"No. They're takin' him down now."

"Who's takin' him down?"

"The Birnie Brothers. You know, undertakers?"

"You wanna watch that?"

"Looks like they're mad at each other."

"Darn it, Maud!"

"The cute one's mad about something."

I wuz fed up so's I stepped back from the wall.

"Archeee! I'm not done looking."

"Yer skirt's a suffocatin' me."

"I want to see!"

"I ain't starin' at this here wall no more!" Ignorin' her squeals, I backed away and pulled on her ankles. She slid down onto my shoulders until she wuz a straddlin' the back of my neck.

She pounded my head with her fists. "I hate you, Archie."

Along about then, I decided I didn't like her much. "Then git offa me."

"Fine!" She held onto my head while she uncurled first one leg and then the other and then slid down my back. "What's this?"

Blushin', I turned to face her. "What's what?"

"This!" She held up my lil green book.

"You picked my pocket?"

"Don't be persnickety, Archie." She opened it and thumbed through the pages. "It's not even in English. Where'd you get it?"

"None of yer business!" I grabbed it away from her and stormed off.

"Archieeee, wait!"

Purty as Maud wuz, I didn't like her much.

*   *   *

Back at The Bailey, I knocked on the door to the Sprinkles' office.

"Who is it?"

"It's me, Miz Lydia. Archie Biggs in room 30?"

"Come on in."

I pushed open the door. Lydia Sprinkles didn't look up from her paperwork, "You still havin' trouble with Sarge?"

"No, ma'am. Me and Sarge is fine now. I didn't come fer that."

"What is it then?" Lydia removed her spectacles and rubbed her eyes before facin' me.

"I brought you a new boarder." I shoved Maud toward Miz Sprinkles. "See?"

"Well, hello." Lydia stood up. "How can I help you?"

"I wanna place where my husband cain't find me, ma'am," Maud said as I backed out of the room and closed the door behind me.

*   *   *

1:10 PM

Without Sarge and the carnival barker a'sawin' logs, my room wuz quiet. Tired from the execution I didn't get to see, I stretched out on my bed. Soon I wuz dreamin' that it wuz a rockin' back and forth and then I heard a kid cryin' behind me. Then I realized there wuz lotsa little ones around me...all of 'em hungry and..."

28

"Archie!"

Someone wuz a bangin' on my door. I opened my eyes.

"Archie!"

"What?" I sat up.

"You're late."

"Huh?"

"It's Sam. You're late for work."

I glanced at the clock on the wall over Sarge's bed. It said 2:20. "Dammit!"

"You awake?"

"I am now." I felt under the bed fer my shoes. "Come on in."

Sam pushed open the door but stayed in the hall while's I laced up my brogans.

"Am I in trouble?"

"Not yet. Mr. Fagan ain't there now either, but you better get yourself together."

"I got up early this mornin' and wore myself out a wanderin' around over by the gallows." I buttoned my shirt up under my chin and smoothed my hair with both hands.

"Enough with the primpin'. We got work to do before you get busy in the saloon."

"I'm ready." I jammed my cap on my head. "Let's go."

We hurried across the street to where Belle and the wagon full of goods waited. James and Cap wuz already sittin' on the wooden boardwalk in front of the store, rummagin' through a box.

Jes as we got there, George Allen busted outta the store, pullin' Maud by her wrist. She wuz cussin' a blue streak and tryin' to jerk away. Morty came out behind 'em and stood in the door, hands on his hips. Gertie started barkin'. James jes sat there watchin' it all happen, but Cap backed aginst the wall of the store lookin' like he wuz gonna cry.

As soon as she seen me, Maud stretched out her other arm and cried, "Help Maud, Archie. George's gonna beat the tar outta her when he gets her home."

Neither me or Sam knowed what to do so's we jes stopped in the middle of South Sixth Street.

"For God's sake, Maud. No one's ever laid a hand on you." George pulled her away from us.

"Help!" Maud kicked over a small box and walnuts spilled out onto the wooden sidewalk. "Archieeee..."

George seen us and frowned.

Me and Sam backed away to let 'em pass.

"Coward," Maud hissed at me. "You're like the rest of 'em, Archie. You're just the same."

"Food and a nap'll make you feel better," George said to her.

"Maud needs her medicine, George. Pleazzzze."

"You've had enough of that crap for today."

She fought him. "No! No"

He picked her up and threw her kickin' and a squealin' over his shoulder.

James stood up. "What's wrong with her, Morty?"

Morty shrugged. "Crazy, I reckon."

"Maud needs her medicine," Maud called as George headed up Sixth. "Archieeeee."

People stepped aside to let 'em pass. Heads popped outta windows and kids pointed and laughed. As they got close to Parker Street, Maud's screams skeered a horse tied up by the courthouse. It tore loose from its tether and galloped toward us with Cephas Rush a chasin' after it. That got Belle goin' too. As she stamped her hooves and brayed, Sam grabbed her reins. "Yo there, girl. Ain't nothin' gonna hurt you."

Wide-eyed, Cap pressed agin the wall of the store as the horse and Cephas rounded the corner headin' fer the river. Holdin' Gertie under one arm, James tried to comfort the lil feller. "Hey, hey, hey. You're okay."

Belle rolled her eyes and heehawed until Sam unhitched her from the wagon and led her to the barn a few yards away.

Me and Morty glanced at each other and busted out laughin' in spite of the chaos around us.

"Ya think that gal's crazy?"

"As a bedbug." Morty chuckled.

"What's going on?" Julia Bourland came a runnin' down Sixth with a pistol in her hand. Pantin' and red-cheeked, she probably thought there wuz a fire or someone robbin' the place...and she came prepared to protect her kids.

"Mama!" Cap ran to her.

Julia put her arms around her youngest. "Shush, baby. Mama's not gonna let anyone hurt you."

"That lady's got a devil inside her," Cap pointed at Maud and George.

"Folks and devils are two different things, sweetheart." She patted Cap's head and then looked up at Morty. "What happened?"

"Some crazy girl that Miz Lydia turned away from the hotel." Morty stepped aside so that his mother and brother could go inside the store. "Turned out she'd run away from her husband."

Cap tugged at her skirt. "She's got funny eyes, Mama."

Julia wrapped her arms around him and kissed the top of his head. "What do you mean, baby?"

"She's always watchin' to see if you're a-watchin' her."

"Oh?"

"Like a cat eyin' a rat."

"She's probably far away from her mama and she's lonely." Julia looked up at me. "What was she doing here?"

I took off my hat. "Don't know, ma'am. I overslept and Sam came to roust me. We'd jes got here when all holy hell...excuse me, Miz Julia...when that woman started throwin' a fit. Skeered everyone pert near to death."

Julia put her pistol inside her skirt pocket. "James?"

"I was going through this box of new books when the ruckus started inside."

"I don't like her, Mama," Cap said.

Julia sighed and picked a cotton bag from a box of them by the front window. "It's rude to say things like that out loud, baby."

"Can I just think it?"

Julia caught my eye and we both choked back a snicker. "You can think anything you want."

She turned to Morty. "Got any beans today? We got a nice piece of leftover pork to season 'em with. Tawny says pintos are best if we got 'em."

"Over by the door to the saloon." He pointed.

"There's Sam a comin' back," I said to no one in particular.

Julia glanced out the window as she inspected the produce. "Where was he?"

"That squallin' girl skeered a horse up the street and he came a runnin' this way with Cephas a chasin' after 'em—and that got Belle a goin' so's Sam put her in the barn."

Julia chuckled. "Sounds like there was a three-ring circus going on here."

"Yes, ma'am. Shore wuz."

"It's all over now, Cap," Julia smoothed his hair offa his forehead. "Why don't you go back out front and help James unpack boxes while Sam unloads them from the wagon."

"Aw, Mama."

She gave him a gentle push. "Go on out there, baby. Shoo!"

Cap went outside and when she could see him through the front window, Julia turned to me and Morty. "Okay, what went on here?"

Me and Morty glanced at each other.

"You first," I mouthed.

"Okay," Morty rubbed his hands together. "This woman named Maud Allen showed up at the boarding house wanting a room. Miz Sprinkle tried to accommodate her, but the woman didn't have a penny on her and no income that Miz Sprinkle could figure. She called The Euper Boarding House where Miz Allen said she'd been living to see if she'd paid them on time. That's when she found out that gal had a husband who was looking for her."

"And that was her?"

"Yes, ma'am." Morty bobbed his head. "She was wanting Pop to change Miz Sprinkle's mind about renting to her."

"Never happen." Julia scooped dried beans into the cloth bag.

"No offense, ma'am," I said, "...but why not?"

"Yeah, Ma." Morty threw a towel over his shoulder. "Every body needs a place to stay. Isn't that why we own a hotel?"

"Women with no known source of income don't always have rent money. And pretty soon they start trying to get the men in the house to help them out. And before you know it, we got tenants fighting each other and... and what all...." She let her voice fade away.

"And what all what?"

There wuz a long pause. "Prostitutes."

"Aw, Ma! Don't say that." Morty blushed. "What would Reverend Mathews say? Or Reverend Culpepper if'n he was around?"

I stared at my shoes, as scandalized as Morty wuz.

"The word 'prostitute' is in the bible, Morty."

"I know but..."

"There are much uglier words for it." Julia glanced out the front window at James and Cap who wuz focused on the crates of vegetables Sam wuz unloadin'.

"What does Pop say?"

"Stop trouble before it starts."

"Meaning?"

"Meaning we don't rent to young women with no source of income. They're trouble."

I glanced at Morty. "Miz Julia's got that right. Maud's more trouble'n anybody I ever runned into."

"So why'd she pick us to hustle?"

I sighed. "I'm sorry, Miz Julia. That wuz me."

"You?"

I avoided Morty's eyes...and Julia's. "I didn't realize it warn't proper. I ran into her at the execution today. She told me she wuz a leavin' her husband and needed a place to stay. So's I introduced her to Miz Lydia. I never thought about Maud not havin' money."

Julia tied the top of the bag into a knot and weighed it. "Women like that want some man to keep them but don't want what goes along with being kept. What she really needs is a mother to reel her in some."

"Yes, ma'am."

"Mark me down for taking two pounds and a quarter, Morty." She held up her basket.

"Sure thing."

"And Archie, you were late?"

My face burned. "Yes, ma'am."

"Don't let Fagan know because then he'll have to lie to me about it tonight."

It took me a bit to figger that one out, then I grinned, "Yes, ma'am."

She paused at the door. "Before you do anything else, Archie, rescue these poor walnuts out here before someone steps on them."

"Right away, ma'am."

"Send the boys home if that woman shows up again, Morty. I don't want James and Cap seeing things like that."

"Should've thought about that myself but things got out of hand before I knew it."

Julia put her hand on Morty's shoulder. "You did good, sweetheart. A grown man might not have thought of it."

The screen door slammed behind her.

Morty looked worried. "Think that girl'll come back here?"

I shrugged. "I don't know much about her except that she's pushy."

"Better tell her not to mess with Mama." Morty filled a big jar with candy.

"I doubt I'll ever see her agin. She don't wanna be around a feller lessen he's got a pocket full of change. Besides, there's somethin' wrong with her."

"What do you mean?"

"She...ain't right." I tapped my own temple.

Morty frowned. "Awww, she just didn't wanna go back to her old man."

"Look at her eyes next time," I said.

Morty stopped unwrappin' a box of taffy fer a moment. "You shoulda seen the fit she threw when he walked in." He sighed. "Our lady shoppers backed away like they thought he was gonna rob us or something."

"Why wuz Maud even here?"

"She was too much for Lydia to handle. I'm glad she sent her here instead of our house though. Mama woulda sent her packing right off the bat if'n she showed up there."

"Miz Julia?" I laughed. "Why she's sweet as pie."

"Sure she is but to get to one of us—including Pop, you gotta get past her and she's one heck of a shot. Grandpa was a deputy U.S. Marshall fer awhile. So's one of our uncles. With the war and all that went on back in the day, they made sure the Bailey girls could shoot."

I wuz impressed. I coulda used someone like Julia a time or two back...well, jes back in Pope County."Let's get to work." Morty picked up the inventory logbook. "We got that wagon load of stuff to log and put away before Pop gets back."

"I'm on it."

Julia stuck her head back in the door. "The boys've decided to go home with me for now. We'll be back later this afternoon. If your father shows, tell him to stay put until I talk with him."

Morty nodded and waved.

*   *   *

By four o'clock, me and Sam'd unloaded the wagon and parked it inside the barn...and with Morty's help...put everythin' away but the big sacks of flour and potatoes. They wuz still on the boardwalk outside the store. Aside from the dry goods and specialty items, I'd unloaded and stowed five cases of liquor in the saloon. And in the store proper, I'd replaced all the wiltin' vegetables with fresh and I had a case of older carrots, cabbages and corn set aside to take to The Bailey Hotel. Tawny used 'em to make stew fer those of us who lived there.

I hoisted the first bag of potatoes over one shoulder. "Where to?"

Morty pointed. "There."

I emptied the potatoes into a display bin, folded the bag and put it in the storage room. I wuz headin' back fer the last of the load, when Julia showed back up with James and Cap.

"Pop's still not here, Mama," Morty said.

"Where is that man now?" Julia put her hands on her hips.

"He said he wuz gonna look at a horse Mr. Shaw has fer sale."

"Must be quite a beast," Julia looked at the clock on the wall behind the counter. "He's been gone for hours."

"Can I have candy, Mama?" Cap tugged at her skirt.

"One, baby."

He ran over to the bowl Morty'd filled and rummaged through the wrapped squares of taffy.

"One, Goober!" Morty smacked his brother on the head with a towel.

33

Cap pulled out a piece, peeled back the wrappin', and popped it into his mouth.

"You want one too, James?"

"I don't like stuff that sticks to my teeth."

"Are you really a kid?" I nudged him with my elbow.

James looked confused. "Of course. What do you think?"

"Never knowed a lil feller that didn't like taffy."

James wrinkled his nose. "I'm not little anymore."

Morty took another piece of taffy from the jar and juggled it. "Which hand, James?"

"I don't care."

The little boy jumped up and down, "I'll take the ones James won't."

"Left or right?"

"Left!" Cap's mouth wuz still full from his first piece.

"Left it is!" Morty opened his left hand and Cap grabbed the treat.

"Tell your no-good father to call me when he shows up, Morty. We have plans for this evening that I'm sure he's forgotten." Julia reached fer Cap's hand. "And, Morty, try to finish up before your father gets back with whatever Tillman Shaw sold him."

"It's a bit late for that!"

Everyone—includin' me—turned toward Fagan Bourland's voice. Standin' in the doorway, he flipped his straw hat across the room and it landed on a wall hook behind Morty's head.

"How does he do that?" I asked Sam who'd follered Fagan into the store.

"Luck. Ain't that so, boy?" Fagan winked at Cap who ran to hug him.

"Practice," Julia corrected him.

Gertie danced around Fagan, a waggin' her tail.

"Hey, poochie." He leaned down and scratched her ears. "How ya doing, James," he said as patted his second son on the head.

James rolled his eyes. "Aw, Pa!"

Fagan kissed Julia on the cheek. "How about you, ole thing?"

"Good enough for a Wednesday. Where's the horse?"

"Left her over in the barn. The guys are gonna give her a rubdown."

"You wore that poor thing plumb out?" Julia put her hands on her hips.

"More like she wore me out," Fagan chuckled. "Rode her from Till's place."

"Where's Lilith?"

"Tied up at Till's."

"Better send someone for her," Julia sighed. "She probably thinks you've abandoned her."

"She knows I'll be back. Like you."

"I wouldn't push either of us too far."

Cap tugged at Fagan's jacket. "What's the new horse's name, Pop?"

"Aurora."

"That's a silly name for a horse."

"Might be, son, but I didn't name her."

Julia frowned. "I'd stick with Lilith. She's tried and true. No need to replace her."

"Not to replace Lilith, sugar. I bought Aurora for you. "

"Oh?"

"You been harping about wanting to get out on your own more. When I saw this little filly, I thought she'd be perfect for you."

"Is she broke for carriage?"

"A little feisty but you can handle her."

Julia sighed. "I wish you'd asked me first."

"Don't you want her?"

"I don't know yet. Show her to me."

"Come on then. Let's go meet the little darling." Fagan held out his arm and Julia took it.

"I wanna come too," Cap cried."

Julia glanced over her shoulder. "Leave the taffy behind."

"It's gone, Mama." His cheeks a bulgin', Cap held both hands palm up.

Julia nodded and Cap chased after 'em.

"So what's this news you have for me?" Fagan asked as they went out the door.

"Dinner with Judge Bryant and the Breedlove's tonight. I knew you'd forget. We need to be there by six."

"I didn't forget. We can make it by six, no problem."

"Really?" Julia raised one eyebrow.

"Eddie'll never even notice if we're late."

"The others might though."

They took a couple steps off the boardwalk. "Julia, my love?"

"Yes?"

"Who exactly is coming to this shindig?"

Arm in arm, they wandered off toward the corral with Cap skippin' along behind 'em.

"Yer folks are great," I said to Morty.

He chuckled. "A powder keg and a spark."

Chapter Three

Maud Meets the Bourlands

July 16, 1894

One of Fagan Bourland's telephone operators, a Miss Arabella Plummer, was attacked on South 6th last evening. The assailant beat her unconscious, stole $1.10 from her purse and took off with her bicycle. The victim described her attacker as 'ugly as sin' and that he 'stunk like a billygoat.' Unescorted ladies are advised to keep an eye out for a short, heavy-set balding fellow, carrying a lady's handbag under his left arm.

Flyer posted in Window of Fagan Bourland's Store

* * *

July 30, 1894

Crawford Goldsby (Cherokee Bill) robbed the Lincoln County Bank in Chandler, Oklahoma, and made off with $500. J.B. Mitchell was killed.

The Guthrie Daily Dealer, August 1, 1894

* * *

Friday, August 1, 1894
10:15 am

A group of girls passed me as I crossed the intersection of South Sixth and "A" Street. When they seen me, they giggled. I pretended I didn't know they wuz a makin' fun of me and hurried into Fagan's store.

"Mornin'," I took off my hat at the door.

"Why're you here so early?" Morty sat behind the counter, porin' over a stack of papers.

"Yer Pop asked me to help you with them books."

"Kinda hard for two people to add, subtract, and multiply in the same book at the same time."

"He said I could take care of customers while you work the figgers."

"Pop said that?"

"I ain't as good with people as I am at cypherin' though."

"Is that so?" Morty stared at me fer a while. "If'n I had fifteen hams and I sold seven of 'em last week and two are set aside for Miz Berry, how many should be hangin' in the storeroom waiting to be sold?"

"Six, I reckon."

"How'd you do that so fast?"

"Fingers." I held up my left hand.

"How's about if I had eight more down in the cellar packed in salt?"

"Fourteen."

"You didn't use your fingers that time."

"Shore did. Same as the first time."

"I watched you. You never touched them."

"That don't mean I don't keep track of 'em in my head."

Morty stared at me fer a bit. "Okay, come on back here."

I squeezed into the office and sat on a stool across the table from Morty.

"Here's this week's record of what we had and what we sold." Morty pointed to a thick book opened in front of him. "That there column's for things Pop's holding for folks."

"Whatcha mean 'hold?'"

"Say the Berrys order something for a certain day and time. When the shipment comes in, we call Mr. Artie and he comes by and picks it up and pays us right then and there. Then there are the Cooks. It takes Miz Emily awhile to put back enough to buy a ham."

"So holdin' 'em means they gotta buyer but you ain't got the money yet."

"Something like that."

"How long you hold 'em?"

"A week."

"So them two hangin' back there'll be paid fer today?"

"Well, one for sure. The other's iffy."

"Iffy?"

"If'n Miz Emily's got the money by four this afternoon, she'll come get it."

"What if she don't?"

"Pop'll have me put it back in inventory. Then Mama'll come in and buy it, Tawny'll cook it and Reverend Mathews'll pick it up and take it to the Cooks anyway. It's Mama's way of tithing."

"Does it happen a lot?"

"Naw. Usually, Miz Emily comes in and buys their ham right before four."

"So's you jes want me to keep track of it all?"

"Do ya mind?"

"Heck no. More fun than liftin' and totin'."

A smile broke out over Morty's face. "That's finer than frog's hair, Archie. Nothin' I hate more than keepin' them books. You want me to close the curtains? I had 'em open to keep an eye on the store in case someone came in."

"Yeah, sure." I said. "I like workin' alone. Get more done that-a-way."

He closed the curtain behind him and I started down the long list of numbers.

*　*　*

I'd been at it fifteen or twenty minutes when I heard a familiar voice. "I'm lookin' for Mr. Bourland."

"You and your mister ain't gonna cause trouble, are ya?"

"Naw. George is working and won't be looking for me."

There wuz a long silence, then Morty said, "What can I do for you, Miz Allen?"

"Talk to the Sprinkles. Tell them to give Maud a room."

"That ain't my business, ma'am."

37

"Sure it is, sweetie. Get your Daddy to okay it."

"The Sprinkles are lookin' out for Pop. If you move in there and can't pay, he loses money."

"I hear your Daddy's rich. What's one little room for Maud when he's got so much?"

"Now, Miz Allen. That ain't for me to say one way or another. That's business and even if you got Pop to change his mind, Mama wouldn't hear of it."

"Why does she have a say at all?"

Morty laughed. "Because she does."

"Maybe you could help Maud convince her?"

"Um..." Morty sounded confused and skeered.

Something bumped into the wall beside the curtained openin' to the back office where I sat.

"Love that peach fuzz on your lip, baby boy."

"Miz Allen! Stop it. This is a place of bus..."

I stood up.

There wuz a crash.

I threw open the curtain to see Morty backed into a corner and the tiny woman trying to get around an upset stool between them.

"MAUD!"

Maud looked back at me. "What're you doin' here, Archie?"

"Workin'. The question is, what're you doin' here?"

She jerked a thumb over her shoulder at Morty who wuz backed up agin the wall. "This here boy's tryin' to take advantage of Maud, Archie."

We'd been down this road before. "No." I frowned. "He warn't."

"Yes, he was! And I'm gonna tell everyone all about it."

"Go right ahead, Miz Allen. You tell 'em. Nobody'll believe you." Morty's voice cracked.

"Say Maud, honey. That's how Maud likes it."

I stepped between 'em. "Stop it!"

His face red, Morty hissed over my shoulder. "My parents know me. My brothers and uncles know me. Heck, most of the folks in this town know me."

"And they don't know you, Maud." I wanted to shake a finger in her face, but from the look in her eyes, I wuz afeared she'd bite it.

"I think you better go now, Miz Allen and not come back." Morty stuck out his lower lip.

Breathin' heavily, Maud started toward the door. Halfway down the aisle, she bumped into a bin of tomatas. She glanced over her shoulder like a dog eyin' a sausage on someone's dinner plate. Then she looked back at me, a grin a spreadin' across her face.

"Stop," I raised my voice fer the first time. "I see what yer up to!"

"You mean this?" She held up a tomata and smirked.

"Why you little thief!" Morty's eyes liked ta popped outta they's sockets.

"Put it down, Maud." I blocked Morty with my arm or he'd have charged her, right then and there. "Put it down and go away and don't come back."

"You can't talk to poor lil Maud that way, Archie."

"Go on. Get outta here before there's trouble."

"You mean like this?" She hurled the tomata at me and ran out the door. It hit me square in the nose, busted and bounced off my chest.

"Damn it, Maud!" I started after her and stepped on what wuz left of the dadgum tomata. One foot slid out from under me and I fell hard, a hittin' my cheek on one of the display bins and a jammin' a finger tryin' to catch myself.

"Archie!" Morty knelt down beside me. "Oh, you're bleeding, stay still."

"It ain't blood," I growled. "It's tomata juice."

"I better get Pop over here. And Mama." Morty stood up. "Stay still."

"Where am I gonna go?"

He got on the telephone and talked to his mother. Then he ran out onto the boardwalk and yelled fer Sam. When he came back in, he said, "You ain't gonna believe it. That crazy girl's up the block screaming and carrying on like nothing I ever saw before."

"Worse'n when George carried her outta here?"

"Excepting George ain't around this time."

Sam came to the door, took one look at me and raced off to find Julia and Fagan.

"I cain't believe it," I rubbed my eyes tryin' to get tomata seeds outta them.

*　*　*

"You say all this woman wants is a room?" Fagan paced back and forth while Julia and Tawny tended to me. "She's doing all this for that?"

"She's crazy, Pop," Morty said. "Won't take no for an answer. Thinks she's gorgeous but she ain't. Liked to scared me to death. Except for Archie standing up to her, I don't know what woulda happened."

"You did all anyone could've done," Julia picked a tomata seed off'n his apron. "Who'd think a grown woman'd act that way?"

Tawny dabbed at my eyes with a damp cloth. "I can't say I ever seen anyone hit in the face by a tomato before. Don't think it was firm enough or thrown hard enough to do much damage but where you bumped yourself when you fell is puffin' up."

I couldn't see clearly from either eye and my finger hurt like the dickens. "I gotta get cleaned up before the saloon opens." I struggled to get up.

"Stop it, Archie. No sense in falling again." Julia put a hand on my shoulder. "Morty, fetch a bucket and a mop."

"Okay, Mama."

"Is that finger broken, Tawny?"

"Don't think so, ma'am, but we might oughta see if Doc Southard will come take a look."

Fagan leaned over the two women tendin' to me. "Not Dr. Breedlove?"

"That poor soul has a hard time getting around these days," Julia said. "He'll never know we called Doc Southard."

"I hope not."

I tried flexin' and unflexin' my hand. "Can I get up, now?"

Tawny's eyes wuz enough to keep me layin' on my back, but she put her hand on my chest in case I tried it. "What if that there bin knocked you crazy,

39

ever think of that? What if you got up and passed out? What if you started puking?"

"My God, Tawny. Can we not talk about puking?" Fagan wrinkled his nose. "Archie, do what these ladies tell you. I'll send Sam to find Doc Southard. Won't be too long. They live up the street on the other side of Garrison."

"I ain't movin', Mr. Fagan."

"Good. Now what you want to do about that girl?"

I glanced at Morty who wuz in the back room fetchin' a mop. "She knowed yer boy's a youngster and she went after him anyways."

Julia put her hand on Fagan's. "This is the second time that girl's caused trouble."

"Sounds like she ain't much more than a kid herself," he sighed.

"She's a grown woman with a husband. Let him take care of her. We have to protect our boys. Who knows what might've happened if Archie hadn't been here?"

"Hell, Morty's as tall as you are."

"He's still my baby."

"She pert near skeered him to death, Miz Julia," I said, "But I gotta say the boy rallied and stood up fer himself."

"See!" Fagan helped Julia to her feet. "The kid did fine."

"A thirteen-year-old child shouldn't have to fend off a crazy woman." Julia patted her hair back in place and brushed lint off her skirt.

Fagan eyes rested on mine. "Thank you, Archie, for looking after my boy."

*   *   *

Tom Sprinkle wuz a standin' in the arch between the parlor and the hallway when I opened the front door. "What the Sam Hill happened to you, Archie?"

"It looks worse than it is, sir. Mostly tomata juice."

He pushed his glasses down his nose and peered over them. "Uh huh."

"I wuz fussin' with that girl who wants to stay here. She backed Morty Bourland into a corner and lied about it."

"You know that or heard about it?"

I held out my red-stained sleeve. "I seen it, sir."

"What did the Bourlands do?"

Lydia Sprinkle came outta her office. When she seen me, she put both hands to her cheeks. "Oh my goodness, Archie. What happened?"

Embarrassed, I avoided her eyes. "That girl that wanted a room came back and went after Morty Bourland. Skeered him silly."

"Oh that poor dear. He's such a well-mannered child. Won't say boo unless he has to."

"Yes, ma'am. Wuz real hard on him."

"And you took up for him?"

"He took up fer himself, ma'am. I jes...uh...backed him up a bit."

"And that tiny girl did this to you?" She raised one eyebrow.

"With a tomata, ma'am. It hit me in the face and dropped on the floor. I stepped on it."

The corners of Lydia's mouth twitched.

"Don't do it, Lydia," Tom covered his mouth with one hand.

"It's okay, sir." I took off my cap and lowered my head. I been laughin' about it my own self." Avoidin' they's eyes, I waited until they wuz done a chucklin'.

"I'm sorry, son." Tom took off his glasses and wiped his eyes with his handkerchief. "Just the idea of a tomato fight in Julia Bourland's spotless store...well, it's ..." He bit his lip.

"Sir."

"Me too, Archie. We're not laughing at you." Lydia said.

"I know." They wuz of course, but I let it go.

"I imagine Miz Julia's pretty mad?"

"I thought she might go after Maud herself, ceptin' Morty wuz still worked up."

"And Fagan?" Tom stood up.

"Says he's gonna give that girl what fer."

"He oughta take you with him, Tom," Lydia said. "There's something wrong with that girl."

"What?" He turned to her and then back to me.

"She's mad," Lydia said. "And she's out to make everyone feel as bad as she does."

"That how you see it, Archie?"

"She'd steal a nickel off'n a dead man's eye. But..."

"But what, boy?" Tom frowned.

"I feel right sorry fer her, sir."

He sighed. "Guess I better go talk with Fagan."

"Be careful, sweetheart," Lydia said under her breath as he closed the door behind him.

"I'm sorry about all this, ma'am," I said when he wuz gone.

"How's this your fault, Archie?"

"The day I brought her here, I seen her do the same thing to some kids over by the gallows. She told 'em that she'd tell everyone they tried to...well, you know."

"And they didn't in anyway approach her?"

"I wuz right there. And that's what she wuz a tryin' to pull on Morty Bourland too."

"Oh my," Lydia wrung her hands. "You're right, Archie. That poor child's going to get herself in serious trouble sooner or later."

"She ain't never gonna get what she wants neither."

"And what is that?"

"I got no idea."

She stared at me fer a bit. "Are you okay, Archie?"

"Embarrassed mostly. Doc says to wash up and take a nap. Should be okay in a couple hours."

"Better get on upstairs, then."

"Yes, ma'am."

"I'll warm up some ham and beans for you."

"I'd be obliged."

Lydia Sprinkle wuz good people.

* * *

I startled awake.

"Heard you had a bad day," Sarge said.

I sat up and threw my legs over the side of my bed. "What'd ya hear?"

"That you had a row with a lady over at Bourland's Store."

"A row, eh?" I yawned and stretched.

"That pretty young thing's a tellin' anyone that'll listen that you was gonna rape her right there in the middle of the store in front of the Bourland boy."

"Aw, fer Pete's sake, Sarge. You believe that?"

"Not for a minute but thought you oughta know. She was over at Bob Wyatt's saloon when Fagan and Tom found her."

"How'd ya know that, Sarge?"

"Cause I was there too. Hee hee. Sittin' at the bar a mindin' my own bizness. Yessiree, she got to tellin' 'em about how you was tryin' to get at her when she threw that 'mater atcha." Sarge rocked back and forth on his bed, cacklin'. "All's I can say is that sucker musta weighed five pounds to do that much damage."

I squinted up at him, "Is it that bad?"

"Naw, not so bad. Ya look like you did a few rounds with John L. Sullivan's all."

I groaned and stood up. "Fagan and Tom? Are they back yet?"

"Hoo, yes. They're a-waitin' for ya down in the parlor."

"They sent you to fetch me and you didn't tell me?"

"I'm doin' that part right now, boy," he chuckled. "They wanted me to ask you to join 'em."

I got up, poured water from a pitcher into the basin and splashed it on my face. Pattin' my sore cheekbone and swollen eyes with a towel, I said, "What happened to the girl?"

"Whatcha mean?"

"She still drinkin' down at the bar?"

"Don't rightly know. She wuz havin' fun when I left. It don't seem fair though, ya know?"

"Fair?" My spare shirt wuz short in the arms and tight between my shoulder blades, but my only other one wuz still damp." What're you talkin' about?"

"If'n a man runs outta money, the barkeep'll show him the door. If'n you're a pretty lassie though, you can stay till the cows come home and all them men hangin' around'll buy her drinks the livelong day and night. Ain't fair."

"Maybe you need to show off that skinny leg of yers, Sarge." I tried to wink as I headed out the door, but neither eye'd close right.

* * *

"Sarge said you wanted to talk to me?" I stood in the archway to the parlor.

"Come on in, Archie." Tom waved.

42

"I-I'm not too good-lookin' right now, sir."

"No, no. Not so bad." Fagan pointed to a couch. "Take a seat."

"What'd ya want to talk to me about, Mr. Fagan?"

"About what you did for my boy this afternoon. I want to thank you."

I tried to smile. "Ole Morty did good on his own."

"That lil gal's got no limits going after a kid like Morty."

"No, sir. She shore don't."

Tom put a hand on my shoulder. "We saw how she was at the bar. She'd get a man in trouble for sport."

"I never thought of it thataway, sir, but now that ya mention it, that sounds about right."

Fagan stood up. "Two things. First, that woman's not to set foot on any of my properties. Not my store or the barn or my hotel. You understand?"

"Yes, sir."

"My wife's a sweet woman, unless you mess with one of her chicks. Anyone fool enough to cross that line...well, none of us has ever been brave enough to try."

The idea of Julia Bourland as the big bad wolf made me chuckle.

"So if that girl shows up at any of the businesses—or gets anywhere near one of my kids, you get Sam to help you protect them. And get ahold of Brizzolara. He'll know what to do."

"Yes, sir."

"What was the second thing, Tom? This here business has my head spinning."

Tom rubbed his thumb and forefinger together and grinned.

"Ah, yes. I was lucky to run into you at the train station that day, Archie. My wife likes you. Hell, my wife loves you. My kids like you too. Even Mr. Snootypants, James likes that you been reading his castoff books."

"Yes sir."

"Sam says you're a good man too. And Tawny says you are...and I quote...awful damn cute for a white boy...unquote."

I blushed but knowin' Tawny said somethin' nice about me felt good.

"They all want you to keep on workin' at the store."

"I...uh...I warn't plannin' on leavin' anytime soon, sir."

"No, probably not yet. But soon enough you might get bored or find some sweet little someone you want to court and boom, you'll be out the door."

I frowned, tryin' to work out what he wuz a gettin' at.

"It's like this, son. Everyone says you got potential and everyone in my life that matters likes you. So, I'm gonna make it worth your while to stay with us as long as possible."

"Uh, how so sir?"

"Pay you, of course."

"Aw, you already pay me a fair salary, sir."

"Here's how it'll work. Tom and Lydia here are gonna clean out a room that we use as storage right now. That'll be your room...free of charge...until you leave my employment."

"My own room, sir?" My voice broke. "You mean by myself?"

"It's small, but it'll have a bed and a closet. Maybe we can find you a little dresser. Nice and private. That work for you?"

That caught my attention and I grinned. "Yes, sir!" I'd never had a room to myself.

"Good."

"Thank you, sir." I grabbed his hand and pumped it.

Fagan winced and pulled his hand outta mine. "There's a couple other things we need to talk about besides crushing the bones in a man's hand."

"I'm sorry, sir. I..."

"I'm going to get someone else to help Bill Hatcher in the saloon. I want you to keep on doing the books—not just for the hotel and store and bar but for the horse business and the wood and the phone company too. Tom here'll teach you. Then we'll all rely on you for numbers."

"I do like cypherin', sir."

"Good. And for all that, I'll double what I'm paying you now. And we'll see how you're doing next year and talk about the future then."

My ship'd come in. "Thank you, sir. I'll do my level best to live up..."

"You already have. Julia said you should think of yourself as an honorary Bourland."

"Miz Julia said that?"

"Well, I think James suggested it."

I grinned. "He likes that I like his books."

"And Cap likes that you sneak him candy when the missus isn't looking."

"Me? Sir?"

"You."

I remembered not to squeeze his hand when I shook it this time.

*　*　*

After Fagan left, I wuz feelin' high on the hog...and hungry. I stuck my nose into the kitchen and wuz surprised to see Tawny at the stove. "What're you doin' here?"

"Filling in for Mary. Someone in her family's sick and she needed to check on 'em."

I sat down at the kitchen table. "I...uh...I...thank you fer patchin' me up."

"You'd have done the same for me and mine, Archie."

"Let's hope I never have to do that, though."

"We're all proud of Mr. Morty...and grateful you was there to back him up." Tawny sprinkled flour on the dough, put it in a ceramic bowl, and covered it with a cloth. "You want to eat?"

"I could eat a rhinoceros right now."

"Hoo, now. You even know what one of them critters looks like?" Tawny nodded fer me to sit down at a small table by the back window.

"I seen a drawin' in one of James' books. Ugly son of a gun."

"So you ain't jes a playin' along with Mr. James?"

"Naw, I like his books. Gives me somethin' new to think about."

"Good." She put a big slab of cornbread onto a plate, cut up some green onions, ladled beans and a chunk of ham onto it. "You like butter?"

44

Tryin' not to seem as eager as I wuz, I nodded.

"You look like the kinda kid that'd go for that." She put a big chunk of butter on it and stuck the whole thing in the oven to warm up. "We got regular milk, and we got buttermilk."

My stomach growled. "Buttermilk, please."

She poured me a glass and I took a big swaller before she could get the beans outta the oven and set 'em down in front of me. "It's been a hard day, ain't it?"

"Not what I expected when I got up this mornin', that's fer sure."

"Miz Julia's mighty grateful you stood up for Mr. Morty. That crazy woman embarrassed the peewaddlin' out of him."

"Me and Morty...we're a good team."

"You got that right." She set the plate of food down in front of me.

"That woman scares me to death, Tawny," I said as I tackled the beans. "She ain't got no more sense than that old rhino we wuz talkin' about. Goes through life knockin' folks down and tramplin' 'em."

"Mm, Mm, Mm." She turned her attention back to cookin'. "Never heard of such a thing."

After a few bites, I stopped long enough to say, "Must be a big job, cookin' fer everybody."

"Mary's got the touch, but I can manage. It ain't no harder to cook for thirty than it is for five. Jes bigger pots." When she laughed, the little dimples in her cheeks got deeper.

"Did you hear what Fagan did fer me?" I said before I thought better of it.

"I mighta heard somethin' about tyin' you down and makin' you an honorary Bourland—like me and Sam. They're so good to us, we'd never think about leavin' 'em."

"They seem like everyday folks to be so rich."

"The Baileys are tight. Miz Julia keeps up with her brothers and sisters...there's eleven or twelve of 'em, I think. And a whole bunch of cousins too. They're spread out all over the country these days. Miz Julia...well, she takes care of everybody. I heard Mr. Fagan say that's cause of her little brother gettin' kilt."

"Aw, now ain't that too bad," I said with my mouth full. "How'd it happen?"

"Name was Robert E. Lee like ever other kid born in the South after the war. You know how kids are, by the time Bobby Lee was sixteen, he was begging for a horse of his own. And Mr. Wiley, Miz Julia's pa—he gave him one for Christmas. That boy was so excited he couldn't hardly eat his dinner. He jes had to take that horse out. I don't know if it threw him or he jes fell off and hit his head on a rock. He wasn't but seventeen years old."

I swallered. "That's mighty sad."

"Miz Julia never did get over it. Mr. and Miz Wiley neither." A tear tickled down Tawny's cheek like Bobby Lee up'n died yesterday afternoon.

"Maybe that's why she watches over them boys like she does."

"Probably so," Tawny sighed. "And that's why she appreciates you taking up for Mr. Morty the way you did. Want some more buttermilk?"

I held up my glass.

"Her pa, Mr. Wiley, he died in June, right before you showed up," she said as she refilled my glass. "Stomach cancer. Must run in that family. His sister, Miz Julia's favorite aunt, died of the same damn affliction. Tore Miz Julia up bad. She don't let go easy. Now she's worrying her mother, Miz Lucinda, to death, afraid something might happen to her too."

"Well, it will sooner'n most of us want."

"That's the problem. Which is better? Losing someone out of the blue? Or livin' for years expecting it?"

"Both, I guess." I laid down my spoon. "I never lost anyone I knowed really well. Hard to figger how I'd feel about it."

"That mean all your kin are still above ground?"

I stirred my coffee fer a bit. "How'd Mr. Bourland get so rich?"

* * *

"Miz Emily! Hold on and I'll help you."

A woman, leanin' on her cane, wuz havin' a time with the single step up onto our boardwalk.

"Thank you, Archie. These spectacles make it hard to keep my balance anymore. When I first got 'em after me and Babe moved here, they made everything clear as a bell. But I can't tell how close or faraway or high that step up is anymore."

"How'd you get here all by yerself?" I got behind her and cupped her elbows.

"That nice Cal Whitson brought me up in his wagon."

"Well, that wuz mighty nice of Cal," I said as I guided her forward. "Yer toes are about an inch away now. Can you feel the riser?"

She tapped it with her left foot. "I feel it." Leanin' back agin me to keep her balance, she follered the riser up until she found the top of the step.

"Jes put yer weight on that foot. I ain't gonna let you fall backward."

"Step ups are mighty nerve-wrackin', Archie." Her voice quivered.

"Yes, ma'am. They shore are."

The door opened and Morty hightailed it out onto the boardwalk.

I leaned sideways and winked at him. "Here's the cavalry come to rescue us, Miz Emily."

"Morning, Miz Emily," Morty said as he took her arms.

"Is that you, Morty Bourland?"

"In the flesh."

"You're taller than last week."

"By a hair."

"Mebbe I'm shorter this week," she chuckled.

Morty winked at me over her head. "Only so much height in the world and Archie got it all."

"I'm a hoggin' all the inches I kin get." I lifted her up from behind and Morty steadied her.

"Oh my!" She swayed back and forth between me and Morty, tryin' to find her balance. I put out my arm fer her to grab but she shook her head.

"Nothing like a little excitement," she puffed. "Draws a crowd...specially if I fall on my face. Good for business."

46

"Yes, ma'am." I stood behind her until she got her balance. "Excitement beats boredom."

"That's because you're young, Archie. Nothing hurts yet." She straightened her hat and waited fer Morty to grab her cane before it rolled off the boardwalk. "At my age, excitement ain't all that different from aggravation."

I grinned. "Yes, ma'am."

Morty opened the door.

Emily Cook smoothed her skirt. Then, chin high, she went in.

He follered her. "How's Babe these days, Miz Emily?"

"She's still blind, Morty."

"Yes, ma'am," he said. "I spose she is."

"She can't see at all and what I see is blurry. It's a wonder one of us ain't burned the house down yet."

I guided her around a table full of produce. "You need any help, Miz Emily, you jes send fer me. I don't mind lendin' a hand."

"Ain't you the sweetest thing, Archie, but don't offer less'n you mean it."

"I mean it, ma'am."

"And if Archie can't make it, I'll come a running too," Morty said.

"Thank you, boys. I appreciate that, I surely do."

"We got some of Miz Homann's jelly that Babe likes so much." Morty held up a jar.

"She's gonna have to pass today. I've got to pay for that ham we put aside." She handed the jelly back to him. "And maybe get a potato or two."

Me and Morty exchanged glances.

I shrugged and stuck my hand into my pants pocket. "This yers, Miz Emily?" I held up a quarter.

Her eyes went from the coin to my face and then back to the money. "Don't think so, Archie."

"Sure it is. It fell outta yer pocket back when you dropped yer cane."

Behind her spectacles, her eyes wuz a waterin'. "Thank you, Archie, for findin' it for me. There's a blessin' in it for you."

"Must be my lucky day." I smiled at her even though I warn't sure she could see it.

*   *   *

Miz Emily wuz standin' on the corner when I came out the door. It wuz hotter'n blue blazes and she wuz sufferin' from the heat.

"You okay, ma'am?"

"Just tired. Was hoping to find someone heading my way. It's not far as the crow flies, but I ain't much of a crow these days."

"Let's get you back inside where the sun's not beatin' down on you. I'll go see if Sam kin bring the wagon around."

"I'm thinkin' this might be my last trip up here. I don't have the strength anymore."

"No problem, ma'am. I'll be glad to deliver whatever you want, includin' you."

"Thank you, Archie."

Whiles I wuz a helpin' her back up on the boardwalk, Morty came to the door, a lookin' worried.

"How about a glass of water, Miz Emily," he said as I passed her to him. "You can rest in the bar while Archie finds Sam."

* * *

Belle stood outside the barn door, already harnessed to the wagon. She looked up at me.

"You ain't gonna bite me, are ya?"

"Eeeeee awwwwww!" She turned to look into the barn and then back at me.

I took a step and her ears went back. "Eeeeeeee!" I stopped agin. "Aw, Belle. I ain't got time fer this." Actually, the ole mule didn't look like she wuz gonna eat me alive. She looked...well, she looked nervous. "Awwwww!"

"Somethin' scarin' you, old girl?"

Belle stamped her feet and swished her tail.

I started past her...

She brayed so loud I about jumped outta my skin.

"WHAT?"

She moved the wagon forward and back, makin' a wheezin' sound. Then, somewhere deep inside the barn, Gertie howled.

Goosebumps rose on my arms. Something wuz definitely wrong! I broke into a run. "SAM?"

"Archie..." Sam's voice echoed in the high-ceiling barn. "Archie, come lend a hand!"

I took a few steps and stopped. "Where are you?"

"Loft. Back of the barn. Where Bill Hatcher plays cards? Hurry. It's coming after us."

"What is?"

"A great big snake."

"Does it got rattles?"

"Don't see any."

I wuz a tryin' not to breathe so fast. "At least it ain't poisonous."

"It's hungry though."

"What makes you think that, Sam?"

"It went after Gertie."

My mouth went dry. "She okay?"

"One of Cap's roosters startled the thing and it came after us. Me and Gertie climbed up into the loft. Never seen a dog scurry up a ladder like that before. The rooster's snake food though. I can hear its bones apoppin'."

"Maybe that'll be enough to keep it quiet fer awhile." My heart wuz a thumpin' so hard I wuz a feared it wuz gonna bust outta my chest. "Where is it?"

"Underneath us. Hatcher must have the ladder nailed down. It won't move."

"Why in the world did he do that?"

"I'm sure he has his reasons."

"How...uh...how big is this critter?"

"I never seen a snake this big. That color neither. Must've come in with our last load of gear, cause this thing sure ain't from Arkansas."

48

It wuz darker toward the back of the barn. And it wuz downright spooky a knowin' somethin' had Sam treed thataway. The horses and mules rustled around in they's stalls—stampin' and cryin' like they knowed all about the snake. Halfway down the length of the buildin', the old barn cat, Violet, screamed and hissed. A second later she runned past me, her hair a standin' up on her back.

"Skeeredy cat," I muttered.

Deep in the barn, Gertie's barkin' turned into almost a scream.

I grabbed a hoe off a rack. "Where is it, Sam? Exactly?"

"Bottom of the ladder to the back loft. It went after Violet, but she slapped at it and took off."

I stopped. "Jes how big is that critter?"

"Big. Maybe fifteen feet? And big around…like a cantaloupe or a watermelon. Don't think that chicken's gonna fill it up." Sam's voice cracked.

I leaned aginst the wall, my heart a poundin'. Biggest snake I ever came across wuz in an outhouse back in Pope County. I warn't but eight or nine at the time and that critter wuz longer than I wuz tall. The memory still made my skin crawl.

"Archie?"

"Yeah?"

"When you plan on coming in here?"

"Jes figgerin' things out…"

"Maybe figure them out faster?"

"Why?"

"It's coming up the ladder after us."

The hoe wuz sharp and had a long handle, but it wuz meant fer weeds—not a snake as big around as a watermelon. What if'n it broke?

Gertie's barkin' got shriller.

"Archie?" Sam sounded skeered.

Not knowin' what else to do, I ran back to the loft. The snake's head wuz already three rungs from the top of the ladder. I chopped at it with the hoe. It moved faster. Before it could get back around the ladder and either bite me or get to Sam and Gertie, I swung at it. Agin and agin.

"Archie!" Sam's voice seemed a long ways away.

I kept on a choppin' until it fell on the ground beside me, thrashin' around—coilin' and uncoilin'. Finally, I slammed the hoe down on it one more time, slicin' off its head.

Sam crawled down the ladder and kicked the carcass.

I still held the hoe over my shoulder like'n it wuz a baseball bat.

"It's dead, son."

I breathed faster and faster.

Sam put his hand on my shoulder. "Put the hoe down."

"I c-c-cain't."

"Sure you can. Just give it to me." He reached up and took the handle.

Voices outside the barn and a loud heehaw caught my attention.

"Let go, boy. Relax your hand. There ya go." Sam took the hoe and leaned it up aginst the wall. "Let's sit down a bit."

I grabbed a hold of the ladder and bent over, a gaspin' fer air.

"Everything okay in there?" The voice wuz familiar but I couldn't bring to mind who it wuz.

"A big old snake tried to eat me and Gertie, Mister Fagan," Sam called back, "And Archie here kilt it right before it got to us up in the loft."

"Well, well, well. Look at this..." Bill Hatcher, a shotgun over one shoulder, nudged what wuz left of the critter with one toe. "Looks like you took care of business, boy."

Fagan, a few steps behind Bill, took in the situation. "We owe this young man another debt of gratitude, don't we, Sam?"

"Yes sir, we do."

I couldn't stop a pantin'.

Fagan peered at me over his glasses. "You ain't gonna pass out on me, are you?"

"N-No, sir, I-I don't plan..."

*　*　*

Morty and Miz Emily stood over me. I squatted outside the barn, heart a poundin' and hands a shakin'. Belle wuz still harnessed to the wagon. She'd calmed down a mite, but still flenched when anyone got close to her.

"I shore didn't mean to scare y'all." I waved away the water Morty offered me. "Wuz excited, that's all."

Fagan and Bill came outta the barn. Sam follered, a pushin' a wheel barrow filled with giant yeller-skinned chunks of meat.

Belle shied and screamed, but Sam'd tethered her to a post.

"Shush, Belle!" Morty grabbed her reins. "This thing ain't gonna hurt no one now."

Miz Emily took off her glasses and squinted. "What is it?"

"A snake, ma'am," Morty said. "A great big one."

"Yellow?

"Yes, ma'am."

"I never seen anything like it." Sam poked at a big piece of snake meat with the pitchfork. "That son of a gun was big enough to swallow a billygoat."

"James reads all the time. Maybe he'll have an idea," Morty said. "We can ask him when he gets here with Mama and Cap."

"Sure hope that critter don't have friends." Miz Emily bent over the wheel barrel. "Living down on the Poteau like Babe and I do, we've had lotsa Water Moccasins ... and a Copperhead once in awhile. But never in my life did I see a critter like this one."

"My family worked these rivers for years, first with riverboats and then with the ferry business," Fagan said. "A snake like this one'd stand out like a sore thumb."

"My guess is it escaped from a circus," Bill said. "Maybe it belonged to one of them Gypsies camped out on Rogers. They got all kinds of things we don't find around here."

Morty nudged the wheel narrow with his toe. "Were you scared?"

"I was," Sam said. "Thought for sure me and Gertie was gonna be this feller's dinner. Wasn't anyplace to run to up in that loft."

50

They turned to me.

"I-I never been so skeered in my life."

Fagan clapped me on the back. "That's two times you came through for the Bourlands, Archie. I knew you were somebody special the day I saw you on that train."

"You're quite a kid, aren't you?" Miz Emily dabbed at my sweaty cheeks with her kerchief.

"Lots a kids ki-kill snakes, ma'am."

"Never knew any around here to go after something like that." She pointed at the dead critter in the wheelbarrow.

Morty offered me the cup agin. "Neither have I."

My hand wuz still shakin,' so's when I took a swaller, it spillt down my chin.

*　*　*

When I stowed Miz Emily's groceries in the back of the wagon, Belle stamped her front hooves and shook her head. I stepped back, heart poundin'.

Miz Emily patted my hand."You scared of old Belle?"

"Don't think she likes me much."

"Horses?"

"Don't think they care much fer me neither."

Sam took hold of Belle's harness. "She's loud but she ain't never hurt no one."

"Just get to know her," Morty said.

Fagan folded his arms across his chest. "Go ahead. Pet her."

"W...what if'n she don't..."

"Belle's not gonna bite you."

"You think?"

"Why Belle's as sweet as the live-long day," Miz Emily said. "Just don't startle her."

I put my hand out. Belle turned to watch me. I stopped.

"Come on, Archie. If'n you can kill a giant snake, you can pet a sweet ole gal like Belle." Sam took my hand and placed it on Belle's shoulder. "There, ya go."

Belle turned to look at me.

I froze, my hand an inch or so from her shoulder.

Then, Belle bobbed her head and after I seen she warn't gonna bite me, I petted her agin.

Fagan slapped his straw hat aginst his thigh and laughed. Miz Emily and Morty did too.

"C'mon. Let's get Miz Emily on home." Sam stowed her groceries in the wagon while's I helped her up on the wooden seat.

"I didn't take up nearly so much space back in the day." She fussed with her hat and squirmed.

Belle turned to watch as I climbed into the bed of the wagon and squatted behind Sam and Miz Emily.

Sam took the reins and clicked and Belle started forward.

"Wait!"

Sam pulled back on the reins. "What in tarnation?"

51

Morty ran up to the wagon. "This was in the barn. Musta fallen outta your pocket when you passed ou...uh...you musta dropped it." He held up my little green book.

I patted my pockets, but of course since Morty wuz a holdin' it wuz proof I'd dropped it.

Miz Emily reached down and took it from Morty, adjusted her glasses, looked it over...and then handed it to me."

"Thanks." Avoidin' her eyes, I tucked it into my pocket.

"What language is that, Archie?"

"I got no idea, ma'am."

"What is it then?"

"Jes somethin' been with me ever since I kin remember."

"Can't read it?"

"Kin you?"

"Half-blind folks can't make out writing like that." She turned to face front as Sam urged Belle to start. "Might know someone who can though."

I thought about the possibilities as we rode toward the river. "What d'you think it is, ma'am?"

"Can't tell too much. The ink's faded but I'm thinkin' maybe a hymnal."

"Ain't English though."

"Some reason you got it... "Her voice trailed off into a question.

"I don't knowed what though."

She turned to look at me. "Is that so?"

"Yes, ma'am."

She turned to face forward. "From your family, maybe?"

I shrugged. "Mebbe."

"Pardon my nosiness, Archie, but you're an orphan, aren't you?"

Sam glanced at me over his shoulder.

Wuz it written on my face? "Yes, ma'am. Guess so."

"Where you from?"

"I don't really knowed where. I remember ridin' in a train but I wuz a little feller."

"And you've always had that book?"

"Yes, ma'am."

We rode a little further.

"Who did you live with?"

I wuz gettin' embarrassed. "Anyone what needed cheap help, I guess."

"Schooling?"

"Some. Unless whoever I wuz stayin' with had work fer me."

"Uh huh."

We turned the corner and started on down South Sixth. It wuz only two or three blocks before we stopped in front of her house. I jumped down to help her outta the wagon while Sam gathered up her bag of groceries. He carried 'em up to the porch of the old house and wuz already headed back to the wagon by the time me and Miz Emily started across the yard.

"I don't like to poke into other folks' business," she said as we walked through ankle high grass. "...but that book's yours for a reason."

I wuz barely listenin'. After my fight with that big yeller monster in Fagan's barn, I wuz eyeballin' the weeds fer anythin' that might bite.

"Your mama—whoever she wuz—left that with you for a reason," she repeated. "You need to keep it safe because someday, you'll find someone who knows what it says and what it means."

Everyone ever seen my green book said somethin' like that. I used to dream that one day, some sweet woman a lot like Miz Emily or Miz Julia, maybe, would show up—and like magic, she'd see my book and know it wuz me. "I'm a guessin' that ain't never happenin', ma'am. Even if'n she wuz lookin' fer me, she ain't never gonna find me now." I took Miz Emily's elbow and helped her up onto the wooden step up to her front door.

"You don't know that Archie. Coulda been all kinds of reasons she left you. She wuz probably hoping someone else could do better by you. You hold onto that, you hear me?" She patted my hand.

"I don't even know why I'm a keepin' a book nobody kin read."

"Hope, maybe?"

"Mebbe."

"You know my Babe's blind?"

"Blind?"

"She was real little when I realized she wasn't like other babies and that she wasn't ever gonna be, you know, normal. Things are tough. They've always been tough, but especially so since her daddy ain't with us no more. I don't know what I'd do without that sweet thing."

I could hear Belle stampin' the ground and movin' the wagon forwards a bit. "Guess, I better go, ma'am. Sam's awaitin'."

She looked around me and caught Sam's attention, holdin' up one finger and mouthin', "Give us a minute?"

Sam nodded.

"I have a Bible with my Mama and Daddy's names and their Mama's and Daddy's names and so on all the way back to the old country. I kept it because I thought it was important to know where I came from." She looked me right in the eye. "It's nice to know stuff like that, but in real life, who they were makes not one lick of difference. Knowing someone's name ain't like spending time with her or talking to her."

"No, ma'am, it sure ain't."

She shook her finger in my face, but her eyes wuz kind. "Your history is made up of all the people you know and will know whether they be blood or not. You make life good or bad because of you... not your ancestors."

Then, not knowin' why I wuz a doin' it, I fished my book outta my pocket and handed it to her.

"Archie!"

"Maybe that friend of yers' kin read it."

*   *   *

I wuz headin' back to the store when I seen a feller ridin' a feisty stallion a comin' my way. "Mornin', Cephas." I lifted my cap and started to pass him by.

He pulled back on the reins with one hand and pointed at me with the other, "Hold on, Archie. I been looking for you."

"I ain't goin' any wheres fast," I said. "Somethin' wrong?"

"I don't rightly know."

"Oh?"

"You see, I got kin down in Pope County and one of them passed last week."

My heart pounded. "S-Sorry, to h-hear that."

"While I was down there for the funeral, I heard a story."

"Oh?"

"A son of a bitch named Jethro Barnes took off with some red-headed kid back in January. Nobody knew where they went...but fact was, nobody much cared. Jethro was the kinda feller who pissed off everyone including the preacher man."

I ducked my head and waited.

Cephas went on, "Some say it was the war that made him so mean, but the older folks in town say he was born thataway."

Still starin' at my toes, I blinked to keep from tearin' up. "Uh huh."

He leaned forward in his saddle. "Someone said the whole town was worried when he took in that kid a few years before that."

I coughed into my fist.

"And sure as shooting, Jethro was a sonofabitch to that boy. Beat the bejesus outta him at least twice, they say. And pert near worked him to death too."

"Starved him..." I said softly.

"That's what I hear. Booze costs money, you know."

"I know..."

"Thing is, Archie, they disappeared last May. Both of them."

"Uh huh."

"And then last week, they found Jethro..."

I thought about runnin', but where wuz there to go?

"...dogs'd dug him up. Looked like someone beat him to death with ..."

"A rock?"

Cephas nodded. "Something like that."

"S-so what happens n-now?"

"Oh, he stunk to high heaven. They reburied him."

"And...?"

"They figure that boy's buried around there somewhere too. But after Jethro stunk up the place, no one was up for digging in them woods. No one knew that kid anyway."

"You gonna...?"

"Ain't none of my business. Just thought I'd tell you about what I been hearing." Cephas jiggled the reins and rode off down toward the river.

I watched him fer awhile and then went on to the store.

Chapter Four

The Explosion

Saturday August 18, 1894
8:55 PM

It'd been a long day. I stepped out onto South Sixth Street in front of
Bourland's Store. I wuz so sweaty that my shirt stuck to me. I stretched and
yawned. I had a couple more chores before quitin' time. Sam, first, I decided
and headed toward the stables. I didn't go more'n a couple steps when a flash
of light blinded me. Then I wuz a flyin'. It happened too fast to be skeered or
to even wonder what wuz happenin'. Jes when I figgered I wuz dead and
headin' to Jesus, I landed on my belly. I couldn't get a breath and my ears wuz
achin'. Then nothin'.

*   *   *

Somethin' bounced off the back of my head. I opened my eyes. A big ole
boot wuz on the ground a couple inches aways from my nose. Am I dead?
"Archie?" Hatcher sounded like he wuz a long ways away.
Somethin' warm and wet trickled through my eyebrow and into my left
eye.
"Archie!"
Gruntin', I rolled over and touched my cheekbone. My fingers came away
covered in blood. "What the hell," I muttered.
A red-haired woman holdin' a giant feathered hat leaned over me. Her
puffy sleeve'd tore loose from the rest of her dress.
Miz Abigail?" I tried not to stare at her bare shoulder.
"Archie!"
I couldn't hear her voice but I knowed she wuz shoutin' at me. What?
"Where's Garland?"
I stared at her mouth.
She leaned forward and feathers fluttered down onto me. "GARLAND?"
Who? My head throbbed but it didn't hurt. The bow on her hat dangled off
the brim. Finally, I said, "What's makin' that noise?"
She pulled the bow off and stared at it. "What noise?

*   *   *

I opened my eyes. Snow? Cain't be snow. There ain't no snow in Arkansas.
Not in August. I tried to sit up. I'm in Arkansas, right?
"Archie, help me!"
I closed my eyes.

*   *   *

BONG! BONG! BONG!

My head. No. Not my head. A bell?

"Archie!" This time it wuz Sam's voice and it wuz closer.

I winced.

Sam put his hand on my shoulder and his lips moved. "You hurt?"

"Wuz it a tornado?"

Blood trickled from Sam's nostril down his upper lip. "No idea."

"Archie!"

"Hatcher?" My mind cleared. "Gotta check on him." Oh God! Whut's happenin'?

Sam touched my shoulder and I opened my eyes agin.

"Hatcher's in the bar," he said. "Can you get up?"

Bong! Bong! Bong!

"What?"

Sam held out his arm to me.

I stared at it.

"Get up?"

I reached fer his arm but fell sideways onto my elbow.

"Hold on there, boy."

I stared at his lips.

"Uhn, uhn, uhn. You wait right here whiles I go check on Mr. Hatcher. I'll be back in no time."

I sat cross-legged in the road. People wuz a runnin' this way and that. Where wuz everyone goin' in such a god-awful rush? I shook my head. Tiny shards of glass and bits of wood fell outta my hair. Then I seen it. Somethin' wuz a stickin' outa my thigh! I reached fer it, my hand a shakin'.

"Don't touch it, Archie. You pull that out now, you might bleed to death."

*　　*　　*

"BONG! BONG! BONG!"

I looked up at Fagan Bourland. "What?"

He knelt beside me. "Everyone else alive?"

"What?"

"Any customers in the bar?"

Where wuz his glasses?

"Customers?" He shouted.

"Uh, Sarge Eacret."

"Who else?"

"Garland Talbot and some feller he brought in with him. Said Till kicked 'em outta his place..."

Someone bent over me. "You ain't dead yet are ya, young man?"

It hurt to blink. "Doc Breedlove?"

"Looks like you ain't too addled to recognize me."

Things went fuzzy agin...

*　　*　　*

BONG! BONG! BONG!

I wuz still layin' in the middle of "A" Street. "Wh-what happened?"

"You passed out," Doc Breedlove said. "Seen it dozens of times in the war. It's nature's way of making you lay down."

I couldn't figger out why nature wanted that, but I took his word fer it.

"You gave us a good scare, Archie." It wuz Julia Bourland's voice. "Sam's gone to check on the livestock but once he gets them calmed down, he'll bring Belle to carry you home."

"No need fer that, ma'am." I fought to sit up. "It ain't that far..."

Doc Breedlove put his hand on my chest. "Whoa, boy. No need to get up if you're gonna fall right back down. Once they make sure The Bailey won't come down around you, we'll get a stretcher out here and tuck you in for the night."

Restin' on my own soft bed didn't sound like a bad idea at that. "What happened?"

Julia knelt beside me while Doc Breedlove cut my pant leg open and leaned down to inspect whatever wuz stickin' outta my thigh. He turned and whispered into her ear. "Need a light, good lady. The brightest lantern you can find. And some whiskey."

"I don't need no whiskey." I tried to sit back up,

"Ain't for you, young man." Doc Breedlove rested a hand on my chest with jes enough pressure so's I couldn't get up. "An old feller like me needs a nip now and again to keep perky, don't ya know."

Julia gathered her skirts around her and stood up. "Anything else?"

"Tear up a sheet or towel. It might get messy when I pull that thing outta his leg."

*   *   *

BONG! BONG! BONG!

I ground my teeth and put my hands over my ears. "Ow. What is that?"

"It's the courthouse bell," Julia said. "Been ringing ever since the explosion."

"Explosion?"

"Probably loosened the fittings around the cupola," the doctor said.

I squeezed by eyes shut. "Make it stop."

"Now, now, boy. None of us standing here's got time to worry about a damned bell." Doc Breedlove turned to Julia. "We're gonna need a belt and a cloth—and a stick about yay long."

*   *   *

BONG! BONG! BONG!

Somethin' wuz in my left eye. I tried to rub it but my arm didn't move the way I expected it to. "What's that smell?"

"Whiskey." Someone wuz holdin' my right hand.

I opened my good eye.

"It's me, Archie."

"Hatcher?" His eyelashes wuz caked with dust. "You hurt?"

57

"I'm fine and dandy." I could see his lips a movin' but that bell! That goldurn bell. "WHAT?"

"The bar fell over!"

"The bar?"

"It fell over on us, Archie! Me and Sarge. Sam had to lift it off of us."

"Sarge okay?"

"I'm fine, boy."

My eyes cleared. I could jes make out Sarge a leanin' on Garland Talbot's shoulder a few feet away. Both of 'em looked pretty banged up.

"Broke my damn crutch is all. Knocked old Garland here flat of his back."

"I was still in my chair, just upside down," Garland grunted. "Sam thought I was dead at first."

"Miz Abigail wuz lookin' fer you, Garland."

"She okay?"

"Best I could tell." I tried to sit up, but everythin' wuz blurred.

"Archie!" Sam reached fer me as I fell backwards...

*　*　*

BONG! BONG! BONG!

Echoes. Far away and close by.

Did I die?

I moved my leg.

"Lay still, Archie."

I opened my eyes. "Miz Julia?"

People wuz a runnin' back and forth across the road. Why am I in the road?

Doc Breedlove said, "A little higher, Miz Bourland."

Julia stood at my feet, a holdin' a lantern.

"Okay, let's see what we got here." Doc Breedlove tugged at the tear in my pants.

I screamed and tried to pull away. Then I realized Fagan wuz a holdin' my feet. I jerked my legs, tryin' to get loose, but he held 'em even tighter.

BONG! BONG! BONG!

Doc Breedlove yelled somethin' to Julia.

She seemed confused. "I got ... don...ry...ca...do...it."

He gestured upwards with his thumb.

Julia lifted the light even higher. Her hair came undone and fell forward over her shoulders.

"READY?" Doc Breedlove wrapped somethin' long and soft around his hand. "Close your eyes, Archie."

"Why?"

"Trust me."

Beyond my feet, Abigail and Garland Talbot hurried through the light throwed by the lantern. Her mouth wuz a movin'. His head wuz bowed. I craned my neck, a wonderin' where they wuz goin'.

Doc Breedlove touched my arm. "Close 'em, son."

I laid back down and squeezed my eyes tight.

When he touched whatever it wuz in my thigh, my leg quivered. Then there wuz pressure.

"Not much longer…"

Please jes do it. DO IT!

Doc Breedlove grunted. "Here we go!"

I opened my eyes.

Doc Breedlove held up a piece of metal.

"What is that?" Hatcher held the lantern closer to it.

"A nail. Missing its head. Most of the buildings around here lost a few shingles." Doc Breedlove cackled like a rooster. "If'n it'd hit you in the temple, woulda killed you quicker'n a minute, young man."

I sat upright to look. It wuz two inches long and round with no head or tip.

Julia leaned forward. "Where'd it come from?"

Doc Breedlove shrugged and slipped it into his vest pocket. "Who knows? The force of the blast tore the roof off buildings between here and the Arkansas river."

I reached fer the wound, but he knocked my hand away and squeezed the flesh around the hole. "Just blood and grit. You'll be fine. Maybe three or four stitches once we get you inside somewhere."

Long about then, the smell of my own blood made me roll over and puke on Bill Hatcher's feet.

*   *   *

BONG! BONG!

"He's gonna be down for a couple days, but he'll be good as new if no pus forms," Doc Breedlove said.

"Ewww." Cap stuck out his tongue and shuddered.

Someone with another lantern crossed the street aways.

"Mr. Whitson!" James called out. Gertie whimpered and wiggled in his arms.

Suddenly Cal wuz squattin' on the other side of me. "The Talbots tell me you got hurt, Archie."

"I'll live, sir."

"Anyone know what happened?" Julia's voice came from somewhere in the darkness.

"An explosion on the Poteau River they're saying." Cal took off his hat and wiped his forehead with the back of his hand. "Lucy and me, we felt it all the way out on Mill Creek Road. Got all my critters a-squawking and a-neighing. I hear it wuz them powder houses Speer Hardware has down there."

"You got much damage, Cal?"

"Naw, nothin' like here. Garrison's got glass and wood splinters layin' everywhere though. Dogs is howlin' to beat the band. Guess the noise hurt their ears."

"So that's what all that racket is about," Hatcher said.

"HOW KIN ANY OF YOU HEAR ANYTHIN' FER THAT GOLDURN BELL?"

They stared at me like I wuz the crazy one.

"Relax, son." Doc Breedlove patted my shoulder. "Let Cal fill us in on what's going on."

"Some folks and critters got tossed around like Archie here," Cal said. "Lots of broken glass.

The Grand Opera and First National Bank had windows blowed out. Same with the Arcade and JJ Little's. Miz Rogers had some damage. Vaughan Hardware lost shingles. How about you, Fagan? Anything worse than shingles and broken glass? And Archie, here of course."

"Still figuring it out," Fagan said. "Got Sam checking the animals."

"Well if you don't need anything, thought I'd head on down toward the river," Cal said. "Miz Emily and her daughter live pretty close to them powder houses. She mighta lost her roof or some of her critters. Poor soul ain't got much to begin with. This is gonna set her back a bit, I reckon."

BONG!

"Can I go?"

"James!" Julia frowned. "It might be dangerous down there."

"Aw, Mama. I wanna see what's going on!"

"We need to take care of our own buildings firs…"

"Julia, darlin'." Fagan took her hand. "The boy wants to see what's going on. Maybe help folks who need it. That makes him a good man in my book."

Julia still seemed worried, but she nodded.

Cal elbowed James playfully. "I'll keep an eye on him, Julia, just like he was one of mine."

"We could all go down there together," Morty said.

"We're going to need you here, Morty. With Archie down for the count, you and Sam and me need to check our buildings and inventory. And your mother and Lydia'll see about folks at the hotel. And if our house isn't safe to stay in tonight, we'll have to figure that out too."

"Aw, Pa." Morty sighed so's we all knowed cleanin' up the store warn't his idea of fun.

James set Gertie down and the two of 'em follered Cal down toward the Poteau River.

Fagan turned to Hatcher. "Let's you and me see just how bad it is."

Bill stood up and dusted off his trousers. "What would you like me to do?"

"Straighten up the bar mostly. Morty'll help you with anything needing a lift. And maybe you can help us get the grocery store back in order too."

Hatcher nudged me with his toe. "You gonna be okay?"

"Yeah," I growled. "I guess so."

"Let's get you out of the street, boy." Doc Breedlove struggled to get up. "My leg's asleep." He rubbed it and then limped in a circle. "Where's my damned cane?"

*   *   *

Turned out, The Bailey warn't too bad. Tom Sprinkle'd already climbed up on the roof and while there wuz damage…missing shingles and trash everywhere, it warn't about to fall in on us anytime soon.

"We lost a few windows," Lydia said as she helped me lay down on a couch in the front parlor "And everything's a mess."

"I should be helpin' Tom with all that." I tried to sit up.

"Just lay back now." Lydia put her hand on my chest. "Don't try to get up by yourself."

"I got to, ma'am." I didn't feel especially cold, but my teeth wuz chatterin' anyways. "The Bourlands don't pay me to lay around. They'll kick me out and I don't got nowhere else to go."

"Dear, Archie." Julia stood in the doorway with a quilt over her arm. "You're breathing too fast. Slow it down some."

"Cain't help it. My nerves is shot. Cain't seem to calm down."

"You'll be fine soon as you get some rest."

"But work..."

"Put your mind at ease, son. We won't kick you out."

I wuz still panicky fer a bit...until what Julia'd said sunk in. Then I said, "Yes, ma'am" and took another deep breath and laid back.

She covered me with the quilt. "There now, give it a minute." She put her palm on my forehead. "Close your eyes. Come on, close 'em."

Fer a bit, I wuz afeared I'd die if'n I closed my eyes, but when that didn't happen, I relaxed.

"There now, better?"

"Better'n bein' dead, I reckon."

"How about some water?"

"Don't go to no trouble fer me, Miz Lydia."

Julia pulled the quilt up under my chin. "Warm it a bit, Lydia, if the kitchen's functional."

This must be what it feels like to have mothers, I thought.

"I'll figure out a way," Lydia said.

Bong!

I startled and put my hands over my ears.

"It's just the bell rocking back and forth on its moorings. You're okay."

"That goldurn thing'd shake a sinner loose from the Devil's clutches."

Julia laughed. "You'll never have to deal with the Devil, young man.

*　*　*

Monday, August 20, 1894

11:30 AM

Squeak!

I smacked my lips.

Squeak, squeak, squeak.

There wuz somethin' gritty in my mouth. I raised up on one elbow and put the other hand on my upper lip. "Goldurn it."

"You awake?" Fagan Bourland said over his shoulder. He wuz sittin' at a small desk beside the open window, writin' somethin'. Every time he moved, that blasted chair squeaked.

"Part of my tooth is gone." I ran my tongue over the rough edge.

61

"Does it hurt?" He laid down his pen, picked up the paper and blew on it.

"No."

"What's your problem then?"

I sat up and swung my legs over the edge of the cot they'd set up fer me. "I wuz kinda partial to that tooth. One of my...well, someone I used to know told me that I'd live longer if'n my teeth stayed in my mouth."

"What's done is done. Compared to what might've happened, consider yourself lucky." He waved the paper back and forth to dry the ink and then laid it back down.

Outside the window, the sun wuz high in the sky. A man and a woman wuz arguin' in the middle of South Sixth. Someone wuz hammerin' on the roof over our heads. A wagon rattled by. I wiped a bead of sweat off my forehead. "I don't remember ever sleepin' so late."

"Doc Breedlove said you'd be down a couple days or so."

"I'm sorry about that. I'll get cleaned up and git to work."

Fagan turned around to look at me. "Nonsense. You're weak after all that pukin' last night."

I hunched over, starin' at my bare feet. "Sorry about that too, sir."

"Good Lord, haven't you ever been hurt before?"

"Had chicken pox once. Wuz about eight or nine. About scratched myself bloody." Jes the memory made the insides of my ears itch. "But I worked anyways."

The light from the window reflectin' off of Fagan's spectacles made it hard fer me to tell what he wuz thinkin'. After a minute, he said, "Not the same as getting hurt, now is it?"

"I'm sorry, sir. Did I do somethin' wrong?"

"You'll get used to bein' human soon enough." He turned back to his desk.

"Sir?"

"Un huh?" He held the paper up to the light from the window, squinted at it and laid it back down. "What is it, Archie?"

"I been a layin' here tryin' to figger out what happened the other night...and it...it jes won't come to me."

"Speer Hardware's Powder House blew up."

"Where exactly wuz it?"

"On the Poteau River? You probably saw it when you took Miz Emily home. It wasn't all that far from where she and her daughter lived."

"Oh? How big wuz it?"

"A mighty big boom. Almost all the businesses on Garrison had some kind of damage. Not as bad as those of us closer to the river, mind you, but bad enough. Had some horses knocked down, a buggy turned over. Put a kink in the bar businesses all over town what with windows being blown out and a lot of the paying customers rushing home to take care of their properties."

"Miz Abigail looked pretty ragged the other night. She okay?"

"That woman's tough as nails. Don't you worry about her. She and Garland are fine. Hatcher and Sam and the boys have about got the store put back in order. Business has been good what with everyone needing to replace something. We had some damage to the roof, but we got Sam working on it. Gonna take a couple days to fix but if'n it don't rain, we oughta be fine."

They wuz doing fine without me! "How about Miz Emily and Babe? The blast musta messed up they's place pretty bad. They ain't got a pot to piss in on good days. They's gonna need help findin' somewhere else to live while its is bein' worked on?"

Fagan turned around to face me. "That's not gonna be necessary."

"Oh?" I cocked my head. "Somebody's gonna take 'em in? Churches' helpin' out?"

"Their house was blown to smithereens."

"Is Babe okay? You know she cain't see nothin'."

"Archie, Miz Emily and Babe were blown to smithereens too."

I chewed on that fer a minute. "Hurt bad?"

He got up and put his hand on my shoulder. "They're dead, son. The Birnie brothers been out there picking up parts of 'em for two days now. Every time they think they got everything that's left, someone finds something else."

I opened my mouth, but nothing came out. And I couldn't take a breath neither.

"LYDIA? TOM? Get in here." Fagan's voice cracked.

*   *   *

There wuz somethin' wet on my face.

"What were you thinking, Fagan? The boy's not an insensitive clod like you." That wuz Julia's voice.

"Someone had to tell him sometime. Never thought he'd pass out on me."

"He'd taken a liking to Miz Emily and Babe these last few weeks. Always volunteering to take them their groceries. He even bought them a ham with his own money."

I opened my eyes.

"There he is. Bout time you came back around, Archie." Fagan wiped his upper lip with the big white handkerchief Julia always tucked into the pockets of his suit jackets. "Scared the daylights out of us."

"You feel like sitting up?" Julia took a wet cloth offa my forehead and used it to bathe the rest of my face and the back of my neck.

I put my hand on her wrist. "I..I'm fine, Miz Julia. Really."

She dropped the cloth into a small pail of water beside my cot. "Let's see if that dizzy spell's gone now. If you feel woozy, we'll get Doc Breedlove over here."

"Is it true? Miz Emily? Babe? They's dead?

Julia's eyes told that they wuz gone before her mouth could.

Fagan grunted, "You aren't going to keel over, are you, boy?"

Julia elbowed Fagan. "The man's an elephant in a china closet, but he means well, Archie."

I pulled myself up on one elbow. "Is there nothin' left?"

"I haven't been down there today, but there's not much left but trash," Fagan said.

"I need to go see fer myself."

63

"It's hot out there. No way can you walk down to the river and back in your condition. Doc Breedlove would have my hide if I let you out of The Bailey any time soon."

"I need to go, sir. It's personal, but I need to go. Maybe Sam kin help me?" I sat up and put my feet on the floor.

Julia and Fagan exchanged glances.

"Can you stand up by yourself?"

"Fagan!"

"Shush, my dear. We were about to send for Dr. Breedlove a few minutes ago, knowing that he's a busy man. Archie needs to decide if he's sick or if he's well enough to go poke through that mess down on the Poteau."

"I…"

Julia put her hand on top of my throbbing head. "Archie's not well, Fagan. He's reacting to the loss of two innocent ladies, but he can't go anywhere."

"But I…"

This time it wuz Fagan who shushed me. "He's a grown man, Julia."

"He's a boy! A hurt one. No way will I allow him to cross the street in this heat, let alone to go down to what's left of Miz Emily's property."

"Miz Julia?"

They both turned to me. "Miz Emily had somethin' that belonged to me. A hymnal. At least that's what she thought it might be."

Fagan peered at me over his glasses "Why did you give her your book?"

"She wuz gonna have someone translate it."

Julia sat down on the edge of the couch beside me. "What kind of hymnal was it, Archie?"

"I don't know. Miz Emily thought it might be Russian."

She patted my shoulder, her eyes filled with curiosity. "Where were you born?"

"Pennsylvania? New York? Overseas? Mebbe?"

"How the hell did you get to Arkansas?" Fagan pushed his glasses higher on his nose.

"Train."

"An Orphan Train?

I looked up at Julia. "Guess so. I wuz little."

"Where the train come from?"

I shrugged. "Philadelphia?"

"Why do you think that?"

I turned to Fagan. "I don't remember."

"German? Swedish?"

"Mebbe," I said. "It shore ain't English though."

"It might be in the rubble," Julia said to Fagan.

"It probably is rubble."

"It probably belonged to his mother."

"You don't know that."

"It's all he has, Fagan."

He frowned. "Julia."

"We have to look at least."

"Julia…" It wuz almost a whisper that time.

"We could go together." She tugged at the hem of his jacket. "Morty can manage without us. It'll be like a treasure hunt. You know, old times."

"Julia." His shook his head and sighed.

She turned back to me. "What color is the cover if it still exists?"

"Green when I gave it to Miz Emily. Who knows now? I'll recognize it though."

"You aren't going, Archie." Julia wuz stern and determined so's I turned to Fagan.

"You're gonna stay right here and heal up," he said. "We need you back at the store."

I leaned back on the couch and sighed. Someone besides me cared about findin' it! I never had anyone care about me like that before. The Bourlands didn't owe me nothin'. I didn't know what to do with that. A few minutes later, they's left to look fer it.

I rolled over to face the wall, swallerin' back tears. Don't get too wrapped up with the Bourlands, I told myself. They's like anyone else. They'll be nice as long as they want somethin'.

*　*　*

"Archie!"

I opened my eyes. "Maud?"

She stood in the doorway to the parlor. "I heard you got hurt."

I raised up on one elbow. "You ain't oughta be here."

"Maud's worried about you." She sat down beside me and put her hand on mine.

I frowned and pulled away.

"Maud don't want you to be laid up. What if she needs you?"

Ah yes, I thought. What if Maud needs somethin'? Nothin's changed. Everythin's still about Maud. "I'm fine." I relaxed back into my pillow. "Don't like layin' around with nothin' to do."

"It was a scary night," she said. "I couldn't find George."

"Is he okay?"

"I thought he might be dead or hurt bad." A tear trickled down her cheek.

"And?"

Her face crumpled. "He was having breakfast with another girl."

I sighed. "What didja expect?"

She took a ragged breath. "He promised to take care of Maud."

"Maud…"

"George knew Maud wasn't like everyone else. He knew it and said he didn't care. He said he'd always take care of her."

"But you ain't been there fer him."

"That's different."

I sat up. "Why?"

"Because Maud needs a lot and George don't need nothin'."

"Ah."

"And now he's let Maud down. Like everyone else. What should Maud do now?"

"How would I know?"

"Maybe you could take care of Maud? Do a better job than George?"

"I'm a kid. I kin barely take care of myself."

"Fine!" She scowled and stood up. "Remember Maud came to you first, Archie."

I doubted that but not wantin' to get her goin', I kept my mouth shut.

"Maud can have someone better than you, just like that." She snapped her fingers in my face. "Richer. Smarter. Someone who'll buy her pretty things and call her 'Honey' and 'Sweetheart.' Someone who'll put her up in a fine house with velvet curtains and gold-framed mirrors. Lots of mirrors."

"PERFECT! Go get 'em."

At the door, she turned around. "You're nobody, Archie Biggs! And Maud's special. People'll remember her a hundred years from now, but not a soul'll know you ever lived at all."

"Fine." I punched my pillow a time or two and pulled the covers up over my head.

"I'm going now."

I ignored her.

"Archie!"

It wuz quiet fer a bit. Then I heard the front door open and slam shut.

*   *   *

I wuz still dozin' when Julia came back from her trip down to Miz Emily's house on the river.

"I'm awake Miz Julia," I called, when she knocked.

The office door opened a crack and Julia stuck her head in. "Fagan stopped at the store but told me to come on back and talk to you. Is it okay if I come in?"

I sat up. "Yes, ma'am, that'd be fine."

She came on in and straight away, I seen she had my book in her hand. It's cover wuz even more ragged than the last time I seen it, but at least it wuz in one piece. I reached fer it.

"We found this too," she held up a pair of glasses. "Since Miz Emily didn't have anyone but Babe, I thought maybe you'd like them? To remember her by?"

When I reached fer 'em, I wuz the saddest I ever been.

*   *   *

August 21, 1894
Fort Smith Daily News Record

The last thing the council did was pass a resolution that hereafter, no powder or dynamite magazine shall be used or established within three miles of the courthouse and that all the present magazines be removed within the next thirty days.

*   *   *

August, 1894

Fort Smith Ark., special: Four powder houses containing 1,200 pounds of dynamite and 300 kegs of powder belonging to the Speer Hardware Company located two miles from here in the Poteau River exploded. A small cabin nearby, the home of Mrs. Cook, was blown to splinters. Mrs. Cook and daughter Babe were blown into eternity. The shock was felt at Van Buren, Alma, Greenwood, Jenny Lind, Hackett, Kavanaugh and many other places twenty miles away. In Fort Smith, many thousands of dollars' worth of property was destroyed. Tall buildings swayed to and fro and the crash of falling and cracking glass was like the discharge of artillery. The Opera House, the Boston Store, Arcade, J.J. Little, Ayers and Co., Vaughan Hardware Store, Fagan Bourland and the Western Union buildings were severely damaged, while along Sixth Street and Garrison Avenue is a continuous story of wrecks. There is no explanation for the explosion.

*   *   *

Weiser, Kathy. *Cherokee Bill - Terror of Indian Territory.*
September 2007. *Legends of America.* Accessed 31 January 2009

On November 8, 1894, when the men robbed the Shufeldt and Son General Store, Goldsby shot and killed Ernest Melton, who happened to enter the store during the robbery

Chapter Five

The Book and the Barn

Wednesday, December 12, 1894

Tony Homann pulled up in front of the store and set the brake on his wagon. He tied his rig to a pole out front and kicked mud off'n his boots. Then he clumped across the porch and into the store.

"Howdy, Miz Southard!" Mr. Homann took off his hat and held it to his chest. "Miz Talbot. Miz Keating. Miz Rogers."

Our customers smiled back or nodded a greetin' and turned back to they's shoppin'.

"How're you doing, Tony?" Fagan shook his hand. "You got our potato order?"

"I do."

Fagan put his hand on Morty's shoulder. "If you don't mind, I'm gonna let my son handle this transaction."

The farmer turned to Morty and shook his hand. "I'm mighty proud to work with you."

"Thank you, sir." Morty opened up the order book. "We ordered thirty pounds of potatoes. Is that right?"

"Got 'em in the wagon. 'Course we're gonna need to weigh 'em."

"Hold on a minute." Morty turned to me and nodded.

I reached up and pulled the line that rang the bell in the barn.

"If ya got 'em, we'll take an extra ten pounds for the Bailey Hotel residents," Morty said.

"We got plenty of 'em this year. Set a hog out to loosen the ground and what she didn't eat still left us with more'n we could store and plenty left over for folding money."

"Yes, sir?" Sam stood in the doorway.

"Afternoon, Sam." Mr. Homann waved.

"Thanks, Sam," Morty said. "I need you to heft those potato baskets off Mr. Homann's wagon and weigh out thirty pounds of 'em for us."

"Yes, sir." Sam grabbed a wooden cart from the saloon and pushed it back onto South Sixth where Mr. Homann's wagon sat.

"Got some of Mary's canned peaches and some dried peppers too, if'n you're interested," Mr. Homann said to Morty.

Morty glanced at Fagan, who nodded."Yes, sir. We sure would be." Tongue sticking outta the corner of his mouth, Morty concentrated on the list of items Fagan planned on buyin' from Mr. Homann.

"I heard you slaughtered that hog your kid's been raising." Fagan put down *The Elevator* he'd been reading. "How about some Leberwurst or Blutwurst, Tony?"

Mr. Homann's face brightened. "We got both, Mr. Bourland. How much you need?"

"How much you got out in that wagon right now?"

"About ten pounds of the Leberwurst. Only about six of the Blatwurst. Savin' the rest for the family, you know."

Fagan put a hand on Morty's shoulder. "Keeping up, son?"

"Yes, sir." Morty never took his eyes off the paper he wuz writin' on. "Got any ham, Mr. Homann?"

"No. Interested in sauerbraten?"

Morty looked over his shoulder at his father. Fagan nodded.

"Wait. Is that ham and sauerbraten or are they the same thing?"

"Don't have any ham, young man," Mr. Homann corrected him. "Only have sauerbraten."

"Got it, sir."

"Got any Christmas trees?" Fagan mouthed to Morty.

Morty turned back to Mr. Homann. "Got any Christmas trees for sale?"

"Three four-foot ones in the wagon. A six-footer back at the house."

"You keep that big one for Mary and the kids." Fagan took his handkerchief outta his pocket and cleaned his glasses. "I'll...we'll take the ones you got in the wagon though."

"Thank you, sir." It wuz then that I realized Mr. Homann wuz makin' marks in a tiny dogeared book. It made me think of the little green one I almost lost when Miz Emily and Babe got kilt. The book wuz pretty dinged up and covered with soot now, but if'n you held it up to the sun and squinted, you could make out the writin' on most pages. Figgerin' out what it wuz sayin' wuz another thing... but that's how it'd been all my life anyways.

Morty looked at Fagan who mouthed, "Jelly?" He turned back to the man standin' in front of the counter. "Miz Homann make any of that good peach jelly like last year?"

"Yes, sir. She sure did."

"Give us about ten jars," Fagan mouthed.

Morty turned back to Mr. Homann. "Can we have ten jars?"

The man beamed.

I guessed the jelly sale put Mr. Homann in the black.

"Did I miss anything?" Morty glanced over his shoulder once agin.

"Sauerkraut, young man?"

"Sauerkraut, Pa?"

Fagan smacked himself in the forehead with the heel of his hand. "How could I have forgotten sauerkraut? Julia would've killed me if I forgot that."

I chuckled to myself. Sauerkraut indeed! I never seen any of the Bourlands eat much of the stuff, but it showed up on the table at The Bailey Hotel all the time. At first, when Mary ladled me a big servin' of it with potatoes and carrots and onions and some kind of seeds, I wuz leery. But when yer hungry, you'll try anythin' and after a bit sauerkraut got to be downright tasty—either by itself or with sausages if'n Fagan wuz feelin' charitable toward us boarders.

"Okay, that's about it," Fagan said. "Tony, would you like a beer while Morty and Sam unload your wagon and Archie here does the bookwork?"

"Speaking of books," Mr. Homann turned to me. "I hear tell you got one written in a foreign language."

"Yes sir."

"Ain't German is it?"

I glanced at Fagan. The corners of his mouth almost curled into a grin. After going down to rummage through what wuz left of Miz Emily and Babe's belongings to find my book, Fagan and Julia wuz invested now. They wuz determined to help me figger out what it said.

"Rabbi Moses said it warn't Hebrew or Yiddish or Polish. And Father Smyth wuz definite about it not being Latin, but didn't know about German."

"Ain't Cherokee is it? You know they had a whole alphabet and schools, the whole nine yards, back before President Johnson kicked their butts outta the Carolinas."

"Don't know, sir. Ain't never been in the Carolinas or met any Cherokee that I knowed of."

"All kinds of Cherokee around here. Good decent folks. Just have to ask one of 'em to take a look."

"I'll do that."

"Got your book nearby?"

I dug it outta my pocket.

In Mr. Homann's big calloused hands, it looked little. He opened it and held it up to the window, squintin'. "Not German, Archie. Sorry to say. Was kinda hoping it was."

"I appreciate at least knowin' that, sir."

"Don't think it's Russian neither, but you might check with the Pahotskis. I think they're from Poland."

"Hadn't thought of Russian or Polish," Fagan said. "I'll ask Lou next time I see him."

"Good luck with this, Archie." Mr. Homann handed the book back to me.

"Thank you, sir." I wuz touched at everyone wantin' to help me in some way.

"Let's get you a beer, Tony." Fagan clapped the farmer on the back as they headed fer the saloon. "Didja hear about Doc Breedlove's dog?"

"Didn't know he had one," Mr. Homann said.

"That hound's about as old as the doc is. Goes everywhere with him. But I saw him yesterday without his pooch so's I says, 'Doc, where's yer dog?'"

Mr. Homann raised one brow. "And?"

"Well, the doc said that he had to put the poor pup down. So, I asked the obvious question, was he mad? And old Breedlove gave me the evil eye and says, 'Well, he wasn't too pleased about it.'"

They disappeared into the bar leaving me to figure how much we needed to pay Mr. Homann and Morty to manage the scale as Sam unloaded the wagon and brought in the goods.

"How long before I can buy some of Miz Homann's Leberwurst, Archie? Miz Abigail tapped on the counter with her fingernails. Her basket wuz half-filled with Miz Rosemary's cookies, some taffy, a can of coffee beans and a pound of sugar. "You know how Garland loves the stuff."

"Soon's they unload it, I'll slice a hunk off fer you, Miz Abigail."

"Imagine the luck, being here when that man brings in Leberwurst."

"Mr. Talbot likes liver does he?"

"Can't stand the stuff—but you should see him go after Mary Homann's Leberwurst. Likes it with mustard. I never told him how it was made or what it was made from. So don't you go telling him my secrets."

"Yer wiles is safe with us, Miz Abigail." I winked at Morty who smirked as he weighed potatoes and put 'em into a basket.

I got busy turnin' Morty's list of the stuff we wuz buyin' into a statement of purchase. Usin' my notes about how much we'd paid fer the same stuff in the past, I printed each item into our ledger, how much or how many, and the price we wuz payin'.

Sam set a box of jelly down on the counter. "What else?"

I ran my finger down Morty's list. "Another box of jelly."

He turned around to go back to the wagon, just as Fagan called from the saloon, "Dammit, Sam. What happened to the new set of shot glasses I bought last month."

"Go ahead," I said to Sam. "I'll go get the jelly."

"Sam!"

Sam grinned. "Thanks, Mr. Archie."

"SAM!"

"Comin', Mr. Fagan."

I watched him disappear into the saloon before I headed outside.

A scrawny kid stood beside a mule hitched to our front posts.

"You Mr. Homann's boy?"

"Who's askin'?"

"My name's Archie. I work here."

"I'm Kate."

"That ain't no boy's name."

She frowned. "So, what's that tell you, mister?"

"That you're a sassy lil devil. Want some candy?"

"Cain't."

"Why not?"

"Cause I got a job tendin' to Clyde here. Doin' rounds makes him cranky what with all the traffic up on Garrison."

I reached out to pet Clyde.

"I wouldn't do that if'n I was you," the little girl said. "Clyde done bit the postman twice."

I drew back my hand. The critter did have a mean look in his eye... meaner'n any Belle'd ever gave me.

"How come he don't eat up a lil thing like you?"

"'Cause he knows I'll knock him seven ways to Sunday if'n he even thinks about trying it."

"I kin see that." I chuckled.

"So, what you want?"

"Jelly."

"Peach or blackberry?"

I scratched my head. "I don't think we ever bought blackberry from y'all before. Is it good?"

She sighed. "A course, it's good, whatcha think?"

"Okay then, Miz Kate. Give me ten jars of blackberry."

"Get 'em yourself. You don't want to see what might happen if'n I walk off where Clyde cain't see me."

I chuckled and stared down at her. "How old are you, sweetheart?"

"Eight. What d'you care?"

"Who's home with yer ma?"

"My brother and sister."

"You the oldest?"

"A course, I'm the oldest. I'm takin' care of Clyde, ain't I?"

"You are. I'll be right back if'n you keep Clyde from eat'n me up."

She sighed agin.

Guess she thought I wuz a half-wit. I climbed up on the wagon and found the crate with the blackberry jelly. I gathered up ten jars, got 'em back inside the store and set 'em on the counter with our other purchases. Then I rummaged through the candy jar, picked me out six pieces... and went back out to Mr. Homann's wagon.

"Why you givin' me candy, Mister?" Kate stared at the pieces I gave her. "You lookin' to trade for somethin'?"

"Naw, this is fer you and the kids back home."

She looked at the candy on my hand then back into my eyes. "I ain't got no money."

"That's okay. Mr. Bourland, the man that owns this store, is rich. He said to give it to you cause he likes doin' business with yer daddy so much."

She reached out and took the candy. "Thanks."

"You're welcome, Miz Kate Homann."

As I stood up, I glimpsed a skinny young woman standin' on the corner talkin' to Pappy Brown. "Oh, Lord." I muttered under my breath. "Maud."

"Daddy says it's not nice to talk about Jesus like that."

I glanced down at Kate. "Yer daddy's right. Don't you ever do that."

"Why did you?"

I stared down at her. "Cause I'm a damned fool."

"Then stop it."

"I promise, Miz Kate, to never do that agin. You watch after Clyde now, okay?"

"What you think I'm gonna do?"

* * *

After Mr. Homann and Kate left, I went back to my bookkeepin' while keepin' an eye out in case Maud decided to come our way.

"Archie?"

I looked up. Morty wuz nowhere to be seen and a pretty young woman toting a baby on her hip stood at the counter with a basket full of groceries. "I'll be right there, Miz Keating."

"Take your time. My Larry's working nights this month so he's sleeping now."

I closed the ledger and laid down my pencil. "I hear Mr. Keating's real popular with prisoners."

"He's a Godfearin' soul, my Larry."

"I look forward to meetin' him someday," I said as I wrote down the items she wanted to buy. "I only been to the federal jail once, but they wouldn't let me go in or nothin'. Wanted to watch ole Louis Holder hang but that didn't..."

"Put that down, Mary," she called to one of her kids who'd picked up a piece of taffy.

I lowered my voice. "Is there a reason you don't want yer little ones to have candy, Miz Keating?"

She glanced around to see who else wuz in the store and then lowered her voice. "With a big family, we try to be frugal."

"No problem, ma'am. I jes didn't know if'n it made 'em sick or anythin'."

She laughed. "No, like any little kids, they love the stuff."

"Good, have each of them pick out a piece. Curtesy of yers truly."

"Why thank you, Archie. But you're just a young fella, startin' out. Why are you being so good to my babies?"

"Because orphans never got anythin' extra. Wuz a time, I'd have crammed taffy down my throat until the cows came home, but I never got that chance."

"Why don't you have as many as you want now?"

I shrugged. "Once I tried 'em, I realized I ain't partial to 'em. But I didn't know that until I started workin' fer Mr. Fagan."

"Actually, they hurt my teeth," she chuckled. "You know, I couldn't help but overhear your conversation with Tony Homann earlier. Have you ever thought that the writin' in your little book might be Gaelic?"

"What's Gaelic?"

"Original language in Scotland and Ireland. The reason I mention it is that my husband Larry was born in Ireland. He was a little scamp back then, but he's sure to know someone who'd recognize it..."

"I'll show it to him the next time he comes in."

"You do that, Archie."

*　*　*

A couple hours later, Morty stuck his head into my cubby hole. "Where'd Pop go?"

I shrugged. "Ain't seen him since Tony Homann left. Sam neither."

"He's talking about buying another telephone company. Maybe he's meeting someone about that?"

"Another telephone company?" I leaned back in my chair. "Y'all make that much money from it?"

"I heard him tell Mama that there'll be a day when everyone'll have one. Said they'll make a killing off being one of the first to invest."

"I admire that."

"Why?"

"It's...it's brave, ya know?"

73

Morty shrugged. "Pop's always looking for new ways to make money."

"Not you?"

"Naw. I'm happy with the store."

"You're young yet, but it's probably gonna be yours one of these days anyway."

"Not as long as Pop's alive. What's his is his until...well, forever. I'm not lookin' for that though. I'm like Mama. I like it when things stay the same."

"Don't ya have any dreams fer yerself, Morty?"

"I dunno. Might like watchin' you play baseball one of these days."

"Doncha wanna play yerself?"

"Naw. Not me. I used to think about being a cop or a US Marshal."

"Not anymore?"

"Lot's to do here, I guess."

I knowed how that wuz. Somedays anythin' seemed possible. Others...well, I wuz lucky to be where I wuz. "Guess we better get all this stuff put away." I pretended I warn't chokin' back a tear or two. "If'n you slice and wrap up Miz Abigail's Leberwurst, I'll pack up the rest of her stuff fer when Sam comes back from wherever he went with yer Pa."

*   *   *

Morty'd already gone home when Sam came back around five o'clock. Most of our customers'd gone home too. Hatcher wuz in the saloon with a few customers, but we wuz alone in the store.

"Sam?"

He picked up Mr. Homann's potatoes and put them in the bins, avoidin' my eyes.

"You okay?"

He ignored me.

"Sam?"

He shook his head.

I sighed, got up, and put the "Closed," sign in the window. Then I went back to my tiny office, picked up the take of the day.

"Night," I said as I came back out front.

When Sam looked up, I realized he wuz boiling mad.

"Kin I help?"

"Get on home, Archie. Ain't nothin' to do here."

"I..I didn't mean to intrude."

He ignored me, slammin' boxes down on the floor and grumblin' to himself.

Irritated, I let the door slam behind me. I aimed to leave the day's take with Julia...but, as I passed the barn, I seen that the door wuz wide open. Sam musta forgot to close and lock it.

Thinkin' he'd get to it as soon as he worked off whatever got him steamed up, I headed toward the Bourlands' house further up on South Sixth. I stopped. What if one of them horses got out? I turned around and went back. At the barn door, I got to thinkin' about that big yeller snake that treed Sam and

Gertie the summer before and shuddered. But then after a minute or two, I pulled myself together and went in.

The horses hadn't been fed and they wuz low on water. What's going on? I set the satchel of sales slips on the ground, fetched a lantern and a pail and headed back out to get water. As I passed the tackle room, I heard a soft squeak. I froze. Another snake? Heart apoundin', I went back and pushed open the door. Two people wuz a layin' half-dressed on the floor. They startled and jumped back from each other.

"Is that you, Archie?" It wuz a girl's voice.

I raised the lantern and squinted into the dark room. "This here's private property. Ain't no place fer hanky panky."

A skinny little gal stood up, leavin' whoever she'd been a messin' with hidin' in the dark.

My face burned. "This here place belongs to Mr. Bourland."

"Maud knows that, silly." Her skirt wuz twisted and there wuz straw in her hair.

"What're you doin' here?"

"Silly boy!" She put her hand on my cheek. "What's it look like I'm doing?"

I flinched and pulled away. "Don't touch me."

"Doncha want poor little Maud anymore, Archie?"

"Straighten up yer clothes and get on home. George'll be lookin' fer you."

"Poor old George," she giggled. "He's only twenty-six but he acts like he's older than Dr. Breedlove."

"Go home, Maud!"

"Maud's going, sugar." She turned back toward the tackle room and blew a kiss to whoever wuz in there.

"Tomorrow? Same time?"

A familiar voice grunted.

Maud threw a thick shawl over her shoulder and blew me a kiss. Grittin' my teeth, I watched her mosey on up the street. When she passed The Bourland a headin' on up toward Rogers Avenue, I sucked in the cold evenin' air and turned back to the tackle room. "It's a dangerous game yer playin', sir."

"It's none of your business."

"That ain't true."

"Things'll be okay if you keep what you saw tonight to yourself."

"No one'll ever hear about this from me. It's Maud you have to worry about."

Fagan Bourland stepped into the light, puttin' on his glasses. "Believe me, Archie. I know it."

"She won't stop, sir. She don't know how."

He dusted straw of off'n his pants. "I didn't ask for this."

"Then stop it. When she shows up like this, send one of us to tell George to come get her!"

"It's more complicated than that."

"Oh sir, don't tell me that you love her…"

"No. It's not that…"

"What about Miz Julia?"

He straightened his shoulders. "If it's any of your business, I love my wife. Dearly."

"Then why do this with Maud?"

He shrugged. "That little girl's like...like..."

"Glue?"

He sighed."Like glue."

"Is she...you know, pregnant?"

"NO!" He avoided my eyes. 'It's not gotten that far. Yet."

"Don't gotta be yers to cause trouble, ya know."

"I'm not a mark, Archie. Just a damn fool. She's unhappy...with no one to turn to."

"She acts simpleminded, but she ain't."

Fagan closed and locked the door to the tackle room. "I know..."

"She'll eatcha up, sir."

"It's my mess, Archie. I got myself into it. I'll get myself out of it."

"What about yer boys? They adore you."

He bowed his head and took a breath. "I'm probably not worth their adoration."

"Don't hurt 'em..."

"I'm trying not to."

"Don't then."

"She's going back to Missouri day after tomorrow. To spend Christmas with her family. She and George aren't on good terms. She might never come back for all I know."

"That'd be best."

Fagan sighed. "That'd definitely be best."

CA and HC Birnie
Embalmers and Undertakers
Fort Smith Times, December 16, 1894

* * *

December 21, 1894
8:30 AM

As usual, I went to the back door and knocked. "Miz Julia?"

No answer.

She'd insisted I pick up her order soon as Mr. Kimmons opened fer business. I tapped agin. Hearin' nothin' movin' inside, I backed away, stuffin' the small package back into my pocket.

A voice inside stopped me. "Is that you, Archie?"

I turned around. "Yes, ma'am. I got yer order from Kimmons."

Julia opened the door and looked both ways before steppin' out onto the porch.

"You okay, ma'am?"

Her face wuz puffy, like she'd been cryin'. Not lookin' me in the eyes, she stretched out her hand.

76

"Oh, Miz Julia. What kin I do fer ya?"

"Do?" She seemed confused.

"Should I call Doc Breedlove? Or Doc Southard?"

"Not much a doctor can do, Archie." She peeked into the bag I'd handed her and sighed. "I'm tired. That's all."

"Want me to tell Mr. Fagan that yer feelin' poorly?"

"Fagan's a busy man." It wuz almost a whisper.

"Yes, ma'am." I turned to go.

"Archie?"

I turned back to her. "Yes, ma'am?"

"Tell Sam that when he picks up James and Cap after school, he should take them to my mother's house. This is our first Christmas since Daddy died and she's lonely. The boys'll cheer her up."

I touched my cap brim and started to leave.

"One more thing." Her voice wuz lower.

"Ma'am?"

"Tell Fagan that I'm going to nap now."

"I'll take care of it fer you, Miz Julia. You get some rest."

"Go on, now!" She shooed me away with the back of her left hand. "They need you at the store."

At the corner, I turned to look back. The house wuz dark.

*　*　*

11:30 AM

I wuz focused on inventory, when I heard Fagan Bourland boom, "How's it goin, son?"

"Pretty good, Pop," Morty said. "Been a busy mornin'."

"How are you, Mrs. Keating?"

"I'm good, Mr. Bourland. Larry and I missed you and Miz Julia at the Christmas Social the other night."

"Julia's been down in the dumps lately, ma'am. She rallied right after Wiley passed, but the holidays've been hard."

"The poor thing. We do miss our dearly departed more during the holidays, don't we?"

The register rang. "That'll be $1.75," Morty said.

"Oh my, 'tis very dear, isn't it?"

"Yes, ma'am," Morty said.

"How's that man of yours, Miz Keating?" Fagan broke in.

"Larry's just fine, sir."

"We all appreciate him keepin' those bandits locked up in Judge Parker's jail."

"He'll like hearing that, Mr. Bourland. I worry about him looking after robbers and murderers. But he says it's not as dangerous as what the Marshals do, tracking them down and all. They can't shoot you locked up in their cells. And besides, the pay's good. And the good Lord knows, we need his salary."

77

As Fagan and Miz Keating chatted about Larry Keating's job, I focused on my cypherin', but the image of Julia Bourland, shiverin' on her back porch niggled around in my head. She wuz thinner than usual. And she seemed...sad.

Outside my little nook, the register dinged and I heard Morty say, "Thank you, ma'am."

A moment after the bell on the outside door told me Miz Keating'd left, Fagan said to Morty, "Have you heard from your mother this morning?"

"No, sir. Should I have?"

"I got a call at my office at The Bourland a few minutes ago. It was from Miz Sally at the church. Your mama didn't show up for choir practice this mornin'."

"Maybe she forgot?"

"You know how Julia loves church activities during the holidays."

"Mama's been awful blue lately...about Grandpa passin', like you said to Miz Keating."

"Did she tell you that?"

I coughed to remind 'em that I wuz there—and could hear 'em.

Fagan pulled back the curtain. "How're things going back here, Archie?"

I laid down my pencil. "The books're fine, sir."

"Have you seen my wife today?"

"Yes, sir. She had me pick up a package from Kimmons' this mornin'. She said she wuz havin' trouble sleepin' at night and planned on nappin'."

"What kind of medicine?"

"It warn't my business so's I didn't ask."

Fagan frowned. "Guess I better check on her," he said after a bit. He picked up the phone. "Is that you, Arabella? Yes, it is. Yes. Can you please ring my home?"

Neither me or Morty went back to work. And neither of us said anythin' to each other. I don't know about him, but my heart wuz a poundin' even though I couldn't come up with a reason why. We both jes stood there watchin' Fagan.

"Thank you," Fagan finally said. "You keep on ringing her. Archie says she had him bring her some pills from Kimmons this morning. Maybe she's napping but I better go check on her anyway." He wuz pale when he hung up.

"Want me to..."

He grabbed his hat and coat off they's hooks. "No, you stay here with Morty."

Morty and I watched him hurry out the front door.

"You think there's something really wrong?" Morty said as we watched Fagan tip his hat to Eliza Rogers who wuz headed our way with a fat canvas bag under her arm.

"Naw," I murmured. "Yer Mama jes seemed a mite blue. And maybe a little tired."

Morty opened the door fer Miz Rogers.

"Top of the mornin' to ya, Morty. Archie."

"Mornin', ma'am," we chorused.

"I've brought ya me coins...to trade for me foldin' money, doncha know."

* * *

On December 23, 1894, Goldsby and an accomplice Jim French held up and robbed
Nowata, Oklahoma, Station Agent Bristow of $190.00.
The Morning Call, December 24, 1894

*   *   *

Fort Smith, Ark.
Mrs. Fagan Bourland attempted to commit suicide Friday by taking morphine.
Indian Chieftain, December 27, 1894

Section II

1895

Chapter Six

The Bourland Hotel

Sunday, January 13, 1895

Somewhere someone wuz a hammerin'. I woke up and stretched. The bangin' stopped. "What in tarnation?" Rubbin' my eyes, I sat up in bed. The clock said 8:14. Way too early fer such a racket on Sunday mornin'. I pulled my blanket up to my chin and rolled to face the wall.

I hadn't even dozed back off before the hammerin' started agin. This time it seemed further away. I barefooted it across the cold floor to peek out my window. Nothin'. I rubbed the glass with my sleeve. Still nothin'. Figgerin' it must be too early fer the usual Sunday crowd, I pulled yesterday's clothes back on and headed downstairs.

Lydia Sprinkle wuz a holdin' a sign sayin', "The Bailey Hotel," that used to hang outside by the front door. She looked up at me, "Morning, Archie."

"Mornin', Miz Sprinkle. What's goin' on, if'n ya don't mind my askin'?"

"The new sign came in yesterday. Since Mr. Bailey passed last year, Miz Julia and Mr. Fagan've been discussing whether to rename the place now that it's officially theirs. Fagan convinced Julia it was a better business decision to change it. The new sign showed up yesterday, but this morning's the first chance we've had to switch it out."

My jaw tightened. Fagan probably decided that while Julia wuz gettin' over whatever made her take all that morphine. And I probably warn't the only one thinkin' that neither.

Tom stuck his head inside the doorway. "Mornin', Archie," he said as he reached fer the new sign Lydia wuz a holdin' with her other hand. It didn't take him but a couple minutes to hang it. "Come take a look." He folded his arms and cocked his head sideways as he inspected his work. "What do ya think?"

I shivered when the chilly morning air hit me. In big letters, the sign read, "The Bourland Hotel." I bit back a chuckle. "Wonder whose idea that wuz?"

Tom chuckled. "Don't ya now?"

"Maud seen it yet?"

"You're the first, boy." Tom came inside, rubbing his hands together to warm them.

"You know how she's gonna read this," I said.

*   *   *

The knock on my door surprised me. Usually no one who had business with me wanted to climb them stairs. "Who is it?"

Another knock, this one firmer.

I got up and threw open the door.

Maud leaned agin the door jam. "I didn't know you wore glasses."

"What're you doin' here?"

"Maud lives here." She sauntered past me. "Second floor right below you"

"That's Miz French's room. And Miz McGinnis's."

"Only rich people and Bourland favorites get rooms of their own. Remember?"

"That's up to the Bourlands."

"Ah, yes." She picked up a book James Bourland'd lent me and thumbed through the pages. "So why you?"

"Part of my salary."

"I see." She set the book back down. "Look at you with all those freckles and baby chin hairs popping out all over the place." She reached fer my glasses.

I flinched and backed away. "You changed yer hair."

"You like it?"

I folded my arms. "Hair is hair."

"Why're you so mean to Maud?"

"You're like a bug bite between my shoulder blades."

"Most folks adore Maud."

"Not me."

"You do too!" She lowered her lashes, lifted her chin and then slowly opened her eyes wide.

I backed way from her. "We got no business, you and me."

"Of course, we do. Our business is just...unfinished."

"I'm broke."

"No, you're not." She stood on tiptoe to kiss my cheek, but it landed on my chin.

Embarrassed, I backed away. "What do you want?"

"Buy Maud something?"

"I ain't got money fer no lady's clothes."

"You had money for them glasses."

"That's none of yer business." My voice cracked.

She wandered around my room, pickin' up my things and lookin' 'em over. "Maud needs a dress, Archie. George's mad and Fagan won't talk to her since she got back from Missoura."

"If'n I went shoppin' with you, it'd be all over Fort Smith before we bought anythin'."

"I don't need you to go with me, I just need money."

"No."

"You got it." She opened the little cabinet by my bed and pulled out my flannel under drawers. "Look at these," she shook them at me. "They're brand new."

"I don't got money fer no lady's outfit. You kin find someone better off'n me."

"Maud's got business in town."

I wuz startin' to panic. "Get outta my room."

She ignored me and kept right on pokin' through my stuff.

"Does Fagan even know you're back?"

"Not yet. Miz Sprinkle ..."

"You're gonna get Lydia in trouble."

"Fagan'll be glad to see his little Maud."

"Fagan's got family to take care of. Miz Julia needs him right now. The boys ne..."

She stiffened. "Maud's got family too. They need stuff too."

"What kinda stuff?"

"...food, clothes...money..., you know."

"Get a job waitin' tables at one of them places on Garrison."

"Them plain Fort Smith housewives in their fancy Boston Store clothes don't wait tables. They got husbands who take care of them."

"If'n that's so, then why ain't you makin' up with George? He's got prospects."

"In ten years. Maybe. Maud needs money now."

"Why?"

"Maud needs a dress that's nicer than what that bitch Jooolia wears."

"No matter what you wear, Maud, you cain't compare to her."

She drew back. "Why not?"

"Julia's got heart."

"And Maud don't?"

"Julia looks after folks what ain't even her family. You cain't take care of yerself, let alone yer ma."

"He said Maud was his sweet darlin'."

"Uh huh."

Maud stamped her foot. "He gave Maud presents."

"Then why're you askin' me fer stuff?"

The sparkle in her eyes turned hard. "Because you got money, Archie."

"Go away."

"Or what?"

I elbowed past her and slammed the door behind me. Clompin' down the stairs to the first floor, I pounded on the office door.

"What is it?"

"Miz Lydia..." my voice cracked,"... you gotta keep that girl outta my room."

"You got a lock." She looked up from her desk. "Why'd you open your door?"

"Cause it never occurred to me she'd be livin' here, of all places. Thought it mighta been you or Mr. Tom needin' somethin'."

"Tom and I have keys."

"Meanin' anyone kin jes waltz in to my room anytime they want?"

Lydia rolled her eyes. "I know Maud's a problem, but..."

"How'd she even know which room is mine?"

"I don't know, Archie." Lydia stood up. "I'll speak to her."

"Jes get her outta my room?"

Lydia patted my arm. "I promise."

"Don't let her take anythin'."

"I won't."

My heart wuz a beatin' so fast I couldn't catch my breath.

"Sit down, Archie."

"I'm...I'm sorry." Dizzy, I grabbed hold of the back of a chair and panted.

"Mary!" Lydia put an arm around me and guided me into the seat. "Mary, get in here, please and bring a cold cloth."

Mary peeked into the dinin' room. "Lawd Almighty, Archie, you sick?"

"I'm fine."

"You ain't fine. You're white as a sheet. Stay right where you are and I'll bring you some water." Mary hustled off.

"Don't get up." Lydia shook her finger at me. "I'll take care of Maud."

*　*　*

Mary sat down beside me at the table. "Now, what's up with you?"

"That girl agin."

"What did Maud do this time?"

"She's sackin' my room as we sit here."

Mary seemed shocked. "You got a thing for Maud, Archie?"

"If'n hate's a thing."

"What happened this time?"

"She's livin' here."

Mary sighed. "I know."

"She came up to my room and wanted me to take her shoppin'."

"For what?"

"Who knows? Lady stuff."

Mary sat down beside me. "This ain't gonna end well, is it?"

"Julia's bound to find out she's here sooner or later."

"And she's gonna be mad none of us told her." Mary took off her spectacles and rubbed her eyes. "She already suspects something's up. Maybe someone oughta tell her outright."

Afraid she thought that someone oughta be me, I took a quick gander at my toes.

"It's not like Fagan don't enjoy the town ladies from time to time," Mary said. "Or that Julia don't expect it. That's how it works after married folk have as many kids as they want."

"I try not to think about stuff that ain't my business."

The corners of Mary's mouth twitched. "Don't go turnin' all red in the face on me. We all look the other way."

"That girl don't plan on bein' no second fiddle."

"She's a fool then."

"Especially if'n she thinks Fagan'll give up his family and marry her."

Mary chuckled. "Okay, sugar, naive. Is that better?"

A loud crash made us both jump. In the front hall at the foot of the stairs, Lydia stood over an open suitcase of patched-up, frilly women's clothes.

Maud stood on the top landing. "You ain't tellin' Maud who she can visit."

"That boy deserves privacy."

"He lured me up to his room."

I gasped. "Why that little..."

Lydia glanced my way and frowned.

Mary put her hand on my arm. "Shhh."

"But..."

86

"Let Lydia deal with her, sugar."

"She's lyin'."

"Of course she is. Everyone knows that."

I wuz still steamed. "Crazy damn girl."

Mary raised an eyebrow. "How about a cookie with your coffee?"

Jaws clenched, I follered her back to the kitchen. "Don't let Maud get your goat," she said. "That gives her the upper hand in this game the two of you play." She glanced over her shoulder at me as she set a big pot of water on the stove. "You can sull up if you want to, but that don't change nothin'. Maud's gonna do what Maud's gonna do and Mr. Fagan's gonna do what he's gonna do. Ain't our place to get involved."

* * *

I wuz hurryin' up South Third carryin' our weekly take to the First National Bank when I passed Corrine Southard and Abigail Talbot standin' on the corner of Third and Garrison.

"I was dressed for calling and if I do say so myself, I looked mighty nice in my new black dress with a bunch of big red roses. I invited Mama and Mrs. John Rogers to accompany me and expected to pay thirty-two calls from three until six...Why mornin', Archie. How are you this fine day?"

"Mornin', Miz Southard." I took off my cap. "Mornin', Miz Talbot."

"You're the person to ask." Abigail grabbed my sleeve.

I glanced at Miz Southard who sighed and rolled her eyes. "Ma'am?"

"Urie Ann Johnston's maid told Caroline McGrath's handyman that Fagan Bourland's keepin' a young girl over at The Bourland Hotel. Bold as brass. Shares a room with the woman that brother of his sees."

"Oh?"

"Don't give me that look, Archie Biggs. You know something! What's going on at The Bourland?"

"Don't know nothin' about Mr. Fagan keepin' no girl."

"Julia's a proud woman," Miz Southard said. "This must be tearing her heart out."

"Miz Julia's fine, ma'am."

"I can't imagine she's fine with Fagan keeping a tart in her daddy's hotel," Abigail said.

"I'm only tellin' ya what I know," I pulled away from her. "They's no girl!"

"He's brazen, putting her there." Abigail's voice'd wake snakes.

Miz Southard blushed. "Abigail..."

Abigail kept right on talkin'. She wuz so loud that folks on the other side of Garrison looked our way. "If he was discreet, he'd put her in Edward's place and no one would know the difference."

"Edward's place?"

"Down there." Abigail pointed to a dilapidated old hotel a block away.

"The Fitzgerald?"

"Edward told Garland it was bleeding him dry what with the constant repairs. Only the wrong kind of people'll stay there now."

"Is that so?"

"You know...people without financial resources?"

Miz Southard seemed embarrassed by Abigail's gossip. "I'm sorry, Archie," she said. "The doctor's expecting me to meet him at The Hotel Main for lunch."

Abigail grunted. "Nonsense, Corrine, it's not even 10:30 yet. You've got plenty of time."

"No, dear, I've got errands to run before I meet him."

Abigail narrowed her eyes. "What kind of errands?"

I took a step back. "I need to get this to the bank, if'n you fine ladies'll excuse me."

"Nice seein' you again, Archie," Miz Southard said.

"Yes, ma'am." I put my hat back on, turned and walked away.

"Did you see how that boy reacted, Corrine?"

"Eager to get on with his day?"

"Wouldn't look me in the eye. That's how you tell someone's lying."

"Oh, Abigail," Miz Southard said, "It's horrible to think about what Julia's going through. No wonder she took all that morphine..."

"And I thought Fagan was such a fine man." Abigail made sure she said it loud enough fer me...and everyone on Garrison Avenue...to hear.

A block further up Garrison, a girl waved as she passed me on her bicycle. "Hello, Archie!"

I flushed. "Hi, Arabella."

Chapter Seven

Ain't Got No Secrets Now!

Monday, February 4, 1895

I wuz workin' in my cubby hole, addin' up numbers. The last I looked, some of our regulars wuz fingerin' the new items I'd put out fer sale yesterday evenin'. Morty wuz at the register, sortin' through Miz Keating's items while her youngest son eyed the taffy jar. Fagan sat in his rockin' chair beside the front window readin' *The Elevator*.

The bell tinkled as someone came in the front door.

"What do you think?" A familiar voice floated over the chatter of the other customers. "Don't they look pretty on Maud?"

"You ain't allowed here, Miz Allen," Morty warned.

"Is that so, Fagan?"

I pulled back the curtain so's I could see the front of the store. Several customers stood around, groceries in hand—mouths open. Maud stared down at Fagan, her glove-covered hand stretched toward him, palm up. Morty stood behind his father, hands on hips.

"MAUD!" It slipped out before I thought better of it.

She gave me the evil eye and turned back to Fagan.

My God, I thought. She's goin' fer broke right here in the man's place of business!

Tears streamed down her cheeks. "You gonna let that boy talk to Maud thataway?"

Fagan stood up, brushed past her and marched out the front door. Through the window, we watched him head up Sixth Street toward the courthouse, his arms tight agin his sides, his hands clenched into fists.

"You best be goin' wherever it is you go, Miz Allen." Morty pointed to the front door.

I walked up behind him. "Morty's right, Maud. Get outta here."

Fagan's secret wuz out. Warn't much anyone could do about it now. Maud knowed it too. She looked around the room and wagged a finger. "Y'all are my witnesses if'n they hurt me."

Miz McGrath laid her items on the nearest display table, grabbed her son's shoulder and hustled him out the front door. I wondered if'n Julian told her about how Maud treated him and Burley the day they hanged Lewis Holder. Whether he had or not, I figgered he warn't gonna tell her now that she seen Maud goin' after Fagan thataway.

Adaline Keating's groceries wuz already on the counter waitin' fer Morty to take her money. Without waitin' fer her food to be packed up, she grabbed the hand of her youngest boy and headed fer the door.

"But Mama, I want candy!" Her little one cried.

She stopped and found Larry, Jr. with her eyes.

"Go on, Mama," he said. "I'll bring it home when they get everything back on track here."

"You're sure?"

"Go on. It'll be okay."

She handed Larry, Jr. the money and hurried out the front door, mutterin' about that "Jezebel."

I follered Miz Keating outside and tugged at the rope connected to the bell in the barn. Sam stuck his head out the door, his eyebrows arched. I waved him over.

"What's wrong, Archie?"

"Maud's here agin. Teased Fagan until he left. In front of everyone."

"Lawd almighty." Sam frowned. "Where's Miz Julia?"

"Dunno. I figger she'll hear about it soon enough. Miz Keating done headed home in a huff. Miz Southard's still inside the store though and you know Miz Southard and Abigail Talbot's thick as thieves. And Miz Talbot'll break her neck gettin' over to Julia's to share the news once she hears what Miz Southard's got to say. And even if Miz Talbot misses the catch, Morty'll tell his mama."

"That girl's goin' for a homer, Archie."

I sighed. "And in front of the man's kids."

"What you thinkin' we oughta do?"

It wuz the first time Sam'd ever asked me a question like that. It made me feel like we wuz partners in this here deal. Problem wuz though, I had no idea what to do next. "Go get Miz Sprinkle," I said finally. "Maybe she kin herd Maud back to her room."

Sam set out fer The Bourland Hotel and I went back inside the store.

"You ain't gonna shoot Maud."

Maud wagged a finger at Morty who wuz pointin' a pistol at her.

"I can and I will, Miz Allen."

"Whoa!" I stepped between them. "Ain't nobody gonna do no shootin'."

Larry, Jr. stood behind Morty, his fists clenched and his jaw set.

"Shoot her, son," Sarge cackled from the door of the saloon.

I frowned at him and he wheeled around and limped back into the bar.

"This here girl ain't allowed anywhere near our property." The pistol shook in Morty's hands. "If'n she ain't gone soon, we'll roll her corpse out onto "A" Street and tie it to the back of a skittish horse."

I choked back a chuckle. A skittish horse? Morty Bourland sure had a good imagination, but I didn't reckon he'd pull that trigger. I turned to Maud. "You heard him. Sam's gettin' Miz Sprinkle. You better skedaddle."

"Why're you doin' this to Maud, Archie? Why's Fagan ignoring her?"

I looked around. Our remaining customers wuz scowlin'. "Ain't you got the sense God gave a goose?" I grabbed her elbow and hustled her outta the store.

In the middle of Sixth Street, she jerked her arm outta my hand. "You hurt Maud, Archie."

"I ain't hurt you yet, but you better get yer butt outta here before I do."

She puckered up and bawled. "Everyone is m-m-mean to Maud. All the time."

Maud bossed me around or flirted with me. Cryin' wuz the last thing I expected. Like every other time she'd caused trouble, people wuz a watchin'. In the street, men wuz a waitin' to see if she needed defendin'. Women wuz a standin' on the corner a gossipin' about her.

And then Lily French busted outta The Bourland Hotel and ran into the intersection right in front of a boy leadin' a lame horse down Sixth. "Maud, dear," she cried as she elbowed her way into the store. What's wrong?"

"Archie ki-kicked me out of the sto-store."

Lily turned on me. "How could you be so mean?"

"I hustled her away from a bad situation...which she caused...to keep her from gettin' shot."

"He-he hurt me!" Maud pulled up her sleeve and held up her skinny arm. Sure enough, there wuz bruises half-way between her wrist and her elbow.

"Look at her." Lily turned on me. "You don't know your own strength."

"Them bruises is old."

"You're tellin' me that this little thing is lying?"

Lily wuz spoilin' fer a fight and I didn't have a taste fer it. I turned to Maud. "I'm sorry you're hurt. Now stay away from the Bourlands and all they's properties or there'll be trouble."

Tears dripped down her chin. "You threatenin' Maud, Archie?"

"You keep doin' what ya been doin', bad things're bound to happen."

"You heard him, Lily. He's plannin' on hurtin' Maud. Again..."

"He's gonna do no such thing, are you, Archie?"

The kid with the horse looked from Lily to Maud to me and back at Lily agin.

I folded my arms over my chest. "Ain't me this here girl oughta be afeared of."

"Oh, Archie." Lily turned back to Maud. "Come inside, dear." She herded the snifflin' girl toward The Bourland Hotel. Jes before they went in the door, Maud looked over her shoulder and stuck her tongue out at me.

I growled and headed back to the store. The kid follered me across the intersection and tied his horse up out front. "What the Sam Hill was that about?"

I glanced down at him. "None of yer business."

"You don't know me well enough to know that." The boy had more freckles than me and lots more sass.

"You're right, I don't. But it ain't none of yer business whoever you are."

Morty still had the pistol all cocked and ready to go, but then his eyes went past me. "Yo, Freckles, how ya doin'?"

I turned around to see the same kid standin' in the doorway, hat in hand.

"I'm good, Morty. What's goin' on here?"

Morty put the gun in its little box behind the brass register on the counter. "Craziness."

"Who was that girl makin' a fuss out there in the road?"

"A two-bit she-devil who's set her sights on my dad."

"Fagan?" The boy snorted. "Why he ain't that much bigger'n me. Think that lil old gal'd chase after me?"

"Maybe if you waved a dollar bill at her." Morty finally cracked a smile.

"What would you do with that lil firecracker, Milt?" Sarge Eacret said from the bar door.

The boy puffed up like a rooster about to hustle a hen. "What any man would."

Morty, Larry, Jr. and Sarge busted out laughin'...and, okay, I confess. I gotta kick outta him, too. Even Freckles hisself got tickled. And when he laughed, it wuz open mouthed and all out, his shoulders a shakin' and his eyes turnin' into slits.

We went on longer'n the joke warranted, but we wuz blowin' off steam, doncha know.

I stuck out my hand. "Nice to meet you, Freckles. Sorry about bein' stuffy. That girl's been a thorn in my backside fer a while now. I'm Archie."

"Yo, Archie. Milt Hinckle here." He pumped my hand. "Miz Annie Shaffer told me about you killin' that big ole yeller snake last year. She said you got all the pretty young gals of Fort Smith pantin' after you. Cain't think why now that I've laid eyes on your ugly mug."

"If'n that wuz so, I'd have picked me one out by now." I laughed but my mind wuz whirlin'. Who wuz Annie Shaffer?

"Don't do that! You'll break Annie's heart."

I snorted because I warn't no hit with the ladies. Except'n fer Maud, none of 'em ever paid me no nevermind.

"Milt and I've known each other since we was knee-high to old Belle," Morty said. "I got bigger, but Freckles here's a slow starter."

Milt elbowed Morty. "We been raisin' one ruckus after another since we was little—Larry, Jr. too."

Larry tipped Milt's hat down over his eyes. "So now you gonna mouth off about when we tried to hang you?"

Freckles' shoulder-shakin' snorts got the rest of us a laughin' agin.

"Okay, what's the story?" I wiped my eyes with my knuckle

"We tried to sneak in and watch a hangin' over at the gallows by Judge Parker's Court," Morty said. "It was all Freckle's idea."

"We wasn't more'n nine or ten," Larry elbowed Milt. "Of course, the guard chased us away."

"Must be part of bein' a kid." I thought about Maud standin' on my shoulders a watchin' Holder die.

"So's we decided to have a trial of our own. Guess who was the outlaw?" Milt grinned.

"Hmm, I wonder."

"We found Freckles guilty of stealin' candy outta Pop's jar there," Morty pointed.

"They convicted and sentenced me on the spot!" The way Milt told it, it sounded like a happy memory.

"So's we put a rope around his neck and threaded it through a sign that hung over that stable up on Garrison," Larry said. "We'd just got him up on a nail keg and tied the rope to the stable, when Freckles loses his balance, and the keg falls over."

"And them little bastards ran off. I hadda hold onto the rope to keep from stranglin'."

Why Milt wuz chucklin' escaped me. But since he obviously didn't die, it wuz pretty funny, I reckon. I'd a been peeved if'n it'd been me, but Freckles didn't seem to hold a grudge.

"It's a good thing we never thought to tie his hands together," Morty went on. "Freckles was swinging back and forth kicking and a gurgling. He made such a racket that Cephas who was getting a horse shoed came running and cut him down. Lucky for us. A minute more and Judge Parker'd been hangin' five or six of us for murdering Freckles."

"Lucky for them?" Milt's voiceless shoulder-shaking laugh got me and Morty and Sarge goin' agin too.

And then the fun wuz over. "So what's with that crazy girl?" Freckles gestured toward The Bourland Hotel with his head.

Morty's grin melted off'n his face. "Who knows. She's like a mad dog. Once she starts bitin', she cain't bite you enough."

"So's why she goin' after Fagan?"

"Cause she's dead broke," I said.

"Cause she wants to hurt my mother," Morty said at the same time.

Milt's whistle wuz more like a breathy sigh, "What do you think, Larry?"

"I think she's a bitch," he said. "And that's what bitches do."

"Who knew ole Larry was up on bitches?" Morty elbowed Larry, Jr. in the side.

* * *

Sam met me in front of the store. "Mr. Fagan musta took off for quieter places."

"I woulda too if'n I coulda, but this here's his mess. Not mine or Morty's or yers."

"Mr. Fagan ain't careful with other people's feelins'. If'n he sees somethin' pretty, he takes it. And when it ain't pretty no more, he leaves by the side of the road."

"He might graze, but he always comes home. Don't he?"

"So far." Sam's eyes wuz hard.

"He won't leave Julia and the boys."

"How do ya know that?"

"I jes do, Sam."

"Mmmm."

"He won't."

"He better not. That's all I gotta say about it." He headed back to the barn.

I watched him as he crossed the street in front of Ollie Fields' rig, causing ole Ollie to pull back on the reins so hard one of his mules reared up. "Sam, you gonna git yerself runned over one of these days."

Sam waved and hustled over to the side of the road so's Ollie could pass.

There wuz only a few customers in the store when I got back. Miz Mathews and her oldest daughters, Lula, Jesse, and Sadie, wuz rummagin' through bolts of material that'd come in a few days back. And Miz Martin and her little boy, Cy, wuz a pokin' through Miz Homann's jellies. None of 'em'd been around

93

when Maud pulled her latest stunt, so's they busied themselves with shoppin' rather than gossipin'.

Morty sat on a stool behind the register, his jaw twitchin'.

"You, okay?"

"Do I look okay?"

"You look like yer best friend done stole Gertie." I gestured at the little dog curled up behind the register where she usually slept until James got outta school and came to fetch her every day.

"That's about it."

"What're you gonna do?"

"Honestly, I ain't got a clue. Killin' her might make me feel better for a day or two."

"Yeah, well, then comes day three."

"Yup."

The gun wuz layin' on the counter. I picked it up.

"It ain't loaded," he grunted.

I chuckled. "Jes wanted to scare her?"

"Couldn't find any bullets."

"Don't give me that. You ain't a killer."

"Right now, I wish I was."

"Gettin' yerself hanged ain't gonna help yer folks get past this."

"I hate him."

"No, ya don't. You jes don't wanna to see yer mama hurt."

"She'll kill him when she finds out."

"I ain't gonna tell her...and you ain't neither."

"Miz Talbot or Miz Sprinkle or any of the local housewives that shop in this store'll know by sunset, if'n they didn't already suspect it. One of 'em's bound to tell her. And if they don't tell her, Maud'll make sure she knows sooner or later." Morty rubbed the corner of one eye with his knuckle and we got back to work.

* * *

February 22, 1895

Me and Julia'd jes spent a couple hours at Goldman's Warehouse on Garrison. They wuz overstocked and sellin' off old merchandise. We wuz headin' back to the store when we ran into Abigail Talbot and Adaline Keating and a feller I never seen before.

"Archie, have you met my husband?" Miz Adaline touched the man's sleeve.

"No, ma'am, I shore haven't." I wuz excited to finally meet Larry's pa. He wuz one of Judge Parker's jailers and I wuz jes dyin' to ask him about ole Cherokee Bill.

"Darlin', this is Archie Biggs. He works for the Bourlands. He's the one who fought off that yellow serpent in their barn."

Lawrence Keating, Sr. had mebbe ten years on Fagan Bourland. Except'n fer his beard, there warn't no doubt he wuz Larry's pa. "Well, ain't you a strong big lad," he said as he clasped my hand. "Nice to meet you, Archie. My sweetheart here tells me you've got a book she thinks is from Ireland."

94

"Nice to meet you, sir. I do have one my mother…or someone…wrapped up with me in a shawl of some kind. Or so the story goes. I keep it close but no one I ever met kin read it. As I told yer Missus here, I ain't got a clue what it means or why I have it. Or where I come from fer that matter. Don't even know why I keep the blamed thing."

"My family came here from Ireland when I was a but a lad. I don't remember too much about them days. Remember that ship though." Mr. Keating rocked sideways back and forth and grinned. "Was quite a ride."

"You don't remember Ireland?"

"Oh sure. The old house, of course. In Tipperary."

"That cape is gorgeous, Julia," Abigail interrupted. "Fur lined?"

"Fox I believe. Not sure."

"Only you, Julia," Abigail chuckled. "Every other woman in town would know the details, down to the last button. And is that brocade you're wearing black or purple?"

"Purple." Julia didn't actually say 'of course,' but I seen it in her eyes.

Abigail ran her fingers across Julia's sleeve. "Yes, with a bit of silver woven into it."

Julia stepped back outta Abigail's reach. I didn't blame her. Someone feelin' of my clothes with me in 'em would give me the heebee jeebees too.

"It's stunning, my dear," Abigail pretended not to notice she'd offended Julia.

"I buy what I like."

"You buy the best."

"I like nice things."

"We all do, my dear." Abigail sniffed. "But not all can afford what you can."

Julia raised her chin. "We work hard for what we have."

"Everyone knows that. The women of this town love your beautiful things. Makes us push our own husbands to do better."

Lawrence Keating glanced at Adaline and raised an eyebrow.

She bit her lip to keep from laughin'.

My toes wuz as cold as my nose. With a crate of boots and shoes and small items on one shoulder, listenin' to Abigail Talbot yammer on wuz icy hell.

"Garland buys you lovely things, dear. You're always pretty as a picture." Julia pulled her cape closer and stepped to the side as if to go around.

"By the way, have you seen Colonel Crump?" Abigail's voice rose a bit.

"Not lately."

"They say he sprained his ankle trying to get on a moving train up near St. Louis.

"Oh dear. I'm sorry to hear it." Julia shifted from foot to foot. "Why would he try such a thing?"

"Men." Abigail rolled her eyes. "You'd think they'd have better sense."

I thought about makin' an excuse and headin' on back to work, but I didn't want to abandon Julia less'n she wanted me to…and somehow, I didn't think she did.

"Have any of you seen Gladys Wallace and Joe Cawthorn at the Grand Opera House? Caroline and Wilbur McGrath attended last night, and she said it was funny. Don't know why she didn't tell me they were going. Garland and I could have made it, even on short notice. Anyway, we'll go tonight instead. Do you and Adaline enjoy the theater, Mr. Keating?" Abigail peered at him through her monocle.

Fer a moment, I thought he wuz goin' to laugh. But then he looked down at Adaline and patted her hand. "We do when we can, but as a guard over at the Federal prison, I work nights mostly. And of course, with the children and all..."

"Yes, it must be difficult." Abigail turned to Julia. "How about you and Fagan? Perhaps we could have dinner beforehand?"

"No, no, dear. We can't. We have plans for this evening," Julia said. "And Archie and I must go now. We have another engagement in ten minutes."

"Oh? With whom, might I ask?"

"No one you know, dear. Has to do with the store and I know how tiresome you find that."

Abigail seemed disappointed. "We'll do dinner one night next week then?"

"That sounds lovely." Julia touched cheeks with Abigail and hurried off down the street.

"Nice to see you, Archie." Adaline Keating waved.

I nodded and took off after Julia. Larry Keating's ma and pa wuz nice and all, but a minute of Abigail Talbot's company wuz a minute too much fer me.

*　*　*

"Send Sam back up to Goldman's to pick up the other boxes of odds and ends I bought," Julia said to Fagan as we came into the store. "There's a partial set of china. And a framed mirror. And a couple silver coffee pots. A nice lamp too."

Fagan kissed Julia's cheek. "Good work."

"Archie and I'll take these things upstairs and see what we got for our money."

"Good. I'm going to take Lilith out to run off some of that winter fat."

"Don't be gone long. John's bringing his new woman over for dinner tonight. Don't leave me to make conversation by myself. You know how I hate that."

"What time?"

"Same as usual."

Fagan took out his pocket watch. "Hour out to the Homann farm. Talk an hour. An hour back. That gets me home by five."

"I mean it, Fagan. I don't like what John's doing to Lulu and the kids. They aren't officially divorced yet."

"It's none of our business, sweetheart."

"It is when he shows off this Lily woman in front of our boys. Morty knows what's up. And James is smart enough to figure it out, too. How will you explain it?"

I grunted to remind them that I wuz still standin' there.

Fagan chuckled. "It's okay, Archie. Surely living at the hotel, you've seen my brother come and go? Visiting that pretty minx that lives there?"

I avoided his eyes. "Yes, sir."

"You got an opinion about John and Lily French?"

I did but I figgered it wuz best to shrug and say nothin'.

96

Fagan laughed. "See there, my love? Archie doesn't give two figs what John does with Lily."

"There'll be trouble, Fagan. Mark my words."

"Yes, well, at least it'll liven up the place. Been months since anyone had anything to gossip about." Fagan put on his coat and hat.

I choked back a snort over that one.

"Be back by five," Julia said. "And don't forget to send Sam to Goldman's with the wagon."

"I will, I will, I will." The door closed behind him.

"That man'll be the death of me yet." Julia gathered up her skirts and we climbed the back stairs to the second floor. I set the crate on a long table. Julia took off her hat and cape and hung them on a rack beside the front window. "Did you know about John?" Julia dumped the box of shoes and boots and odds and ends onto the table.

"Yes, ma'am."

She examined a pair of high-topped men's shoes. "What's she like?"

"A little nosy fer my taste, but nice enough."

"How so nosy?"

"She already found Sarge a woman."

"What did Sarge say?"

"To her or to me?" I grinned.

"Both."

"He said that the woman in question wuz too old, too fat, and too selfish."

"He said that to Lily?"

"No, to me. He told Miz Lily he needed a woman who warn't always gettin' into his chew."

"Sarge cares about three things in life...food, drink, and tobacco," Julia laughed. "I can't imagine he'd share any of them."

When Julia laughed, I couldn't help but laugh too. I loved the days she came down to the store. She seemed a lot more interested in it than Fagan. He spread his time and energy between the saloon and horses and hotels and coal and telephone service and who knowed what else. She told me once that he couldn't sit still or be satisfied with what they had. He wuz always lookin' fer somethin' new.

I picked up a pair of red leather baby shoes. "Like brand new. How much do you think?"

She examined them. "Originally from the Montgomery Ward Catalog, I should think."

"They's hardly worn at all."

"Fifty cents?"

"Okay. I'll log 'em and tag 'em."

"If they don't sell right away, we'll donate them to the Methodists."

The little kids I'd growed up with in Southern Arkansas went barefoot mostly. No one could spare fifty cents fer fancy baby shoes. "They might catch Miz Southard's eye," I said. "Her boy might be jes about that size by now."

The sound of men's voices and horse's hooves echoed up from the street. Julia looked out the window agin. "Fagan's off to chat with Tony Homann," she said. "And Sam and Belle are heading up to Goldman's."

"Hope it warms up soon. Me and Sam wanna play some ball this spring."

"With a team?"

"We kin try. Depends on…you know…my leg."

"It still gives you trouble?"

I avoided her eyes. "Not all the time."

"You and Sam get along pretty good."

"Yes, ma'am. We got lotsa things in common."

"Like baseball?"

"Like baseball."

"Perhaps the two of you can go see some of League teams play one of these days."

"I'd shore like that."

We sorted the items spread out over the table while we waited fer Sam to come back.

"These are scuffed up, but a good polish and they'll be good as new. The soles are barely worn." Julia held up a pair of thick-soled boots. "What size do you wear?"

"I-I don't know."

"Try them on."

"I reckon I got some miles left in these." I glanced down at my shoes. The heel on the left one wuz worn down a mite and my big toe wuz stickin' through the hole on the right. "Jes need to clean 'em up."

"Now, Archie. We want you looking nice at the store. Come on over and let's see if these fit."

I only had one pair of socks and they had more holes than my shoes.

"Come on now."

My cheeks burned. "Yes, ma'am." I picked up the mate to the boot she held and placed the sole agin my foot.

"Looks about right."

"No no, try them on."

I sat down on a small bench beside the table and slipped my foot into the boot.

"There now," Julia said. "That wasn't so hard."

"No, ma'am. Fits fine."

"Good. Now buff them up and wear them to work tomorrow."

I looked up at her and grinned. "Thank you, ma'am."

Julia wandered over to the front window while I put my own shoe back on and set the boots aside to take home. She stiffened and then leaned forward, pressin' her face aginst the glass. "Who's that coming out of our hotel?"

"Ma'am?"

"Is that the girl that caused the hullabaloo last fall? The one who gave Morty such a scare?"

I walked over to the window. "That's Maud Allen, ma'am."

"What's she doing at The Bourland?"

Tryin' not to spill the beans about Maud alivin' there, I shrugged.

"She's headed this way." She stood up. "I don't want her here. She's troubled Morty enough."

"I'll go tell her to leave."

"No! I will this time." She threw her cape around her shoulders and headed down the stairs.

My heart dropped to my stomach. Julia and Maud in the same room? I thought about hidin' under the table until that ruckus wuz over, but figgered someone'd have to referee.

I hit the first floor just about the time, Julia confronted Maud as she opened the door to the store. "Mrs. Allen, after the hubbub you caused last summer, I thought you understood that you're not welcome here."

Morty stood behind the counter, eyes wide.

Outside, Sam pulled the rig up front. He got down off the wagon and wrapped the reins around a post. Just inside the door, rubbing his hands together to warm them, he stopped. "What the he..."

Maud turned to look at him and then me and then Morty in turn.

"Mrs. Allen!"

Maud's thin cotton clothes wuz dowdy up agin Julia's fancy wool outfit. I expected her to throw a conniption fit right there in the middle of the store. But she ducked her chin, elbowed her way around Sam...and ran out the front door.

I glanced at Morty who seemed relieved but unsurprised.

"Now then," Julia slipped on her gloves. "That's how it's done." She turned to me. "Don't let that woman set foot on any of our properties."

Feelin' like a fool, I said. "Yes, ma'am."

"Did you hear me, Morty?"

"Yes, Mama."

"Sam?"

"I'll throw her over Belle and carry her off to the trash heap where she belongs."

There wuz a long silence. Then we all laughed.

✳   ✳   ✳

February 23, 1895

"Which wuz worse?" I said as we opened the store.

"Definitely the discussion about Maud Allen."

I sighed and put down my pencil.

"Mama insisted that Maud not be allowed on any property we own. And Miz Lily says, 'So what're you gonna do? Just kick her out?' and Uncle John tried to catch Miz Lily's eye and shake his head. And then Mama says, 'What are you talking about?' And Pop's avoidin' Mama's eyes and I'm jes sittin' there until Mama figures it all out, blows up, throws her napkin at Pop—and goes out into the yard."

"Dang."

Morty sat down across from me. "Eventually, Pop follows her out there. And Uncle John and Miz Lily and I sit at the table not knowing what to say while James and Cap chase after Mama and Pop in the yard. Half the

99

neighborhood comes out on their porches or opens their windows to listen. Mama's screamin' at Pop. Cap's a bawlin' ...and James, well, he just sits down on the porch with his hands under his chin and watches. And as Mama's giving him what for, Pop's got his arms crossed and his head bowed. And while that's goin' on right outside the dining room window, Uncle John looks at me and says, how's business at the store?"

"So what did Fagan say?"

"About the store?"

"About Maud livin' at The Bourland?"

Morty sighed. "He lied. Smooth as a whistle. With all of us listening, he told Mama that he didn't have any idea Maud was there and he was sure it was Miz Sprinkle's doing and he'd take care of it."

"Julia buy it?"

"You can't trick Mama no more'n you can catch a weasel sleeping."

I laid down my pencil. "I'm sorry, Morty."

"So, everybody knows everything now. Aunt Lulu knows Uncle John's seeing Lily French. All the hotel residents know Lily's friends with Maud Allen. And Maud knows Pop ain't Uncle John but she thinks she has him hooked just the same. Mama's got it all figured out and even though Pop says he's done with Maud, Maud probably don't know that yet. And Mama's gonna be watchin' him like a hawk from now on...and no one should underestimate James cause he was born to tell tales. And, Lord-a-Mighty, don't even think about talking with Mama or Pop anytime soon cause either one of 'em'll bite your head off soon as look at you."

"What about Cap?"

"Last I saw him he was suckin' his thumb and tellin' Tawny he ain't goin' to school today."

"So what happens now?"

"Pop says he's gonna send Maud away."

"Easier said than done."

"Mama says she'll shoot her if she ever sees her on any of our properties after today."

"She's bluffin'."

"Archie, folks think Pop's the tough one but that ain't so. He's a starter. He gets interested in a new business, decides he likes it and buys it. Then he's off a starting something else before the first thing he started is goin' good. Mama's the one that keeps things chugging along. One or the other of 'em's always sayin' that they're invested in each other and us and the businesses. Mama ain't gonna allow no dirty-mouthed girl to get in the way of that."

＊　＊　＊

March 2, 1895

"What kin I do fer ya, Miz Julia?"

"Do you know where my husband is right now?"

"No ma'am. He warn't at the store when I left." I started to say he wuz seldom at the store this time of day but figgered that might not be news to her."

100

"Do you know if that girl left town yet?"

"I don't know it fer sure. She threw a tantrum about it. Came up to my room and told me off."

"Why you?"

I shrugged. "Probably cause I wuz home."

Tawny gave us each a mug of coffee. "I'll go now, ma'am."

"You ought to hear this too." Julia nodded toward a chair next to mine.

"Yes, ma'am." Tawny pulled up a chair, sat down and folded her hands in her lap.

They both looked at me.

I blew on my coffee and then took a sip. "That girl's been pokin' into my business ever since I come to town, Miz Julia. I don't much like her, and she jes cain't stand it. She's like that. The more you push her away the more she tries to get a body's attention."

"I was told she went back to her husband."

"Who told you that?" I looked from Julia to Tawny and back to Julia.

Julia narrowed her eyes. "Guess!"

"Ah," I blushed. "I don't know nothin' about that, Miz Julia. But if'n she did go back to George, I doubt she'll stay long. Jes my opinion, you understand. They don't seem to like each other much. Maud's downright mean when she talks about him. And he's frustrated with her. Tired of draggin' her outta bars. Reckon any man'd be."

"Yes, I imagine so."

"I ain't seen her around lately, but I ain't been lookin' fer her neither. She's got family up in Missoura, I think. Maybe she's there."

"You'll tell me if you see her, won't you?"

"If'n that's what you want."

"Divided loyalties?"

I blinked. "A mite."

"At least you're honest."

"Ain't no way of hidin' somethin' like that."

Julia poured cream into her coffee. "Here's the situation. My family's well-known and well off. So's Fagan's. We each brought a lot to this marriage. This house, for example. That hotel over there. They were mine before they were ours. Those boys are mine. And Fagan Bourland? He's mine too."

"Yes, ma'am."

"There's a lot of things that pompous little man does that I pretend I don't see. And there are things about me that he puts up with. You understand?"

"Kinda."

"I don't care what the law says. That's the deal Fagan and I made. That's not to say that we don't have private interests that we each accept. However, looking the other way only works when it's between two people. Third parties have no rights to things Fagan and I agreed to share."

"What do you want from me?"

"Loyalty."

"You and Mr. Fagan been kind to me, Miz Julia. No crazy girl's gonna make me forget that."

"Good."

My hands wuz shakin' and I banged my front tooth on the rim of my mug as I finished my coffee. "Whatcha want me to do?"

"Things that don't change my life or hurt my kids don't matter. Just warn me of...intrusions."

Caught up in her mood, I said, "I promise."

"Good. You can go now, Tawny."

"Yes, ma'am." Tawny pulled on her sweater, picked up the bag of pecans I'd brought, and went out the back door.

"Now, Archie. I expect we'll be examining the books more closely from here on out."

I opened the store ledger. "What're we lookin' fer?"

Julia wrinkled her forehead. "I expect I'll recognize it when I see it."

"You know I don't keep track of the hotels and roomin' houses. Or anything that goes on with Bill Hatcher and that card game he's got goin' on in the barn."

"I think we can work that out."

"Will Mr. Fagan be okay with that?"

Julia smiled fer the first time that morning. "Regardless of how he feels about it, I expect he'll accept our little audits. And I know you're already busy, so we'll adjust your salary accordingly."

*　*　*

March 25, 1895

It wuz a slow day. I wuz in my alcove behind the register, workin' the ledger. Morty and Sam wuz unloadin' goods Sam'd brought over from the train station. Once in awhile, one of 'em would grunt when they picked up somethin' but mostly it wuz quiet. I knowed it wuz good to have lots of customers, but I loved slow days. They gave me time to do stuff we put off on busy days.

"Anybody here?" It wuz Bill Hatcher's voice.

I waited, hopin' Morty wuz close enough to answer.

"ANYONE?"

I sighed, stood up and pulled back the curtain.

Hatcher wuz at the register, holdin' a fist full of cash. Startled, he looked up at me and said, "Gotta game set up in the barn tonight. I need cash."

"A game?"

"You know. Cards?" He wuz lookin' straight at me but his eyes shifted from side-to-side so's it made me wonder what exactly that varmint wuz up to. "What kinda cards?"

"Fagan never told you?"

I'd never seen anything about them card games actually in the books so's I said, "Maybe you should wait until Mr. Fagan gets back?"

Hatcher slowly closed the cash drawer. "Ask Morty. He knows the score."

"Morty ain't here right now."

He narrowed his eyes. "I need that money, boy."

"Even if'n Fagan wuz here and said it wuz okay, I'd still need to put it in the books or Miz Julia'll have my butt." I walked over and eyed the cash drawer.

102

"Okay, okay." He put the money back in the drawer and held up both hands. "Don't wanna get the man in trouble with his missus."

We stood there fer a moment, starin' at each other...and the money in the cash drawer.

The front door opened.

"...and so we left Babe with Mama while Dear and I went to Dr. Bailey's. Mrs. Main, Mrs. Bailey's mother'd died, don't ya know. But Dear had to make three stops along the way which delayed us. And then... no sooner do we get to the Bailey's than a boy on horseback rides up and says there's been an accident at Miz Sher..."

Two ladies stopped in they's tracks. Corinne Southard stayed close to the front door like she might bolt if'n things didn't suit her, but Abigail Talbot stood up straighter. "You okay, Archie?"

I kept my eyes on Hatcher. "Jes fine, Miz Abigail. How are you and Mr. Talbot doin'?"

"We're doing fine. Was just saying to Miz Southard here how nice it was to have dinner with the Bourlands and the Breedloves at The Hotel Main the other evening. Even Cal and Lucy were there." Abigail folded her arms across her chest. "In fact, Corrine and I saw Cal a minute ago. Didn't we, dear?" She turned to Miz Southard who nodded. Then she looked back at me and narrowed her eyes. "He said he was heading this way as soon as he finished his business with Mr. Brizzolara."

Hatcher glared at me, stuffed his hands in his pockets and left.

*　*　*

3:30 PM

I wuz late. I ran up the steps, unbuttonin' my shirt, and wuz already bare-chested when I threw open the door to my room.

"Why, Archie! You're downright purdy."

I frowned. "Get outta my room, Maud." I hung up my good shirt and pulled on an older, softer one. "You ain't supposed to be here at all. If'n Julia finds out, there'll be hell to pay."

"It's none of her business."

"Tell Julia that."

"Fagan said..."

I sighed.

"He did."

"If'n you wuz smart, you'd get yerself on back to Missoura."

"C'mon, Archie, say it. You'd miss Maud if she left town for good."

I dug my glove and baseball outta the closet. "Ain't I made it clear I don't like you?"

"But..."

"I mean it, Maud. Get outta here."

She sighed and sat up. "Where's Maud gonna go?"

"I don't care." I put on my practice shirt and started buttonin' it up. "Why don't you go on home to George?"

103

"He's mad at Maud. All the time."

"Surprise, surprise."

"Don't you be mean too."

"You stay outta them bars and start actin' like a wife, he might not be thataway." I grabbed her elbow and pulled her off my bed. "C'mon now, get yer shoes on."

"Don't," She jerked her arm away and swayed backwards.

I wrinkled my nose. "You smell like whiskey and cigars. Where you been?"

"The Corner Saloon...," she swayed forward, caught herself and then swayed back agin. "Think maybe The Morning Call before that. Not sure. They ain't nice to Maud there. Coulda been Till Shaw's place though. Maybe?"

"Uh huh. So how'd you get up here?"

"That bitch Julia...ain't that a funny name? Jooooliah. She came in while Maud was visitin' with Lily so's Lily hustled Maud outta her room and this was the only hidey-hole left."

"I didn't see Miz Julia when I came in. How long you been here?"

"Dunno. Awhile."

"Neither you or Lily have a key to my room."

Maud smirked. "There are ways."

"Yeah, and you know 'em all, doncha?"

"Don't be mad at Maud, Archie."

"Cain't help it. You're always doin' stupid things to get yerself in trouble."

"Doncha like girls?"

"Nice ones."

She flinched.

"Of all the crap you pulled since I met you, that hurt yer feelins'?"

"Maud ain't no rock, ya know." A tear trickled down her cheek.

"I'm meetin' somebody. Get outta my room."

"A girl?"

"What?"

"You meetin' a girl?"

"None of yer business."

"Why not Maud?"

"You're married."

"Maud's lonely, Archie. And that bitch Joooliah's been sayin' mean things about her to everyone."

"Don't you think you deserve it after you went after her boy and then her husband?"

"Fagan don't love her anyway."

I laughed.

Her eyes widened. "What do you know?"

"They's thick as thieves same as always."

"That's work stuff."

"Ha."

"No. He told me."

"How dumb kin you be, girl?"

"He sleeps in his own room." It wuz a question masqueradin' as a fact.

“They ain’t got no extra room.”

“That’s not what Fagan...”

“No, it probably ain’t.” I had no idea if’n the Bourlands shared a bed, but I got a tickle outta the look on Maud’s face.

She frowned. “He’s gonna keep Maud, Archie. Buy her pretty things. Put her up somewhere better’n this old place.”

“What’s George say about that?”

“George’s got someone else.” She sounded like she wuz gonna cry.

I laughed and shook my head. “You gotta heap of trouble comin’ yer way, girl.”

The clock in the hallway dinged four times.

“You goin’ on yer own?”

Maud stuck out her lower lip.

“Or do I have to throw you down them stairs?” I grabbed her arm.

“Fine.” She jerked away and felt around on my bed, her fingers slippin’ under my pillow.

“What in tarnation are you lookin’ fer?”

She avoided my eyes. “What’s it matter, it ain’t there anyway.”

“It wuz you!”

“Course it was me, who’d ya think?” She crawled off my bed and straightened her clothes. “What else can a body do while hidin’ up here? Besides, who puts something like that under a pillow anyway? That’s the first place a thief’d look.”

“Jes how many times you been up here goin’ through my stuff?”

She covered her ears. “Don’t yell!”

“If’n I ever catch you in my room agin, I’ll boot you down them stairs”

“Oooo,” she held her hands either side if her face and wiggled her fingers, “Oooooo.”

“There ain’t no money here. And that book ain’t yer business.”

“Maud couldn’t make hide nor hair out of that scribble anyhow.”

“Imagine!”

“Maud was gonna show it to Miz Sprinkle. She can read real good, ya know.”

“Go.”

She folded her arms over her chest. “What if Maud stays put? What would you do? Hurt her?”

“Fine!” I picked up my glove and left.

March 27, 1895

Early morn.

Our darling sits on his little chair (with the hole in it). Dear is over at St. John's Hospital performing an amputation of limb—a woman shot—didn't know it was loaded!! During the night, a drunken man fell from the trestle at the edge of town—fifty feet—terribly hurt. Dear amputated an arm— then, so worn out this morn. & this is pension day. Always a busy one. Work is progressing nicely on our new home.

Corrine Southard

* * *

March 29, 1895
8:00 AM

"Mornin' Reverend Mathews, Mary." You'd have thought I'd walked in on a funeral. "Somethin' wrong?"

"Archie, have you ever heard of Reverend Culpepper?" Mary Kirkpatrick poured coffee into my cup and offered me a biscuit to go with it. "Does a big tent revival over on North Tenth every ten years or so?"

"Um..." I glanced at Sarge who avoided my eyes.

"Ever been to a revival? I hear it's a moving experience..."

The back of my neck burned. "Um...a time or two."

"Did you see the Lord?"

"Jes a lot of people all stirred up."

"That's okay, Archie." Mary patted my hand. "It ain't the only way to God."

"Julia Bourland does love Reverend Culpepper's events though." Reverend Mathews said.

"She's told me several times how much his revivals move her."

Mary set a plate of fried eggs and ham down in front of me. I poked at them and watched the yeller egg yoke spill out over the ham, before I dug in.

"Don't you worry, Archie," she said. "Reverend Culpepper ain't due back in Fort Smith for a couple years."

That she thought I'd be worried made me worried. I took my first bite of egg and looked around the table. "Okay."

Reverend Mathews sighed. "Sorry that made you uncomfortable, Archie. It's just that Julia's been through a lot lately. And she always enjoys Reverend Culpepper's sermons so much, I thought maybe you could cheer her up by askin' her about him."

"Sir, I mean no disrespect but I never heard tell of no Culpepper preacher. Besides, wouldn't it be better if'n you remind her about him? I ain't much fer religion."

Sarge laid his napkin down on the table, picked up his crutch and left.

I took another bite. "Somethin' wrong with Sarge?"

"Sarge is still mad at the Almighty," Mary said. "About the war, you know. And his leg."

"Hmm," I digested that before takin' another bite.

After Mary Kirkpatrick went back into the kitchen, Reverend Mathews leaned forward, "Not religious, son?"

"Ain't that, sir," I said hopin' he'd leave it at that.

"What then?"

I felt the back of my neck gettin' red. "Seems to me that a body's ideas about the Almighty oughta be private."

"I got no problem with that, but if you ever need to talk..."

My heart pounded. Did he know about Culpepper? "Thank you, sir, but I'm fine."

Chapter Eight

Maud's Family

April 9th, 1895

Morty stood beside the cash register with his hands on his hips. "Where you been?"

"Stopped to chat with Miz Rogers. She told me about crossin' the ocean in a ship and all the rockin' and bouncin' around in the waves. Said she didn't sleep fer days. I guess I could sleep through…"

"You need to talk to Lydia Sprinkle. Right now."

"Somethin' wrong?"

He shrugged. "Ain't something always wrong around here?"

I pulled back the curtain to my cubby hole and stopped in my tracks. "Lydia?" When she looked up, I couldn't tell if'n she wuz mad or skeered.

"I'm only talking to you because there ain't no one else to tell."

I opened a foldin' chair and set it down in front of her. "What's goin' on?"

"It's that girl. She's back at The Bailey and she won't leave."

"Did you talk to Fagan?"

"What good would that do? That girl thinks it's gonna be hers someday and she's lording it over everybody. And giving me orders like I work for her."

"Whatcha want me to do about it?"

Her eyes drifted past me. I turned around. While Morty wuz takin' Abigail's order, she wuz leanin' over sideways to get a good look at us. I turned back to Lydia. "It's more private in the bar this time of day."

She got down off the stool.

I collected the bar key off its hook and follered her. Once inside the bar, I closed the door behind us and locked it. "That better?"

She nodded sat down at one of the tables.

"Tell me what's goin' on."

"I feel right sorry for that girl, Archie. I do. She's the loneliest little thing I ever met. And she's…well…lost. And she can't leave well enough alone."

I sat down across from her. "I know…but, what's got you fired up right now?"

"She's mad because Julia kicked her out. She's ranting and raving about how she's gonna take over the whole place. She's lording it over rest of the girls livin' there—even telling me and Tom how we ain't running the place proper."

"Who all she been sayin' it to?"

"To me, of course. And the girls boarding with us. She's even been sassin' Reverend Mathews."

"And Sarge?"

"She and Sarge don't get on."

I tried not to chuckle. "I don't like her much myself. But how kin I fix any of it? That's between Fagan and Julia. I'm a kid. Not even their kid. Ain't nothin' I kin do to fix it."

"If Julia catches her there, there'll be hell to pay."

I leaned my chair onto its back legs. "Yes, ma'am. I reckon so.

"And me and Tom...well, I'll be in trouble for letting her in. Tom's raising all kinds of holy hell about her being there at all. Says she's gonna get us both thrown out on our...our behinds. And everyone else'll get booted out for not telling on her. And Lily's in a tough spot, seeing Mr. Fagan's brother and all. She don't want to rock the boat since she's hoping Mr. John's gonna propose soon. And Fagan...I think he likes his comfortable life with Julia and the boys and while he might like a little...well, you know...on the side, I don't see him jumping course anytime soon."

"Whatcha want me to do?"

"Get her out of the hotel, Archie."

"I got trouble keepin' her outta my own room. What makes you think she'll listen to me?"

"She likes you."

"Naw," I looked at my boots. "...she don't. She likes bossin' me around."

Lydia rolled her eyes. "There's trouble coming."

"Everybody but Maud kin see that."

"She knows what she's doing," Lydia said. "Someone's got to stop her."

"Okay, okay!" I stood up. "I'll talk to her."

"Thanks, Archie."

"Don't thank me yet. That there girl's got a way of comin' out the other side of trouble slicker'n a whistle."

* * *

I found Maud in O'Keeffe and Mulraney's Saloon near Texas Corner. She wuz leanin' aginst Sarge Eacret, needlin' him to buy her a drink...and he warn't happy about it. I figgered Maud'd pester him til his money runned out or he up'n left...but then she seen me.

"Archie, darling!" She gave me one of her tight hugs.

Flustered, I peeled her fingers off'n my neck. "You got no more sense than a dog in heat..."

"Come on, sugar." She walked her fingers up my arm. "Maud ain't gonna hurt her baby boy."

"Go for it!" At the far end of the bar, Will Kaigler wuz red-faced drunk.

Walter, the bartender, pointed at him. "Calm down, Will."

"Guess I'll be spending my money at the Main then." Will slammed his glass on the bar so hard that it shattered.

Walter tapped the bar top with one hand and with the other, rubbed his index finger and thumb together.

"I ain't paying for no cheap glassware." Will kicked over his bar stool.

"Fine with me." The bartender reached under the bar and pulled out a pistol. "But you better not set foot back in here."

"You ain't gonna shoot me."

108

Walt closed one eye and pointed the gun at Will's chest. "Ya, think?"

"Look what's happening here." Will turned to me fer help.

I backed away, hands up. "This here ain't my problem."

He looked around the room. One by one, the other customers either laughed or ignored him.

Maud put her palm on my cheek and forced me to look down at her. "You been missin' Maud?"

"NO!"

"You gonna buy her a whiskey?"

Walter raised his eyebrows. I warn't sure if'n that meant, 'sure buy Maud another drink' or if it meant, 'get her the hell outta my bar.'

"I ain't got money growin' out my ears...and we need to talk somewhere's quieter."

Maud opened and closed her fingers like a duck's beak. "Blah, blah, blah, blah, blah."

Riled up and not knowin' what else to do, I pushed her out onto Garrison. Once out there, she staggered around like she wuz lost or somethin' so's I grabbed her shoulders and pointed her toward the river. I follered her lessen' some drunk think she wuz easy pickin's. We walked about a block before she rallied, "Where you takin' Maud?"

"Someplace to talk."

She swayed toward me. "Why you wanna talk to Maud all of a sudden?"

I wuz gettin' purty riled. "What's wrong with you? Sometimes you're sweet as pie. Sometimes you mope around like an ole hound dog. Sometimes you wear a body out, talkin' crazy and grabbin' at 'em. Ever think that folks don't like bein' manhandled thataway?"

"Most men love getting close to Maud."

"No, Maud. They don't. Most of 'em head fer the hills when they see you a comin'...like they do Abigail Talbot."

"That ain't so, Archie." She puckered up like she wuz gonna cry, but I couldn't make out if'n them wuz real tears or not.

"Course it is!" I felt bad fer hurtin' her and all—but I warn't backin' down neither.

"Ain't nothing wrong with Maud that her medicine won't fix. Been out for days now and nobody'll give her money for more."

"Ever think that that medicine might be what's makin' you wild like this?" I took her arm and we started walkin' agin.

"The druggist said it's good for Maud's nerves."

"Well now, mebbe he's tryin' to make a sale, ever think of that?" We headed down a shallow slope to the Arkansas River.

"It's a respectable store."

"Think maybe that stuff's why you're always in trouble?"

"Maud's not in trouble."

"Why're you hangin' out in bars then? Why ain't you got a home? Where's yer husband? Where's yer babies?"

"George'll come back to Maud."

"Ha!"

"Besides, Maud found someone richer than George. Someone who calls Maud his baby girl."

I laughed. "That ain't gonna get you a cup a stale coffee."

"What do you know about it?"

"You better stay clear of The Bourland and the Bourlands. Ain't no good comin' from what you're a doin'."

"That's Maud's future, Archie. Soon's Joooliah leaves for good."

"That ain't happenin'. Ever. Julia and Fagan are tight." I crossed my fingers and held 'em in her face. "Shared investments she once told me. Kids. Property. Tender feelins'... memories..."

"I didn't mean she'd pack up and skedaddle. She's crazy. Everyone knows what she did..."

I stopped.

Maud kept right on a talkin' fer another step or two before she realized I warn't beside her no more. "What?"

"Don't talk about things you don't know nothin' about!" I folded my arms across my chest.

"That woman ain't right in the head." Maud tried to poke me in the chest with her index finger, but she wuz so short, it ended up in my gut. I stepped back.

She wuz too revved up to notice and kept right on pokin' the air an inch or two in front of me.

"Everyone says she ain't the same since her pa died. Maud knows how that feels—but that ole pisspot Joooliah ain't strong like Maud. One of these mornings, she'll find another druggist who'll give her morphine behind Fagan's back and that ugly old bitch'll do it again. And the next time, Fagan'll be too busy with his darlin' Maud to rescue that whore."

"You'd like that wouldn't you!"

She grinned real slow. "And when that bitch dies, Fagan'll come lookin' for his baby girl."

She reeked of whiskey and onions and ugly. Then, her spunk jes drained away. "I-I don't feel good, Archie."

Fer a minute, I thought she wuz gonna pass out so's I pulled her over to the riverbank. Them big rocks wuz damp but she closed her eyes and leaned agin one of 'em anyways.

"Watch fer snakes," I said.

She covered her mouth with the back of her hand. "Ain't no snake gonna get Maud," she gurgled and her eyes rolled back into her head.

Afeared she might fall into the river, I grabbed her arm and held on while she leaned over the water and retched. Tryin' not to puke myself, I looked away until she stopped a gaggin.' "Is that all?"

She gasped and nodded.

I dug a bandana outta my pocket and handed it to her. She leaned forward to wet it. "Whoa whoa whoa! You wanna fall in head first?"

"I want fresh water."

"The puke's done been warshed downstream." I took the bandana outta her hand. "Let me do it. You sit down."

She backed away from the edge and sat on one of the bigger rocks.

I dampened my bandana and handed it back to her. "You look like you might toss agin. You ain't..."

"You're a pig, Archie." She wiped her face and put the damp cloth around her neck. Then, she murmured, "Course that might speed things up."

"Is that this wuz about?" I expected a mouth full of Maud talk but she retched one more time.

Finally, she wiped her upper lip with the bandana. "Ain't that simple, I guess."

"You ain't gonna have a baby? Cause if'n you are, you better ..."

"Better what?" The color came back into her cheeks.

"Take care of it."

"Why do you care?"

"I jes do!"

She looked up at me and I seen her eyes wuz all swolled up. "After all, what's one more bastard in the world? It ain't like that bitch Joooliah'd take in a kid of mine. And it ain't like Fagan'd pretend it wasn't his."

"What good would that do you?"

"Think of it." She laughed. "An unhookable hook until the day he dies."

"Julia'd kill you."

"The bitch." She sat down on a boulder and stared into the water beneath her.

I picked up a small rock and turned it over in my palm before throwin' it into the river. Hard. As I came down on my front leg, pain shot through my thigh. "Damn!" I limped in a circle.

"It's been months," she murmured.

"Yep," I sat down on a rock and put both hands on my aching thigh.

"What does Doc Breedlove say?" She kept her eyes on the other side of the river.

"Last time I talked to him, he said, 'Nail in the thigh, whatdya expect?'"

She wrinkled her nose. "Nasty old coot."

"He took care of guys hurt a lot worse'n me durin' the war. He knows what's what, I reckon."

After a bit, a tear trickled down her cheek.

"What is it?'

"Maud has energy, Archie, ya know?"

"What's that mean?"

"Maud knows things."

"Things?"

"Maud knows you got an ache...jes like Maud."

I felt like I wuz gonna cry. "What's that mean?"

"It means you ain't never gonna play baseball with no team."

I flinched. "So now you're a fortune teller?"

She closed her eyes a long time...so long that I figgered whatever she'd been takin' had kicked in agin. "Don't think so," she said finally. "But there're some things that Maud jes knows."

"Like what?"

"For starters, you ain't no nineteen years old. You ain't even seventeen."

I shrugged. "Ain't nobody knows fer sure."

"And you do remember your mama."

"I remember someone with red hair...dunno know if'n that wuz her or one of the babysitters."

"You gonna find her and get even?"

"Naw. She had her reasons, I reckon."

"Maud'd get even."

"You a throwaway, too?"

She stared at the water flowin' past us. "Maud's got a mother," she finally said.

"You got a pa, too?"

"The selfish bastard cashed in."

"What happened?"

The little line between her eyes deepened. "It was jes after Mabel died."

"Who's that? A girlfriend?"

"Maud's sister. Mama said his heart was broken, but he had other kids. He still had Maud."

"How many..."

"To Hell with anyone else, what about Maud?"

"At least you knowed yer dad. Had a chance to talk to him ...about, you know...stuff..."

"He was a little bitty kid when he went to war. A bugler. Didja know that?"

I shook my head. "I don't know nothin' about yer family."

"Went all down the east coast a blowin' that horn."

"And after the war?"

"Played drums around town. Until she got sick."

"Who?"

"My sister. The little bitch got sick and died on us."

I tossed a smaller stone into the river. "Do you miss her?"

"What good would that do?"

"Why're you so mad at her?"

"I'm not mad. I hate her's all."

"Why?"

"Because Pa got sick and died too. Not a month later. Left us with nothin'. NOTHIN'! No money. No house. He didn't even say goodbye. He just up and died."

The river suddenly seemed louder. I never had nobody to lose, but I guess I understood. "I'm sorry."

"Maud's kin are as poor as Job's turkey. And now that George's got another girl, Maud's gotta figure some other way to take care of 'em."

"You got kids?"

She shook her head, real slow like.

"What then?"

"Mother, little brothers."

"Ain't takin' care of them kids her job?"

"You don't know nothin', Archie."

I stood up and reached down to help her to her feet. "You got that right."

"So why'd you bring Maud down to this stinkin' river bank?" She brushed wet leaves and twigs off her skirt.

"Leave the Bourlands alone. They's respectable people. They got kids to raise too. Find another place to live. Find another mark."

"Mr. John's got Lily French stowed away at The Bourland."

"Move on, Maud."

"Ain't fair," she grumbled. "If'n Mr. John can do it, why can't someone keep Maud there?"

"Someone?"

"If'n it wasn't for Joooliah Bourland, no one would give a damn if Maud stayed there."

"Julia's family owned that place. It's still hers. Hers and Fagan's. She's got a say who kin stay and who cain't."

"Maud don't like her. All dressed up in them fancy clothes, all high and mighty."

"You jealous?"

"Maud's prettier."

I rolled my eyes.

She stamped her foot. "Maud's younger."

"You cain't win this time."

"Don't seem right that that bitch Joooliah has all them fine things and Maud has to scramble and beg …" Her voice trailed off.

"Find yer own man. You'll always be number two to Fagan. Or three or four as you get older."

"I hate you, Archie!" She flounced off through the weeds…stopped and turned back at me. "I hate you!"

"Watch out fer snakes," I laughed.

She stopped, looked back at me—took another couple steps and stopped agin. "Come get Maud."

"Naw. I ain't partial to them critters myself." I started back up the path we came on.

"Archie!"

Suddenly she wuz beside me trying to hold my hand. "Maud's scared of snakes."

I brushed her hand away. "Me too."

Chapter Nine

Hanging Freckles

April 10, 1895

Fight at the Hotel Main

Last night at about 8 o'clock, Will Kaigler, laboring under some mental aberration, walked into the bar at the Hotel Main and with the words, "You are the cause of it all," hurled a great sharp-cornered rock at Mr. Dave Mayo. It hit the bar, bounced off and slashed Mr. Mayo's arm to the bone. Mr. Kaigler must surely be insane as he had no earthly reason for this attack. He was arrested and is currently lodged in our jail.

May 16, 1895

9:00 AM

Eliza Rogers wuz a snorin' away in Fagan's chair, a stray flower on her straw hat danglin' in front of her face. I could see her through the window as I got closer to the store. Once agin, I wondered if'n she might have any idea what wuz written in my book. I'd hesitated to ask her because although Miz Rogers knowed her kin, it'd been years since she left Ireland. And it'd been a while since her husband, Captain Hugh Rogers, died. Some folks...Abigail Talbot to be exact... claimed Eliza wuz daft. Maybe so. But she warn't near as crazy as Abigail her own self, if'n the truth be knowed. Accordin' to Fagan, Miz Rogers owned a lot of property in Fort Smith and I put more stock in Fagan's opinion than Abigail's. Even so, I wuz shy about approachin' Miz Eliza with the question.

As I came into the store, a broad-shoulder feller stood at the counter, hat in hand.

"Afternoon, Archie. How are things in Bourland land?"

"Mornin' Mr. Brizzolara. I ain't seen hide nor hair of a single Bourland this mornin'. Maybe they's takin' time to cool off."

"That's the best track. Been times in my life when I let my passions get in the way of common sense. I advise against jumping the gun. It's never as satisfying as folks think it's going to be."

"No, sir." I had no idea what he wuz talkin' about, but I played along jes the same. "Kin I help you with somethin'?"

"Just thought I'd drop by and see how Julia's doing. It felt wrong to go to their house. They might not welcome nosy friends poking into their business. I just wanted them both to know that if there's anything Stella and I can do..." he shifted his hat from one hand to the other. "...well, you know."

"Yes, sir."

"Hello, Brizz, 'tiz nice to see you, me boy." Eliza struggled to get outta Fagan's chair.

Brizz reached fer her hand. "Lovely to see you, Eliza. How'd you get down here? Walk?"

114

"Well, of course, lad. I sure didn't fly, now did I?"

He chuckled. "Well, it being such a warm day, I thought maybe you hired a carriage."

"A carriage is way too dear for me blood!" She straightened her hat. "Besides, I took a wee nap while I was awaitin' for Archie here to fetch me foldin' money."

"I have it right here, ma'am." I took out a small roll of ten dollar bills and handed 'em to her.

"Didja count 'em?"

I blushed. "Jes got in the door but I watched the bank feller with the shade count 'em."

"Not to worry, boyo." She set her bag on the counter beside the register and patted the bills into a neat pile. "Now let's see what we have." She licked her thumb and started countin'.

I caught Mr. Brizzolara's twinklin' eye and bit my lip to keep from chucklin' as we watched the dear lady inspect each bill before placin' it into a new and neater stack. When she finished, she took a tiny book outta her bag and wrote down the number before she'd look at us agin. "There now," she said. "That's settled."

"You need anythin' else, ma'am?"

"I have me own store, don't you know, Archie. Don't need much else."

"Yes, ma'am."

"Can I give you a ride back to Texas corner, Eliza?" Mr. Brizzolara smiled at her.

She put the money in her bag. "I wouldn't want to be a bother."

"Why it'd be my pleasure, ma'am." He held out his arm.

She beamed before she took it. "You're a darlin' man, Brizz."

As they went out the door, they passed Freckles practicin' rope tricks in the intersection. As Mr. Brizzolara helped her into his carriage, I heard her say, "I can walk it just fine, you know, but this town is full of young hooligans tossin' rocks and stealin' candy."

"That's why I'm happy to escort fine ladies such as yourself home." Brizz climbed into the carriage beside her and took up the reins.

A minute later, Freckles walked into the store. "Why does that old lady give me the evil eye every time she sees me?"

"She probably thinks you're gonna steal her money."

Freckles laughed. "Poor thing. She probably ain't got a pot to pee in."

I bit my tongue. "Lot's of folks like that around town. Maybe you oughta do a kind deed and offer to help a few of 'em from time to time. Like Mr. Brizzolara jes did."

"I would, you see, but I ain't gonna be around long. I plan to get on with Buffalo Bill's rodeo."

"You know how to ride a horse like they do?"

"Mebbe not quite as fancy yet. I'm workin' on some tricks though."

"Jes don't go puttin' any more ropes around yer neck."

"You been spendin' too much time with Morty Bourland," Freckles chuckled.

Cherokee Bill's Escape Attempt

Corrine Southard's Diary
July 19, 1895
Have moved in new home!! everything is so nicely fixed, despite the extreme heat I am enjoying it to the utmost. I am so proud of possessing one of the most beautiful homes in the Ft.

July 26, 1895
Federal Prison Guard, Lawrence Keating, Sr., shot and killed by Cherokee Bill during an attempted prison break.

Freckles wuz waitin' fer me at the door of Bourland's Store when I got there at 9 o'clock. "Did you hear about Mr. Keating?"

"Everyone what's got ears've heard." I unlocked the door and he follered me inside.

"What should we do?"

I went about openin' the shades. "Ain't much we kin do about Mr. Keating bein' dead but maybe we should send a note to Larry, Jr. I'm sure the Bourlands'll send groceries and flowers and every lady in town'll send a home-cooked meal, so no need to worry about 'em eatin' fer awhile."

"I cain't even imagine what's happenin' in that house this morning," Freckles said. "Think Larry, Jr.'s up to being the head of his family?"

"Don't reckon he's got much choice."

"Think they got money put back?"

I shrugged. "I don't know 'em very well. Do you?"

Freckles sat down in the rocker near the front window. "Jes Larry, Jr. This ain't the first family havin' to make do because of that bastard Cherokee Bill."

"And he ain't the only murderin' outlaw runnin' around the Territory," I said. "The marshals' got they's hands full. 'Course you'd think bein' locked up would've done the trick."

"Wish I was the kinda fella who could take out mad dogs needin' a bullet in the head," Freckles leaned back, and the chair squeaked. "But I ain't got it in me to do nothin' but tell Larry and his folks what they already know and probably don't care."

"What's that?"

Freckles sighed. "How sorry I am."

* * *

116

Cal Whitson nodded as he came in the door of the Bourland Bar. The sound of chairs scrapin' and shufflin' feet told me this shindig wuz about to start. I put a sign in the front window sayin' that we wuz closed and locked the door. The chairs toward the front of the bar wuz all taken so's I headed toward the back.

"Mornin', Mr. Homann." I nodded as I stepped over his feet and the shotgun he'd propped aginst the arm of his chair.

He nodded but I knowed how mad he wuz. Of course, he warn't the only one upset about what happened to Larry's pa. Jes about everyone I seen on the street wuz either a frownin' or cryin'.

I squeezed in beside Garland Talbot who wuz leanin' agin the back wall, a chewin' on an unlit cigar.

"Mornin, Garland. Reverend Mathews."

Garland Talbot nodded but he didn't move or say anything.

"Mornin', Archie." Reverend Mathews moved aside to make room fer me.

"Sad news about Larry Keating's pa," I said as I squeezed past Garland.

"The worst," he said. "My heart goes out to Adeline and the kids. They're good people. They deserve better than this."

"Yessir." I tried to imagine what Larry, Jr. wuz a feelin'. It wuz hard fer me to know, never havin' had a pa and all.

"Hell of a thing when a slimy bastard like Crawford Goldsby can kill a guard yards from his cell in a Federal Prison," Garland growled. "If an armed lawman like Keating's not safe, what about ordinary citizens living nearby? What about our women?"

I bit my tongue to keep from sayin' that Garland needn't worry. Abigail Talbot'd probably scare Goldsby right back into Oklahoma or Kansas or wherever his gang wuz a hidin' now.

Morty wuz sittin' with Fagan, his Uncle John, Mr. Sprinkle and Sarge Eacret, two tables over.

He caught my eye and mouthed, "Didja put the money in the register away?"

I nodded.

"Locked the door?"

I held up my thumb.

Toward the front of the room, Cal Whitson drank half a glass of water, wiped his mouth on the cuff of his shirt sleeve and turned toward the men a waitin' to hear what he had to say. "So you wanted to know what happened the night Larry Keating wuz killed and I got it for you. I just talked with Campbell Eoff about it and as you know, he had a front row seat." Cal wuz calm but I could tell he wuz mad enough to wake snakes.

I leaned agin the back wall and folded my arms across my chest. Abigail Talbot'd told me her "like-it-wuz-gospel" version the mornin' after it happened. She said she heard it straight from the sister-in-law of one of the women at her church who'd heard it from the maid of one of Judge Parker's wife's closest friends. I figgered Cal's story'd be closer to how it really went down than hers...and shorter.

"So here's what I found out." Cal rubbed his palms together. "As you know, tensions been runnin' high from the day the judge set Cherokee Bill's date with the noose. It's a known fact that Goldsby tried to escape at Nowata, in the territories, when Deputies Ike Rogers and Clint Scales first caught him. So the head jailer then... what was his name?" He snapped his fingers a couple times and frowned, "Uh...Berry! So Berry figured he might try again and ordered a sweep of the place. Sure enough, they found cartridges in Goldsby's cell and a pistol in the jail privy."

"Howd'ya think that stuff got inside the jail?" Freckles said from the door between the grocery store and the bar.

"Ain't you ever heard of the good fairy, Milt?"

"Is that the gal whose grandpa owns half of Sebastian County?" Freckles popped back.

We snickered, mostly cause we didn't know what else to do. Everyone liked Mr. Keating. And of course, young fellers like Morty and Freckles and me wuz friends with Larry, Jr. And none of us knowed what to say to him, what with his dad gettin' kilt and all.

Tony Homann raised his hand. "So who did stash that stuff in the jail, Cal?"

"They're thinkin' it was a trustee by the name of Vann."

Everyone got quiet.

"Never heard of him," Freckles said.

"Me neither," Morty whispered to me. "You?"

I shook my head.

"Sadly for Keating, they didn't find a second pistol that Goldsby'd hidden in his cell," Cal continued. "That evening, July 26th, Eoff and Keating was makin' their usual rounds, lockin' the prisoners in their cells for the night. Now ya gotta visualize this. Each cell block's enclosed by bars. Thataway, prisoners can move around during the day, outside their assigned cells, but still in an enclosure. And there's a corridor outside the blocks so's the jailers can keep an eye on these characters. There's two levels of cells, on the east and west sides of the jail. They call the lower west side "murderers' row.""

"Bastards," Morty murmured so loud we heard him from where we stood.

"You see, there's a lever they can throw on each row," Cal went on, "that latches the doors across the top. Then the jailer can turn a key to lock or unlock each cell—and of course, while he's doin' that, he's covered by another jailer outside in the corridor."

"Why do prisoners have so much freedom in a Federal jail," Hatcher groused.

"Before this newer jail was built back in 1886, they kept all them prisoners in two big rooms in the basement. It was dark and dirty down there and the biggest, meanest bastards down there ran the show. So some Senator's daughter from back east, Dawes I think it was, she wrote about it being like a dungeon and sent it to the damned newspapers. Next thing you know, they was buildin' that modern jail you see today."

"Doesn't sound like it helped much," Fagan said.

We wuz quiet fer a bit as everyone thought about what this had meant fer the Keatings.

Finally, Cal sighed and moved on, "So, Campbell Eoff threw the lever on the lower east side, while Keating covered him and locked them cells without a problem. Then they made their way around the south end of the cell block. Eoff threw that lever and commenced to lock the first cell, where they kept that murderin' scoundrel Dennis Davis. But the key stuck in the lock. By the time Eoff realized something was off, Keating had moved real close to the bars and could see into Cherokee Bill's cell, which was the next one in line. At that point, Goldsby jumped up brandishin' a pistol and demandin' that Keating turn over his gun and throw up his hands."

"Sheee-it!" Freckles muttered under his breath.

"Keating drew his weapon but Goldsby fired first, hittin' the poor feller in the belly. He staggered down the corridor towards the jailer's office door, but Cherokee Bill fired again. And that stopped Keating for good."

I wondered if'n Mr. Keating'd had time fer one last thought about Miz Keating and his kids.

Cal took a quick swaller of water before he said, "So then, Eoff ducked behind the cell door and ran around the south end of the cell block. Keep in mind that he was still inside with the prisoners."

I thought about what that musta felt like—and the hairs on my arms stood up.

"Goldsby turned and shot at him. Then another murderer, George Pierce, chased him with a club made from a table leg," Cal went on.

"Was there more to this plan than just Goldsby escaping?" Father Horan's voice boomed, and everyone jumped.

"Oh yeah. Thanks, Father. Pierce was supposed to throw the levers for the other rows and let all the prisoners loose. But the jailer, George Lawson, heard the commotion and got there in time to cover Eoff. That surely saved his life. And then Lawson drove Goldsby and Pierce back into their cells with his pistol. More jailers and a few deputy marshals—Heck Bruner among them, by the way—joined the fight. Not only did Goldsby not escape, but none of the others did either."

"Thank God," Fagan murmured. "They would've turned this town upside down."

"What might've happened if all them cutthroats and bandits decided to take on Garrison Avenue or one of the neighborhoods?" Sarge said it, but I wuz a ponderin' the same thing.

"Relax, fellas." Cal held up his hands. "There's enough Marshals and police here in Fort Smith to keep everyone safe. We got veterans from both sides. We'd have taken 'em down!"

I wuz glad to hear it but still nervous. Them bastards'd kilt Mr. Keating in the blink of an eye and went after Mr. Eoff too. Sure, veterans had guns and knowed how to use 'em, but I didn't have a clue. Neither did Freckles. Maybe not even Larry, Jr.

People started gettin' up and talkin' with each other in smaller groups.

"One more thing..." Cal held up his hand. "They said Goldsby gobbled like a turkey between shots."

"What? Why?" I warn't the one what said it but I shore wanted to know what that wuz about too.

"It's a "death cry" or a "death curse" among the Indians, Archie," Tom Sprinkles said.

Morty's eyebrows shot up. "Gobblin'?"

We's all looked at each other not knowin' whether to laugh or cry.

"Over hundred rounds was fired in the jail before Henry Starr himself talked Bill down. Once everything was back in order, they moved Goldsby to a more private cell." Cal took a deep breath and blew it out through his clenched teeth. "Coulda been worse. A lot worse."

"How?" I turned to him.

"Well, a crowd of citizens was outside makin' their voices heard. They were upset about Larry Keating, you know. They were yellin', "Lynch him!" until a few deputy marshals and District Attorney Read quieted them. He promised that they'd prosecute Cherokee Bill and avenge Keating. So the rest of the night passed without any more ruckus from the citizens at least."

I chewed on that fer awhile. I didn't have no sympathy fer Goldsby, but no matter what they done to him, Larry, Jr. still didn't have no pa.

*   *   *

"You have had a fair trial, notwithstanding the howls and shrieks to the contrary. There is no doubt of your guilt of a wicked, foul and unprovoked murder, shocking to every good man and woman in the land. Your case is one where justice should not walk with leaden feet. It should be swift. It should be certain."

Judge Parker sentencing Crawford Goldsby, also known as
Cherokee Bill, to death for the murder of Federal Prison Guard,
Lawrence Keating
September 10, 1895

Chapter Ten

Fury at the Bourland Hotel

September 14, 1895

It wuz Saturday around noon and the store wuz busy. I wuz at the counter chattin' with Miz McGrath, Miz Southard and Miz Talbot, when I seen Fagan Bourland through our front window. His jaws and fists were clenched and I knowed the pot wuz finally boilin'.

"What?" Abigail turned to see what I wuz lookin' at.

"What is going on?" Miz Corrine glanced over her shoulder.

Morty wuz sweepin' up the store. "Hey, Pop! What should I buy from Mr. Homann when he ge..."

Fagan walked past him, crossed Sixth and went into The Bourland Hotel.

What now? I kept my eye on what wuz goin' on outside while's I put several ears of corn into Abigail's cloth bag.

Morty propped his broom up aginst a display table and hurried out the door. Elbowin' past Milt, I heard him grumble, "Get outta my way, Freckles."

We all watched Morty hurry across the intersection after Fagan.

Milt looked back at me. "Archie..."

"I see."

"Should we do somethin'?""

"Not we, Milt. You stay out of it." I turned to Miz Southard. "Excuse me, ma'am. Maybe you should go home now? I mean it might be safer..." I flushed.

She froze, her eyes movin' from my face to the front window. She seemed torn between curiosity and fear of what might be about to happen outside.

"Ma'am, yer husband'll have my hide if'n I don't get you outta here right this minute."

She picked up her bundle. "Thanks for caring, Archie."

I opened a side door and shooed her out into the street. "That way. NOW!" I pointed toward South "B" Street. I reached the front door jes as Morty follered Fagan into the Hotel. By the time I got to the intersection, he wuz comin' back out. Jaw set and brows lowered, he brushed past me and into the store.

"Morty?"

He stormed past me into the back room. Then I heard him on the telephone talkin' to Arabella.

I turned back around to see Abigail and Caroline still starin' at me. Guess they planned on watchin' whatever wuz about to happen, no matter what I said. I sighed and stuck my head into the bar. "Hatcher, will you watch the store?"

He nodded and hurried to the counter to take Caroline McGrath's order.

I peeked in the back room. Morty wuz hangin' up the phone. "What kin I do?"

"Not much any of us can do, is there?" He sat down and covered his eyes with his hands.

"Maybe I should get Maud away from The Bourland?"

"If you could do that, you'd have done it months ago."

121

He had that right. "That girl's like glue, Morty. It ain't yer pa's fault."

"No?" Morty sighed. "Whoever's fault it is, it's between the three of them. I'd stay out of it if I was you. Unless you want to get caught in the crossfire."

"Call the police?"

"You mean, turn my parents into the law?"

"Someone's gonna get hurt."

"Someone's already been hurt, Archie."

"Someone could die!"

His bottom lip quivered. "I'm fourteen years old. No one cares what I think."

"Sure is hard to watch though."

He fought back tears. "Over the last year, that girl tormented my mother—not just by carrying on with Pop, but by embarrassin' her. Callin' her ugly names. Sendin' her dirty pictures. Makin' up things about her—horrible things—and spreading them all over town. People who used to be friendly with Ma avoid her now. It ain't right, Archie. It jes ain't."

"Oh my God!" It wuz Abigail Talbot.

I pulled back the curtain that separated the back office from the store.

Abigail looked back at us from the door. "There's Julia! And she has a gun!"

Miz Abigail, Miz Caroline and Freckles crowded in front of the store window, blockin' my view. Me and Morty squeezed through them in time to see Julia go into the hotel.

"Take the customers outta here, Hatcher," I said softly. "And tell Sam to come right now. He should be in the corral."

Hatcher scowled. I guess he didn't take kindly to a kid like me tellin' him what to do. But when he seen what wuz happenin' outside, he set to herdin' the ladies what wuz shoppin' out the back way.

I grabbed Morty's arm as he ran past us, headin' out into the Intersection of Sixth and "A." "Do you really wanna see this?"

"They're my folks." He tugged to get away from me.

"Hadn't you better lay low in case there's trouble?"

He froze. "Why?"

"Someone's gotta watch after yer bro—"

KAPOW!

We both startled.

Caroline McGrath crossed herself, "God in Heaven!"

I wuz almost to the door of the hotel when Julia bumped into me comin' out. She held her gun muzzle down, pressed aginst her thigh.

A moment later, Fagan busted out the door after her. "Julia!" He held out his arms.

She stopped.

"Come to me, sweetheart," he put his hand on her shoulder.

Inside the hotel, Maud screamed, "THAT BITCH TRIED TO KILL ME!"

"If I wanted to kill you, you'd be dead now!" Julia yelled back.

"Julia, darlin'." Fagan tried to embrace her but she squirmed away and turned on him.

"You promised, Fagan. You said you'd get rid of her."

"That's what I was trying to do."

"He's lyin'!" Maud appeared at the open door of the hotel, the first four buttons on her bodice unbuttoned. "Fagan loves Maud."

Lydia tugged on her arm. "Get back in here, you fool."

"Maud's prettier than you. She's Fagan's baby girl. His sweet love."

Julia raised her gun toward the door. Her lower lip trembled but her aim wuz steady.

I warn't but a step away from Maud. What if Julia missed? I put out my arms. "NO…"

Fagan wrestled the gun outta Julia's hand, threw it on the ground and embraced her.

Without thinkin' it through, I rushed out into the street and scooped it up.

Then Sam came runnin' from the barn. Together, Sam on one side of the Bourlands and me on the other, we all stopped in our tracks, unsure what we should do next.

Fagan held Julia tightly, kissing her hair and rocking back and forth as she sobbed.

Inside hotel, Maud wuz squealin'. "That whore shot at me!"

"Mama!" Tears streamin' down his cheeks, Morty elbowed around me to get to his parents.

Mr. Homann wuz drivin' down South Sixth with a wagon full of vegetables. Seein' the commotion in the middle of the street ahead, he pulled hard on the reins and stopped, turnin' to tell Kate to duck down.

Mr. Brizzolara ran past them, gun in hand. Fagan beckoned fer him to stop. Then he turned his attention back to Julia. "Shhh," he murmured as she sobbed in his arms. "We got a crowd here. It's over now."

"What should I do?" Brizz said to Fagan. "Go after that girl or stay here with the two of you?"

The door of the hotel swung open. "Maud's gonna kill that ugly bitch!"

"Shut up!" Lydia's voice carried as she pulled Maud back inside and slammed the door.

"Get that tramp outta Daddy's hotel, Fagan."

"I promise, sweetheart." He kissed Julia's forehead and nodded to Morty.

"Come on, Mama." Morty took his mother's hand and led her away.

Fagan turned to Brizz. "Here's what's been happening," and explained the situation. "What should we do now?"

As Julia and Morty reached the Bourland home on the corner of Parker and South Sixth, we seen them pass Tom Sprinkle who wuz a runnin' back toward The Bourland where we all wuz standin'. "What is it?" He panted. "What's happened?"

"Julia took a shot at that …that Maud woman," Abigail told him.

Tom's eyebrows rose. "Did she hit her?"

"Don't think she was aimin' to do that." Mr. Homann lifted Kate back up onto her seat. "Wylie Bailey taught his kids to shoot an eyelash off'n a gnat."

"Everyone knows that," Kate chimed in as they drove away. "She jes wanted to teach that girl a lesson."

Fagan turned around from his private conversation with Brizz. "Tom, would you please go help Lydia with the other guests? I imagine the ones who were in their rooms a few minutes ago might be pretty riled."

Tom bristled. I didn't blame him. What wuz he gonna do? Kick his boss outta his own establishment?

"If anyone wants to leave, offer them my apologies," Fagan continued. "And then let them. No charge for last night."

"Ain't no one hurt, is there?"

"Naw, Julia just meant to scare Maud outta there."

"From the looks of it, she did an excellent job of scaring everyone," Brizz said.

Fagan gestured fer me to come closer. "Archie, I don't dare go back in there right now. That girl'll be all over me. I gotta see to Julia first. Then I need to call our lawyer to meet us at the courthouse. And honestly, I don't have time or energy for Maud's bull right this second. Would you get her out of there? Letting her stay there in the first place was the worst decision of my life."

"Yes sir! It shore wuz."

He shook his head, trying to choke back a chuckle. "Swear to God, Archie, I'll listen to you next time." He dug into his pocket and gave me a wad of money. "Maud's gonna fight you, but you tell Lydia to pack Maud's bags and send them over to wherever you stash her. Get her out NOW though. You might try The Fitzgerald over on Garrison. Mr. Fitzgerald's talking about selling it because it's in bad shape and he's not got many folks staying there. He needs the money. But if he balks, just put her as far away from my house as you can."

"Yes sir." I stuffed the money in my pocket. "Anything else?"

"Give her whatever's left over."

"Pardon my sayin' this, sir, but she'll jes spend it on booze and that stuff the druggist sells her." I expected him to fire me fer that one.

"She's got family obligations, Archie," Fagan said softly.

"I'm jes tellin…"

"I know, son. She's a complicated kid…but her mother's countin' on her."

A little confused by that, I lowered my voice, "Okay?"

"And get back here and help Hatcher close the store. We'll be swamped with folks wantin' to know what happened. Jes tell them it's a private matter for now."

I doubted that would stop the gossip. I went into the hotel and as I closed the door behind me, I heard Fagan say, "Okay, Brizz, what do we do now?"

*   *   *

Maud stopped in the middle of Sixth Street. "Fagan never said no such thing!"

I stopped too. "She'll kill you if she catches you in her daddy's hotel agin."

"It ain't hers. It's Fagan's."

"Hoo boy, I'd like to see you tell her that."

She folded her arms across her chest. "Maud don't like her."

"Looks to me like the feelin's mutual. You're banned from goin' back to that place, understand?"

"Maud needs Fagan."

"He'll always belong to someone else. Is that what you want?"

"I'll get rid of that old piss pot …sooner or later."

"Don't count on it. Even if'n you got her to leave, what's hers and what's Fagan's gonna always be mixed. You'll never have him…or the Bourland properties…to yerself."

124

"Maybe she'll die."

"Maud!"

She stuck out her lower lip. "Well ain't that what's she's wishing will happen to Maud?"

"Don't go makin' it happen. You're young. There are hundreds...no thousands...of rich fellers you could go after. And Fort Smith ain't the only place to look. There's lotsa places you kin go..."

"Time ain't on my side," she muttered as I led her toward The Fitzgerald. She stopped dead still. "You're putting Maud up here?"

"Fagan's friends with the guy that owns it."

"Maud wouldn't be caught dead in a place like that."

I looked down at her. Whatever she'd tried to pull at The Bourland'd blown up in her face and now she wuz facin' a night in poorer digs. "Where ya wanna stay?"

She folded her arms across her chest. "Not here."

I racked my brain. "There's Mr. West's. Small compared to The Bourland but the food's good. Besides, you won't be there long."

She put up a fuss, but in the long run, she didn't have a choice. Fagan wuz sendin' her back up to her mother in Missoura whether she like it or not.

*   *   *

On the way back to the store, I stopped at the Bourland house and knocked on the front door. "Miz Julia! You okay? Miz Julia?"

"Take care of the boys, Archie." Fagan called from deep in the house.

"Is Miz Julia..."

"No, Archie. She's not okay. Tell Morty to stay at the store. You go get James and Cap. Take them to my mother-in-law's."

"Should I...?"

"No, I'll explain what's happened later."

I pressed my cap aginst my chest. "Want me to send fer Reverend Mathews?"

They's voices wuz buzzy deep inside the house. "We'll be fine for now," Fagan finally said.

"Okay." I turned to go.

"Archie?"

"Yessir?"

"Thank you for caring."

I wanted to scream that this wuz his fault...that he knowed damned well Maud wuz crazy... that jes because she offered it, he didn't have to take it... that it warn't Maud all by herself that drove Julia mad. But after a bit, I jes said, "Yessir."

"There's a bottle of good brandy under the bar at Bourland's."

"Yessir?"

"Bring it back?"

I started to tell him what he could do with his brandy but thought better of it. "Okay."

I turned to go.

The front door opened behind me.

"Archie?"

I turned.

125

Julia stood in the doorway, her eyes red and swollen. Fagan wuz behind her, his hands on her shoulders.

"Anythin' I kin do fer you, ma'am?"

"Tell her next time, I'll kill her."

"Ma'am?"

"You heard me."

I lowered my eyes. "Yes, ma'am."

Julia's breath wuz more of a wheeze. "Good." She stepped back and closed the door.

I stared at it fer a minute before headin' back to the store.

* * *

"Are they gonna put Mama in jail?"

I swung Cap up into the back of the wagon and climbed in after him. "Why'd ya say that?"

"A kid in school told me so."

Sam and James turned around to look at us from the front seat. I raised an eyebrow. There really warn't much I could say to comfort the Bourland boys. "Ain't happened yet, Poot. Might never happen."

Cap teared up as we settled in. "I don't want Mama to go away."

"Me neither."

"Where's Pop?"

"He's at home with yer mama. They's both feelin' kinda blue right now."

James turned back to face Old Belle's behind. "That's where he shoulda been all along." James Bourland always did have a way with words.

The Fort Smith Elevator September 20, 1895

Mrs. Fagan Bourland was arrested last week and fined $50. Mrs. Bourland had recently become convinced that her husband had become too intimate with another woman, so last Saturday she put a pistol in her pocket and went to the house where she thought the couple were staying. Finding them together, she drew the pistol and fired several shots at the disturber of the peace of her family, one or two shots coming very near the intended victim.

Corrine Southard's Diary
October 30, 1895

The most important event in our home was the arrival, All Saints Day, Halloween Eve, Oct. 30th, 1895, of a big bouncing boy, Jefferson Sherlock Southard - The loveliest, finest, fattest, smartest babe in the world, & to him I dedicate this diary and leave the remaining pages for his remarks.

November 7, 1895
Lily French marries John Bourland

Chapter Eleven

Maud's Letters

December 20, 1895

To Julia Bourland:

...he is a hun for your whiskers. Mrs jul shit ass dog fucking niger prigging hoar poor little woman has to sleep with the nigers and frig with dogs fagan gave his best to maud any what you get from him is so week and thin he is maud best love. fagan is awful good to maud...he wont let her do no thing...he say her hand look so sweet and soft...get her such a fine brown dress cape hat to match it is just butifull...fagan say she look like a angel in it...an he give her a fine diamond ring for christmas...why bet ever time fagan takes you to the hotell he give maud a dollar...your old dam bastads have to go like begger kids ...you arent nothing but a low down clap eaten whoar you have got the pock so bad you have to walk all spradled out...we are going to write and tell that inspectors wife about him getting your mail and that will raise hell...we arent one bit afraid of that post office man...you low down yeller face thing old piss pot...fagan never will quit keeping maud an if ever it is found out fagan

will spend his last dollar on his darlin maud. we will kick your ass...fagan yet you ______ glad to wash ______ you before you did

we will close calin you some sweet name. you are a god dam daughter of a bitch...you are a whoar an a clap eaten hoar and a niger fuckin bitch...good by little niger frigin angel...you wish...youu an Houk the son of a bitch in hell. Fagan is all OK

From Maud's Letters to Julia sent through U.S. Mail, December 20, 1895

It wuz just past four in the afternoon when I knocked at the kitchen door. "Miz Julia?"

Silence.

"Miz Julia, It's me. Archie? I'm here to show you the books?"

My heart beat faster. Where wuz Tawny?

The door wuz unlocked. "Miz Julia?"

This ain't right. I stepped back and looked in the front window. Heavy drapes hid what wuz inside. Afeared Julia'd tried to do herself in agin, I played with runnin' back to the store. But Fagan warn't around. And James and Cap wuz at they's grandma's house. I didn't want to scare Morty before I knowed fer sure...

I twisted the knob. "Miz Julia?"

No answer. The kitchen curtains wuz closed too. A pot sat on the stove but there wuz no fire under it. I lifted the lid. Uncooked fat back. Settin' the lid back down, I closed the door behind me and took a deep breath.

In the hall, a board squeaked. "Miz Julia?

The parlor wuz dark. I could hear her in there though. Bawlin'. I sucked in air and blowed it out. At least she warn't dead. I felt my way to the window and opened the drapes.

"NO!"

I turned to look at her.

Her eyes wuz all swolled up.

"Oh, Miz Julia. What's happened now?"

She didn't answer.

"Do you want me to leave?"

"Leave?" She blew her nose and took a deep breath. "No, now that you're here, I think not."

Unsure what to do, I waited.

"Close the drapes," she said agin, "... and light the lamp."

"Yes, ma'am."

"And then sit down." She pointed at Fagan's straight-backed chair.

I did but that chair warn't meant fer someone as long in bone as me. The light from the lamp gave everythin' a yeller tint—even our faces.

"Can you keep a secret, Archie?"

"Yes, ma'am."

"Good." She handed me an envelope. "Take a look."

It wuz covered with a smeared pencil scratchin's. I held it under the lamp. It wuz addressed to "Julia Bourland the bitch hoar."

I glanced at her. A single tear trickled down her left cheek. "Oh, Miz Julia!"

"Keep reading, Archie."

There wuz writin' along the edges that looked like a note to the mailman. Don't give it to Fagan but give it to her. Another line of words inched around the edge of the envelope. If you give to him, he won't let her see it. I opened the envelope and unfolded the paper inside. "...he is a hun for yer whiskers.

Mrs jul shit ass dog fucking niger prigging hoar ..." I swallered and swallered agin. "Um...Miz Julia, she's crazy. You do know she's crazy, don't you?"

"Is that supposed to make me feel better?" She stared at her hands. Her nails wuz buried in the flesh below her thumbs.

"No, ma,am, nothin' I say'll do that."

We sat fer a minute, each of us thinkin' about crazy, I expect.

"You gonna read the rest of it?"

"Do you want me to?"

"Yes, Archie. I think I do want you to read the rest."

"Why?"

"So you never forget what she is."

"Yes, ma'am," I said as I picked up the letter and started readin'."...fagan is awful good to maud...he won't let her do no thing he say her hand look so sweet and soft get her a fine brown dress cape hat to match it is just butifull..." I looked up. Fer the first time, I seen sadness in Julia's eyes along with her anger. "Maud lies, Miz Julia," I said. "All the time. She sniffs that crap up her nose and she cain't tell the difference between what she's dreamin' and what's real. And she's jealous, ya know? Of you. Of what you got."

"I expect all that's true enough, but you tell her that she's not getting anything that's mine—not my home or our businesses or my clothes or my kids...or my husband."

"I expect she knows that ma'am."

"You tell her anyway."

"Yes, ma'am. I know what she's done might seem unforgivab..."

"You tell her that I don't believe in forgiveness. People who say they can forgive are lying."

"Surely when she's gon..." I looked into her eyes as I handed her back the letter and what I meant to say got lost. "Yes, ma'am."

"And don't tell my boys."

"Never." I opened the front door, and she shrank from the light that streamed through.

"Go get Brizz. Tell him I need to talk to him."

I touched my cap. "Yes, ma'am."

"Now."

I closed the door behind me and set out at a run.

*　*　*

When I got to the store, Morty wuz countin' out dollar bills fer Miz Rogers, who wuz eyin' every dollar he laid down on the counter.

Annie Shaffer wuz nosin' through the produce. "Good afternoon, Archie," she sang out.

I nodded to her.

Fagan sat in his rocker, readin' *The Elevator*.

I knelt beside his chair and whispered, "It's Miz Julia, sir. You might oughta get on home."

He startled. "What now?"

"She got an ugly letter from Maud."

129

“Ugly?”

“Pert near the meanest thing I ever read, sir.”

He stood up and put on his coat. “What’s wrong with that girl?”

“Desperate.”

“Desperate?”

“And mean as a rattlesnake.”

He sighed and nodded. “Yes, I guess she is.”

“She said she’s got kin to take care of...”

“Nonsense, Archie. I gave her money for her mother last week.”

“It warn’t enough, sir.”

He put his hat on. “Not enough?”

“Ain’t never gonna be enough fer Maud.”

Fagan caught Morty’s eye. “If I’m not back before two, call the house.”

Morty looked worried but he nodded as me and Fagan hurried out the door.

“That girl’s gonna be the death of me,” Fagan said as we started up the front steps at his house.

“Should I go get Mr. Brizzolara?”

“Brizz?” He stopped. “Why?”

“You gotta see that letter.”

Fagan grimaced, “Oh, for God’s sake!”

“You want me to go get him?”

“You get on back to the hotel and have some of Lydia’s coffee. If I need you, I can call the hotel. Thataway, we won’t be feedin’ the gossips.”

“Best ought to send that girl packin,’ sir.”

He spun around. “Mind your business, Archie!”

I froze. “I-I-I....”

He softened. “Guess I’m a bit over my head right now.” He patted my shoulder. “I got myself into this mess, guess I oughta get myself out of it. Don’t you worry. I’ll look after Julia.”

December 20, 1895

Section III

1896

here comes snider out wonder if you will get through it.

Chapter Twelve

A New Year—More Letters

January 10, 1896

We see you have a new cape...cant call you old browny any more... what tickles us you dont go to the hotel like you did for awhile...who says maud cant put a stop to fagans taking you old bitch ...

we wont make a picture of you this time...

*   *   *

mrs julia Bourland and the dog... Ha Ha here you are fucking with a dog is it good out of sight

more of Maud's artwork

*   *   *

The Bourland Store
6:00 AM

After I unhitched the wagon, I put Belle in the barn and fed and watered her. Then I checked in at the store.

"Thought you'd never get back!"

I could tell by Bill Hatcher's voice that he wuz het up about somethin'.

"Where's Morty?"

He frowned and shrugged.

"James?"

"You here alone?"

"This place is falling apart," he said. "Getting to be hard to make myself come in everyday what with all them bad feelings and never sure who's gonna

133

show up. I'm supposed to tend bar, not play backup fer you and Morty Bourland."

"It's been a tough few months," I said, eyein' his pockets.

"If I didn't need this job, I'd been gone the day Miz Bourland rousted that girl outta the hotel." Bill looked around the room. "I still got nightmares about the look on her face. Swingin' that gun around like that. We was lucky them kids playin' in the street didn't get kilt."

"Ain't likely Julia's gonna hit someone she ain't aimin' to kill," I said.

"You think it matters to me whether she's out to kill me or jes give me a good scare? I don't appreciate either possibility."

"Are you goin' or stayin'?"

Bill put on his Bowler and examined his reflection in the mirror that hung on the wall behind the counter. "I cain't afford to go." He fished what looked like a tiny fiddle out if his pocket, flicked opened a blade with his thumb and used it to pick his teeth.

"So where ya goin' now?"

"Ain't your business, Archie, but it ain't time to open the bar and I got things to do."

I watched him saunter up Sixth Street, before I checked the cash drawer. There wuz more money in it, than there'd been when I opened that mornin'. Figgerin' Morty...or Bill hisself... musta made a few private sales whiles I wuz fetchin' our new shipment of dry goods from the train station. I started unloadin' the wagon.

Somethin' about Bill never set right with me. I couldn't put my finger on what it wuz exactly. If'n the store wuz still closed, how come there wuz more money in the register than when I left an hour or so ago? Did Morty sell somethin' before the store even opened fer the day? And why would Morty leave Bill alone in the store? That didn't make no sense any more'n Bill bein up at the crack of dawn did. I got all the new items unloaded and settin' in the middle of the store. I opened the cash drawer and counted agin. Fer a minute, I thought I musta miscounted the night before. But that dog didn't hunt. I knowed exactly how much we had in there. So's Bill really did put more money into the cash box?

*   *   *

9:00 PM

Before I locked up fer the night, I thumbed through the books agin. Wuz folks a stayin' away because of the ruckus? I'd not noticed much of a change in the sales numbers. To be sure, I ran my thumb down the rows. Even allowin' fer Hatcher's extra money, there wuz a slight bump in sales. "Nosey damned people," I grunted. "God bless 'em."

134

Chapter Thirteen

The Execution of Crawford Goldsby

March 17, 1896

I woke up at daybreak, grabbed a hunk of cornbread leftover from last night's supper and headed toward the old fort. Even though I'd had trouble sleepin', I couldn't stay away. The Federal jail on the second floor...where Cherokee Bill'd murdered Larry Keating...made my skin crawl. So did the gallows where they planned on hangin' him. The last time I came to watch a hangin' wuz different. I wuz different. I'd never laid eyes on Lewis Holder's victim. In fact, I'd never laid eyes on Lewis Holder hisself, that is, if'n you don't count watchin' the Birnie brothers totin' his sorry carcass off in they's wagon.

At the fort, everyone wuz a talkin' about how Cherokee Bill'd finally run outta time. People wuz already a gatherin' fer what wuz supposed to be a noontime hangin'. Young fellers wuz arguin' over the best spots on the fort wall. A couple small boys'd claimed the lower tree limbs near the gallows. Without Maud bossin' me around like she did when they hung Lewis Holder, I found a big Elm with a thick branch that almost extended into the east side of the gallows enclosure. I shimmied up the trunk and settled in to wait fer the big event.

Around 9:30, there wuz a commotion around the jail as guards escorted two older women into the buildin'. Warn't til later, I found out them women wuz Cherokee Bill's ma and an old nurse from when he wuz a baby. At least the bastard knowed his ma. At least he had a nurse. I squinted. Both them ladies's clothes wuz neat and clean. They wore nice hats too. Around 11:00 o'clock, I dug out the sandwich Miz Kirkpatrick'd made me. Across the jail yard, it looked like Marshal Crump wuz makin' some kind of announcement. Fer a moment, I thought mebbe the execution wuz bein' called off, but I warn't gonna risk my tree limb to climb down and go find out. So's I ate my lunch and waited. By noon, there wuz still nothin' happenin' at the gallows—but a youngster climbed up onto a limb right below me.

"Hey boy," I called to him.

"What?"

"What's goin' on here. They gonna cancel?"

"Naw. They's waitin' for the two o'clock train to come in. His sister wants to see him one more time before they carry out the sentence."

I understood a sister wantin' to do that, of course, but Goldsby didn't deserve more time. Only reason the son of a gun kilt Larry's pa wuz cause he got tired waitin' on his appeal fer killin' someone else. I didn't know how to square all that so's I tried not to think about that part. I rubbed my eyes and looked around. The whole town'd come out to see the son of a bitch die. I heard later that there wuz close to three thousand people competin' fer a place to watch Cherokee Bill's trip into eternity. I wuz startin' to feel ashamed bein' there, but not enough to give up my limb.

Warn't but a few minutes after Goldsby's family got there, the jail door opened. Guards and deputy marshals cleared a path through the crowd. Then out came Goldsby, shackled and cuffed. He warn't nearly as big as I'd imagined. Jes rough and pissed off at the world. Made me wonder where all that meanness came from. I felt sorry fer the bastard even though he kilt Larry's pa fer no reason 'ceptin' he wuz in the way and old Bill wuz in the mood.

Goldsby's ma walked on one side of him, and Father Pius follered. Reporters a writin' on they's tablets brought up the rear of the parade. A jam of people wuz crowded around the gallows' fence gate. Folks who bought tickets wuz allowed inside to eyeball the doin's up close. When those with permission wuz all in and accounted fer, someone shut the door to keep everyone else out on the grass.

Cherokee Bill climbed the gallows and took his place on the west side. Marshal Crump offered him a seat, but I guess he warn't tired because he shook his head and kept right on standin' where he wuz. He warn't in the mood to say anythin' to the crowd, I guess, so's Father Pius did some prayin'.

Then it wuz time. As Goldsby stepped on the trapdoor, the crowd got real quiet. I heared him say, "Goodbye all you chumps down that way."

George Lawson, who'd helped deliver Campbell Eoff from certain death in the jail shootout, pulled the lever. The fall wuz about six feet, which broke Crawford Goldsby's rotten neck. His body twitched once or twice, and then jes dangled.

A thousand ugly thoughts went through my mind, but I cain't exactly remember 'em now. But I'll never forget the sound of them jailers unlockin' Goldsby's shackles and cuffs...and the thump his body made when they hefted him into his coffin. The whole thing—from the time Goldsby stepped onto the trap door—took less'n fifteen minutes. The crowd dispersed, Goldsby wuz dead, justice wuz served. Not much'd changed. Larry's pa wuz still dead.

I climbed down the tree and went to find something to eat.

Chapter Fourteen

Sending Smut Through the Mail

mad god damn dog you how did you like those holes in your umbrella it cost just about as much as the ring did I bet fagan dont get you any new one either you old ______ that son of a bitch of a Houk is workin just to please when are you goin to get on a tare again why dont you ride some more "ha ha " how did you like those names on your sadle did you see that name on a sack of flour
well I will quite am tired writing to such an old hoar as you

I remain highly kept
Ta Ta
baby girl
clap pock eaten niger fuckin friggin

Letter from Maud to Julia, March 29, 1896

* * *

March 30, 1896
The United States of America, Western District of Arkansas
I do solemnly swear and believe from reliable information in my possession, that Maud Allen within the City of Fort Smith, Western District of Arkansas, on or about the 10th of January 1896, and at other times, did send obscene letters through the mail in violation of Postal Laws and Regulations

* * *

James Brizzolara, Commissioner
of the Western District of the United States
versus
Maud Allen
Violating Postal Laws
March 31, 1896

Fort Smith *Elevator*
April 3, 1896, page 3, col 7

One of the arrivals at the [federal] jail this week was Maude Allen, who was arrested on a charge of sending obscene letters through the mails. Maude is the woman who figured last fall in a shooting scrape in which Mrs. Fagan Bourland handled the pistol. Some time after the shooting scrape Mrs. Bourland began receiving letters, the contents of which were simply horrible. They were placed in the hands of Inspector Houck, who went to work and collected testimony enough to warrant Maude's arrest. She was before Commissioner Brizzolara Tuesday. She denies writing the letters in question, but the commissioner thought the testimony against her was strong enough to warrant her being placed under a bond of $1000 in default of which she was placed in jail.

Maud wiggled her fingers at me when I stuck my head into the room. "Archieee!"

That goldurned girl had a way of embarrassin' me ever time our paths crossed. I ducked my head and took a seat. Brizz sat behind a desk in the front of the room a talkin' with Mr. Osborn who wuz Maud's lawyer. By the door, Tom Sprinkle stood beside John and Lily Bourland who seemed as embarrassed to be there as I wuz. Next to the windows, I recognized Viola Wade even though she wore an old-fashioned bonnet with a brim that hid most of her face. I'd only met her once when she came into the store. Mr. West and Mollie Frazier sat together, not speakin' to each other or anyone else. I figgered Maud's latest escapade had Mr. West worried about her bringin' trouble his way too. I didn't see Fagan but knowed he had to be around somewhere.

"Imagine finding you here," Sarge said. "Mind if I sit next to you?"

Warn't much I could've said if'n I'd a minded. He'd already made hisself at home.

"How many stew pots of trouble can that gal get herself into?"

I shrugged.

"You ever see them dirty letters she sent Miz Bourland?"

"Nary a one," I lied.

"Then why they got you here?"

"No idea. Why are you?"

"They sent me a letter to show up, so's I did." He scratched his beard. "They say the ones she sent Miz Bourland are filthy. They say even a whore don't talk like that."

"I guess."

"You think she sent 'em to get back at Julia for breakin' up that lil love fest last fall?"

I turned on him. "That girl's crazy as a loon! Who knows what's a goin' on in her head? Maybe she's jes plain mean, ever think of that? Or maybe she really thinks Fagan'll throw his wife and kids over and marry her. Or maybe she's aimin' to get Miz Julia so upset she'll leave—so she kin move right into Fagan's house—sleep with him in Julia's bed. Who knows what crazy thinks?"

"Hell, boy. Your eyes are bulgin' out. Calm down. People are lookin'."

I glanced around. Sure enough, even Brizz wuz a squintin' at me like he wuz tryin' to figger out who I wuz and where he'd met me. Maud's lawyer, Mr. Osborn, glanced my way and then went back to work. Since we never laid eyes on each other before, I warn't nothin' to him, I guess.

"Think Miz Julia'll be here today?" Sarge looked behind us.

"That'd be a bad idea."

"What's got caught in your craw, boy?"

"This ain't no party where you kin hoot and holler and throw peanuts, ya know."

"Ain't you the hoity-toity one."

"Shush!" I hissed at him.

Sarge folded his arms across his chest and sulked.

When the time wuz right, the bailiff stood up and called the room to order. The folks who'd been a standin' around gossipin', shuffled to they's seats.

Maud wuz bein' charged fer sendin' her filthy letters through the mail. I guess it wuz agin the law—not that Maud woulda knowed that when she done it. Or cared.

"You okay, boy?" Sarge elbowed me.

I felt bad. I'd been pretty mean to him, I reckon. "Sorry, Sarge. This fightin' back and forth's got me on edge. Don't it bother you?"

"Naw, what they gonna do? Cut my leg off?" He cackled.

I hid a grin behind my fist and changed the subject. "I ain't never had to testify before."

"Nervous?"

"A mite."

"What you think they're gonna ask you about?"

"No idea. I ain't seen that girl since she came back from Missoura. And she never sent me no dirty letters." I'd never told anyone about the one Miz Julia showed me last December. After that, I could barely look at her or Fagan without blushin'. Or Maud neither. Especially Maud.

Brizz banged on his desk and the young bailiff called someone named W.P. Houck to testify.

A feller with thick glasses stood up. With his hat under one arm, he swore on the good book.

"He's got the best lookin' mustache in town." Sarge muttered under his breath. "Bet you can do him one better in a few years though.

I felt my lip. "A mustache?"

"Ain't never seen me no red one before."

Tryin' not to grin, I elbowed him. "Quiet."

The bailiff went back to his seat, a takin' the Bible with him...and Houck sat down in a chair in front of Brizz's desk.

Brizz leaned forward. "Mr. Houck, what's your role here?"

"My official capacity is Post Office Inspector."

"Well, ain't Houck high on his nut?" Sarge muttered.

Mary Kirkpatrick glanced over her shoulder and hissed, "Quiet, you old buzzard."

"Don't be that way, darling. This ain't church, ya know."

Mary held her finger over her lips.

I elbowed him. "You been at the bottle already, Sarge?"

"Not yet. You got any?"

That time everyone around us chuckled.

Brizz waited until folks calmed down a mite. Then he focused on a piece of paper a layin' on the desk in front of him. "Did you come to be aware of some letters sent to Miz Julia Bourland, wife of Fagan Bourland of this city?"

"Yes sir."

"Can you explain why they were called to your attention?"

"They were called to my attention for two reasons. First, the address on 'em's not proper. Inspector Williams and myself took these letters to Miss Allen here...," Houck tipped his head toward Maud.

She wiggled her fingers at him first and then at Brizz.

"That girl done seen the elephant," Sarge cackled and everyone in the room laughed until Brizz banged his mallet on his desk.

Houck went right on talkin' through it all. "...and then there are the drawings and the interlineations."

Maud giggled behind her hand and—jes like she planned it—everyone looked at her instead of Brizz or this Houck feller. Osborn scowled at her and shook his head. Everyone in the room laughed until Brizz banged on his desk.

Mary Kirkpatrick turned around in her seat. "What's an interlineation?"

I shrugged.

"Not a clue," Sarge snickered. "Is it dirty too?"

Brizz squinted to see who'd asked the question. I guess he figgered us fer a bunch of hicks cause he said, "For everyone's information, an interlineation is when someone writes something in between the lines of an existing document."

Sarge elbowed me. "Why would anyone want to do that?"

I shrugged. "Maybe she got her dander up and had somethin' more to say?"

Brizz banged on his desk until we all settled down. "Go on, Mr. Houck."

Houck raised his chin. "As I said, myself and Inspector Williams showed her these letters and Miz Maud acknowledged to the interlineation on this one. You can see that the two had writings and they are the same. She admits to this interlineation but nothing about this one," he tapped another paper on Brizz's desk. "...or the other one that we have. The other one, the interlineation that we have is just the same. Miz Maud says she knows nothing about it."

"Jes how many of them filthy letters they got?" Sarge cackled.

Everyone in the room laughed. The bailiff scowled and patted the baton on his belt. We knowed he warn't gonna hit anyone with it but we all quieted down jes the same.

Brizz frowned at Sarge, then turned his attention back to Houck. "Go on."

"The day before yesterday, Miz Bourland received another letter." Houck looked snooty and outraged. "These letters were all the same handwriting—or they have the appearance of the same handwriting." He held up a piece of paper. "This has the same kind of interlineation and the same kind of handwriting in the main part of the letter."

I couldn't see the handwritin' from where I sat but I knowed he wuz right. Unless of course, some other crazy girl, bent on messin' with Julia Bourland, had sent her letters too.

Houck held up another paper. "I have one here—written at Seneca Missouri and addressed to Mr. Fagan Bourland—that Miz Maud acknowledges to writing and sending. And that is a violation of the law."

"Think that one's as bad as the ones she sent Julia?" Sarge elbowed me.

Miz Kirkpatrick turned around and glared at Sarge. "Shush, Sarge. Just shush!"

He winked at her. "This is better than them plays over at the Grand Opera House that you have to pay through the nose to see."

The bailiff glared at both of 'em.

Brizz ignored us and held up the first letter. "Where was this mailed from, Mr. Houck?"

"Seneca, Missouri, sir."

"Who wrote it?"

"Miz Maud acknowledged writing it and mailing it."

"And when did all of this take place?"

"This began in April 1895—and has continued right up until the present time."

"How were they sent? And from where?"

"These letters were mailed at the post office where the stamps were cancelled."

Brizz nodded to Mr. Osborn, who stood up and straightened his vest.

Sarge elbowed me agin. "Ooo, boy. Here we go."

Aggravated, I moved my chair outta Sarge's reach. The woman left of me scooted hers too. The sound of our chairs scrapin' across the floor made several people turn to look at us...includin' Maud who threw me a kiss. I looked around, worried that folks thought maybe...well, you know.

"Mr. Houck." Osborn held up a thin piece of paper. "Is this the letter that was written in Seneca, Missouri?"

Everyone turned to the front of the room where Houck sat.

He didn't even look at it. "Yes. That's her handwriting. And she admits to writing it."

Now the roomful of curious eyes turned back to Maud.

She giggled fer no earthly reason.

"Did Maude Allen say she mailed it?"

Houck stiffened. "I don't know that there was anything said about the mailing of it."

Osborn folded his arms across his chest. "You're sure?"

"I would not say positive..." Houck'd jes told Brizz that Maud mailed it—and he shore looked like he was shore then, despite what he wuz sayin' now. "...I would not say she mentioned that definitely."

I couldn't put my finger on it exactly, but somethin' about Houck bothered me. I believed him over Maud, of course. That girl'd lie when the truth'd suit her better. I jes didn't like him lookin' down his nose at her thataway. And then, I realized I'd been doin' the exact same thing. She embarrassed me and all, but she warn't no bug fer me to flick away. Like Lydia said, Maud wuz lookin' fer a friendly face in an unfriendly world. I stole a quick glance her way. With everyone else listenin' to Houck, she seemed sad.

"So how do you know...for certain...that Maud herself mailed these letters?"

"Mr. Bourland said he got it out of the mail—and I supposed that she mailed it. I don't know that she said she mailed it. Mr. Williams would know more about that because he talked with her mostly. I know because I got them out of the mail." He squirmed in his seat. "She admitted to the interlineation in one of these letters."

Osborn wrote somethin' in a little notebook and then nodded to Brizz.

Brizzolara tapped his desk and excused Houck.

Houck got up—straightened his tie, checked his pocket watch—and put on his hat.

When the door closed behind him, the bailiff stood up and said, "Fagan Bourland."

Maud brightened and looked around the room. I hadn't seen the boss yet that day neither, but figgered he wuz around somewhere.

Sure enough, a door behind Brizz's desk opened and Fagan came in, all decked out in a new suit, head high. Without lookin' left or right, he walked around Brizz's desk and stood in front of the chair beside it. In short order, he put his hand on the good book and swore to tell the truth. I glanced at Maud—and then back at him. He wuz ignorin' her. Good!

Brizz shuffled some papers before he stood up—towerin' over Fagan. "Where do you live, Mr. Bourland?"

What a dumb question. Brizz and Fagan went way back.

"I live in Fort Smith."

"Do you know the defendant, Maud Allen?"

"I'm acquainted with her."

"Acquainted my foot!" Sarge snorted.

Brizz ignored Sarge and pushed on. "Did Maud Allen send you letters from Seneca, Missouri?"

Fagan sighed. "Yes, I...uh...received letters from her from Seneca, Missoura."

The room wuz quiet. Not even Sarge made a peep.

Brizz waited another heartbeat before pickin' up a pile of paper layin' on his desk. "Are these the letters Maud Allen sent you?"

Fagan shuffled through them. "These look like the ones I received."

"You're sure, Mr. Bourland?"

Fagan took a deep breath. "I...uh...I got several from her when she was living in Seneca. I know her handwriting and that is her handwriting."

"There's one or two words here...," Brizz held one of the letters so that Fagan could see it and pointed, "...especially the word 'frig.' Is that her handwriting?"

Everyone in the room laughed.

Fagan waited until we all settled down before sayin', "That's her handwriting."

Brizz took 'em back from Fagan and laid 'em on his desk. "Now, I'll ask you to examine some of these letters." He pointed at a particular line on a particular page. "Is that her handwriting?"

Fagan glanced at it and then looked back up at Brizz. "Yes, sir."

Brizzolara held a hand to his ear. "How is that?"

"That is her handwriting!"

I glanced at Maud. She wuz starin' at Fagan like a bird eyin' a worm. I couldn't tell if'n she wuz proud everyone knowed he recognized her handwritin'—or if'n she wuz upset he warn't gonna lie fer her.

After a few more questions, Brizz waved to Osborn who got up and stood in front of Fagan's chair. "Mr. Bourland," Osborn said. "Here is a word…" he tapped the thin paper. "…that you said looked something like the other handwriting. I will ask you if it is the same kind of a 'G' as in the other words?"

"It looks like it to me."

"Are you sure?" Osborn pressed.

Fagan took a deep breath. "She has written me lots of letters."

"How many?"

"A hundred, I suppose. She has written me notes from here in town as if they were written in Missouri —and those were never in the mail."

"Why would she do that?"

"She said she did it to keep my wife from knowing where she was."

Osborn waited until we all stopped laughin' before sayin' he wuz done. Brizz didn't have anymore questions neither, I guess, because he told Fagan he could leave.

We wuz all quiet while Fagan stood up and put on his hat. Avoidin' everyone's eyes…includin' Maud's, he walked out with his chin up.

"Nothin' more embarrassin' than bein' made a fool of in front of old friends." Sarge's voice echoed in the silence Fagan left behind.

And then…Maud giggled.

*　*　*

There wuz a short break while Brizz and Osborn huddled over somethin' on the desk.

I stood up.

"You leaving, boy?"

I turned around to see a short, stout gentleman sitting behind me. "No, sir. Jes stretchin' my legs. Ain't used to sittin' all day."

"He's a big boy, Mr. West," Mary turned around to join the conversation. "These chairs ain't comfortable for any of us, but they got his knees pushed pert near up to his ears."

"I stuck out my hand. I'm Archie Biggs, sir."

"I'm Bill West, Archie. I own the West boarding house. I'm guessing they got me down here because that girl's been stayin' at my place."

I looked at Mary in surprise. I'd assumed Maud'd gone back to her house when she didn't show up at The Bourland agin.

143

Mary leaned forward and lowered her voice. "I could only keep her so long, Archie. She don't believe in rules. And she ain't exactly neat, leavin' her stuff around all messy like. And while the extra money was nice, I wasn't set up to keep her long term."

"That's okay, ma'am. I don't care where she is as long as it ain't The Bourland."

"I thought it was for the best when she went to her mother's place in Missoura. But when she came back, she was hell-bent to get in good graces with Mr. Bourland agin. I'm guessin' things ain't goin' so well for her mother and brothers. Don't know if they was fightin' with Maud or if they was countin' on her for money or what."

"She kin barely read an' write, ma'am."

West shook his head. "Nonsense! I hear she's one hell of a letter writer."

Sarge slapped his thigh and roared.

Mary covered her mouth but her eyes wuz a laughin' as much as mine probably wuz.

Brizz looked up from whatever he wuz a doin' and shook his head ever so slightly.

I nodded and shushed everyone.

Mary lowered her voice. "Maud was always askin' what was goin' on at The Bourland—you know, who was sleepin' in whose room and the like. Wanted to know if Fagan had made up with Julia and if'n they was still goin' to church together. She even asked if Fagan was seein' anyone else. Like I'd know any of them things. She's like a piece of gum stuck on your shoe, Archie. Getting rid of her ain't that easy. So I set her up to board with Bill West."

I turned to Mr. West. "We all appreciate it, sir."

"She's a cantankerous little thing, but other than throwing a fit over getting arrested, she ain't been a bunch of trouble yet. Maybe this scrape'll settle her down some."

I doubted Mr. West'd be sayin' that after they let Maud go. She'd really be on a tear then.

The bailiff stood up. "Mary Kirkpatrick!"

Brizz and Osborn musta finished they's conversation because they wuz sittin' down. Seein' that, we all took our seats too.

Mary turned to me. "Why do they want to talk to me? I don't know nothin'."

"Mary Kirkptrick?"

She faced forward and raised her hand.

The bailiff gestured toward the chair where Houck and Fagan'd been.

Mary glanced back at me.

I gestured fer her to go on up front.

The bailiff held up the Bible. When Mary swore on it, she wuz tremblin'.

Once she settled into the chair, Brizz stood up and walked toward her. "Calm down now, Miz Mary. We'll take this real easy."

She took a deep breath and nodded.

"Now can you tell us where you live?'

She looked up at Brizz and said, "Fort Smith, of course."

We all laughed including Brizz.

"That wasn't hard, now was it?"

Mary smiled. "No sir."

"Do you know the defendant?"

Mary looked blank.

"Do you know Maud Allen?"

"Yes, yes. I know Maud."

"Do you know her handwriting?"

"I think I know her handwriting. I've seen lots of her letters."

Brizz held out a piece of paper. "Is this her handwriting?"

Mary took it from him and stared at it.

"Well?" Brizz folded his arms across his chest.

"I cain't tell…," she handed it back to him. 'I don't know it well enough to swear it's hers. I think that would be hard to do."

He took it and laid it back on the desk. "Did you ever see any of her letters that she mailed to Fagan?"

"I've seen lots."

"Have you seen her writing them?"

Mary seemed puzzled. "Have I seen her writing letters to him?"

"Did she ever read them to you?"

Mary looked up at him, wide-eyed. "No, sir."

"Did you ever see her writing any letters and you helped her to make interlineations?"

"No, sir."

Brizz held up another paper. "Here is a letter that it is claimed you helped her make this interlineation." He pointed to somethin' on it.

"When she stayed at my house she did all my letter writing." Mary kept her voice low. "I don..cain't write very well."

Brizz tapped the paper. "Did you ever see that paper before?"

She squinted at it. "Not until I saw it in the inspector's hands."

"You did not get Maud to make an interlineation of that kind?"

"No, sir."

Brizz raised his voice. "Did you have anything to do with mailing these letters?"

"No sir!" She cried. "Never in my life!"

"Why does he have to embarrass her that way," I said to Sarge.

"I don't know why, but if he does it one more time, he's gonna be eatin' my fist," Sarge growled.

While I appreciated the sentiment, I had to choke back a snicker at the idea of little one-legged, half-drunk Sarge takin' on Brizz.

"Mary, did you have anything to do with writing those letters?"

"No, sir!"

He turned to Osborn and said, "She's yours."

Mr. Osborn stood up. "Mary, how are you involved in all of this?"

"Maud was staying at my house because she didn…"

"Mary, did you write those letters?"

"Why're they beatin' a dead horse?" Sarge clenched his fists. "Mary's a good-hearted woman who's never done nothin' wrong in her life."

I held a finger over my lips. "Shush!"

He bristled. "Want me to take you down first, boy—before I go after them two sonsabitches?"

I chewed on my bottom lip to keep from grinnin'. Both Brizz and Osborn wuz at least a foot taller'n Sarge. And I wuz bigger 'n all of 'em. Warn't no way Sarge could take even one of us down. I liked his spunk though. In the war, when he wuz young and healthy, he musta been fierce.

Mary looked up at Osborn and sniffed, "I don't know that I could tell handwriting exactly." She held up the letter in her hand. "This doesn't look like this handwriting here." She pointed to the one Osborn wuz holding. "And I don't know anything about when this letter was written."

He leaned over her. "Did you mail it for her, Miz Kirkpatrick?"

"I don't know when it was mailed. I never saw it until the Inspector showed it to me."

Osborn said, "Thank you, Miz Kirkpatrick."

She looked up at him as if in a daze. "Can I go now?"

*   *   *

The bailiff waited until Mary left the room. Then he said, "Lily Bourland?"

Fer a moment, I wuz confused. I warn't used to Lily French bein' a Bourland yet. There wuz some whisperin' and rustlin' behind me. I turned around jes in time to see John Bourland squeeze her hand. Then she got up, straightened her fancy new hat—and headed toward the front of the room. After they swore her in, she glanced toward John.

"Think he's giving her smoke signals," Sarge muttered under his breath fer once.

I didn't even bother to say, "Shush," this time.

Brizz got up and straightened his tie. "Miz Bourland, do you live at The Bourland Hotel?"

"Yes, sir." Lily smiled at John and everyone turned around to see who she wuz flirtin' with.

"Do you have roommates?"

"Well, not anymore, of course. My husband and I have a room there together."

"Of course." Brizz's sounded amused. In fact, everyone laughed, includin' Maud and Lily herself.

"Did you live there before you were married? Last year, maybe?"

"Yes, sir."

"Did Maud Avery stay in the same room with you there?"

Lily glanced at John, worriedly. "Sometimes."

"Did she pay rent?"

"No, sir. She was a guest."

"She didn't pay to stay there?"

"Well, Miz Bourland didn't want her there so's she kind of snuck in, you know."

"By Miz Bourland, you mean Julia Bourland?"

She lowered her eyes. "Yes, sir."

146

"So during the time that Maud Avery was hiding in your room…"

"Visiting, sir. She was just visiting."

The corners of Brizz's mouth twitched. "Yes, of course. During the time Miz Avery was visiting with the rest of you single women at The Bourland Hotel, did you ever see her mailing letters?"

Lily stared straight in front of herself. "I don't know nothing about Maud mailing letters."

"Did you see her writing letters?"

Lily glanced at John. "Well, yes. I did see Maud writing letters. She was always writing something."

"What was she writing?"

Lily shrugged. "She never read me what she was writing."

Brizz tried another way. "Did you ever ask her what she was doing?"

"I once saw her writing and asked her what she was doing."

"And what did she say she was doing?"

Maud stared at Lily like an egg-suckin' dog eyin' a hen on her nest.

"She said she was writing backhand and practicing so that no one could detect her handwriting." Lily fidgeted. "That's all she told me."

"Are you sure?"

"Well…" Lily responded to Brizz's gentle tone. "She said she was going to shoot a letter to Mrs. Bourland."

"Thank you, ma'am." I guess ole Brizz thought he'd got all he was gonna get outta Lily.

Osborn stood up. "When did you see Maud practicing ways to disguise her handwriting?"

"I don't remember the exact date, Mr. Osborn—but I think it was along in October sometime."

"Did you ever mail anything for Maud Allen?'

Lily glanced at Maud. "I mailed one to the Arbuckle Coffee Company for her."

Osborn faced those of us in the wooden chairs. "Was that all?"

"I don't remember mailing more than one for her."

"Did you ever see Maud get any mail?"

Lily folded her arms. "Yes, sir. I sure did."

"Who was it from?" Osborn sounded like he already knowed the answer to that one.

"I seen her get letters from Mrs. Bourland."

"Your sister-in-law, Mrs. Julia Bourland?"

"Yes."

"And what did they say?"

I could see Maud over Lily's shoulder. She leaned forward, her lips curlin' downward. "Julia wrote that she was going to shoot Maud!"

"Damn fool women," Sarge murmured.

"And what did Maud do?" Osborn knelt beside Lily's chair.

"Maud'd fill great sheets of paper—and tear 'em up. Practicing."

Suddenly, I knowed. Maybe not when or how, but I knowed. It wuz gonna happen because Maud wanted it…arranged it. Julia wuz the way. It wuz her husband, her weapon, her fate. She'd pull the trigger like her pa taught her.

The rest of us wuz jes bystanders drawn to a bonfire. No one could stop it. All we could do wuz see it through.

*   *   *

After Brizz declared the "Government" wuz finished presentin' its case, there wuz a break. We all got up to stretch our legs or find a privy. John Bourland escorted Lily outta the courthouse right after she wuz done testifyin'. She wuz probably already tellin' folks back at The Bourland what wuz happenin'. That meant most of Fort Smith knowed by now too.

I stood at the end of the hall, starin' out a tall window, tryin' to figger out what to do, when I heard a familiar clump step clump step behind me. I glanced down as Sarge joined me.

"Hoo, boy! Look at them clouds. One of these days a cyclone's gonna blow in from Oklahoma and knock down these fine buildings—and carry off anything not nailed down."

"What should we do, Sarge?"

"I guess you ain't talkin' about no tornado," he sighed.

I shook my head.

"This here reminds me of the buildup to the war, Archie. Anyone with half a brain could see them arrogant pissant Rebs was gonna make it a shootin' match eventually."

"But why?"

We stared down into the courtyard below. Finally, he said, "Some folk jes don't like each other, I guess."

"Fagan ain't never gonna leave Julia fer Maud."

"Never in a million years." He never took his eyes off the intersection a few blocks away where the Bourlands' hotel and store sat catty-corner across from each other.

"Or any other woman."

"Nope."

"Think Julia knows that?"

"Sure she does, boy. Julia ain't afraid of losing Fagan. They got too many connections."

"So why don't Julia jes ignore Maud?"

Sarge laughed. "You ever tried ignorin' her?"

"Most aggravatin' person ever...and the most pitiful."

"Lonely. Maybe skeered. Whatever. She's a pain in the behind to everyone."

We stood there—each lost in our own thoughts—until Brizz banged on his desk and everyone headed back into the courtroom."

As we settled back down in our seats, I said, "So it's got nothin' to do with Fagan?"

"Sure it does, boy. He's Maud's weapon."

*   *   *

As soon as we got settled in our seats, the bailiff huddled with Osborn. Then he stood up and faced those of us still sittin' in the room. "Mollie Frasier."

A woman I never seen before stood up. As soon as she wuz sworn in and settled into her seat beside Brizz's desk, Osborn said, "Good afternoon, Miz Frasier."

"Morning, Mr. Osborn."

"Miz Frazier, do you know the defendant, Maud Allen?"

"Yes, I been rooming with her at Mr. West's."

Osborn put his hands behind his back. "In the last week, have you seen Maud Allen writing letters?"

"In the last week, I seen Maud write but one letter and it was to her mother. I ain't seen her write any letters other'n that one."

"What about the letters Maud's been accused of writing to Miz Bourland?"

"I don't know anything about them other ones," she said.

At that point, Osborn said he didn't have anything else fer the defense and sat down.

"What wuz that," I said to Sarge. "Osborn called a woman who don't know nothin'?"

Sarge shrugged.

It didn't make sense. As I understood how this hearin' stuff wuz supposed to work, the side that calls a witness generally thinks that witness has somethin' important to say. So far, Miz Frasier didn't.

Brizz got up, straightened his jacket and smiled at her.

"What do you do for a living, ma'am?"

"I'm cooking at Mr.West's."

"And do you know Maud Allen?"

"Her and I are rooming together, Mr. Brizzolara. We sleep together every night."

"So, you're around her all the time?"

"Well, she's with me most of the time in the room where I'm cooking."

"Does she help with the cooking?"

"Oh, she doesn't cook." The very idea seemed to upset Miz Frasier. "She's boarding there."

"I see. So how many people live at Mr. West's Boarding House?"

"There's five that I cook for—three meals a day."

"And you and Maud sleep where you cook, do you?"

"We don't sleep in the kitchen, Mr. Brizzolara!" Miz Frasier's patience with Brizz's ignorance about the West establishment wuz runnin' thin. "We sleep in the front room."

"Yes, of course. And in all that time, you only saw her write but one letter?"

She folded her arms and stuck out her lower lip. "I don't know of her writing anything but this one letter to her mother."

"That was a standoff Brizz wasn't gonna win," Sarge chuckled as Brizz excused Miz Frasier.

The bailiff waited until the lady disappeared into the hallway before calling, "W.T.L. West!"

Once Mr. West wuz sworn in, Osborn stood up. "Mr. West, were you aware that Miss Maud here wrote letters to Seneca, Missouri?'

"Yes, sir. Not very long ago, I mailed one for her."

"To whom was it addressed?"

"It was written to her mother in Seneca, Missoura."

"Are you sure about that?"

"It wasn't written to anyone in town, Mr. Osborn. That's the only letter I know of."

"How about the letters that the Commissioner has shown us today?"

"I don't know anything about them."

*　*　*

I glanced around the room. After bein' questioned, most of the women left. I guess they didn't much like bein' a part of such dirty doin's. The men that wuz still there looked sad or disgusted or curious about what might come next.

The bailiff stood up. "Maud Allen?"

Every eye in the room drifted over to the left where Maud sat. Her eyes roamed over the lot of us, sitting in front of the Commissioner's desk. Someone behind us must've responded in a friendly manner because she batted her lashes and giggled.

"That girl'd laugh at her own funeral," Sarge whispered.

"Cain't tell if'n she's about to face the music or dance to it," I muttered back.

"Well ain't you the funny one these days?"

Brizzolara banged on his desk and glared at us. Then he nodded to the bailiff who swore Maud in.

Once she wuz settled into the witness chair, Osborn approached her. "Miz Allen, what do you know about this letter?" He handed it to her and she stared at it a bit, with the corners of her lips curlin' upwards. She always done that when she thought someone wuz watchin' her.

She glanced at it and handed it right back to Osborn. "It's a letter I sent to my mother."

Osborn laid that one on Brizz's desk and picked up a pile of other ones. "What about these?" He fanned them out and held them up in one hand fer everyone to see.

"Wouldn't ya wanna see what's in them suckers?" Sarge whispered this time.

Maud smirked, "I wrote those letters to Fagan Bourland when I was stayin' with my mother in Seneca, Missouri, Mr. Osborn."

"Did you tell Mr. Houck that?"

"I told Mr. Houck that I wrote them."

Osborn laid them down on the desk agin. "Did you mail them?"

I leaned over and whispered to Sarge. "She's not referrin' to herself as 'Maud.'"

He chuckled behind his hand. "Osborn probably told her to can it."

"I didn't tell Mr. Houck that I mailed them."

Osborn fished a particular letter out if the ones he had in his hand. "Did you make the interlineations in this letter?"

"Yes. But those other letters, I know nothing about."

Osborn held up the rest. "And these? Did you write these?"

150

Maud smiled up at him. "Some of those are in my handwriting and some ain't."

Osborn gave Brizz the floor and sat down.

"She's the dumbest creature on the face of the earth," Sarge whispered to me.

While I wuz leanin' that way in my thinkin' too, I had to ask, "Why?"

"It ain't just us that thinks she's a liar now."

Brizz pushed back his chair and stood up. "Mrs. Allen, when did you go to Seneca, Missoura?"

"I don't know exactly when I went there, Mr. Brizzolara. But I got back here on the 29th of May."

"Where were you on the 4th and 5th of April?"

"I don't know exactly."

"Now, Miz Allen. Think hard. Weren't you in Seneca when you wrote these letters?"

Her eyes went from flirty to angry. "I can't tell you exactly when I got to Seneca!"

Brizz handed several letters to her. "These are your handwriting, aren't they?"

Maud glanced through them, before handing one back to him. "This one's in my handwriting."

"Dated April 4, 1896?" Brizz held it up. "Did you mail it there?"

"In Seneca? I don't remember if I did or not."

"It's postmarked Seneca, Missouri," he said.

"I was at my mother's when I wrote it. If I didn't mail it myself, some of my folks did."

"Who's it addressed to, Miz Allen?"

She grinned like a egg-suckin' hound. "It was stamped by me, Mr. Brizzolara, and addressed to Fagan Bourland."

Sarge leaned over and whispered loudly in my ear. "I'm sure Julia Bourland loved that."

The bailiff scowled at Sarge. "One more word, Mr. Eacret, and you're outta here."

Sarge leaned back in his seat and folded his arms across his chest.

Brizz held up another envelope. "How about this one?"

Maud seen me alookin' her way and wiggled her fingers at me.

"Miz Allen!"

"Yes, Mr. Brizzolara, I hear you plain as day."

"How about this letter?"

"That letter's not in my handwriting."

"Are you sure?"

"I know writing vulgar letters and sending them through the mail's wrong."

Brizz held the two letters up, side by side. He wuz a ways away so's those of us sittin' in the chairs couldn't tell fer sure, but they shore looked the same to me. "Now, Miz Allen. Are you sure you didn't write both these letters?"

"I'm sure."

"How can you be sure?"

"I know it's wrong, Mr. Brizzolara. So this isn't my handwriting and I didn't send them."

"This isn't your handwriting?" Brizz said through clenched teeth.

"I always write in a plain hand," she paused. "Well, I made that one interlineation in the letter to Fagan."

The room wuz quiet.

"But I didn't write these letters."

Silence.

"I interlined that letter for Miz Kirkpatrick. I didn't know who mailed it though."

Someone in the back row coughed.

Maud turned to Brizz. "I didn't mail it."

A door down the hall slammed.

"I didn't...I didn't ask anyone..." Her voice trailed off.

The bailiff stood up. "Witness excused."

*　*　*

I turned to Sarge. "That's it?"

He shook his head and cupped his ear with one hand.

At first, I wuz at a loss as to what the old son of a gun wuz sayin'. Then he jerked his thumb toward Brizzolara's desk.

"What?" I mouthed.

Brizz sat quietly, one hand under his chin. The bailiff stood to one side of him—and Osborn stood beside Maud.

"Does this mean we don't have to testify?"

Sarge ignored me.

Brizz reached fer his mallet, paused like he wuz thinkin' about somethin' important—and then said, "Defendant held to court. $1000." Then he banged the mallet on his desk.

I glanced at Maud. She wuz pretendin' that there wuz nothin' wrong.

Everyone stood up.

Brizz and Osborn left the room. Then the bailiff herded Maud out too.

"Guess we're free and clear." Sarge held onto the chair in front of him. "Don't know what they thought I might say anyway."

"Me neither." I held up a hand and people that wuz filing out stopped long enough fer Sarge to make his way to the door. "Brizz musta thought he'd already made his case without us."

"This ain't over yet, Archie. Mark my words." He turned and headed down the hall.

Not sure why, I watched him hobble along. I wondered how he'd get down them stairs. Then I wondered how he got up'em in the first place. I started to go after him. Then I felt bad...like mebbe helpin' wuz insultin' him. It'd been over thirty years since Sarge'd lost that leg. A lot longer than I'd been alive. And he got along without me jes fine all that time. Still, I didn't want to find the cranky lil feller at the bottom of the stairs with his head split open.

*　*　*

Defendant held for trial.
April 10, 1896

*　*　*

Maud's Fort Smith Trial for sending Smut through the mail Begins.
April 12, 1896

As I came down the steps at the courthouse, I seen a group of people on the corner of Rogers and South Sixth. As I got closer, I realized that it wuz Abigail and Garland Talbot, Eliza Rogers and Corrine and Doc Southard, Doc Breedlove and Mary Kirkpatrick wuz there too.

"Last Sunday, Sherlock got Dear's pistol," Miz Southard wuz saying. "And it was loaded."

"Oh, my Saints in Heaven!" Miz Rogers' eyes widened.

"Yes, and he ran down the hall to the nurse's room with it."

Abigail folded her arms across her bosoms, "Little ones don't recognize danger, Corrine. You need to keep a closer eye."

Garland leaned over and muttered something to her.

"Why Garland Talbot, what do you know about children?" Abigail's voice bounced aginst the courthouse walls and echoed back at us.

Embarrassed, Corrine tried to rescue her story. "That child passed right by my door on his way down the hall and at the door to her room, that naughty boy pointed the gun directly at Miz Bea…"

Abigail looked up. "What's going on in there, Archie?"

They all turned to look at me.

"Pretty much the same as the hearin', ma'am. Don't know why they put me on the witness list. I don't know the answers to any of them questions they's askin'."

Abigail leaned forward and said so loud that folks up on Garrison, two blocks away could probably hear her, "No one likes that Maud, you know."

"She's not had a good life," I tried to explain.

Miz Southard said, "Surely that's no excuse for going after another woman's husband…"

"No, but unhappy people sometimes do stupid things."

"So you think that means she's got a right to do the things she does?" Mary Fitzpatrick's voice broke with the outrage she wuz tryin' to choke back.

"No, ma'am. I didn't mean fer you to take it thataway. I jes think a body cain't help bein' crazy. There's reasons."

"What reasons, Archie?"

"There's lots of tragedy in her family, Miz Southard. She's from somewheres up in Kansas or Missoura. Her pop wuz a Yank vet strugglin' with all that war does to a feller."

"What did he do for a living, Archie?"

"She said he wuz a bugler, ma'am. He wuz tryin' to feed his family makin' music…but folks wuz too poor to pay fer that."

"Not much call for bugling these days."

"No, Miz Abigail, they sure ain't."

153

"Then he should just learn another trade." She shook her lornette at me like I should go give Maud's pa what fer."

"Well, ma'am. He done died real early, leavin' his family to scrape by on almost nothin.' All Maud's got to sell is her young years, ya know. She ain't all that bright. And she ain't all that nice to be around. Freshness fades fast—and the next batch of young'ens is already startin' to bloom."

"But goin' after a man that's got a wife and kids ..."

"I don't like that any better than you, Miz Abigail, but...."

"Why would she go after Fagan Bourland? It ain't like he's brawny or good lookin'," Mary Fitzpatrick snorted. "And there are richer targets out there too."

"Love may be blind, Missus Fitzpatrick," Miz Rogers said. "...but the neighbors always see through it, don't you know."

There wuz a moment of surprised silence and then everyone burst out laughing.

"Eliza, you do have a quaint turn of phrase," Doc Breedlove chuckled.

"Archie's right," Miz Rogers said. "Miz Avery's what we call "aistreach" back in Ireland. Odd. The girl doesn't fit anywhere—and she's achin' to be liked and respected."

"Well, that's never going to happen after all of this," Abigail Talbot sniffed. "At least not in Fort Smith."

Fer once, I agreed with her. "So what happens to someone like Maud?"

"They end up tradin' their services for cash," Doc Breedlove said. "And that leads to disease or motherhood or both."

I thought about that. Mebbe that wuz all Maud could hope fer. And then I wondered if that's why she wuz so eager to make whatever wuz between her and Fagan seem like more...and why Fagan, even without his family obligations, would never see her as anythin' more'n a whore. Jes like everyone else in Fort Smith, I wanted to pity her. That seemed like the right thing to feel, but I jes couldn't find any fer her.

*　*　*

Maude Allen acquitted. Trial lasted a couple of days.
Maude a rather attractive looking young woman moved to Missouri after Mrs. Bourland tried to shoot her. After the move, Mrs. Bourland received letters "the contents of which were so obscene as to cause some of the spectators to blush when they were read." Maude admitted to writing a portion of the letters but claims she did not send objectionable ones.

The Fort Smith Elevator, May 29, 1896

*　*　*

Maude rearrested on her release for same offense committed in Missouri.
Mrs. Bourland had sympathy of everyone in courtroom.
Newspaper, May 29, 1896

Chapter Fifteen

Maud's War of Words

Indian Chieftain, April 9, 1896
Maud Allen, a well-known woman about town, was arrested last week for sending obscene letters through the mail. A young businessman became infatuated with her, and she has been writing his wife vulgar letters.

*   *   *

Indian Chieftain, June 4, 1896
Maud Avery; mailing obscene letters, not guilty

*   *   *

old juli you old shit ass niger fucking hoar and clap eaten bitch how did you like your picture that was in that note that was thowed in your yard last week while you went to hotel main to discuss a certain little bow saw as you were leaving home (Fagan) he is not able to do much because he gives his best to his darling little Maud she is the daintiest little darling ever Fagan had and Fagan is the sweetest stiffest fucker that ever loved.
O he is a darling he is her baby
Letter from Maud to Julia, June 1896

Gertie started barkin' soon as I knocked. Tawny opened the door and the little dog raced out to sniff my toes. I picked her up and tucked her under one arm so's I could scratch her ears. "What's with you, girl?"

Gertie wriggled, raisin' her snout up to smell first my chin and then my breath.

Tawny held open the door. "Come on in,"

"Mornin' Tawny. How are you this fine..."

There wuz tears on her cheeks.

"Tawny?"

"Thank you for coming, Archie." She sniffed and wiped her eyes on her apron. "I'm at my wits end."

"What's wrong?"

"Maud Allen." She looked over her shoulder. "She's back here in town and up to her old tricks. I said it before and I'm saying it now. There's something wrong with that girl!"

"I know. I seen her last night. How's..." I tilted my head toward the hall outside the sitting room.

"Packing."

I wuz shocked. "She's leavin' him?"

Tawny wrung her hands. "I thought she'd fight for him."

"Morning, Archie." Julia came into the kitchen with a small valise. "I need you to do a few things for me."

"Yes, ma'am?"

"I'm heading south to spend time with friends. I have no idea where Fagan is, so I need you to keep an eye on the boys." She picked up a small tin of something and tucked it into her bag.

"Y..,You're a plannin' on bein' gone long?"

"Whatever's necessary."

I glanced over her shoulder at Tawny.

"Will the boys be here alone if Mr. Fagan don't get back from wherever he is?"

Tawny frowned and shook her head.

Julia smoothed her hair with her hands before carefully puttin' on a small black hat with silk flowers on the brim. "That's why I sent for you, Archie. In case Fagan doesn't come home tonight, I need you to take care of his sons."

"Yes, ma'am." I wuz more'n a lil shocked that Julia wanted me to look after her boys. As far as I knowed, I warn't more'n a few months older'n Morty. But I wuz willin' to do whatever the Bourlands' asked even if'n I didn't understand why they wuz a askin' it.

"At least, there'll be someone here who gives a damn about them."

Gertie squirmed in my arms. I set her down and she scurried off down the hallway. "Yes, ma'am."

"In the meantime, keep an eye on the businesses. Fagan's been...distracted..."

"Um, how long you gonna be gone?"

Julia slipped on a pair of fancy lady's gloves.

"Miz Julia?"

"What is it for Heaven's sake, Archie?"

I flinched and stepped back.

She sighed, "I'm sorry." She patted my arm. "I've got business on my mind right now."

"I understand." But of course, I didn't. Me and Tawny wuz both skeered somethin' bad wuz about to happen with the Bourlands, but we wuz also afeared of what would happen to our jobs.

"My boys, Archie, if things don't turn out like...if things...," she took a deep breath. "If I ...um...never come back...take them to my mother..." Julia's eyes wuz dry fer the first time in months.

"Pardon my askin', Miz Julia," I said, "... but what brought this on?"

"It's too long to get into that right now." Her calmness wuz scary, especially after all them months sobbin' over Fagan's spendin' time with Maud. "Where will you be if'n somethin' happens?"

"What could happen?" She picked up the bag.

"But Miz Julia..."

The door closed behind her.

Neither me nor Tawny knowed what to do. "Where's Fagan?"

Tawny shook her head. "He been outta town for a couple days now."

"Is she goin' out lookin' fer him?"

About then, we heard a faint yip and Gertie's toes a skitterin' around on the hardwood floor.

I stuck my head into the hallway. Light spilled from an open door at the far end.

"What's that dog up to, now?" Tawny hurried past me.

I follered her down the long hallway. Gertie wuz in the small room where the Bourlands' stowed they's papers...and she wuz pouncin' on what looked like a ripped-up envelope.

Tawny put her hands her cheeks and said, "My God, look at this here mess!"

Bits of paper wuz scattered all over Julia's braided rug.

"What you doin', girl?" Tawny tried to pick the little dog up, but she squirmed away, grabbed a larger scrap of the paper and shook her head.

I squatted and rubbed behind Gertie's ears until she dropped it. Holdin' it up to the window, I recognized that writin', '...ain't no post office man gon ...' "That crazy girl cain't leave it alone," I murmured.

Tawny smoothed out another shred and handed it to me.

"...son of a bitch in hell Fagan is..."

Avoidin' my eyes, Tawny gave me another page, half-filled with pencil-scribbles.

At the bottom, Maud'd drawn a woman with a huge belly filled with what looked to be puppies. "Dogs?" I couldn't look Tawny in the eye.

She placed her hands on her cheeks. "Sh...she's sayin' Miz Julia...sleeps with dogs?"

My heart thumped in my chest. "Tawny, where does Julia keep that gun?"

"In the parlor?"

We rushed back down the hall to the room where Julia sat alone in the dark when she wuz sad or angry or hurt. I threw open the curtains and pulled up the shades to let light into her hidy-hole. "Where, Tawny? Where should we look?"

"Check around her chair and under it."

I pulled out Julia's chair and then tipped it forward to look under it. "Nothin'"

Me and Tawny stared at each other.

She wuz suckin' her lips and her mouth looked like a puffy line. "Sometimes she keeps it in the dresser by their bed."

We clomped up them stairs. The Bourland's bedroom wuz neat as a pin. Except'n fer a drawer that wuz dumped upside down on the bed. There wuz a half-empty box of bullets on the bedspread and a pocket knife like the ones we sold at the store.

"My God, Archie," Tawny muttered. "Miz Julia's gonna kill her, ain't she?"

"I...I'm afeared...," my throat wuz too dry to make more'n a squeak. "Mebbe?"

"Lawdy, Mr. Archie. What should we do?"

My mind wuz a swirlin'. "Ain't been that long since she left. Maybe we kin stop her. See if'n you kin get Morty on the telephone. Tell him to have Bill Hatcher take the store. And tell him I'm comin' his way but I gotta stop at the barn first."

"The barn?"

"To talk to Sam," I said. "They's close. Maybe he'll know where she went."

*　*　*

Letter from Maud to Julia, June 10, 1896

*　*　*

Thursday, June 11, 1896
9:00 PM

"Where could yer mother be," I asked Morty as I put the 'Closed' sign in the front window and locked the door to the store. "Even Sam don't know…or won't say if'n he does."

"I got no idea, Archie." He unlocked the cash drawer under the counter and took the money out and laid it on the counter fer me to count. "Pretty sure Pop's got a good idea but he ain't sharing it with us. When James asked him about it, he said, 'Your mother needs a break from us. Don't worry, she'll be back.'"

Cephas Rush tapped on the window.

Morty shook his head and mouthed, "We're closed."

Cephas waved and took off up Sixth Street.

"When do you 'spose she'll come back?"

"A day or so more, I guess." Morty shrugged.

No one seemed as worried as they oughta be and it wuz infuriatin'. "How long you figger that'll take?" I laid the bills in stacks and started countin' the coins.

"She's religious, you know," Morty said as he wrote the amounts of money we wuz closin' with in a big ledger. "So if I were a betting man, I'd bet she's somewhere figuring things out. She loves Reverend Culpepper's tent revivals. Maybe she went to find him."

"Reverend Culpepper?"

"What's the matter, Archie?"

"It's nuthin'."

Morty laid down his pencil and looked up. "Archie?"

"Jes a bad memory, I reckon." I chewed on the inside of my cheek before I made myself look at Morty. "I…uh…I got lost at one of Reverend Culpepper's doin's when I wuz little. Younger'n Cap."

"That must've been scary." Morty pointed fer me to sit on the other stool.

I felt my face a gettin' hot. "I…I warn't exactly lost, Morty. One of them families what took me from the orphan train got tired a feedin' me, so's they left me there."

Morty's eyebrow shot up. "What?"

158

"At the Culpepper revival. I warn't more'n four or five. I remember a bunch of strangers dancin' around, callin' on the Lord to have mercy. They wuz a worshippin' so loud they couldn't hear me bawlin.' Finally, I laid down under a table and went to sleep. Next thing I knowed, the Reverand hisself wuz a liftin' me up onto the table top, askin' me where my folks wuz. I hadn't been with that last bunch long enough to know they's Christian names so's I guess I jes stared at him."

"You were scared."

"I reckon I wuz."

"I'm sorry."

"Warn't yer fault."

"I'm still sorry, Archie."

I stared at my shoes what Julia Bourland had give me. "Thanks fer that."

"What happened?"

"He took me home with him and his woman fed me. And jes as I wuz startin' to warm up to him, that farmer from Pope country showed up. I cried and begged but I still ended up in Pope County with that son of a bitch, Jethro Barnes."

"Who's that?"

"Sorry, Morty." I kept on eyein' my shoes. "You don't need to hear about all this stuff."

He stared at my feet too…fer a minute…and then sighed. "It's okay, Archie. I wanna hear anything you wanna tell me."

I warn't sure if'n he wuz really okay with it or not, but I couldn't stop a talkin' now that I started. "Where you 'spose Reverend Culpepper is these days?"

Morty shrugged. "I don't keep up with him. If'n I need help dealin' with the Good Lord, I talk with Reverend Mathews."

"Why?" Me and Morty'd never talked religion before.

"I know Reverend Mathews. His family knows my family. I never met this Culpepper fellow."

I nodded. "I'd druther take my troubles to someone I knowed than a stranger too."

"Mama sets a lotta store on religion."

"What about your pop?"

"He goes with her and all…" Morty's voice trailed off.

I raised an eyebrow.

"Well, you know…lately…"

"Sorry, Morty." I felt bad about embarrassin' him like that. So's I shrugged and said, "Ain't none of that my business."

"It's okay. I don't understand it either. I asked him once…when I was really mad at him for hurtin' Mama over and over like he's done lately…and he said he didn't understand it himself."

"Think he'll leave your mama like your Uncle John left …?"

"I don't know. Maybe?" He sounded like he wuz about to cry…and I felt like it my ownself if'n the truth be knowed. "Naw," Morty shook his head. "I can't see it." Maud's what Mama calls poor white trash. And she's a mean drunk. Fort Smith folks are getting mighty tired of her mouthin' off the way she does. And Pop ain't shy about telling folks he has an eye for politics."

"And Maud don't have the makin's fer a politican's wife." The idea of that selfish filthy-mouthed girl being the mayor's wife wuz horrifyin'...and funny. I swallered a bellylaugh.

The corner of Morty's mouth twitched and then he got to laughin' as well.

"Think yer mother'll kick yer dad out?

Morty snorted. "She might make him think she will for a while, but we all know...even he knows... she'll keep the door open for him."

"You too?"

"He's my pop, Archie."

I tried to imagine what that might be like, havin' yer own pa and all. "We's runnin' low on cash," I said when things got too quiet between us.

"How low?"

"Ten in ones and coins'd do us."

"That much?" Morty scowled. "Hatcher must be raidin' the cash drawer again."

"He always says yer pa sent him."

"I don't care what he says, Archie. If you can't stop him, tell me or Pa."

"He don't do it when I'm around or I would...but well, one time, I caught him puttin' money into the till. I still ain't figgered that one out. What's the story with this Faro stuff?"

"Reverend Mathews says Faro's just another kind of jail arithmetic."

"You mean cheatin'?"

Morty shrugged.

"Good then," I said. "I cain't wait to kick old Bill's bu..."

Outside on the street, a woman screamed. Long and shrill. Then it sounded like a stampede with folks a'runnin' this a way and that.

I turned to Morty. "What's happenin'?"

He shrugged. "Who knows. Maybe the drunks're out already?"

The ruckus in the street got louder. I switched off the electric lights inside the store and the intersection got even darker. Me and Morty pushed our faces agin the window glass. We could jes make out a dozen or so people ... mebbe more... a runnin' around the intersection, a screamin' and a hollerin'. Fer a bit there, I couldn't fer the life of me figger out what wuz a goin' on, but then I seen it. A little feller and two women wuz a fightin' in the middle of South Sixth and A. Jes behind 'em, Lilith, hooked to a carriage, wuz tied up in front of the Bourland Hotel. And that pretty lil horse wuz a neigh'n and dancin' around, tryin' to get loose and run off. Then, jes the other side of Lilith, we seen a couple women a screamin' and goin' at each other. The taller woman wuz dressed in black from head to toe. The smaller one wuz a gesturin' and yellin' at her. Then we seen the woman in black's arm come forward.

BANG!

The front windows shook and me and Morty ducked. I guess we wuz too young and stupid to be as scared as we shoulda been because we both stood right back up. At first, it seemed black as tar out there, but then we heard feet a runnin' out in the dark.

BANG!

"What the hell..." Morty screamed.

"What?"

He pointed out the window. "There's Pop."

I peeked out the door. Folks wuz a screamin' and a runnin' ever which-a-way. Fagan's carriage wuz parked across the street, in front of the Bourland Hotel and the commotion had Lilith a rearin' and a fightin' the harness. Folks wuz a comin' outta they's roomin' houses and bars and gatherin' in the intersection. Through the horses' legs, I seen a skinny woman lay'n on the other side of South Sixth. She wuz a screamin' and tryin' to cover her face with one arm and a callin' fer someone to help her. And the other woman...dressed all in black and lookin' like some kinda witch ... wuz a kneelin' over her and wallopin' the holy hell outta her with a gun butt.

I yelled, "What's goin' on over there?"

The woman on the ground went on a dodgin' and kickin' and the woman on top kept right on a givin' her what fer.

"My God! Look there! It's Pop!" Morty opened the door and ran out into the street toward a small feller a limpin' our way.

I didn't know what to do. The cash box wuz still open. Drunks and lookyloos wuz a pourin' outta the front door of the bar and into the intersection. And Hatcher wuz a standin' in the doorway between the bar and the store, jes watchin' to see what I wuz gonna do. The damn thief! I went back inside, closed the door between the bar and the grocery store in his face...and locked it. I locked the cash box too and put it away in the safe. Only then did I think to call Brizz. By the time, I done all that and found the old lantern we kept in the back room, Fagan wuz a sittin' on the front step of the store, holdin' his leg.

I glanced across the intersection. Maud wuz layin' on her belly a whimperin'. The taller woman, gun in hand, wuz leanin' over her like a big black crow.

Heart a poundin' in my chest, I ran toward them a'yellin', "Hey, hey, hey!"

The taller woman glanced up at me. She looked familiar but I still couldn't figger out who she wuz and what wuz happenin'. Without a word, she got up and walked past me, the white's of her eyes a glintin' in the moonlight. Wuz she a demon? A ghost? A murderer? A robber?

Then I heard Fagan say, "What the hell'd you do that for?"

And it wuz Julia's voice what said, "I never meant to hurt you!"

I went back inside the store and called Doc Southard. Once he said he wuz a comin', I picked up a new pocketknife off the shelf and a handful of tea towels...and went back outside. A crowd wuz standin' in front of the store, most of 'em drunks outta our own bar, a watchin' Fagan and Julia. I elbowed a couple of 'em outta my way and squatted down in front of Fagan. Usin' the tip of the blade, I ripped his torn pant leg from the knee to the ankle. To my eye, the wound didn't look bad...more like a deep scratch. It'd already stopped bleedin'. But when Julia seen it, she wailed and told him how sorry she wuz.

I looked around. "Where'd Morty go," I said to no one in particular.

Fagan winced and grunted. "I sent him to his grandmother's to watch after James and Cap."

"Good." I tied a tea towel around his leg.

"Call Doc Breedlove and tell him what's happened."

"I...I already called Doc Southard."

"That's fine," he gritted his teeth and tried to straighten that leg. "Call Dr. Breedlove too. Tell him what's happened."

"Yes sir."

Fagan relaxed and leaned back on his elbows.

I guess Julia musta thought he wuz passin' out or somethin' because she screamed agin and reached out fer him.

"I'm okay, sweetheart." He caressed her hair. "It'll be okay. But you gotta quit doing this. Someone's gonna get killed."

She leaned forward and said through clenched teeth, "I'll quit if you will."

"You done beat the Dutch outta her, Old Thing. You win. Hands down." He picked up one of the tea towels I'd brought out and wiped the black grease off'n her face. "But I will, this time, sugar. I promise. I love you."

"Someone needs to get over here," a familiar voice called.

Fagan looked at me over Julia's shoulder and jerked his eyes to the left. "What?"

"Go see if Henry needs something, Archie."

"Who?"

"Henry!" He used his head to point to the left again.

"But, sir..."

"Julia'll take care of me. Don't worry. I'll be fine, son."

Suddenly, I realized what he wuz askin'. "Yes, sir."

As soon as I stood up, Julia elbowed me out of the way so's she could focus on Fagan. "Are you okay?"

"I'm fine. You nicked me but nothin's broken."

She put her arms around his neck and looked into his eyes, "Fagan, darling. I love you."

You'd have thought he'd a been mad, but he rocked back n' forth with her in his lap. "I know you do. I know."

"I did it for you."

With the back of his hand, he wiped at the black stuff she'd smeared on her face. "Shush now."

"I love you too much to hurt you...shoot you."

I fished the handkerchief I kept in my pocket and handed it to him. He nodded his thanks and turned back to the business of wipin' what turned out to be oiled charcoal off'n her cheeks.

Seein' that the Bourlands wuz a takin' care of each other, I stood up and crossed the street to find out what wuz happenin' over there. I figgered it surely warn't good news. Whatever'd happened, I wuz madder'n a pea hen at both Bourlands and Maud. Then I realized that Maud'd stopped screamin fer someone to kill Julia a while back. I walked around the carriage. Several people wuz crowded around her, includin' Henry Surrat who wuz the Chief of Police. I wuz surprized to see him and hurried over to where she lay. Since she warn't pitchin' a fit, I figgered she'd be colder'n a wagon tire. Her eyes wuz open though and she wuz a moanin'.

Chief Surrat put up his hand. "Stay back, boy!"

"Yes, sir." I stopped in my tracks. "I-uh-I called Doc Southard."

"Good. You know who this little gal is?"

"Yes sir. That there's Maud Allen."

I guess Maud recognized my voice cause she turned her head toward me and showed her teeth.

Henry leaned forward. "Lay still, Miz Allen. We got a doctor on the way."

"Is that..."

"Be still now," Henry said agin.

"Archie?"

"I touched her hand. "I'm here. What kin I do fer ya?"

"You tell her...," her cheeks shook. "You tell that bitch I'm better than her..."

"Maud! This ain't the ti..."

"I'm better than her...and Fagan knows it!"

Chief Surrat glanced at me and one more time, I shrugged. Crazy ain't somethin' you kin describe but you shore know it when you see it.

* * *

Fort Smith *Elevator* Friday, June 12, 1896

Shortly before 9 o'clock on Friday night, Mrs. Fagan Bourland met Maud Allen in front of Bourland's place of business and shot her down. After Maud had fallen, Mrs. Bourland pounded her on the head with a pistol and was getting in some pretty good work when Chief Henry Surrat who happened to be in the council room, ran up and pulled the two women apart. Mrs. Bourland then went to her home while Maud was taken to the residence of her husband's mother. After Doctors Kaliem and Dailey had examined her wounds, she was taken to St. John's Hospital where she yet lies. She was very badly wounded but will recover. The bullet struck her in the left side above the heart and passed downward toward the back. The wounds inflicted on her head from the blows of the pistol were severe but not dangerous...

* * *

Julia surrendered herself to the Chief of Police, who immediately released her in her own recognizance.

* * *

Fort Smith *News Record* June 17, 1896
NEW FOSTER BUILDING

The work of tearing down the old Fitzgerald House goes rapidly on. The old landmark will soon be a thing of the past and the work of putting up the new Foster Building will go forward. Captain Foster is very modest in talking about his new building and will not commit himself very broadly as to what it will be like.

*   *   *

Fort Smith *Elevator* June 19, 1896

Maude Allen, the woman who was shot by Mrs. Fagan Bourland a couple of weeks ago, is reported to be convalescing. Maude's narrow escape from death should teach her to forsake the paths of sin and behave herself in the future.

Chapter Sixteen

Judge Parker too ill to Preside over Western District Court

August 1896

I got outta the wagon and unhooked the old mule. "What's goin' on, Belle?"

She gave me an evil eye and brayed.

"What is it, girl? We got another yeller snake in there?" I wrapped her reins around the fence railing and went in cautiously. I could hear Sam toward the back of the barn talkin' to someone. I just couldn't make out who. "Sam?"

"We're back here, Archie."

"Somethin' goin' on?"

Sam and a white-whiskered feller wuz each sittin' on a bale of hay. They looked up.

"It's Judge Parker," Sam said. "Things ain't lookin' good for him."

I took off my hat. "Oh no, I hate to hear that."

"He's been goin' downhill for awhiles now," the second man said. "I almost didn't recognize him this afternoon."

"Do you remember Mr. George Winston, Archie? He was the bailiff in Judge Parker's Court until 1893."

I nodded. "Nice to meet you."

"I been hearin' good things about you," Mr. Winston said.

"Oh?"

"A kind heart is welcome just about everywhere, young man."

I blushed, a wonderin' where he'd heard a thing like that. "Thank you, sir."

Gertie sat down on her haunches and looked up at us, her tongue hangin' out the side of her mouth.

"Look at her," Mr. Winston said. "As long as James Bourland's not around she's everybody's friend. Let that boy walk in, and she don't want nothing to do with anyone but him."

I squatted to scratch her ears. "Yep, Gertie here's my fair-weather friend."

"George was telling me that it ain't likely the judge'll ever be comin' back to the Fort."

I felt my jaw drop. "Whatcha mean?"

"They say he's goin' home to die," Mr. Winston said. "He ain't that old so it's shockin'."

I sat down. "I wuz hopin' to see him in court but the time ain't never been right."

"He's a decent man, Archie. You'd have been impressed."

"You worked with him a long time?"

The old man nodded. "Long enough."

"Long enough to answer a couple questions?"

Mr. Winston scratched at the white hairs on his chin. "Long enough to try, I reckon. What's bothering you, boy?"

"Did you hear about them letters Maud Allen's been sendin' Miz Julia?"

"Just about everyone's heard about them, but nary a person with an opinion ever seen one though." He cocked his head sideways. "You sayin' you did?"

I felt my cheeks burn. "I seen two of 'em. And if'n I wuz Miz Julia, I'd have done the same as she did. And I warn't sad when she did it neither."

The three of us sat quietly fer a moment, listenin' to the critters slurp they's water and chew they's hay.

"Wanna tell us about them?"

I turned to Mr. Winston. "It's jes that everyone's thinkin' bad things about Miz Julia..."

"Nothing's ever quite like it seems, is it?"

I lowered my eyes. "It's confusin'. You see, Maud's desperate. Her ma's a wantin' money. Needin' it bad, I reckon. And Maud don't got nothin' but what she kin wheedle outta the men around her. I ain't got much myself and she knows I'm jes...well, a kid. But she gets up in my face and tries to get me to...you know...give her stuff or help her pull mean tricks on the Bourlands. And...and I feel right sorry fer her sometimes..."

"And other times?" Mr. Winston raised a shaggy eyebrow.

"Pardon me, but I wanna kick her down them stairs outside my room."

Sam and Mr. Winston both busted out a laughin'.

My face burned and I wanted to hide since they knowed what a dunce I wuz.

"Now, now, boy," Mr. Winston said. "People laugh for all kinds of reasons. This time it ain't because you did or said anything wrong...or funny. Most of us woulda run for the hills if we saw what this girl's been doing...especially when we were your age."

"I'm sorry too, Archie." Sam clapped me on the back. "We needed to know."

"Sam's right," Mr. Winston said. "So, what's this pushy stuff got to do with Julia trying to kill her?"

"Well, Maud takes some kinda medicine that makes her crazy. Not sure why. She don't seem sick. It's more like she's desperate and jealous...and mad."

"Desperate?"

"She wants all them fine things Miz Julia has, Mr. Winston."

"Fagan not buy 'em for her?"

"Not as much as you'd think. Or maybe not as much as Maud wants. So's she says things I know ain't true. And then...after a bit, she starts to rub a feller the wrong way, ya know?"

"So you think Fagan's losin' interest?"

"They's easy women out there not nearly as big a pain in the butt as Maud."

"So why feel sorry for her?"

"Because ..." I flushed. "I don't think she's ever gonna get what she's a wantin'."

* * *

September 1896
Miss Annie Shaffer rode a saddle bronc for a Fort Smith, Arkansas,
crowd at the rodeo.

* * *

November 25, 1896
George Allen marries Sarah Nixon

Section IV

1897

Osborne, Thomas S. Atty, 506 Garrison Ave, res 417 n 16th

St. John's Surgical Hospital
(North B cor 10th Street)
Founded 1887.
IC Parker pres; Wm M Mellette, secy, Stephen Wheeler, treas; board of directors,
I.C. Parker, Wm M Mellette, Stephen Wheeler, JA Hoffman, FT Reynolds, Eugene
Adler and Geo T. Williams.

Chapter Seventeen

The Fitzgerald

April 4, 1897
Daily telegraph report of all league baseball games begins.
Fort Smith *Times Record*

* * *

April 5, 1897
The Fitzgerald has been moved to South Fifth Street.

* * *

April 21, 1897

Lightnin' flashed, and the wind picked up. I stood in front of The Fitzgerald and squinted. The move from Garrison to South Fifth Street hadn't made it look any better. It wuz as beaten down as I imagined Maud felt. I knowed it warn't fittin' fer Fagan to make this visit, especially since The Fitzgerald warn't more'n a block behind all the Bourland businesses now. But him askin' me to go in his place wuz aggravatin' all the same.

A door opened on the left side of the buildin' and Lydia Sprinkle came out.

"Miz Sprinkle, what're you doin' here?"

She hurried toward me, lookin' both skeered and mad. "Don't cause trouble, Archie. We already had enough of it."

"I'm here at Fagan's ask, ma'am. Not Julia's."

She relaxed. "Thank God."

"He don't want no more of her. She's not here because he sent fer her."

Lydia frowned. "That's not what that girl in there thinks."

"That's what I figgered when he didn't want to give her this money hisself." I held up the wad of cash he'd given me.

"She won't leave. She's stubborn as a deer tick."

"One of them fellers at the stable said she's a tellin' everyone she's gonna get even."

Lydia glanced over her shoulder and lowered her voice. "Scares me to death, Archie. She's got herself a gun. Been out trying to learn how to shoot it 'til the weather turned bad. But I wouldn't worry too much. She's got a ways to go before she can hit the side of a barn."

"Cain't count on that, Miz Lydia, crazy finds a way."

"You'll be in good company if she does add you to her list. Julia Bourland's at the top, of course. That at least makes sense since Julia's gone after her twice now. I'm guessing she's got others in her sights—Mr. Brizzolara and Mr. Houck, for instance."

"I ain't heard nothin' like that, ma'am."

"How about Mr. Osborn? She's mad at him too. And Sarge Eacret."

"Don't mean she's gonna shoot 'em all."

"I keep wondering how she thinks sending Julia dirty pictures through the mail is going to win Fagan's heart. How long does she think he'll put up with shenanigans like that?"

Lightnin' flashed.

"I'm guessin'—from what he said when he sent me over here—Fagan done made his choice long time ago. It ain't Maud and never wuz. And I'm guessin' she ain't takin' that well. But if'n she'd jes go back to Seneca and stay there…"

"What's she gonna do when she realizes Fagan's never gonna leave Julia?" Lydia shuddered. "That scares me more than anything else."

"Don't take that talk too seriously, ma'am. Maud makes up things. Then she gets to thinkin' what she made up is real. And then she gets all riled about what she made up. She's never on the winnin' side of any of them fights she picks cause there ain't no winnin' side to be had."

"Sometimes I wonder if that girl's ever been happy a day in her life." A light rain started and Miz Sprinkle put up her umbrella.

"Is she back takin' that crap she gets at the drug store?" I asked before she could leave.

Miz Sprinkle sighed. "She says it hurts where Julia shot her."

"Probably does."

"You're bitter about all this, aren't you, Archie."

"Yes, ma'am, I shore am."

"You think Julia knows Maud's here?"

It started raining harder. "There's no tellin' what Julia knows or who's tellin' her what."

"Maybe you can convince Maud to take Fagan's money and leave. But I'm betting you'll be gone when I get back and she'll still be in there plotting."

"Probably so." I muttered as she walked away.

After a few paces, Miz Sprinkle turned back to look at me. "Archie?"

"Yes, ma'am?"

"When you see my husband, don't mention that you saw me here."

I tipped my cap. "Yes, ma'am."

The rain suddenly pounded down harder, and I hunched into my collar like a turtle.

"Thank you, Archie." Miz Sprinkle angled her umbrella into the wind and hurried off.

Mutterin' under my breath, I splashed across the street and up onto The Fitzgerald's covered veranda. I looked around. Maud's door wuz on my left and across from it wuz another, smaller one. Somethin' rustled behind it. Heart poundin', I put my hand on the latch. A crack of thunder made me jump back. Lookin' around, I shivered but decided to try agin. It squeaked but opened easy enough. A rat scurried between my feet and down the hall toward the back of the building. It took my eyes a minute to adjust to the dark. Then I relaxed. It wuz jes a closet—half filled with Mr. Fitzgerald's old broken picture frames and garden tools. The wind jerked the door outta my hands and banged it open and shut a time or two before I got it to latch.

A moan echoed from the room on the other side of the hallway.

I crossed the hall and put my ear aginst the door. "Maud?"

The sound stopped.

"It's Archie."

She opened the door. "Archie?" Her eyes wuz red and swollen—and she'd gotten even skinnier since Julia shot her. "What d'ya want?"

A clap of thunder rattled the porch. "Let me in. I'm gettin' blowed away out here."

"He's sendin' you to give Maud bad news?"

I sighed.

"Okay." She closed the door, sat down on the settee. "Just do it, then."

I dug the envelope outta my pocket. "He's sendin' you enough money to go home...and then some. Take it and run."

She reached fer it. "That ugly old Joooliah's makin' him do this?"

"I'm sure she won't miss you."

She tapped the edge of the envelop agin the palm of her hand. "What'll Fagan do without his baby girl?"

"Probably what he did before you came to town...and while you wuz here too."

She flinched.

I knowed that hurt her, and I felt real good about it.

With the unopened envelop in hand, she hugged herself and rocked back and forth. I'd never seen her lookin' so lost. There wuz a wooden crate at her feet. And a small pile of clothes, hair combs, paper and a thick pencil lay on the thread-bare rug beside it. "Maud don't like this ratty old place, Geor...Archie."

"There's rooms on the north side of town. Hell, there's rooms in Seneca, Missoura."

She glared at me. "Too close to the store to suit you?"

"Go home," I said. "Would be better fer you and fer the Bourlands."

"And you?" A tear trickled down her cheek.

"That stuff don't work on me."

"What does work, Archie?"

"Fer me or fer Fagan?"

"Either of you. Both of you."

"Go on back to George. Tell him you're sorry."

"Now that he's got that money the court made Fagan pay him, he don't want Maud no more." She rubbed the corner of her eye with a knuckle. "He married that other girl."

That didn't surprise me. That it hurt her did. "Then go back to yer ma."

"She got married too and that new man don't like Maud neither. He says feedin' another man's sons is expensive enough. Besides, Maud ain't close with her ma anyways."

"I'm sorry."

"Maud's guessin' that man ain't gonna stick around long. None of 'em ever do."

"Surely he knowed that a built-in family'd cost money when he married yer ma."

"Ain't crossed paths with a man a woman could count on yet."

"Not even yer pa?"

She shrugged.

"I thought you loved him."

"And look how that worked out." She picked up her ragged valise and opened it. "He knew we couldn't get by without him and he up and died anyhow."

"He couldn't help dyin'."

She pulled a shoe with a broken heel outta her bag and dropped it on the floor. "What do you know about being abandoned!"

What did I know? What the hell did she know about that? She had a ma. She knowed who her pa wuz. She growed up with brothers and a sister. I coulda told her all about havin' no one...but I didn't. I turned around and headed fer the door.

"Archeeeeeee..."

"Go home!" I slammed the door behind me so hard it popped back open. The rain'd slowed to a drizzle. I wiped my eyes with my sleeve. When I got to the corner, I looked over my shoulder.

She wuz a shiverin' on the porch...watchin' me. A puff of wind coulda sent her flyin'. I softened. Maybe I'd take her down to the Hotel Main and buy her a good dinner. Fatten her up a mite. It wuz the least I could do. Our eyes locked and I took a step back toward her.

"You tell that bitch Maud's got a gun this time."

I stopped.

"Tell her that after she's dead, that fancy house she lives in will be Maud's...," she stuck out her chin, "...and her jewelry too. And that purple outfit and the fur-lined cape she struts around in."

I seen it all now. It warn't jes Fagan or his money that Maud wanted. It wuz what Sarge said. Maud wuz mad because Julia had friends and power and clothes and stores and hotels and kids and horses and a gun...and an ambitious husband. And she'd have all them things until the day she died. And Maud? She had nothin'...not even a real suitcase. The emptiness in Maud's life made me shiver. Them jealous feelin's visited me at night sometimes too.

Whatever she seen in my face made Maud even madder. She went back inside her room and slammed the door behind her.

I headed up South Fifth Street toward Parker Avenue. At the corner, I seen Abigail Talbot and Eliza Rogers, each huddled under they's own umbrellas.

"That Maud woman's back in town and she has a gun!" Abigail's voice carried over the wind. "Adaline Keating told Sarge Eacret who told Mr. Homann who told me that Miz Allen's tellin' everyone that she's gonna kill Julia Bourland."

"Kill her?" Miz Rogers turned so the wind hit her from behind. "Saints in Heaven, it's another donnybrook we'll be havin', Miz Talbot. Has anyone told Miz Bourland about this?"

"It's only a matter of time." The wind made the feathers on Abigail's hat shiver.

"Archie!" Miz Rogers grabbed my hand as I wuz about to pass them.

"Yes, ma'am?"

"Did you know that Maud woman's back in town? You know, the one Julia Bourland shot last fall?"

I opened my arms to shoo the two of 'em back toward the store. "You fine ladies need to get in outta this storm."

"Did you know?"

"Yes, ma'am. We all know it." I herded them along. "C'mon now, this wind's gettin' worse."

Abigail's umbrella fluttered—and some of them feathers blowed off'n her hat and swirled around us. "Does that post office man know? Or Jimmy Brizzolara? Or Henry Surratt?"

I squinted to keep the water outta my eyes. "Beats me, ma'am." We wuz still half a block from the store.

"Maybe you ought to tell them," she said.

I wanted to say, 'Me? Why don't you do it?' But I knowed, between Abigail and me, Brizz'd be more likely to take me seriously. But what exactky wuz I gonna tell him?

Miz Rogers bent into the wind, put her hand on my forearm and yelled, "You should warn someone that kettle's about to blow, boyo!"

I sighed. "Yes, ma'am, reckon at least Brizz oughta know."

"There's a good boy," she said as I pulled open the door.

The store wuz full of people but I doubted many wuz a shoppin'. I hurried into my cubby hole behind the register, wiped down my umbrella and stowed it in the corner. Pattin' my eyes with my handkerchief, I went back out front to help either Morty in the grocery section or Hatcher in the bar.

The storm blowed and howled outside and more people crowded into Bourland's. They wuz mostly browsers or drinkers—'ceptin' fer Mr. Homann and Kate who stood by the front window, a'watchin' people hurry back and forth in the intersection.

"Hello, Archie," Annie Shaffer smiled at me. She'd been a giggly little girl only last year. Now, I noticed that her lips looked like a bow and that she had a square jaw. And she wuz rounded off in all the right places. In fact, she wuz downright purty. Before I knowed it, despite my worries about Maud and Julia and Fagan, I wuz smilin' back at her. "You cold?"

"A mite."

I hurried back to my desk and found the sweater Miz Julia'd given me fer when I wuz a cypherin' and the back room got chilly. I shook it out a time or two, folded it over my arm and went back out into the store.

Annie wuz standin' in front of the counter, chattin' with Freckles and Morty. She looked upset. I warn't gone but a minute and the two of 'em already elbowed in?

"There's the big man," Freckles winked at me. "Told you he wasn't mad at you or nothin'."

Annie wuz a blushin' and not lookin' at me.

"No, seriously," Morty said. "Archie don't got a mean bone is his body." He jerked his eyes from me to Annie and back to me.

"What's wrong?"

"Annie here's got it in her head that you don't like her. Says you walked out on her on the middle of a conversation," Freckles grinned. "We was telling her that it wasn't personal."

"Oh, no, Annie. I'm sorry. I-I jes noticed that you wuz cold and I..." I held up the sweater. "...I thought this might help."

She smiled up at me.

I blushed while's I draped the sweater around her shoulders.

"Thank you, Archie! That was mighty kind of you."

"Annie?"

We both turned around.

"Cephas!"

"I hear you been practicing over in the field out on Grand."

"You heard right. I'm working on an act where I balance on a pony's back and twirl a lassoo at the same time. Can you do that?"

"Not me," the cowboy laughed. "Best I can do is ride 'em hard til their flanks foam."

She turned to me, smilin'. "Archie, you know Cephas, don't you? He's gonna be breakin' wild ponies for Buffalo Bill's Wild West Show next season."

Cephas stuck his hand out. "Nice to see you again, Archie. I been hearin' a lot about you lately."

After Cephas told me about them folks in Pope County findin' old Jethro's body, I'd been avoidin' him. But here he wuz, a grinnin' like that stuff'd never happened. "Hope you know Milt's a liar," I grinned back at him.

"He says you killed a big yeller snake in the Bourland's barn."

"Never been so skeered in my life."

They's all laughed.

"You a horseman?"

"The best I kin do is feed Belle a carrot once in awhile. And I have to work up the gumption to do that. Naw, no matter what Annie says, I aim to be a ball player, not a cowboy."

"Why ain't you playin' ball then?"

"Got nailed by that explosion down on the river. The one that killed Miz Cook and Babe? That leg ain't been workin' right since."

"I liked Miz Cook," he said. "She was a mighty fine lady."

A feller who spoke kindly of Miz Cook wuz okay by me.

"Why don't we get together and hit some balls one of these days, Archie?"

I glanced at Freckles who grinned. Cephus tellin' me how them folks in Pope County done found ole Jethro'd given me a scare, but it'd been months and so far no one'd come fer me. And as far as I knowed, Cephas hadn't told anyone in Fort Smith about me and Pope County neither. "I'd not mind pitchin' you a few someday."

Annie grinned. "How about tomorrow?"

I'd never noticed jes how pushy that girl wuz . "Um...Annie, I dunno how I'll be tomorrow. I ain't played since I got hurt."

"We don't need to be champions to have fun," Cephas said. "Tomorrow out front of the store."

If'n he hadn't set such store on playin' catch, I mighta turned him down.

He touched Annie's arm. "Grandpa's got some new foals out at the ranch. Wanna go see 'em?"

She looked at me like I wuz a tick on a horse's hind end. "Thanks anyway, Cephas. I've already seen a heap of foals in my life. I think I might like Archie to tell me about baseball."

"Later then." Cephas shrugged and turned to me. "And I'll see you tomorrow, Archie?"

After Cephas left, Freckles nudged me in the ribs. "There ya go!"

I grinned and turned to Annie. "Why doncha have a seat in the bar. I got me some things to take care of until this storm blows itself out. Then we kin go have dinner over at The Main if'n you'd like and I'll tell you all about baseball.

Chapter Eighteen

The Confrontation

Thursday, April 22, 1897

The smell of coffee comin' from the kitchen made my stomach growl. It warn't my day to open the store so's I headed downstairs fer breakfast. On the second landin', I heard Julia's voice in the dinin' room.

"If I find out she's on my property, you'll be shown the door, Tom."

I stopped, unsure whether to go in or to hide.

"I swear, ma'am. I haven't seen that girl in months." Tom Sprinkle sounded het up.

"And where's Lydia?"

I went down the rest of the steps and stood in the foyer. Then I leaned forward jes enough so's I could see the hem of Julia's purple skirt.

"She's running an errand."

I guess Tom warn't gonna fess up that Lydia'd finally left him.

"Mary?"

"I'm here, ma'am. Been here all morning same as usual."

As I went into the dining room, I seen Mary standin' in the doorway to the kitchen.

"And you, Reverend Mathews?"

"Julia, I give you my word. I'll tell you if I ever see that woman here again."

"I give you mine too," Tom's voice wuz so low I could barely hear it.

"This was my daddy's hotel. They were meeting here. In my daddy's hotel."

Reverend Mathews spoke softly. "I know that hurt. But it's over now. Fagan swore to me that it's been over for awhile."

"He's lied so many times that I don't know what to believe," Julia said. "And that woman keeps sending me letters." She tossed an envelope on the table. "This one says she's here again."

"Another letter?" Reverend Mathews seemed shocked. "In Fort Smith, you say?"

"Just look!' Julia's voice rose as she handed it to him. "What if one of the boys got hold of this? What if she hurts one of them? What if she hurts Fagan?"

Reverend Mathews squinted through his specs to make out Maud's scrawl on each page. "Oh, my!" His cheeks wuz red when he looked up agin. "This doesn't say where she is though."

"Exactly! Where is she?" Julia sounded frantic. "And where's Fagan?"

I coughed into my fist.

"Archie," Julia turned to me. "Have you seen this Maud woman?"

I took a deep breath. "Yes, ma'am. I seen her yesterday."

Julia whirled back to Reverend Mathews. "See?"

His eyes focused on me. "Where'd you see her?"

"Was Fagan there too?" Julia asked before I could answer Reverend Mathews.

"No, ma'am. Miz Lydia wuz though."

I glanced at Tom. He wuz starin' into his coffee mug, his jaw muscles a twitchin'.

"Did you know that, Tom?" Reverend Mathews said softly.

Tom shook his head without lookin' up. "Damned fool woman."

"Maud says she's gonna kill me." Julia held up an envelope.

"That girl cain't hit the side of a barn," I said. "She ain't well."

Julia pointed at the envelope. "No sane person would write things like that."

"She's a rattlesnake, ma'am. Filled with poison. I'd stay clear of her, if'n I wuz you."

"Why did you see her?"

My face got hot. "I wuz...um...I wuz runnin' an errand."

The three of them stared at me.

Julia's voice quivered. "Fagan sent you?"

"It..it's not whatcha think, ma'am."

One of her eyebrows went up. "What do you think I think?"

Reverend Mathews laid a hand on my shoulder. "The truth's your best option."

"Yes, sir." A moment ticked by. Warn't no easy way outta this one. "Maud sent Mr. Fagan a letter yesterday mornin.' She wanted him to drop what he wuz a doin' and go meet her. Rather than do that, he sent me to give her money and tell her to go on back to Missoura."

"And did you?"

Her eyes wuz on mine and I warn't about to look away. "He didn't think...none of us knowed..." My voice cracked. "...that she wuz mean enough to keep on a sendin' you them letters."

Julia sat down on one of the dining room chairs.

"That girl's not all the way healed up from the last time you shot her," I said. "She's dangerous. Reminds me of a gut-shot critter. If'n you get too close, she'll tear you apart."

"Where's Fagan?"

"At the store, I reckon. He and Morty get there before me on Thursdays. And then I stay later."

"You sure?"

"I'm jes comin' down fer breakfast, but that's where he is on Thursday mornin's."

"And Maud?"

"She's a leavin.' I'll make sure she goes if'n I gotta drag her to the train station myself."

"Where is she, Archie?"

"Stay out of this, Archie!" Reverend Mathews murmured.

I stared at my boots. Julia'd given 'em to me. My socks too. The first pair I ever had that warn't hand-me-downs with holes already a startin'. I took a breath and opened my mouth.

"Archie…" Tom groweled.

Julia teared up.

Both the Bourlands'd been good to me, a givin' me food, a place to stay, a job, introductions … and … and…trust. Julia'd taken care of me when Maud threw that tomata at me and after my run in with that big yeller snake. And she took care of me when I got blowed up too. Fagan'd paid Doc Breedlove to treat my leg…and…and both of 'em'd trusted me with the financials at they's store. The Bourlands'd even helped me git my little book back after Miz Emily and Babe died. No one ever done nothin' like that fer me before. No one.

And Maud? She never gave me nothin' but aggravation…a lyin' to me and embarrassin' me and stealin' from me. It wuz an easy call. And I ain't gonna lie. I knowed exactly what Julia'd do when I said, "She's a stayin' at The Fitzgerald. On South Fifth where they moved it."

"A block behind the store…" It came outta Julia's mouth like she knowed it all along but didn't know she knowed it.

"What the hell?" Tom frowned.

"Julia!" Reverend Mathews grabbed her by the elbow as she rose from her chair.

"Let go of me, Will!"

"Think about your boys!"

"I am thinking about them." She pulled away from him and turned to me. "Thank you, Archie."

"Ma'am…"

"Now get out of my way!"

I stepped aside and she hurried out the door.

* * *

"What's happenin'?" Sarge wuz makin' his way down the stairs in the foyer.

"Julia's gone after Maud Avery!" Tom ran past him and into the office.

"Again?"

"Agin," I said as me and Mary helped Sarge down the last few steps.

"Where is that damned fool girl now?" He leaned his crutch agin the dinin' room table and sat down.

"The Fitzgerald."

"What was Fagan thinkin' lettin' her come back here?"

"He didn't 'let' her. She showed up on her own and moved into The Fitzpatrick. Yesterday, he sent me over to give her money and tell her to go on home," I said. "Guess she's a wantin' to get back at both Bourlands now. Nothin' I said moved her a smidgen."

Mary patted my arm. "They have you between a rock and a hard spot, don't they?"

"And themselves."

Tom came back into the dining room, pocketin' a pistol.

Reverend Mathews stood up. "Did you call the police?"

"I tried to call Fagan…and then Lydia."

"And?"

"The operator said the line wuz busy at the store. And The Fitzgerald doesn't have a phone."

I glanced at the clock. "Brizz'll know what to do."

"You all do whatever the hell you need to. I'm gonna go get my wife."

"Don't make it worse, Tom." Reverend Mathews called after him.

The front door slammed.

"What now?" I turned to Reverend Mathews.

"Mary, I need a hand with the phone," Reverend Mathews said. "Let's get Brizz in on this."

"Mebbe I oughta go to the store and tell Fagan what's a goin' on," I said.

"And no matter what Fagan does, don't let Morty get involved."

I said "Yes, sir," and all, but I warn't plannin' on bein' there long enough to stop Morty from a doin' nothin'."

*   *   *

I found Fagan and Cal Whitson a lookin' out the front window and sippin' coffee.

"You look like you saw a ghost," Cal said when he seen me.

"It's worse'n a ghost," I puffed. "Maud sent Julia another threatenin' letter."

"And?"

"Julia's gone after her."

Fagan glanced over his shoulder at Morty who wuz sweepin' up in the store. "Gone after her where?"

I lowered my eyes. "The Fitzgerald."

"How the hell did she know about that?" He took off his glasses and wiped 'em with the fresh handkerchief Julia put into his vest pocket every mornin'.

"She asked me straight out and I told her, sir!"

"Ah." Instead of bein' mad, he seemed sad.

"Pa?" Morty dropped the broom.

"Cal and I'll take care of it."

"We got to stop Mama!" Morty ran past us, headed fer the door.

"Stay here, son." Fagan grabbed the back of Morty's shirt.

Morty swung his arms and screamed, "That crazy girl'll kill her!"

Fagan wrapped his arms around him.

"No...no...no!"

"Morty!" Fagan shook him. "Calm down!"

"It's your fault," Morty struggled to get loose. "That girl's gonna kill Mama and it's your fault."

"I have to go take care of your mama," Fagan said, "...and you need to stay here in case you have to look after your brothers."

Morty stopped fightin'. "The boys?"

"Send Sam for your Grandma—but you stay here."

"It's your fault!"

"I know but you gotta let me take care of it, understand? You're the oldest. You have to be here if something happens to your mama—or me."

Tears streamed down Morty's face but he stopped strugglin' and Fagan him let go.

People wuz gatherin' in the intersection, lookin' around and talkin' with each other. Freckles squeezed through 'em. "What is it, Archie?"

"Miz Bourland's goin' after that girl agin."

"Wher..."

KAPOW! A gunshot echoed through the neighborhood.

Me and Freckles looked at each other.

"What the hell?" Cal took off toward the sound.

"MAMA..." Morty fought to get away from Fagan.

"Take him, Archie." Fagan pushed Morty toward me.

I pulled Morty back inside the store and shooed all the shoppers out, lockin' the door behind 'em.

Through the window, we seen Fagan and Cal head up Fifth Street toward The Fitzgerald. I turned to Morty. "Will you promise to stay here if'n I promise to tell you what's happened as soon as I know?"

"No...yes...I don't know."

He wouldn't look me in the eye but there warn't time to worry about him. "The store's closed already. Go home. Call yer grandma to help you take care of James and Cap."

"I'm dang near as old as you! Why can you go see what's happenin' to my family and I can't?"

"Because they need you. They love you. Not a person in the world gives a damn if'n that idiot girl shoots me dead. I doubt you'd wanna be in my shoes."

Morty's mouth dropped open and he stepped back like I'd shoved him or somethin'.

"Whatever happens," I said, "I promise I'll come tell you."

Morty sighed and headed fer home.

Warn't but a moment later, when I wuz lockin' the door, that I heard the second shot.

* * *

As me and Freckles got close enough to see The Fitzgerald, Tom and Lydia came out onto the veranda and headed our way. Her hair'd come loose from its pins and wuz danglin' down her back.

Unsure what to do, me and Freckles stopped as they passed. Lydia stumbled along beside Tom, expressionless. Specks of blood wuz on her face and in her hair.

"What happened?" Freckles turned and ran along side them as they headed back to The Bourland Hotel. "Come on, Miz Sprinkle. What the hell's goin' on?"

Tom turned on him. "Get your ass outta here, Milt. I'm in no mood for your shit."

Our mouths wide in surprise, we watched the Sprinkles walk away. They warn't speakin' or lookin' at or touchin' each other.

182

As we got closer, we seen a crowd around The Fitzgerald. The closet door on the veranda wuz open. "It's gonna be bad!" I warn't sure if'n I said it or jes thought it.

Freckles elbowed me. "Think the two of 'em did a quick draw and they're both dead?"

We squeezed through people standin' in the street. As we got to the veranda, the door to Maud's room opened and Fagan came out. The crowd gave way and he walked through them and back down the street toward me and Freckles.

"Is Miz Julia okay?" It came out a strangled whisper.

"She's over there." He pointed to her carriage parked on South "C" Street.

"Maud?"

He shook his head.

"Dead?"

"Yeah." It wuz a long sad wheezy sigh.

Fer a moment, I couldn't breathe. I knowed it wuz gonna happen fer awhile. But now that it finally had, I didn't know what I wuz feelin'.

"I need to talk to Julia." Fagan dabbed at his upper lip with his handkerchief. "I...uh...just don't know what to say to her."

"Me neither."

"That girl just wouldn't stop, Archie."

"No, sir. She shore wouldn't."

He squared his shoulders and headed down the street where Julia sat in her carriage, messin' with the hem of her skirt.

I didn't think to ask if he wanted me, I jes follered him. When she seen me, Julia dropped her skirt and extended one hand. I ran past Fagan and up to the carriage so fast that Aurora startled. "Are you okay, Miz Julia?"

Julia pulled back the reins. "I am now."

Fagan climbed into the carriage and put an arm around her. "My God, you're brave, Old Thing."

She searched his eyes. "She won't bother us anymore?"

He wuz pale and shiverin' even though it wuz a warm day. "I-I'm—sorry."

"I know."

The quiet wuz so loud I had to say somethin'. "Is there anything I kin do, Miz Julia?"

She met my eyes. "It's already done."

"C'mon, sweetheart," Fagan took the reins from her. "Let's get you home. Archie?"

"Sir?"

"Tell the police we'll be waiting for them at our house."

"Yes, sir."

Aurora took a couple more steps before Julia put her hand on Fagan's. When he slowed, she looked back at me. "Check her, Archie. Make sure."

I nodded.

Fagan clicked softly to Aurora.

*　*　*

Outside The Fitzgerald, Cal wuz talkin' to a red-faced feller whose jacket buttons wuz about to pop. I recognized him right away. He'd been drinkin' with Maud at one of the bars on Garrison a few months back. She threw back shots as long as he wuz payin', but when he ran outta money, which didn't take long, she caused a ruckus. So's the bartender sent someone to tell Fagan, who groaned and sent me over to pay the bill and hustle Maud outta there.

"What's up, Cal?"

"Old Wallace here got into a fuss with Fagan."

"That ain't what happened at all!" Mr. Wallace stuck out his lower lip. "That little pissant yelled at me and came after me with that." He pointed at the stick Cal wuz holdin'. "He disrespected me in front of all them people!" He gestured toward a dozen or so citizens tryin' to get a look at what lay on the other side of the curtained front window of Maud's room. "I'll sue him for every dime he ever earned in Fort Smith. You tell him that."

"Don't bother Fagan," Cal said to me. "Wallace is drunk early today."

I warn't worried. Wallace bein' a jackass warn't new.

"It's all over now," Cal said to the man. "You're goin' home."

Wallace looked at me, back at Cal and then at the beat-up old roomin' house. Finally, he muttered somethin' under his breath and shoved his hands in his pockets.

"Fine." Cal nudged him. "Bye!"

The man stormed off.

After Mr. Wallace disappeared into the crowd, I said to Cal, "Think it'd be okay if'n I see her?"

"That ain't up to me," His voice wuz kind. "Can you handle whatever you see?"

I thought about it. "I'm up to it, I reckon."

He patted me on the back.

I took a breath and stepped up onto the veranda. The closet door across from Maud's room wuz part way open. Somethin' moved in the breeze. I bent down to look. It wuz a shredded piece of purple linen.

*   *   *

I wuz sittin' in the hall, leanin' aginst the closet door and fiddlin' with that little piece of material. Doc Breedlove came out of Maud's room and squatted down in front of me. "I'm sorry, son." He took my chin between his fingers and turned my head one way and then the other.

I put my hand on his wrist. "Did she hurt?"

He stared into my eyes and said, "If she did, it wasn't for long."

Relieved, I let him finish lookin' me over.

Doc Breedlove sighed and patted my head like I wuz a puppy or somethin'. "You're fine, Archie. Nothing you can do now. The Birnie brothers'll be here soon. Might as well go on home."

I nodded but warn't no way wuz I leavin' jes yet.

*   *   *

Fer the fourth or fifth time, I stuck my nose back inside the room where Maud lay on her back. The pool of blood under and around her seemed bigger every time I looked. I warn't sad. I wanted to be but I warn't. And I warn't sorry neither. It wuz over. Finally. And then, all of a sudden, I ran down the corridor to the back of the buildin' where no one could see me...and puked over the railin'. Damned stupid girl!

Wipin' my mouth on my sleeve, I went back up front. A dozen or more folks wuz a waitin' to see what there wuz to see. I recognized the top of Abigail Talbot's feathered hat near the middle of another crowd in the street out front. I wanted to yell at all them fools, but I didn't. I figgered they had as much right to be there eyeballin' Maud's body as I did.

Out in the street, George Allen pushed through the looky-loos, holdin' a pretty girl's hand. They hurried up to Doc Breedlove. The doctor put his hand on George's shoulder and shook his head.

George gasped. The girl tried to put her arms around him but he pushed her away and elbowed his way up onto the porch where I stood. I avoided his eyes as he ran past me into Maud's room. I gave him a minute or two before I follered. He wuz a starin' down at her corpse. I seen that he'd pulled the ragged curtain back and pried open the window. The light made the place seem even more dowdy...and messy.

"You're that kid that works at Bourlands?" George didn't look up at me.

"I'm Archie."

He squatted down next to her. "Did you love her?"

"I didn't even like her. You?"

There wuz a single tear dryin' on his cheek. He reached out to touch her hand, barely grazin' one of her fingers with his. "My lovin' her didn't do either of us any good."

"She warn't exactly lovable, at least, not since I knowed her."

"Think Bourland loved her?"

"Mebbe.' I thought about that fer a minute. "Naw. I think he pitied her."

"I'm willing to bet she didn't love him either. She just..." He took a long shudderin' breath. "She just needed someone to own her. You know, to take care of her—and her alone? She said she never had that. She said it to my face while I was holding her close one night."

"Fagan's got a wife and family. He warn't never gonna leave 'em."

"She wouldn't have stayed with him either, Archie." He wiped his eyes with the back of his hand. "Last thing I told her was 'go back to Seneca,' being as finding and keeping rich men in Fort Smith was iffy at best."

"What'd she say?"

He bit his lower lip. "She said, '"What else is there?"'"

"Maud didn't get on with her ma," I said. "Maybe that's why she didn't like goin' home."

Someone banged on the window.

"Get the Hell away, you sonofabitch!" George's voice broke.

The feller pressed his face aginst the cracked glass and commenced starin' at Maud until someone bigger pushed him aside and took his place. The second feller grinned at us. "That little whore shore got her comeuppance this time."

"Get away!" George waved his arm. "Away!"

"Okay, okay. Don't get yore knickers in a tangle, buster." The man stomped off the veranda and elbowed his way through a growin' bunch of looky-loos

I got up and closed the window, pulled the ragged curtains together and locked the door.

"The cops'll have a fit over that," George said as I came back and stood beside him.

"They better get back up here before them...them assholes break in."

A gruffer voice boomed over the hubub outside, "GET BACK OFF THE PORCH, YOU DAMN FOOLS!"

"Aw, Cal, we was jes tryin' to get a peek."

"Don't you have any respect for the dead? Get out here and leave them people alone."

It took a bit, but eventually the voices outside seemed further away.

Then someone banged on the door and both me and George jumped.

"It's me, Archie. Let me in. The town idiots are at bay for the time bein'."

"Thanks, Cal." I unlocked the door. "I ain't much of a fighter."

"Aw, them clown's are just curious. All you gotta do is be louder'n they are. You're already bigger!" He clapped me on the back and then turned to George. "I'm sorry about all this, Mr. Allen. I know that little gal was your first love."

"I...I moved on, but I ain't never gonna be over this." He looked back at Maud and shuddered.

Someone pounded on the door.

"If you ain't the Birnies, get the hell away from that door," Cal bellowed so loud that both me and George jumped.

"Aw, Cal!"

"I mean it, showboat. This ain't the time."

The voice whined until it faded away along with its' owner's footsteps.

"Guess someone oughta get in touch with Clara," George sighed. "Not sure it should be me anymore."

"Who's Clara?"

"That's Maud's crazy mother."

"Ah," I lowered my eyes. "I didn't know her name."

"I shouldn't have said that. Clara's had a hard life, you know."

Actually, I didn't know.

"Guess we gotta get Maud back to her. Somehow."

I took a step back. "I-I ain't any good with that kinda thing."

"Relax," Cal patted my back. "Fagan'll take care of that."

"Cal's right, Archie." George said. "This ain't your job."

The smell of Maud's blood in the warm closed-in room wuz makin' me queasy.

"Clara was hard on Maud," George said. "Always needin' somethin. Rent, clothes, food. Pushin' Maud to come up with money. She and the kids lived at the corner of 'Broke and Crazy,' Maud used to say."

I avoided his eyes. "I don't know nothin' about that."

"She was mad as hell at her mama," George said, "—but she woulda done anything to get that woman's attention."

"Maud's mama didn't love her?"

"I didn't say that. Clara's strange though. Get's all down in the dumps a couple times a year at least. Ain't nothing Maud can...," he licked his lips, "...could do to please her."

Cal squatted down beside the corpse. "Family can be that way sometimes." He leaned forward and closed Maud's eyes.

"You see Clara ... well...bein' a widow with a bunch of young'ens ...what we could spare from my paycheck wasn't ever enough," George sighed. "And Clara's ...well, she's a nervous ...anxious kind of woman. We'd send her money and then get a letter back begging for—no, demanding more. Someone was always sick or the rent was behind or they needed food." He sighed. "This is goin' to destroy Clara...not just because she's lost another child but because she's also lost her only sure source of income."

"Maud didn't have a penny of her own," I said.

George stood up. "And never will...would have. His face crumpled fer a moment. "Damnit!"

Cal didn't say anything, and I couldn't.

"Anyways," George took a deep breath and went on, "Clara just got married. Guess she finally found someone willing to take on the rest of them kids."

"Any idea on her new married name?"

"Naw, Maud and me ain't been on talkin' terms since she took up with Bourland."

I couldn't think of anything worth sayin' but, "I'm sorry."

We wuz still standin' there not really knowin' what to do next when we heard footsteps clumpin' on the wooden veranda outside the door. A gravelly voice interrupted us. "I don't care why you didn't come when I called you."

Cal opened the door. "Charles."

"Cal." Charles Birnie pushed the door back aginst the wall and shoved a wedge aginst it to hold it open.

Henry Birnie came in behind him, elbowed around me—and squatted down beside Maud. "I got here as fast as I could."

Charles stared down at Maud's corpse. "When we get a call, we roll."

"When we get a call, we do the best that circumstances allow." Henry put his hand around Maud's wrist and his fingers overlapped. "Skinny as a rail." He laid her hands across her body. "At least, we ain't gonna drop this one like we did old Miz Wilcox last month."

"Y'all kin?" Charles looked up at me and George.

I shook my head. "Acquaintance."

"You?" He looked at George.

George nodded. Then he shrugged and shook his head.

"Make up your mind."

"We're divorced."

"So, who do we charge for this?"

George looked at me.

"Fagan Bourland," I said.

Charles Birnie relaxed. "At least we'll get paid what we ask for on this one."

* * *

Arkansas *Gazette*, Little Rock, Arkansas

Fort Smith, April 22, 1897

A few minutes after 2 o'clock this afternoon, Mrs. Fagan Bourland shot and killed Maud Allen, in what is known as the Fitzgerald House, on the Reserve near South 5th Street. Two shots were fired, both of which took effect, one in the throat and one in the breast near the heart. Death resulted almost instantly. It is said that Bourland, who is quite wealthy, has at different times offered Maud money to leave town and remain away, but she persistently refused.

* * *

Thursday, April 22, 1897

Shortly afterward, Mrs. Bourland was taken into custody and escorted by her husband to Esq. Eberle's office, where she waived extradition and gave bond for appearance before the Grand Jury, on a charge of murder. Her bond was set at $5,000. Her husband Fagan Bourland, J.B. McDonough and Henry Surrat are her sureties.

* * *

Hardly anyone who knowed Maud turned up to watch her coffin bein' loaded onto the train. Not even Fagan. I didn't blame him. He wuz tryin' to figger what to do next, I reckon. I warn't even sure why I went. Maybe cause no one should have no one say a last goodbye to 'em? Turned out a whole bunch of strangers showed though. Mostly they jes stood around and said mean things about her. In a way, Maud and I wuz alike. Warn't no one ever gave a damn about either of us or lifted a hand to help us out. Not until we met Fagan Bourland.

Sarge Eacret turned the corner a block away. Leanin' heavily on his crutch, he hobbled up to the Bourland property. "What ya doin' here, boy?"

"Jes passin' by and thought I'd see what wuz happenin'.'"

He frowned at me. "You were at the train station?"

I nodded.

"I saw the Talbots on their way back," he said. "Abigail was carrying on about how there was a bigger crowd at the Birnies' last night...you know, folks trying to get a look at the bloody corpse."

"All they got to see today wuz a coffin bein' loaded onto a train," I muttered. "That and a fistfight across the street."

Sarge rubbed his left eye with his knuckle. "Let me guess. Folks were torn up because they couldn't watch both at the same time."

"Somethin' like that. Ever one of 'em had somethin' nasty to say about Maud, but I didn't see nary a soul what even knowed her."

"She had you."

I shrugged.

"Glad it's over?"

"Sad it happened. Glad she's on her way back to her ma."

He coughed until his eyes bugged out.

"You okay?"

"One of them days."

I opened the gate and waited till he got through it before I follered him.

"After yesterday..." Sarge propped his crutch aginst the railin' on the Bourland's back porch and sat down on the top step, "...I had a hard time sleepin'."

I sat down beside him. "Me too."

The door opened behind us and Morty came out. "Would you like coffee? Tawny's got a pot ready. She's bakin' oatmeal cookies too."

I moved over so's there wuz room fer him to sit with us.

"Nothin' like Tawny's cookies on dark days like this'n," Sarge boomed. Then he said softly, "How're the boys?"

Morty squeezed in between us. "James is in his room with Gertie...reading, I expect. Or maybe just thinking things through. Mad at Pop."

"And Cap?"

"Hanging onto Mama for dear life. Following her around the house. Afraid someone's gonna come take her away. Sucking his thumb. He ain't done that since he was three or four."

"That poor kid's been hearing all the talk." Sarge winced and rubbed his stump. "During the war, you'd see lotsa kids like that. All nervous like. Would flinch if'n you said boo to 'em."

"How about yer pa, Morty?" I hadn't seen Fagan since he and Julia'd left The Fitzgerald yesterday.

"Worried about Mama mostly. Sad. Trying to make it up to us."

"How's that working?" Sarge growled.

Morty took a deep breath. "Gonna take a while."

"For you?"

"For all of us, I'm thinking." A warm breeze made the leaves in a big tree across the street shimmy. "Think they'll put Mama in jail?"

"Not a chance," Sarge said. "That girl poked at Julia for over a year. Bad-mouthed her. Embarrassed her. Humiliated her. And everybody in Fort Smith knows it."

"Them letters..." I sighed.

"Maud threatened to kill Julia in the last one." Sarge avoided our eyes.

"You seen it?"

"Yesterday. After you told Julia where to find Maud, she rushed out so fast that she left it on the table."

"And...?"

"That girl could wear the horns off a billygoat."

"Miz Sprinkle said Maud came back to get even with Julia," I said. "She'd got herself a gun and wuz practicin'. But ya know, them wounds from last time warn't healed up yet. She couldn't keep her arm steady."

"In that case, no wonder she's in a Birnie Brothers' box," Morty sighed.

"That damned fool done her own self in," Sarge grumbled, "...sending threats before she got good enough to have a fighting chance."

"Ever think what happened is what Maud wuz hopin' would happen?"

Morty's eyes widened. "What're you hinting at, Archie?"

"I ain't hintin'. George said Maud's been sendin' most of the money she conned outta Fagan home to her ma. The only nice things Maud ever owned came from men wantin' to look in her drawers. She wuz lonely and jealous of everyone and everythin'—especially yer mama." I blew air between my lips. "Maybe she jes got sick of this nasty old world."

"You mean she didn't have the guts to do it herself?"

"Maybe. That crap she sniffed warn't much help."

"Whew," Morty muttered. "You sure?"

I shrugged. "That's what I figger anyways."

"Whether that girl was trying to get Mama to kill her or not won't matter to a jury."

"Probably not." I wiped my eyes with the back of my hand. "But it matters to me."

Morty got up. "Y'all come on in while the cookies are hot."

"I'm sorry, I didn't mean..."

The screen door slammed behind him.

"Them kids're goin' through hell right now," Sarge said. "It's a lot to swallow."

My own tears finally started. Sarge looked the other way and after a bit they dried on my cheeks. Then, we jes sat there, a listenin' to people movin' around inside the house behind us.

The telephone rang and Morty answered it. "No ma'am. Mama ain't in no mood for visitors. Yes, ma'am. I'll tell her you woulda done it sooner."

I turned to Sarge. "Want me to call the store? Have Sam come get you?"

"Naw, he's busy. I'll walk when the mood hits me."

That warn't a good idea. Even though it wuz cool fer a Spring day in Arkansas, Sarge's face wuz already pale and sweaty. So's we sat on the Bourlands' back step a bit longer. Then, when I couldn't stand the quiet no more, I said, "Whatcha think happened, Sarge?"

"I think that girl planned on shooting Julia dead, hoping Fagan'd get her out of jail."

We sat there a while longer. "Think Fagan fixed that mail thing?"

"Did you see him do it?"

I blinked. "No."

"Until you see evidence don't go believing Abigail Talbot, boy." Sarge hefted himself up, leanin' on my arm and wincin'.

Julia opened the door. "You okay, Sarge?"

"I'm fine, sugar. The question is, how're you?"

"At peace for the first time in a long time." She squeezed my shoulder...and then she turned her attention back to Sarge, wipin' his forehead with her apron. "How'd you get here?"

"Same's anybody else."

"You aren't anybody else, now are you?"

"Just came to see if you or Fagan or the boys need anything."

Together me and Julia eased Sarge back down on the porch step.

"We're fine."

"You shoulda asked me. I'd have taken that girl down for you." Sarge's hands wuz shakin'.

Julia tapped on the back door with her knuckles. "Tawny, bring a glass of water for Sarge."

"Yes, ma'am!" Tawny rustled around the kitchen fer a minute and then pushed open the back door and set several glasses and a pitcher of water on the railin'.

Julia poured a glass and handed it to Sarge. "Here ya go, drink as much as you can."

He drank until his eyes a watered and then handed it back to her. "Where's Fagan?"

"Sending Clara Avery a telegram."

Sarge frowned. "Who?"

"Maud's mother."

I frowned. "How's that play with you, ma'am?"

"The sooner that girl's back with her family the better."

Belle's harness jingled and we seen her and Sam headin' our way.

"Thanks for coming so fast," Julia said as Sam came around the corner to the back porch where we wuz gathered.

He bowed his head. "No trouble at all, Miz Julia."

"We need to get Sarge back to The Bail—uh, The Bourland. Tell Mary to get some food down this old coot...and then have someone help him up to his room."

"Now, Julia. It ain't as bad as all that." Sarge groused but he warn't foolin' no one. He loved bein' fussed over.

"Once he's settled in, tell the Sprinkles to come by here."

The Sprinkles? My heart pounded.

"Tell them it's business. And that they need to come now in case they won't let me stay here after today.

"Yes, ma'am." Sam glanced down at Sarge. "Let's get you on back to the hotel, sir."

I stood up.

"Not yet, Archie." Julia held up her hand. "We need to talk too."

We stood on the porch a watchin' Sam help Sarge out to the wagon.

"Sarge is a good man."

"Yes, ma'am, he shore is. He jes don't want anyone a knowin' about it."

"He said Fagan is a good man."

I chewed in the inside of my lip, tryin' to find somethin' to say about that. "Yes, ma'am. He's always done right by me."

"If it comes to down to it, where do you stand?"

I swallered...and breathed out the poison I wuz a carryin' around. "With you and Mr. Fagan, ma'am."

"And Maud?"

“She’s dead, ma’am.”

“You’re sure.”

“I shore am.”

“That was another kind of war, Archie. One she was never going to win.” Julia’s forehead wrinkled. “I’ll hate her forever for what she did to us…to me. And there’s no forgiving what she made me do.” She took my arm and led me into the kitchen. “And Archie?”

“Yes, ma’am?”

“I…uh…I didn’t kill her for…you know…Fagan.”

“I know.”

She pointed to the chair where I’d sat the day I first met her and the boys. “Coffee?”

I sat down. “Yes, ma’am.”

She rattled around in a cabinet and took down two mugs. “So, are you okay with Maud being dead?”

I chewed on that fer a bit. “I reckon I’m okay with her bein’ gone.”

She filled first my cup and then her own. “No regrets?”

“Fer tellin’ the truth?”

“Yes.”

“The world’s full of monsters, ma’am. Some of ‘em look like pretty young girls.”

*   *   *

Me and Julia wuz back in the kitchen when Fagan joined us.

I half got up. “Mornin’, sir.”

“Sit down, Archie. I need to talk to you.”

I glanced at Julia who nodded…and then sank back into my chair.

Fagan sat down beside her and patted her hand.

I tried not to glare at him. How dare he, I thought. Everythin’ wuz his fault. Me and Julia wuz probably goin’ to Hell fer what we done. How dare he take us fer granted? How dare he seem relieved that Maud wuz in a box on a train back to her mother in Missoura?

Julia poured him some coffee.

He drank half the cup before settin’ the mug down on the table.

The silence made my head ache.

Finally, Fagan cleared his throat and said, “Archie, I let you down.”

“Not me, sir. Her!” I pointed to Julia who wuz avoiding both my eyes and his. “You let her down.”

“And Julia. And the boys.”

That kinda set me back on my heels. I stared into my cup tryin’ to think what to say to him. “And Maud,” I said finally.

“And Maud.” It wuz so soft I warn’t sure he really said it.

“You didn’t do this, Archie.” A tear slid down Julia’s cheek. “I would’ve found her one way or another…or she’d have found me.”

“I already told Reverend Mathews that I ain’t sorry I told you where she wuz, Miz Julia. I’m jes sorry you had to go through any of this at all. Especially since nothin’ seemed to be enough. Them mean nasty pictures shoulda been

192

enough to put that girl...to put her..." I warn't sure where they shoulda put Maud. In prison? An asylum?

Morty stuck his head in the door.

"Go take care of your brothers, Morty," Fagan waved him away.

"You think I didn't know what was goin' on, Pop?"

"I hope what you think you know'll teach you to be a better man than me."

"No." Julia put her hand on Fagan's. "That's not what I want the boys to learn."

Fagan took off his glasses and rubbed the bridge of his nose. "I wanted them to learn to be businessmen and good husbands and maybe politicians. Guess I messed that up."

We wuz all quiet fer a minute. Then Julia scooped both Morty and Fagan into a long hug. No one'd ever hugged me, at least not like that. Embarrassed and jealous, I looked away.

"What's going to happen now?" Morty asked when Julia finally let go of him.

"Brizz is due here in a bit," Fagan said. "And JB. We're goin' to talk about defending your mama in court."

How wuz they gonna do that, I wondered. Julia did it. She meant to do it. And she planned on doin' it...and it wuz the third time she tried. That should count as murder anywhere.

"What're you gonna do about Archie?" Morty sat down at the table with the rest of us.

I startled when he mentioned my name. "Me?"

"Rumor has it you told Mama where to find Maud."

"Who...?"

"They say the police already got that from Tom Sprinkle."

My heart beat so hard I wuz sure the others could hear it. "It wuz more complicated..."

"Don't worry, Archie..." Julia took a deep breath and blew it out through her lips. "...I'd have found her with or without your help."

"You don't understand, Miz Julia. I wanted her dead too. She wouldn't have stopped. Ever."

"Lord, don't I know that..." Fagan muttered under his breath.

The Lord? I'd been so relieved that it wuz all over I hadn't yet pondered the Lord's opinion about what me and Julia done. Would He be understandin'? Or would Julia and Fagan and me have to put up with that crazy girl in Hell too?

*　*　*

Fagan and Mr. Brizzolara and Mr. J.B. McDonough wuz jes settlin' in the parlor when the Sprinkles showed up. Tawny shooed them into the kitchen where me and Julia and Morty wuz a waitin' fer 'em.

Lydia's mouth looked like she'd been suckin' a lemon. I figgered she wuz still mad about nearly gettin' shot her own self. Or maybe she wuz so pissed at Tom that it carried over to everyone else. Either way, I didn't blame her.

Julia stood up...and then Morty did too.

193

It got quiet and everyone looked at me. Lydia wuz like all the rest of them women who'd passed me on to someone else when it got to be too much of a burden to feed me...or when someone younger or cuter or needier showed up. The Bourlands treated me good. I might not be family but they gave me a job and room of my own and shoes that fit and they took care of me when I got hurt. More'n that, I had a place with 'em. They...they liked me. I stood up beside Julia and Morty.

"Yes," Lydia sighed. "I see how this is."

"Lydia, we have two pieces of business to discuss" Julia said. "First, I want you to know that what happened yesterday was not about you. I was there because of Maud..."

"Don't tal..."

Julia stamped her foot. "You can have your say when I'm done. Right now, I have a question."

"What is it?"

"Were you there to help that girl kill me?"

Lydia Sprinkle's jaw dropped. "I was at The Fitzgerald because I was leaving my husband!"

"You went to that dump because of that?" It came outta my mouth before I could stop it.

"I'm not financially indepen..."

"I know what we pay the two of you," Julia said.

"I- I left without telling Tom," she said. "There's a lot we still have to work out."

"You also left without telling me. Who was in charge at The Bourland while you were tending to Maud?"

"Why Tom, of course. And Mary Fitzpatrick kept everyone fed until...you know, we could work everything out."

I frowned when I realized that Lydia hadn't jes walked out on Tom. She'd thrown her job away too. All fer the sake of a selfish girl who wouldn't've given her a second thought after the crisis passed.

"That girl was a foolish child, Miz Julia."

"Lydia!" Tom took her arm jes above the elbow.

"A child with no one to watch over her, to give her advice."

"And what advice did you give her? To threaten me? My family?"

"Of course not, Julia. I saw what was about to happen and tried to stop it."

Morty broke in. "If you wanted to help, why didn't you make her leave town?"

"I tried to get her to go home," Lydia glanced at Tom and then turned back to Morty. "...but she wouldn't listen. I knew things were coming to a head. I tried but..."

None of this made sense. "Why did she come back? You'd think she'd have learned her lesson last year."

Lydia turned to me and fer the first time in a long time, I seen the kind woman who'd welcomed me into The Bailey and took care of me when I wuz hurt. "Because she wasn't perfect anymore, Archie. Those bullets that nearly killed her last year left scars—red welts that were tight and sore. They might have faded with time, but Maud thought no man would ever want her because of them."

“But…”

“She wasn’t the smartest young woman ever came to town, Archie.” Tom Sprinkle folded his arms across his chest.

“What exactly were you trying to do?” Julia said to Lydia. “Why didn’t you talk to me?”

“It was more than that.” Lydia sighed. “Tom and me…well, it don’t look like we’re gonna make it. I knew when that girl showed back up that she couldn’t stay at The Bourland. So, I spoke with Mr. Fitzgerald about something temporary. I didn’t have much put back and as usual, Maud was broke. So we…”

“Made do?”

She turned to me. “Yes, I suppose we did. I didn’t figure Maud would stay longer’n a day or two at The Fitzgerald and that would give me time to figure out what I should do next. Working and staying at The Bourland with Tom that close wasn’t working.”

“You could’ve been killed.” Julia seemed shocked. “And I wouldn’t have wanted to face God with that on my soul.”

“I tried to stop you, Julia. Not for Maud’s sake so much as for your own.”

Julia lifted her chin. “That was between me and God and that girl. You should’ve minded your own business.”

“Lydia’s a fool but she’s not a bad person,” Tom broke in. “We’ve worked for you for years without a problem. Doesn’t that mean anything?”

“It means that Lydia can’t be trusted. And if I can’t even trust her to be a friend, I sure can’t trust her with Daddy’s hotel.”

Lydia flushed. “I…I’m sorry you feel that way, Julia. I’ll get my things and be gone this afternoon.”

Julia held up two fingers. “Two days. I found you a place with Mr. West for a few months. That room won’t be open for two more days though. After that, I never expect to see you here again.”

Lydia’s jaw tensed and relaxed and tensed agin. “I see.”

“What about me,” Tom asked. “Am I out too?”

Julia turned to him. “Which do you need most? A wife or a job?”

The coldness in her voice chilled me. She’d been vulnerable… distraught…since she got that first letter from Maud. Suddenly, she wuz back in charge. And we all knowed where we stood with her.

“I’ll look for work elsewhere then,” Tom sighed and turned to Lydia. “And I’ll help you pack.”

*   *   *

Independence, Kansas
Saturday, April 24, 1897
The remains of Maud Avery came in by the Santa Fe last evening from Fort Smith, Ark., and were at once taken to the cemetery. Most of our readers will remember that Maud was shot in the breast at Fort Smith by a woman who’s enmity she had incurred. She recovered from this wound but as appeared by Globe Democrat of yesterday, she was shot twice and killed instantly by the same woman at Fort Smith Thursday.

*   *   *

Jo Johnson, Attorney at Law
508 Garrison Avenue
District Attorney

*   *   *

June 22, 1897

"Archie!"

I opened my eyes. It wuz dark and I wuz cold even though it wuz summer.

"Archieee!"

I pulled the sheet over my head and prayed Maud'd get tired of hauntin' me and go bother George or Fagan. After all, I wuz a bystander. Warn't me that married her or seduced her. Warn't even me that killed her. I squeezed my eyes shut and let her rant.

*   *   *

It wuz nine in the mornin' when I got up and peeked out my tiny window. Dark clouds in Oklahoma wuz a comin' our way. That's all Fort Smith needed...another blow.

Mary wuz pourin' Reverend Mathews' coffee when I went into the dinin' room. "Imagine seeing you here so early, Archie. They making you go to court this morning too?"

"They sent me one of them letters but they's wastin' they's time. I warn't even there when Fagan got into it with that Wallace feller. In fact, I didn't know this here court thing wuz happenin' til I got paperwork sayin' I gotta show up and testify."

"You never know how long those things are gonna take. Better load up with some extra ham this morning." Mary poured me a cup of coffee and hurried off into the kitchen.

I took a sip before I turned to the Reverend. "Why'd Mr. Wallace make a fuss?"

"Money," Reverend Mathews said. "If Fagan was like me—poor with nine kids, we'd have never heard a peep out of the man."

"Why don't he go out and earn it himself?"

"Why didn't Maud?"

I thought about it a minute. "Too high and mighty?"

"Some folks take advantage of any and every opportunity that comes up. If they get a little something for their trouble, that's a little something they never had before. If they lose, they're no worse off."

"Seems to me they's lazy."

He looked up at me with a twinkle in his eye. "Some of 'em maybe. Seems to me that some of them...like Maud...work mighty hard at being lazy though."

I chewed on that fer a minute. "Yes, sir. I guess she did."

"So, you been havin' nightmares?"

"Who told you that?"

"You've got circles under your eyes and you're getting skinnier."

I stared at my empty plate.

"Want to tell me about it?"

He looked like he cared and all, but what'd needed to be done wuz done. No goin' back on it now.

Mary hustled in with a plate of eggs and ham. "Biscuits'll be out of the oven in just a minute, sugar. You want some too, Reverend Mathews?"

"You got any of that raspberry jam?"

"Opened a brand-new jar for Sarge this morning."

"Bring me it then," he said.

I stared at the plate, my stomach grumblin'.

"Dig in, boy. Don't wait on my account. I already had my first breakfast at home."

I stabbed one of the yolks and it poured out onto the ham. I shuddered and started to take a bite. My hand shook so bad, I laid the dadgum fork down. Fer a moment, I wuz skeered the Reverend wuz gonna start in on that Jesus loves you stuff, but he didn't and I relaxed. No sense expectin' Jesus to forgive me. First off, I warn't one bit sorry—and second, everyone—includin' that crazy girl—wuz better off fer it. But seein' Maud all shot up like that'd made my stomach ache and it hadn't stopped hurtin' since I seen her a layin' there.

"How about trying a biscuit?" Mary set one on my plate.

I looked up at her and she smiled.

"Butter?" The Reverend pushed a bowl of it toward me. He'd already slathered it on his own and had taken a bite. "Mmmm. Mary sure does make 'em good."

I stared at the yoke a spillin' all over my plate and swallered...and swallered agin.

"How about I fry your eggs a mite longer?"

"Um."

"Come on, boy,' the Reverend urged. "Mary tells me you been off your feed bag..."

Mary put her hand on my shoulder. "Let me fix it, Archie."

I looked up at her. "Okay." It came out almost a whisper.

"I'll be right back." She picked up my plate and hustled into the kitchen.

"That was good of you," Reverend Mathews said as he took another bite.

"What do ya mean?"

"That kind woman's been fretting about you not eating. I told her you would when you could, but still..."

"That wuz..." I cleared my throat. "...mighty kind of her...to...to care."

"So you put her mind at ease and eat whatever she beings you."

"Yessir." People bein' nice thataway still choked me up.

*   *   *

Me and Fagan came down the steps of the courthouse to find Sam and Belle a waitin' fer us at the corner. As we climbed into the wagon, Garland Talbot showed up, hat in hand. "How'd it go?"

"A nuisance. Nothing to worry about."

"Abigail and I—well, we wanted you and Julia to know we're on your side."

"That's mighty kind of you."

Sam released the brake on the wagon and Belle took a few steps forward.

Garland put his hand on the side of the wagon and Sam pulled back on the reins. "Everyone knew that girl was trash."

Even though I'd thought so too when Maud wuz alive, I shore didn't like Garland talkin' thataway about her now that she wuz dead. I expected Fagan to take up fer her, but he jes stared at the floor of the wagon.

"Abigail said she even went after Reverend Mathews last summer," Garland went on.

"Hadn't heard that one," Fagan said finally.

"And she heard from Sarabelle who works for the Polks who heard it from the Drennen's maid over in Van Buren that Maud Avery's ma's as dark as Sam there.'"

I glanced at Sam who wuz pretendin' he warn't listenin' to the conversation.

Fagan sighed. "That's a new one too."

"People talk."

"That they do."

"I..uh..I know there's still a lot going on. The trial and all. But..."

"But what, Mr. Talbot?" The back of Fagan's neck wuz turnin' red.

"Will...uh...will Bill Hatcher still be..." Garland's eyes rested on me fer a moment. "...I mean is the Faro game still on same as usual?"

"Same as usual."

"I was afraid what with all that's been goin' on, you'd be shutting him down."

"Hatcher'll be in the barn same as usual."

Garland smiled broadly. "Glad to hear it."

"Good luck, Mr. Talbot."

Sam rattled the reins and Belle took off toward South Sixth.

"Maud's ma ain't no African," I said. "Wuz her daddy?"

"Not that I know of Archie."

"If'n it's true or not, it's all over town if'n Abigail Talbot thinks it's so."

Fer awhile, Fagan didn't answer. But then, a couple minutes later, he sighed.

* * *

June 24, 1897
Baseball games broadcast in Fort Smith

* * *

July 9, 1897

Dr. Southard's Bicycle, mentioned in last week's paper as having been stolen the previous Monday night, was found Friday morning in the Missouri Pacific Stock pen. The bell, lamp and wrench were missing but otherwise, the wheel was uninjured.

* * *

July 17, 1897

THE GALLOWS BURNED

Under the instruction of Mayor Garrett and the board of public affairs, the old gallows in the federal jail yard, which has been the scene of so many executions for crimes committed in the Indian territory, was torn down last week and burned up. This removes an object which, unsightly and gruesome as it might be, was, nevertheless, an interesting one for strangers from abroad.

* * *

August 13, 1897

THE BIG CLOCK STOPS

The clock in the dome of the courthouse was stopped Sunday morning shortly before 5 o'clock by a stroke of lightning. This bolt struck the flagstaff on top of the cupola and tore it into splinters. It also tore up the tin about the base of the dome but did no further damage beyond stopping the clock. The damage was about $150.

Chapter Nineteen

Julia's Justice and Justice for Julia

Fort Smith *News Record* Wednesday, October 6, 1897
The telephone connection with Fort Smith was completed at an early hour
Monday and the first "hello" was given by the phoneman. The first regular
business was from J. W. Breedlove to the American National Bank. The
people here congratulated their neighbor Fort Smith in being able to talk
direct with so busy and sociable a little town as Muldrow.

*   *   *

October 6, 1897
First Day of Julia Bourland Murder Trial

"I tried but it was locked, Mr. Reed."

"What did you do then?"

"I wanted to see if there were any letters from my husband in it. I finally
found the key and opened the trunk...and I did find the letters."

"Did you read them?"

"One or two."

"Were they what you expected?"

Julia gave Mr.Reed her coldest glare.

"I'm sorry, ma'am. I meant were these the letters you came for?"

"Yes."

"What happened next?"

"I heard voices outside."

"What did you do next?"

"I pocketed the letters and picked up my bonnet and pistol from where I'd
laid them on the floor. Then I hid in the closet outside in the hall." Julia bowed
her head so's all we could see wuz the top of her hat. "I heard them come in."

"Speak up, Miz Bourland." Judge Bryant said. "So the jurors can hear
everything you have to say."

Julia looked up at him and nodded.

Mr. Reed lowered his voice. "And then, Mrs. Bourland?"

Julia turned toward the jury. "I thought it was my chance to get away...that
maybe no one would know I'd ever been there."

Freckles elbowed me. "That's bullshit, Archie."

I thought so too, but I shrugged. "It's her story."

"When I pushed the closet door open," Julia continued. "Maud must've
heard it because she came out of her room. When she saw me, she squealed

and ran at me with her arms raised. There was something in one of her hands.” Julia held up her gloved fist like she wuz holdin’ an invisible knife. “At the same time, Maud screamed for Lydia who came out of the kitchen behind me.” Julia twisted in her seat, like she wuz looking over her shoulder…and then turned to face forward agin. “Lydia had once been an employee…and a trusted friend,” Julia’s sigh wuz long and ragged, like maybe when Lydia turned on her, it wuz too much to bear, “…but after she took up with Maud, that was no more.”

“Looks like Maud was chipping away at everything and everyone that Julia cared about,” Freckles said behind his hand.

“Lily French, Lydia Sprinkle…even Mary Kirkpatrick fer awhile,” I said.

Judge Eddie banged his gavel and frowned at us.

“And Fagan,” Freckles said outta the corner of his mouth while he wuz noddin’ and smilin’ at the judge.

I glanced across the aisle to where Fagan sat. The courtroom lights reflected off his glasses. Why’d he mess around with Maud of all people? Had she ever mattered to him? Really?

After we all settled down, Judge Eddie turned back to Mr. Reed. “Go ahead.”

“What happened next, Miz Bourland?”

Everyone leaned forward in they’s seats.

“I was trapped between them. And scared.”

“Why scared?”

“Something big was happening.”

“Did it, Miz Bourland? Did something big happen?”

“When Maud came at me with whatever she had in her hand, the look on her face…” She shuddered.

Mr. Reed seemed surprised. “The look?”

“It was vicious, Mr. Reed. So much hatred. Like a mad dog. It took my breath away.”

“Didn’t you hate her too?”

“Oh yes, I hated her!” Julia lifted her chin. “And in that split second, I decided my life was worth more than hers.”

“What did you do?”

“I fired.”

“At who?”

“At Maud, of course. Lydia Sprinkle was no threat.”

I glanced at Miz Sprinkle. She wuz dabbing at her eyes with a handkerchief.

“What then, Miz Bourland?”

“Maud screamed for Lydia to grab my gun.”

“Did she?”

“Lydia tried to knock it out of my hand, but I wasn’t about to give it up. Maud still had a gun somewhere.”

“How did you know that?”

“She told me in the letter she sent me that morning that’d she bought one and was going to kill me with it.”

“Were you afraid of her?”

"That girl was crazy, Mr. Reed. We'd been going at it for almost two years. I knew she'd kill me if I let her. Or maybe Fagan or the boys."

"Because she wanted your husband?"

Julia sighed. "Because she wanted money," Mr. Reed. "Didn't matter if it was Fagan's money or my money. Just money."

"Why?"

"She and her family are penniless, and no one works. I don't cotton to that. My husband and I earn every penny we make. We don't expect folks to just give it to us."

That stopped me. I understood things about Maud that nary a one of the Bourlands or Baileys ever could. I warn't all that old, but I been hungry lots of times. Sometimes them adoption folks gave me to people that warn't nice. Sometimes they gave me to families so poor they took my clothes and shoes and dinner fer they's own kids. Sometimes they gave me to crazy bastards who took the money and then used me to make more.

Even though she knowed her folks, Maud warn't all that different'n me. Alone and lost. Course, all I had to worry about wuz me. She had a mother and younger brothers wantin' fer a better life...and Maud...well, she worked real hard at not workin' to send 'em what they needed.

I glanced at Clara Avery. She wuz starin' at her hands what wuz folded in her lap. The boy, Maud's brother, musta been real little when his pa and the other sister died. He warn't ragged, but his clothes wuz well-worn, like mine'd been when I first came to Fort Smith.

"What happened next?" Mr. Reed asked Julia.

"Maud was bleeding all over the floor. The three of us were slipping in it. I tried to get her to back off, but she was still fighting...even though I knew she was dying."

"You could tell that?"

"She was done, Mr. Reed."

"You could tell the wound...the first wound was fatal?"

"It was close range and right through her breast."

"Did she fall?"

"Not right away. She was still trying to get at me when Lydia took off running. I could hear her out on the porch yelling for help."

"Was Maud dead at this point?"

"She should have been, but she was still movin'...still comin' at me. Still trying to get the gun."

"And what did you do?"

"I shot her again."

"Why?"

"I didn't dare turn my back on her."

"Thank you, Miz Bourland." Mr. Reed turned toward the prosecution. "Your witness."

*　*　*

While Mr. Johnson flipped through his papers and Julia took another sip of water, Freckles turned to me, "Is she guilty or not?"

"I dunno what to think, Milt."

"I didn't know Maud," Freckles murmured, "What was she like?"

I thought fer a minute. "That girl'd wear the horns off a billygoat."

"That's harsh."

I shrugged.

"Mrs. Bourland." Johnson's voice wuz louder than Reed's had been. "Are you telling this court that you were still afraid of Maud Allen...shot through the chest and layin' in a pool of her own blood?"

"I put nothing past her."

Mr. Johnson shook his finger at Julia. "You killed her because you were jealous!"

Mr. Reed stood up. "That was an accusation, not a question, Your Honor."

"Rephrase, Mr. Johnson," Judge Eddie said.

"Miz Bourland, were you jealous of Maud Allen?"

"NO!"

"What were your feelings about her?"

"As I said before, disgust, fear ..."

"And you hated her?"

"Oh yes." Julia lifted her chin. "I hated her!"

"Why?"

"She was like a stinging bug, Mr. Johnson, who was at me constantly...bite, bite, bite!"

I elbowed Freckles and he nodded.

"Is that why you shot her?"

"I killed her to protect my husband, my family and myself."

Johnson turned to the jury and gestured as if to say, "There you have it."

Judge Eddie tapped his desk lightly. "Is that all, Mr. Johnson?"

"Yes sir."

I thought it wuz over when Julia stood up, but when her eyes met Fagan's, her knees buckled. He jumped to his feet and hurried to put his arms around her. She clung to him, sobbin' out loud.

"Think that's fake?" Freckles whispered.

I shook my head. "Naw, that's as real as real gets."

"Why ain't Fagan mad at her for killin' his girlfriend?"

"Because Maud didn't mean nothin' to him."

"You sure about that, Archie?" Freckles whispered.

That set me back on my heels. Fagan'd always been close-mouthed about Maud...even when he sent me with money fer her to go back to Missoura. He'd a been avoidin' her since Julia shot her last year, but I didn't blame him. Them letters about dogs wuz downright embarrassin'. Outrageous. And ifn' they hadn't hurt Julia so much, they mighta even been funny. There wuz somethin' about Maud...we warn't all that different. She mighta knowed about bein' hungry and...and about dogs, but I knowed about old Jethro Barnes molderin' away in Pope County. The Bourlands'd changed things fer both of us. Guess that warn't enough fer Maud.

* * *

203

After another short break, the lawyers took turns tryin' to convince the jury how to vote. Thing wuz, as long as they wuz talkin', both of 'em sounded right.

Finally, Judge Eddie talked to the jury his own self. "What I'm going to do, gentlemen of the jury, is give you some guidelines. While you must each vote your conscience, to do that you must educate yourselves about what exactly did happen. As you heard from the testimony of several witnesses and from Julia Bourland herself, everyone sees what happened on April 22, 1897, differently. Maud Allen isn't here to tell you her side. However, you do have her words as all these witnesses remembered them. And you have her letters. What she said and did tells you a good deal about the woman. While I encourage you to talk with each other, in the end, you must each make up your own mind.

"So, if from the testimony and evidence you heard during this trial, you believe Julia Bourland went to The Fitzpatrick for the purpose of murdering Maud Allen and in fact, did kill her, you must find Mrs. Bourland guilty of murder."

I blinked back tears. That wuz exactly why Julia went there.

"If however," Judge Eddie continued, "...from the evidence presented, you believe that Julia Bourland reasonably thought Maud Allen intended to kill her that day...for whatever reason...and in the heat of the moment, she fired to protect herself when Maud Allen approached her, you must find Missus Bourland not guilty of first degree murder."

That wuz exactly what happened too.

"On the other hand, if you believe that while Julia Bourland was legally justified in shooting Miz Allen in self-defense, you must also determine whether she committed first degree murder when she then fired on Maud Allen as she lay defenseless on the floor of her room at The Fitzgerald."

Freckles elbowed me in the side. "That means Miz Bourland's gonna hang."

I couldn't see any way past it. Julia did shoot Maud in cold blood while she wuz down. She admitted it. She did it on purpose. Miz Sprinkle heard her do it. Poor Morty, poor James, poor Cap. They's mother wuz gonna hang. I wuz gonna have to watch that dear, kind, dotty woman die. Warn't right. Not after all Maud put her...all of us... through. I glared at Fagan even though he warn't payin' me no never mind jes then. None of this would've happened if'n he'd jes stayed away from Maud.

Judge Eddie droned on. "What people see and remember inevitably varies. You must consider the impact of all the pertinent variables as you evaluate this case."

"Whew," Freckles wiped imaginary sweat off his forehead with the back of his hand. "I'm glad I don't have to decide."

"I wish they'd put me on that jury," I growled. "They cain't know...from what they heard here...what Maud wuz."

Freckles' eyes widened. "And what was that Archie?"

"A monster."

"Really? A monster?"

"You...you had to know her."

"I don't doubt she was crazy, Archie. But you don't think she deserved to be killed, do you? Murdered?"

"She'd have killed Julia in a heartbeat, Freckles. And anyone that got in her way."

"Excepting she didn't have no gun on her."

"It wuz there somewhere…"

Reverend Mathews turned in his seat. "You boys need to keep it down or leave."

"Yes sir," Freckles said.

"Archie?"

Embarrassed to be called out in public thataway, I nodded.

"First, the prosecution claims that Julia Bourland is guilty of first-degree murder," Judge Eddie wuz sayin', "…because she went to The Fitzgerald to confront Maud. They point out that if she'd stayed away, there would have been no shooting at all and Miz Allen would still be with us. They claim Miz Bourland was mad at Maud Allen not just for goin' after her husband, Fagan Bourland, but also for continually writing her taunting, obscene and threatening letters. They talked about how Julia Bourland was humiliated by the talk around town and angry about it. And they've told you that Mrs. Bourland was afraid Fagan might throw her and the boys over for this girl. They referred to Mrs. Sprinkle's testimony and pointed out that Mrs. Allen was not completely healed from the last time Julia Bourland shot her. And they told you how it wasn't a fair fight because Maud Allen wasn't proficient with a gun—especially compared to an experienced shooter like Julia Bourland. And finally, they argued that Maud was still alive when Julia shot her the second time and killed her. You must carefully consider all those circumstances.

"On the other hand, the defense told you that this was a long simmering feud. They said that Mr. Bourland was past his infatuation with Maud Allen. And that infuriated Mrs. Allen and made her even more determined to break up his marriage. They claimed that while he was initially flattered by Mrs. Allen's attentions and sympathetic to her family's dire financial situation, he was appalled by the letters and obscene drawings the girl repeatedly sent to his wife. They were intended to hurt and anger Julia and Fagan found this behavior outrageous and embarrassing. And then, there were the constant demands for money, clothes and jewelry."

I elbowed Freckles in the side. "He's got that right."

Judge Eddie frowned at me and then went right on tellin' the jury what to do.

*   *   *

I sat on the courthouse steps, my arms wrapped around my knees.

"I hear things ain't going well for Miz Julia." Sam took off his cap and held it over his heart.

"I don't know what that jury'll do, Sam."

"Damn."

"I believe…I gotta believe this or I'll cry…I think Fagan'll get Julia out of it somehow."

"If anyone can do it, Mr. Fagan can." Sam put his cap back on. "Call when it's all over and you need me. Tell 'em at the store that I'll be forkin' hay for Belle in the barn."

After Sam left, I leaned back on my elbows and closed my eyes.

"Your mother never told you a lad of your colorin' ought not be spendin' time in the sun?"

"I never met my mother, Miz Rogers."

"Never?"

I opened my eyes and sat up. "Never. It'd be nice to know one way or another. To belong to someone. To be from somewhere."

She smiled. "You're Scotch/Irish, Archie. No question."

"How do you know?"

"Because I'm Irish. Can't you tell? Born and raised in County Cork until I turned seventeen and they sent me here on Father Horan's boat."

As always, Miz Rogers made me smile. "Do you miss it?"

"Lookin' back don't make today any better or worse. I let things that are be."

"Miz Cook and Babe wuz Irish too, I think. Back aways, mebbe."

"Miz Cook's in Heaven lookin' down on us now, boyo."

I nodded, wonderin' if'n Heaven really wuz up...and if'n Miz Cook still remembered me, wherever she went. "Do you think they'll hang Miz Julia?"

"Never you worry, lad." Miz Rogers patted my hand. "Julia's blessed by the saints."

"It's hard to see how that might work right now."

She put her hand on my shoulder. "Take my word for it."

"I shore hope so, ma'am."

She bobbed her head and headed off toward her apartment near Texas Corner.

It warn't but a few minutes later that Freckles came to fetch me. "The jury's coming in."

I looked up at the clock. "It ain't been that long. Whatcha think that means?"

He shrugged. "Be ready for about anything, I guess."

I musta been more tense than I realized. When I stood up, my bad leg cramped. I groaned and rubbed it.

"Come on, no time for that."

"I know, I know," I winced as I tried to put my weight on it.

"Here, let me help you."

I towered over him, but he put one arm around my waist and I leaned on his shoulder. The stairs wuz crowded as folks hurried back to the courtroom, but somehow that boy got me up them steps. The bailiff seen us comin' and held the door, or we'd have been locked out. He pointed to a couple seats up front, and we sat down there.

The cramp wuz jes beginnin' to ease when Fagan and Julia and they's lawyers came in. Lookin' skeered, Julia wuz hangin' on to Fagan's hand fer dear life.

"They seem close," Freckles said. "Is that an act?"

"They's always been close."

"But then why…"
"I don't know, but Julia wuz willin' to kill fer him."
"But would he kill for her?"
I wuz still ponderin' that question when the bailiff brought out the jury.

*   *   *

I came out of the Courthouse, sat down on a step, rubbed my thigh…and cried.
"They gonna hang her?"
I wiped my eyes with the back of my hand and glanced over my shoulder. A dark-haired woman stood under a tree a few feet away. "Ma'am?"
"It's Rosie Lee."
She looked familiar but I couldn't place her. "Did we meet?"
"Not formally, but I know who you are."
I took off my cap, "Sorry, ma'am. I been foggy the last few weeks. Kin I help you?"
"What was the verdict?"
"Not guilty, ma'am."
"Hallelujah!" The woman leaned back aginst a tree and wiped her forehead with the back of her hand. "You had me scared they decided to hang her."
"No, ma'am. Miz Julia's goin' home with Mr. Fagan soon's they sign some papers."
Rosie Lee blew between her lips. "That's about the best news I've heard in a coon's age."
"Yes, ma'am. It shore is." It came out as a sob even though it wuz good news.
"So what's got you so down in the dumps, sugar?" She pulled a hanky out from her bosom and dabbed at my eyes with it.
My lower lip quivered, and I struggled to get a breath. "I-I don't know, ma'am. It's a relief, you know…"
She put her arms around me and pulled my head down onto her shoulder. "There, there. Times been hard for all of us lately."
We wuz in the middle of the Courtyard with people going about they's business all around us…and I didn't know this woman. She had me bent forward so far, I wuz afeared we'd tip over. But she smelled kinda like maple syrup and she stroked my hair…and murmured, "It's all over now, baby. It's okay." And then…no matter how much I tried not to…I bawled on her shoulder. I wuz confused and skeered and sad all at the same time. I didn't like Maud, but I shore didn't want her to be dead. And even though Julia wuz gonna be able to go home, I still felt bad about everythin' that'd happened. Like somehow it wuz my fault.
"Get your hands off that child!"
I looked up.
Abigail Talbot wuz headin' our way, a shakin' her umbrella.
Rosie Lee pushed me back but held onto my wrist. "You best keep your distance, Abigail. This here boy's been through a lot lately and ain't none of you…except maybe Julia Bourland… done a thing for him. He's been scared what might've happened to that fine lady."

207

"That's no excuse to go after an orphan."

"There ain't no excuse for no one watchin' out for him," Rosie Lee shot back.

"He's clean and dressed proper," Abigail said like she'd personally dressed me that very mornin'. "If you turn him upside down and shake him, the change in his pockets'll scatter all over."

"He didn't get that money from you!"

"The point is, he doesn't need anything from YOU!"

Rosie Lee narrowed her eyes. "I think it's time you get on home to Garland before your big mouth gets you in more trouble than you can handle."

I stood there wide-eyed, my head a swivelin' back and forth between the two of 'em.

Abigail's mouth turned down at the corners. "Don't get too worked up here in the courtyard. You come after me they'll throw you in jail again."

"It'd be worth it to black both your eyes, Miss Priss." Rosie Lee let go of my wrist, balled up her fists and took a step forward.

"You wouldn't dare!" Abigail glared at her...but took a step back anyways.

Rosie Lee lowered her head and wuz chargin' past me when I grabbed her sleeve. "Come on, ladies. There ain't nothin' to get all het up about."

"I been wantin' to black both of that bitch's eyes since she and my mama got into it over Garland Talbot.

"Don't look like today's the day fer it." I pointed at Abigail who wuz already a half a block away.

Rosie Lee laughed. "She runs her mouth but she ain't never up for a real fight."

"You took that round then." I glanced at the onlookers.

"Ignore them, sugar. They ain't got nothing better to do with their time than to flap their gums. It's gonna take me years to get round to all the sins they been sayin' I already done." She turned to the crowd starin' at us. "Excitement's over, folks."

Most of 'em jes stood there like they didn't know what else to do. Rosie Lee waved 'em away with the backs of her hands, "Shoo!" Slowly, they all turned back to doin' whatever they wuz at the courthouse to do.

"You feeling better, sweetheart?"

"Some."

"Did you know the girl Julia shot?"

I shrugged.

"She coulda made herself and me a ton of money."

"You knowed Maud?"

"Never laid eyes on her, but I heard plenty. She was notorious and unusual, especially scarred up like they say she was after Julia nailed her last time. She'd have been a draw for a year or two. It's a shame really."

Confused, I cocked my head. Then it dawned on me. Rosie Lee ran a whore house!

"Well, look at you," she laughed, "How old are you, boy?"

Flustered, I couldn't make myself look her in the eye.

"That's okay," she patted my shoulder, "...my business ain't for everyone. You tell Julia I'm real happy it turned out this way."

"Yes, ma'am."

As I watched Rosie Lee head off toward Rogers, I got to thinkin' that bein' a whore mighta been better fer Maud. She'd coulda made a good livin.' One that warn't dependent on Fagan's guilty conscious. She wouldn't have needed anyone and Julia wouldn't have had to kill her. Then I felt bad thinkin' such a thing.

Sam and Belle wuz waitin' by the curb. As I got closer, Sam came out to meet me.

I couldn't hold back once we got in shoutin' distance. "NOT GUILTY!"

Sam clapped his hands together. "Thank the Good Lord!"

"It's over, Sam." I slid my arm through his and we done a jig.

"Can't believe what I'm seeing." Miz Clara stood on the sidewalk a few feet away.

"Mama!" Her son wuz half a head taller than her and as soft as a baby's hind end.

Seein' hard feelin's on they's faces, I hid my joy. "I knowed how this looks, ma'am, but I'm sorry about Maud all the same."

"Of course, you are."

It wuz the first time I seen her up close. "I knowed you ain't happy about how things turned out."

"Happy?"

I flushed and stared at my feet.

"I thought you were my daughter's friend, Mr. Biggs."

I started to say, "Who told you that?" But decided it had a mean tone and I didn't want to hurt this poor lady more'n she'd already been. "No ma'am. Me and Maud hardly knowed each other."

Her shoulders drooped. "We're up against the wall."

"It's over now, ma'am. Time to let go."

"Let go?"

"Let Maud rest in peace," I said. "She tried her best."

"I don't call gettin' herself killed by a maniac 'tryin' her best." Tears streamed down Miz Avery's cheeks. "I still got mouths to feed..."

"Come on, Mama." The boy tried to lead her away. "We need to get a train ticket home."

"With what?"

He took her hand. "We'll find a way."

She jerked away from him. "No! No!" Her voice carried across the courthouse lawn and people turned to look at us.

The boy glanced at me and mouthed, "Sorry."

I nodded.

"We got nothing now," Maud's ma didn't look like she wuz gonna stop her fit anytime soon. "And it'll be the same tomorrow and the day after that."

I looked at the boy. "This ain't the place or time."

He couldn't look me in the eye, "Sorry about the ruckus," he said. "Ma still ain't over this."

Miz Avery pulled a kerchief out of her pocket and blowed her nose. "That woman owes us."

"Owes you?" I'd have thought all that legal stuff'd convinced Maud's folks to jes let go.

"We're de...de...what are we?"

"Desperate, ma."

"Broke and desperate," she repeated.

"This ain't our business, Archie," Sam said out of the corner of his mouth. "We need to get the family outta here."

I glanced around. Abigail Talbot wuz back and yackin' with Corinne Southard, exaggeratin' her run in with Rosie Lee, I figgered. Up near the door, the Bourlands wuz talkin' with the lawyers. Fagan had his hand on Julia's back. It wuz the first time I seen them relaxed and smilin' since before Maud showed up at the store and busted my face with that tomata.

I looked back at Miz Avery. She and Maud didn't jes look alike. They wuz the same inside. Always wantin' fer free what other folks worked hard to get. I filled up with rage, wantin' to say mean things to her, hurt her like Julia'd been hurt..."

"Archie!"

I glanced at Sam and he shook his head ever so slightly. That's when I realized I wuz pantin' and that my fists wuz tight balls. What wuz I gonna do? Beat up on Maud's skinny little mother and brother what wuz grievin'? I took a breath and then blew all that meanness out through the corners of my mouth.

Clara Avery wiped her eyes. "Is that all her friend is gonna do about this?"

"Ain't much anyone kin do, ma'am. It's over."

"It's never going to be over, young man." She took a step my way. "Do you hear me?"

Big deal, I thought. I been beat up on by the best of 'em. I climbed into the back of the wagon, folded my arms across my chest and ignored her, while she screamed and pounded on the side of it. The boy put his hand on her back. "Come on, mama. Let's go get dinner."

"We don't have money for that," she sobbed.

I dug a dollar outta my pocket and handed it to the boy.

"I'm sorry," he avoided my eyes. "And thank you."

As we watched then walk away, Sam muttered under his breath, "Think that woman's gonna be okay?"

"I dunno, Sam. Is Julia okay? Is Fagan? The boys?"

"They be strong. And you be strong too."

"I wuz this far..." I held my thumb and pointer finger close together. "...from punchin' that woman in the nose."

Sam took Belle's reins. "But ya didn't."

*　*　*

"Archie?"

Sam pulled back on the reins. Belle shook her head and looked back at us like she wuz tired and ready to go home too.

I turned around in my seat. "Sir?"

Fagan motioned fer me to climb down outta the wagon.

I climbed back down.

Fagan put a hand on my back and guided me off the sidewalk. "No way should I have ever put you in this position."

I bit my lip and tried not to sob out loud.

210

"I know how hard this was for you," he said.

"Yes sir."

"I want you to know I'm going to be a better husband and father from now on."

I didn't know what to say so's I jes stood there, feelin' sad and confused.

"You don't believe me?"

"No, sir, I believe you."

He cocked his head sideways. "But?"

"You been kind to me since the day we got off that train. I got more food more regular than any time ever. I got work and a room of my own. You and Miz Julia even took care of me when I got hurt. Fact is, you been seein' to me since I set foot in Fort Smith."

"I know you were upset about me and Maud."

"More like confused. And worried about Miz Julia and the boys."

"You were right that night you caught Maud and me in the barn. I was a damned fool. Maud made me think I was a big man right when that's what I wanted to hear. But what started out sweet turned sour soon enough. I'm embarrassed about it now. And I'm sorry it all spilled over on you."

"And Miz Julia and the boys?"

He rubbed the bridge of his nose. "That's going to take a lifetime to fix."

*　*　*

After we got everyone back to home where Tawny had a big dinner a wait'n, I made my excuses and started back toward The Bourland Hotel.

"Archie!"

I turned around.

Morty and James stood on the back porch. "Thank you."

"Fer what?"

"For bein'...," Morty turned to James, "What did you call him?"

"Steadfast."

"Yeah, that's it. Steadfast."

James' fancy word made me grin. I searched fer one jes as fancy to respond with—but nothin' came to mind. Finally, I jes waved.

It wuz over. Julia'd won.

Sssssssssss

Chapter Twenty

You Can't Kill a Dead Person

December 1898

I sat up in bed and stretched. I'd been sad a long time…and kinda lost. What wuz gonna happen to me now? Baseball warn't never gonna work out. I knowed that since the night that nail tore up my thigh back in 1894. It jes took me awhile to know I knowed it.

Of course, I doubted anyone from Pope County gave a damn about me now. The old bastard warn't well-liked down there…not enough fer anyone to go out lookin' fer his killer. And someone else probably owned that farm now. And even if'n folks down there wuz still a lookin' fer me, I doubted anyone'd know me now. I'd growed more'n a foot. And my voice'd changed. With my new name and mustache and chin hair and Miz Emily's specs on my nose, I doubted anyone ever knowed that snot-nosed orphan'd recognize me now. Besides, it warn't what happened in Pope County that kept me in Fort Smith anymore. I had friends here. And Fagan done told me I'd always have a job if'n I stayed.

There wuz Annie, of course, but I took too long windin' up my pitch. She wuz travelin' around the country performin' fer the Buffalo Bill Wild West Show now. She sent me a flyer with her picture on it sayin' the show wuz comin' to Fort Smith. There she wuz all dressed in leather holdin' a whip. A big shot. I sat down to write her back but what wuz there to say? Instead of mailin' it, I ended up pitchin' it into a box I kept under my bed.

Mary knocked on my door. "Archie? Julia's feelin' poorly again and Fagan's in St. Louis."

I opened the door. "What's she need me to do?"

She handed me an envelope and a folded sheet of paper. "I didn't take her call, Tom did."

"Thanks."

The note wuz from Reverend Mathews and said, "I'm downstairs. Come see me first!" I tossed it on the bed. The envelope wuz from Julia. I'd recognize her writin' anywhere. The note inside ended with, "Come by this morning at ten. I have a box of clothes the boys have outgrown, and I need you to take them to the church for me. We are giving them to families in need."

*   *   *

I wuz halfway down the stairs when I heard Reverend Mathews in the dinin' room. "He's about the only one can lift her spirits when she gets this way."

"That should be Fagan's job," Mary said. "Archie's got his own demons. He don't need hers too."

Moved by they's kind words, I coughed before clumpin' down the next few steps.

Reverend Mathews stuck his head into the foyer. "Is that you, boy?"

"Yes, sir?"

"Come get breakfast," Mary called. "I've got biscuits baking."

"I think I will. Thanks."

Reverend Mathews pointed to a feller standin' beside him. "We have a guest for breakfast today."

"Judge Bryant!" I shook his hand. "It's good to see you, sir."

"Same here, young man."

"Bring more coffee, Mary," Tom said as we sat down at the table.

"They tell me you were a blessing to the Bourlands during their recent troubles," Judge Eddie said. "But now that it's over, you've been down in the dumps. Questioning yourself?"

"Who told you that, sir?"

"A flock of magpies." Judge Eddie jerked his eyes toward Reverend Mathews and then toward Tom Sprinkle.

"Ah!" My grin wuz a mask. "Them's some pretty nosey birds you been listenin' to, sir."

"What's got you down, son?"

His concern almost made me tear up agin. "Well, sir, I knowed you made sure them lawyers did everythin' by the rules."

"That's my job," he nodded.

"I want Miz Julia to be free. I do. But I'm confused. How could the verdict be 'Not Guilty?' She went to The Fitzgerald to kill Maud. That's what she meant to do. She said it herself. And that's what she did do. She even shot Maud after she wuz down and couldn't hurt her anymore. Why ain't that murder?"

"I know it's confusing," Judge Eddie said, "...especially since there were two other shootings before this one."

"It was confusing for me too," Reverend Mathews patted my shoulder.

"You see, the first two incidents were already resolved legally," the judge said. "This jury was only dealing with the third encounter between Julia and Maud."

I chewed on that awhile. "I...uh..guess I kin accept that if'n its the law."

"You're still troubled?" Reverend Mathews put his hand on my shoulder.

"Why'd Maud come back? Fagan shore warn't happy to see her."

"Women," Tom shrugged. "Who knows what they're thinking?"

"Maud couldn't hit the side of barn," I said, "...and she knowed it. Why'd she send Julia that threatenin' letter that mornin? Why'd she want a shootout she knowed she'd lose?"

"Even if she'd been a decent shot before this incident...and there wasn't any testimony about that one way or another...," Judge Eddie said. "She wasn't healed up from the last time Julia shot her. By all accounts, the girl was impulsive. And personally, I doubt she was rational."

"You mean maybe she really wuz crazy enough to think she could outshoot Julia?"

"That very day, Maud told several people she was going to kill Julia…" Judge Eddie took a sip of his coffee. "…and she even showed them her gun."

"And the dirk knife," I said.

"Yes," Judge Eddie sighed. "Maybe she thought all those threats would get back to Julia and scare her away?"

"She wuz a barkin' up the wrong tree if'n that's what she thought," I said. "Julia warn't a budgin'. And she shore warn't worried Maud'd beat her in a gunfight."

"Let me ask you this, Archie. Why do you think Maud taunted Julia that way?"

"Well, sir…" I licked my lips. "What if Maud used Julia to do what she couldn't."

"Why do you say that son?" Reverend Mathews seemed shocked by the idea.

"Because that girl…her family…they's been through hell, sir. Between money bein' scarce even before Maud's pa died…and after that, with all they's sicknesses and bouts of crazy and unpaid bills and what all, I wonder if… sometimes…mebbe all they's had wuz what Maud sent 'em."

"You think that's why Maud went after Fagan?"

"She warn't the first to trade…um…comfort fer…."

"Money?"

"Yes, sir." I blushed.

"And Fagan's a generous man?"

I nodded. "I'm sure Maud liked him and all. It ain't that exactly. Fagan and Julia been real good to me too and I'm beholdin' to them. But…"

"What is it, Archie?"

"That jury didn't know everythin' that went on between Julia and Maud. All they knowed from the trial wuz that they'd been fuedin'. Why'd they let Julia go? Did Fagan…you know…pay…"

"No, I seriously doubt that. He didn't need to."

"How so, sir?"

"Remember when Doctor Breedlove testified?"

I leaned back in my chair. "Doc Breedlove?"

"Think about it."

I closed my eyes. Assumin' everyone wuz right about what they seen, there had to be a reason the jury did what they done. Lydia said when she and Maud came back to The Fitzgerald, she checked out Maud's room and no one wuz there. Most likely Julia'd already grabbed Fagan's letters and wuz hidin' in the hall closet with 'em…and her gun.

I thought about Lydia sayin' Maud had somethin' in her hand too. What wuz it? A gun? The knife? A rock? Trapped between Lydia behind her and Maud in front of her, Julia must've figgered Maud wuz a bigger threat. Lydia never hurt a soul in her life. When she said she wuz tryin' to stop them two women from killin' each other…first in the hall and then in Maud's room, I believed her. If'n I knowed somethin' bad wuz gonna happen long before it did, Lydia surely figgered it too. "So did Maud come at Julia with somethin' in her hand," I asked.

"Whatever it was," Judge Eddie said, "...the jury believed Julia thought Maud initiated the attack."

"Maud tried to kill, Julia?"

"The jurors thought so. Especially since Maud seemed to have been the aggressor from the beginning. There was testimony about those taunting letters. And several people testified that Maud told them she was going to kill Julia."

I looked from the judge to Reverend Mathews to Tom. "So they thought Julia acted in self-defense?"

The judge shrugged.

"But she shot her twice!"

"They believed Doc Breedlove's testimony, Archie."

Reverend Mathews seemed shocked too. "What do you mean, Eddie?"

"Both shots were fatal."

I stared at Judge Eddie, opened mouthed. "I still don't get it, sir," I finally said.

"You can't kill a dead person."

*　*　*

After the judge left, I shook hands with Tom Sprinkle. "I'm sorry it turned out this way fer you and Miz Lydia, sir."

"I am too, Archie, but sometimes when things change, they do it so gradual like that a body don't notice until it's too late."

"Where you goin' to be?"

"I'll be workin' in Missoura. Or maybe somewhere's else. Only sure thing, it won't be for the Bourlands."

"Good luck, then," I said.

After Tom left, Reverend Mathews turned to me. "You gonna be okay, son?"

I thought about that fer a bit. "I dunno, sir. There wuz things I done that I had to do. I know it don't seem right, but the only thing that used to bother me wuz that it didn't bother me."

"And now?"

"I've decided my life's more important than ...well, you know, like Miz Julia said durin' the trial?"

Reverend Mathews sighed. "Sometimes what I know don't match up with what I believe."

"No, sir. It shore don't."

Chapter Twenty-one

Eliza Rogers

I wuz sittin' in the Bourland wagon what wuz parked on Garrison near Texas Corner.

"Archie!" It wuz Eliza Rogers' voice. "Archie Biggs!"

I spun my head this way'n that but didn't see her.

"Here, m'boy!" Miz Eliza hollared at me from a window in the buildin' on the far side of Towson.

"Come'on, Belle." I jiggled the reins so's to wake that dang fool mule up. She heehawed to let me know how she felt about bein' disturbed ...but finally she gave in and pulled forward a few steps. I put the brake on and stood up so's I could see Miz Eliza when I wuz a talkin' with her. "You sent fer me, ma'am?"

Her voice wuz squeaky on good days. She once told me she'd "lost me yellin' voice" on the trip over from Ireland back when. I asked her who she wuz a'yellin' at on that boat, but she jes went right on with a topic of her own choosin'. "Take a weight off, Boyo," she said. "I'm a comin' on down to you."

"Yes, Ma'am."

A couple minutes later, I seen her come out a door on my right. Her arms wuz so full of stuff I could barely see the top of her bonnet. "Top of the morning to ya, Archie," she said as she set everythin' at her feet.

"You gotta lot of stuff today, ma'am. You plan on out-Hatcherin' Hatcher?"

She laughed. "Think I could take down that brawny fella, do ya?"

"I think you can do most anythin', ma'am." I still warn't sure why Miz Eliza'd sent fer me, but it shore wuz good to see her. It'd been awhile. "What kin I do fer ya?"

"Just this, lad." She pulled somethin' wapped in brown paper outta her basket. "I found this in the mail this morin'!"

"What is it?"

"You'll see, lad. Open it up."

I pulled at the string and found my little book, lookin' a lot worse fer wear. I opened it. The pages wuz lots more brittle since I last seen it. I put it in my pocket and felt better fer it. "Didja find out anythin'?"

"Nary a thing, lad," she avoided my eyes. "No one ever saw it before. Not in County Tipperary anyway."

"Ah!" I stuffed it in my pocket. It warn't that the kind lady wuz a lyin' to me. She jes warn't tellin' me everythin'. I wuz used to it. People been hidin' stuff from me my whole life. Mebbe it wuz better not knowin' if'n it wuz as bad as all that. Afterall, I done okay on my own. I had a salary now. A place to sleep and food to eat. Maybe I'll jes be Archie a while longer...

And then...

Van Buren *Press* September 25,1897
"For the killing of Maude Allen by Mrs. Fagan Bourland on the 22nd day of last April, the plantiffs, the mother and sister of Maude Allen, are suing Bourland for $25,000.00, believing they are entitled to that amount of money. It is claimed that Maude had been in the habit of sending home as much as $20.00 per month, and this fact is dwelt upon in the complaint. It is said that Mr. Bourland isn't concerned about having to pay it."

* * *

Fort Smith *Times* January 11, 1898
In terms of loss of life, the worst tornado in Fort Smith's history struck, taking 51 lives and destroying dozens of homes and other structures

* * *

April 12, 1898
Fagan and Bill are charged by District Attorney Johnson for dealing Faro

* * *

Fort Smith *Elevator* September 26, 1898

* * *

Fort Smith *Times* Wednesday, September 28, 1901
Well-known employees of Fagan Bourland, Archie Biggs and Arabella Plummer were married this afternoon at the First Methodist Church. They will reside out on Jenny Lind Road where they have purchased a home.

* * *

Fort Smith *News Record* March 6, 1902
Judge Rowe "Hatcher, you are a man of remarkable. reputation," remarked the court to him. "...and it's not a good one. You are said to be the toughest nut in town, and I know that is just about true. You ought to be in the penitentiary now. Someone will kill you soon if you don't change your conduct. I'll fine you $75.

* * *

BILLBOARD MAGAZINE Dec 7, 1907
Annie Shaffer of the *Buffalo Bill Show* was injured at Vincennes, Ind., when thrown from a bucking horse and is now recovering. She will be in Mexico for two months riding bucking horses at various Bull Rings. She will then return to the *Buffalo Bill Show* next season.

* * *

Fort Smith *Times Record* Saturday, March 19, 1910
Contest of Horse Bucking Rules
At Tankersley's Brothers' Pastures
Sunday, 2:30 P
Anna Schaffer and W.W. Dillingham
vs
444 and 111 — One One One
Riders from the above stables will contest with Miss Schaffer who was with the *Buffalo Bill Show* and W W Dillingham, for four years chief of cowboys for Col FT Cummings' *Wild West Show*. They are all to ride for points to be awarded by the audience.
NO COLLECTIONS WILL BE ASKED
ALL FREE
From and through the curtesy of
WILLIAMS BROTHERS
444 and 111

* * *

September 20, 1924

Arabella Biggs was hit by a truck and killed on Friday, 1924. She was a long-time employee of the Bourlands and is the wife of well-known grocer Archie Biggs. Services will be at the First Methodist Church.

*　*　*

Fort Smith *Times Record* February 5, 1932

Capola Fagan "Cap" Bourland died of a self-inflicted gunshot wound. He killed himself at his home on 315 North 15th Street, Fort Smith, Arkansas, while in a period of despondency over what he believed would be a serious illness.

*　*　*

July 15, 1932

Morton Bourland Drowns in Creek

Fort Smith Detective and son of Mayor loses life while swimming.

Morton Bourland age 51, a member of the Detective Bureau of the Fort Smith Police Department, and son of Mayor Fagan Bourland and Mrs. Bourland, of Fort Smith drowned at Deans Ford, Lee's Creek, five miles Northwest of Van Buren about 6 pm today. Details of the tragedy are meager. However, it was said that Bourland was a member of a swimming party and was believed to have been seized with a cramp. Efforts to recover the body were unsuccessful as of midnight. Bourland was not married. Besides his parents, he is survived by a brother James of Fort Smith.

*　*　*

1946

Fagan donates $21,000 to the First Methodist Church
for a Memorial Carillon to honor Julia.

From the Authors

Current Fort Smithians recognize members of the Bourland family as upstanding business and civic leaders. Known for their leadership and political acumen, they are nevertheless notorious for a tragic incident that took place over 120 years ago. This event has become legend. While there are multiple versions of "truth" circulating, Tom Wing and I decided to tackle this story through the historical fiction format, using as many historical perspectives as are available. We include rumors and innuendo from the era, as they were part of this event as well. Then, at the end, we share what we can prove happened and why we believe it happened.

Although most of my books are "historical fiction," I have also written several non-fiction ones. I tend to choose historical fiction when covering an era or an incident where the records are so thin that what really happened is speculative. Or when the story needs to be delicately stitched together so that all the known perspectives can be explored and evaluated. Both of these genres take many years of research.

Professor Tom Wing at the University of Arkansas-Fort Smith is a dyed-in-the-wool historian who carefully documents his non-fiction pieces with original court documents, newspapers from the era and other original sources. He has a long history of working with the Fort Smith Historic Site and has deep knowledge of the history on display there. These resources and experiences made him an invaluable resource for several other projects, but crucial for this one. First, Tom secured images of documents associated with Maud's various court cases, including Maud Allen's provocative letters to Julia Bourland. That these letters are shocking is indisputable. That they are open to interpretation is too. What they suggest about Maud's dark and painful past is heartbreaking.

Julia and Maud has taken more than four years to research, write and edit. While there will always be more to discover, interpret and learn, my team and I have done our best to honor the past, provoke our readers, and tell a fascinating and almost unbelievable story.

Historical Context

Discovery and a story which needed to be told...

Tom Wing first became acquainted with the Maud Avery Allen case shortly after starting work as a park ranger/historian for the National Park Service at Fort Smith National Historic Site. While preparing for tours and programs centered on the history of Fort Smith, he came across the paper copies of the partial case file. Maud's case was intriguing, so Tom inquired about it with other staff members. Long before his time as an interpreter, the story had been declared off limits, due to the mature themes, graphic nature of the evidence, and the possibility of living descendants still in the area. The need for discretion was likely another factor. The story intrigued him, not just due to the scandal, but because it was also a prime example of the diversity of cases heard by the Federal Court in Fort Smith. With the more common murder cases, rape, illegal liquor trafficking, cattle rustling, horse theft, and even admiralty rights on the river, obscenity through the mail was not a typical case. So, while the story was not made into an exhibit, or programming at the site, it was an often discussed and debated topic in the lunchroom and sometimes with staff at the Fort Smith Museum of History.

With the site under repair and the exhibits being redone after the 1996 tornado, Tom went to Fort Worth for a week in the Southwest Regional Branch of the National Archives, where the complete files for the Federal Court for the Western District of Arkansas are housed. His job was to scan and digitize important case files— including testimony— for the purpose of future exhibits and programs. He took a predetermined list of files they needed, then planned on further explorations into little known or other cases that might prove good stories for the public. With a laptop and scanner in tow, he spent eight hours a day for a week pulling files, scanning them, creating CDs and making copies for the archives staff. Fort Smith National Historic Site's paper files were incomplete and somewhat sporadic, so this work would provide all the documents for a particular case, from the grand jury through the petit jury trial, sentencing and in some cases, the appeal process. **His research expanded the Historic Site's knowledge** of Cherokee Bill, Jack Spaniard, Sheppard Busby, Belle Starr, the Rufus Buck Gang, and even Bass Reeves. One of the most interesting cases, and one which became a reenactment for the public was Simon Amonia, who was brought into court for selling American Hops Ale in the Choctaw Nation, an Anheuser-Busch product that required a deposition by August Busch and testimony of the company Brew Meister. One must wonder what an Anheuser -Busch monopoly of liquor sales in Indian Territory would have meant, had the judge and jury decided in Simon's favor.

On the last day of the research trip, after all the "important files" had been scanned, Tom asked to see the Maud Avery Allen file. Immediately, the staff members helping him burst into laughter and asked if he knew the case. Tom responded "yes," but that he was hoping to learn more. They guaranteed more and presented him with the file jacket. Upon opening it, he found the usual writs, subpoenas, and the transcript of testimony. However, he was surprised to find the actual evidence presented at the trial, the obscene letters, in the case file itself. This material formed the basis of *Julia and Maud*, and a chance to tell the story from the evidence, the context of the town, and hopefully without the myths and legends assigned over the years. The staff there knew their collection well and were very helpful. Tom made lasting friendships with many of them. After the renovations at Fort Smith were complete, they stopped by on the way to a conference, and they were allowed to sit in the courtroom jury chairs and get their photos made.

When Joyce Faulkner asked Tom to assist her in telling the story, he was interested but somewhat cautious. Being a historian, and not a fiction writer, he wanted to make sure the story was told with respect and with as much documented fact as possible. While a historian always has questions with no answers, the scandalous nature of the story, and the possibility of offending descendants made credibility, authenticity, and accuracy very important. Joyce and Tom had no desire to sensationalize the story for effect. These are real people, caught in difficult and tragic circumstances. Inside, Tom was very glad the time had come to tell a story that had been hidden to recent generations. Joyce has an eye for detail and a knack for using fictional narrative and dialogue to illuminate historical events. When finished, there is no doubt they will have explored every lead and followed every twist and turn the story holds. Tom felt it a great honor to work with such a talented and accomplished writer as Joyce to bring as much truth and light to the story as possible.

Historical fiction is a good way to cover historical events because it allows readers to experience history in a more engaging and personal way. By weaving factual events and real-life characters into a fictional story, it can provide a deeper understanding of the times, culture, and societal issues of the past. Historical fiction can also make historical events more relatable and understandable to modern readers by showing how people in the past faced challenges and overcame obstacles. Overall, historical fiction can bring history to life in a way that textbooks and academic writing cannot, making it a valuable tool for educating and entertaining readers.

The context of Julia and Maud in the Victorian Era

The Victorian era, named after Queen Victoria of the British Empire, who reigned from 1837 to 1901. It was a time of significant change and development in Britain as well as the United States. As it relates to our story, the two women were daughters of Civil War soldiers. Julia's family found themselves spraddling the issues that tore the nation apart, being slave owners who supported the Union. They owned a store at Bailey's Crossing, Georgia, but postwar, ended up in Fort Smith, Arkansas, by the 1890s. While not super wealthy, they were a family of some means. On the other hand, Maud's father, William DeLoss Avery, was born in Wisconsin and began his service as a twelve-year-old bugler in the Union Army. He served all four years of the Civil War and ended up in Sherman's March to the Sea. He was still a teenager when he married Maud's mother after the War and the family lived in Missouri. He died when Maud was twelve.

The mid to late 1890s, when Julia and Maud's paths crossed, was a period of social, political, and cultural change, marking the end of the Victorian era. One of the defining features of those years was adherence to a strict code of conduct that emphasized the virtues of hard work, self-discipline, and moral uprightness. Julia Bourland was the epitome of those qualities. Maud was not.

Victorian society was highly structured, with a clear hierarchy of social and economic classes. Fort Smith, with Indian Territory just to the west, saw a mix of traditional responses and liberal approaches to morality of the day. Women in Fort Smith in some ways had greater latitude in the workforce than "back east," but still they were subservient to men. Women with wealth had advantages lower class women did not enjoy.

Gambling in Fort Smith was another activity that was widely enjoyed in the open rather than confined to back alleys and dark rooms "back east." Fagan and Hatcher took advantage of local interest in such things and hosted regular Faro Games.

Fashion was an important aspect of Victorian society, with dress codes and clothing trends closely tied to social status. The 1890s were characterized by the rise of the New Woman, who challenged traditional gender roles and wore looser, more comfortable clothing. While still being a "girlie girl," Annie Schaffer showed off her riding skills and her fancy costumes on the rodeo circuit. However, for the most part, Victorian fashion remained highly restrictive, with most women wearing tightly laced corsets, voluminous skirts, and high-necked blouses.

Class relations were a defining feature of Victorian society, with a clear divide between the wealthy upper classes and the working-class poor. This divide was particularly pronounced in the 1890s. The wealthy enjoyed a life of luxury, with access to education, healthcare, and entertainment, while the working classes struggled to make ends meet. Given her widowed mother's difficulty supporting Maud's siblings, Maud must have hoped for a more prosperous life when she married George Allen. That he didn't make enough to support the Averys too, must have been a big disappointment.

The Victorian era of the 1890s in the United States was a time of significant social and economic change. It was a period of rapid industrialization and urbanization, which led to the growth of large cities and the emergence of a new middle class. During this period, the United States experienced a wave of immigration, particularly from Eastern and Southern Europe. This influx of immigrants contributed to the diversity of American society, but it also led to a rise in nativism and anti-immigrant sentiment. Due to employment opportunities in the region's coal fields, and other developing industries, Fort Smith saw an increase in immigrants at this time.

Yet another aspect of the Victorian era was the impact of the Civil War. While the country was reunited, the practical aspects of the reunion were difficult at best, violent at worse. The rise of the Ku Klux Klan, the harsh reality of reconstruction in the years preceding the 1890's and the post war trauma of the survivors on both sides meant that even though the armies weren't fighting, much conflict existed. Both Julia and Maud had fathers who were Civil War veterans. The loss and trauma they likely experienced was passed down to their daughters in ways that are hard to define. The term PTSD did not exist in the years following the Civil War, yet we can assume grief followed the costliest war in American history, not just for the soldiers who came home, but their families as well. Having fathers who were veterans is just one aspect that the ladies shared. They were also from poor farming families, which meant similar backgrounds. They were independent, protective, and resourceful for women of the time. From their photographs, they were both considered quite beautiful then, as well as now. While writing, we wondered if under different circumstances, they might have been friends rather than enemies.

The Victorian era was also marked by significant advancements in technology, including the development of the telephone, the phonograph, and the electric light bulb. These innovations transformed everyday life and paved the way for the modern era. The impact of these advances is still felt today. The speed in which we communicate and the progression from telegraph to telephone made the Victorian world a smaller place.

Overall, the Victorian era of the 1890s in the United States was a complex period characterized by both progress and inequality. Despite these technological advancements, the Victorian era was also a time of significant social inequality. Women had limited rights and were largely excluded from the political and economic spheres. African Americans faced discrimination and violence, and many lived in poverty.

Yearly context, 1893-1898 and beyond...

In 1893, the United States experienced a period of economic depression and political turmoil. The country was recovering from the Panic of 1893, which caused widespread financial hardship and unemployment. In Arkansas, the state was struggling with its own economic challenges, particularly in the agricultural sector, which was hit hard by falling crop prices and drought conditions.

Fort Smith, located in western Arkansas, was a key center of commerce and transportation. The city was home to a large military outpost, which had been established during the Civil War, as well as a thriving river port and railroad hub. In 1871 the Federal court moved from Van Buren to the old barracks building and the money brought into the economy by the court created an economic engine in Gilded Age Fort Smith. The golden age of development of the city occurred at this time. Despite the economic challenges facing the region, Fort Smith remained a bustling hub of activity in 1893.

The city was also undergoing significant social and cultural changes. The late 19th century saw the rise of the women's suffrage movement, and Fort Smith was no exception. Local women's organizations actively advocated for their right to vote and to fully participate in civic life.

Overall, 1893 was a challenging but dynamic period in the history of the United States, Arkansas, and Fort Smith. Despite economic and political upheaval, the region experienced changes that shaped the area for years. Nationally, the Panic of 1893 which began with a run on banks, brought high unemployment, loss of savings, foreclosures, and railroad failures to the United States as a whole. Second only to the Great Depression of the 1930s, it was a time of incredible hardship for many Americans. On a much lighter tone though, the Chicago World's Fair brought people from around the world and all over the United States to the White City to enjoy the cultural, architectural, technological, and culinary marvels of the day. The Southards really did go to the World's Fair and brought back new ideas, like chocolate chip cookies. Closer to Fort Smith, the Cherokee Strip Land Run allowed claims and settlement for lands previously reserved for Native Americans. Women got the right to vote in Colorado while in Fort Smith, the notorious Henry Starr was captured. While Starr was wanted for various crimes himself, he also played a part in the Crawford Goldsby (Cherokee Bill) segment of this book.

In 1894, the Panic of 1893 continued affecting the economy of the United States. In Fort Smith, a new federal building was completed, and the city celebrated it with a parade. At the Fort, Federal executions continued. Johnny Pointer paid for the crime of murder September 24th and on November 2nd, Lewis Holder met his fate at the end of a rope...also for murder. These two executions have additional details. Once the gallows enclosure was built in

1886, executions in Fort Smith were no longer public spectacles. People were allowed in, with a ticket. However, the court issued them… and to receive one, a person had to be connected to the case in some way. One "hanging day" ticket has survived to this day, and it was for Johnny Pointer's execution.

The Lewis Holder trial is among the most memorable for a few reasons. Holder threatened the judge and jury when he was found guilty, not with physical harm, but that he would return from the grave and haunt them. When Tom was hired by the National Park Service in 1996, his aunt told him an amazing story. She had been looking for her grandfather in her family history. All her life, her family told her that he had abandoned her grandmother and mother. They also told her that his name was Joe. After years of searching (pre-internet), she found her grandmother's marriage license. To her surprise, her grandfather was not Joe Holder, as she had been told, but in fact, Lewis Holder, who did indeed abandon her grandmother, but not exactly as the family had said. Weeks after Holder's execution, the town drunk was caught inside the gallows enclosure late one night, but not before his hooting and hollering made the jailers wonder if Lewis Holder's ghost had come back to haunt them after all. For years, Tom told the Holder story with his personal family connections. Knowing that the park ranger was connected to one of the outlaws always got the audience's attention.

In 1895, William McKinley took over at the end of Grover Cleveland's second term as President of the United States. The first patent for the automobile was granted that same year. In Fort Smith, a flood damaged many city buildings and infrastructure. On February 26th, Cherokee Bill was convicted of the murder of Ernest Melton. On July 26th, an escape attempt resulted in the death of guard Larry Keating. On August 5th, Cherokee Bill was tried for murder.

The year of 1896 was an eventful year—for the nation, Arkansas, and Fort Smith. William McKinley defeated William Jennings Bryan for president of the United States. Bryan had family in Van Buren and gave many campaign speeches in Crawford County. The Supreme Court decided Plessy vs. Ferguson and segregation became legal. Internationally, the United States participated in the first modern Olympic Games in Athens. In Fort Smith, Cherokee Bill died for the murder of Larry Keating on March 17. On April 30, Webber Isaacs, and George and John Pearce (brothers) were executed for murder.

July 1 saw one of the most heinous crimes punished on the gallows. Rufus Buck, Lucky Davis, Lewis Davis, Sam Sampson, and Maoma July (The Rufus Buck Gang) were executed for rape. In addition to several other crimes, the Rufus Buck gang, as they were known, held a gun on the husband while each took a turn raping the wife. She testified in court as to the brutality of the crime and her words insured a guilty verdict and federally mandated death sentence. On July 20, George Wilson, aka James Casharego was hanged for murder. His was the last execution in Fort Smith.

On November 17, Judge Isaac C. Parker died at the age of fifty-eight. The stress of his workload and responsibility contributed to Bright's disease, a deterioration of the kidneys.

In 1897, William McKinley became President of the United States. Gold was discovered in Alaska's Klondike region, and the first transit subway opened in Boston. Fort Smith enjoyed the city's first electric streetcar line connecting major points of the city.

In 1898, the Spanish-American War broke out, beginning with the sinking of the *USS Maine* in Havana. Hawaii and Puerto Rico were added as US Territories. In Arkansas, the state's National Guard was called into service for the Spanish-American War effort. In Fort Smith, the city experienced a smallpox outbreak and established a quarantine station.

Throughout our years of researching and writing this book, several myths, legends, and local lore surfaced. There are plenty of opinions about how the Julia and Maud saga played out, yet our team wanted to get to the facts as much as possible. One of the most puzzling myths we found, was that Maud was of African American descent. Over the years, the African American community appeared to embrace and accept Maud, yet the author found no indication that this was true. Her parents and extended family tree point to a Caucasian heritage. We looked for where this assumption started but could not find the origin. Some accounts of the shooting have Maud being killed as she slept in her bed. One legend has her shot in the back. However, the newspaper accounts of the shootings clearly describe it as face to face. Further, while the jury for Julia's trial for Maud's murder was likely filled with prominent men of Fort Smith, and therefore likely contemporaries of Fagan, the fact that Maud threatened Julia's life many times, in the eyes of the court made self-defense a real factor, not just a "good old boy" solution.

Maud's image does indeed attest to her beauty, but she has been made the victim through the years in many interpretations. In the opinion of the authors, beauty does not necessarily translate to virtue and innocence. The team found this troubling and while we can agree she was victimized to the point of death, her actions, provocations, and complete disregard for the fact that Fagan was married, places much of the responsibility on her shoulders. Many newspaper accounts of the specific events show Maud's hostility, jealousy, and anger towards Julia. The discrepancies we found in locations, descriptions, chronologies of events, make inconsistency a factor that will always be a part of the story. While not proven in court to be Maud's handiwork, the drawings and words sent to Julia reveal Maud's real character. The depravity and depth of the letters and drawings indicate a troubled and likely abused writer. With no other participants in the narrative, Joyce and Tom found it hard to believe that the letters and drawings were produced by someone other than Maud.

Loose ends and final thoughts...

As for Fagan Bourland, the team believed from the start that this book would not be about him. It references him and places him in the context since he, of course, set Julia and Maud on their collision course. However, we felt that the book should not make him the center. We tried to keep Julia and Maud in the forefront, both as victims of circumstances and the consequences of their own behavior and the actions of others. In Fort Smith, Fagan is also involved in activities that came under scrutiny in the Victorian era. Owning and operating a saloon complete with gambling, placed him at odds with women's reform initiatives of the day. The anti-saloon league, prohibition movement, and the general disdain for gambling illustrated Fort Smith's slightly more liberal culture than other parts of the country.

Joyce and Tom were somewhat surprised to find the legendary Henry Surratt only mentioned once in the series of events. At the second shooting, Surratt is mentioned as being present at the chaotic scene. This is a bit puzzling as he is mentioned many times throughout his career as a law enforcement officer in Fort Smith. We did find he was the likely victim of politics after being dismissed from the force at one point and reinstated—only to be accused of wrongdoing and dismissed again. He also worked for the Fort Smith Fire Department for a brief period.

Somewhat outside the scope of the book, but part of the story, was Fagan's donation in 1941 of a carillon in Julia's honor to the First Methodist Church. To the authors, this appears to be a way for Fagan to make amends or publicly atone with Julia, many years after the events of the 1890s had passed.

About the Author

Joyce Faulkner grew up in Fort Smith, Arkansas, graduating from Immaculate Conception School in 1962 and St. Anne's Academy in 1966. She attended the University of Arkansas, majoring in writing, from 1966 to 1968. She earned her Chemical Engineering Degree with a specialty in Petroleum Engineering from the University of Pittsburgh in 1983 and her Master of Business Administration from Cleveland State in 1991. She worked in the natural gas industry for twenty years and managed a new department dedicated to adapting corporate functions to a multi-company Intranet—Internet world in the late 1990s.

Interested in a variety of subjects and approaches, Joyce is the author of many award-winning books and articles. However, her main interests are History, Historical Fiction and True Crime. Her Historical Fiction titles include *In the Shadow of Suribachi* about the Battle of Iwo Jima, *Windshift* about the Women's Air Service Pilots (WASPs) in World War II, *Vala's Bed* about the Holocaust, and its aftermath, *Garrison Avenue* (with coauthor Dr. Micki Voelkel) about a lynching that took place on Garrison Avenue in Fort Smith, Arkansas, in 1912. Her Nonfiction History books include *Sunchon Tunnel Massacre Survivors* and *Role Call: Women's Voices*, both with coauthor Pat McGrath Avery. She has also ghosted several books about World War II and Vietnam.

About the Author

Tom Wing is a sixth generation Arkansawyer and currently Assistant Professor of History and Director of the Drennen-Scott Historic Site for the University of Arkansas-Fort Smith. He's been an educator in secondary and higher education class-rooms for thirty-five years, and a museum professional with twenty-seven years in resource interpretation, program planning, exhibit design and visitor services. He's a published author with numerous articles and several books, including *A Rough Introduction to This Sunny Land: The Civil War Diary of Private Henry Albert Strong Company K, 12th Kansas Infantry*, and *Images of America: Van Buren.*

He is a 19th Century scholar having been interviewed on Discovery Channel, History Channel, Smithsonian Channel, and PBS. An award-winning historic preservationist, he possesses diversified skill sets including curriculum design, interpretive planning, client and visitor relations, human resources and recruiting, historical research, grant writing and project management. He has served multiple terms as a board member for Preserve Arkansas and the Arkansas Historical Association.

He cherishes time with Renee, his wife of thirty-four years, his four sons, daughters-in-law and currently six grandchildren with another due soon. He lived for twenty-five years near the Old Wire Road in the hills of Northern Crawford County, but today resides near the confluence of Lee Creek (Papillon to the French fur trappers) and the Arkansas River.

Well-known Historian, Teacher and Author, Tom Wing, found the original documents...and most important, Maud's letters that are used in the historical fiction work, *Julia and Maud.*

Acknowledgments

We would like to thank the many people who gave us insight, information, stories, helped check facts, illuminated court procedures, dug for nuggets of significance, and otherwise helped us go far beyond where we could have gone ourselves. Shelley Blanton at the Pebley Center inside Boreham Library at the University of Arkansas-Fort Smith was a constant help and cheerleader from the beginning of this project to the final edits. Her knowledge of Fort Smith and skill as an archivist makes her an indispensable resource. Also, many thanks to Mindy Lawrence and Dianna Carmel Faulkner who edited and proofed this book several times along the way.

Dusty Hebling gave us insight into many aspects of Fort Smith History and inspired the Annie Shaffer story line. The character of Cal Whitson came from his descendants, Al Whitson and Calvin Evans. Information about Irish immigrant and widow of Hugh Rogers, Eliza Rogers, who is Phil Daggs' great-great-aunt, came from the research of his wife Karen Daggs. Judge Jim Spears gave us important and critical insight to the story from a legal perspective, while Karen Daggs helped make sense of our main characters' family trees. Loren McLane with the National Park Service helped us get copies of the case files, so important in our story. John Skelly, my bother in law who is a behavioral health professional gave us insight into victims of abuse. Sonny and Sue Robison designed an attractive cover that we love, and they helped keep the story of Julia and Maud alive though their work at the Fort Smith Museum of History. And where would we be without the Fort Smith Historic Site itself? Finally, our spouses, John Faulkner and Renee Wing deserve our thanks as they listened, commented, and gave advice throughout our long obsession with Julia and Maud.

www.ingramcontent.com/pod-product-compliance
Lightning Source LLC
Chambersburg PA
CBHW041642010726
47507CB00012B/429